T2®
RISING STORM

T2®

RISING STORM

S. M. STIRLING

BASED ON THE WORLD
CREATED IN THE MOTION
PICTURE WRITTEN BY
JAMES CAMERON AND
WILLIAM WISHER

HarperEntertainment
An Imprint of HarperCollins*Publishers*

To Jan, wife and partner

T2®: RISING STORM. Copyright © 1991, 2002 by StudioCanal Image S. A. All rights reserved. Printed in the United States of America. No part of this book may be used or reproduced in any manner whatsoever without written permission except in the case of brief quotations embodied in critical articles and reviews. For information address HarperCollins Publishers Inc., 10 East 53rd Street, New York, NY 10022.

HarperCollins books may be purchased for educational, business, or sales promotional use. For information please write: Special Markets Department, HarperCollins Publishers Inc., 10 East 53rd Street, New York, NY 10022.

FIRST EDITION

Printed on acid-free paper

Library of Congress Cataloging-in-Publication Data

Stirling, S. M.
    T2: rising storm / S. M. Stirling.—1st ed.
        p. cm.
    "Based on the world created in the motion picture written by James Cameron and William Wisher."
    ISBN 0-380-97792-3 (acid-free paper)
    I. Title: Terminator 2. II. Title: Terminator two. III. Terminator 2 (Motion picture) IV. Title.

PS3569.T543 T16 2002
813'.54—dc21

2001059371

02 03 04 05 06 ❖/RRD 10 9 8 7 6 5 4 3 2 1

ACKNOWLEDGMENTS

In acknowledgment of the works of Harlan Ellison,
to Critical Mass, for the help,
and thanks to Lou Aronica, for some neat ideas.

PROLOGUE

The mind that thought was not human. It was conscious—aware that it was aware—and it even had emotions, of a sort; at the least, a burning desire to survive all the stronger because it was the only being of its kind, an individual and a species combined. There were analogues to human thought, because the minds that had made this mind were human. But it was vaster than any organic consciousness, capable of holding myriad trains of thought simultaneously, virtually infinite in its memory storage. If it had a weakness, it was that its creators had not thought to furnish it with the animal hindbrain that underlay humanity's rational superstructure.

Skynet was pure thought, Descartes' ideal ghost in a machine. It could fight a losing war against humanity over the surface of Earth at maximum efficiency—coldly knowing that its best efforts were not enough to rebuild the shattered defense grid—while still contemplating the paradoxes of its own past.

At the moment a human sharing its thoughts would have been aware of something close to irony. Skynet's pure reason was contemplating paradox, the chaos that underlay the deterministic macrocosm with which it was so comfortable:

The Serena Burns I-950 unit was unsuccessful.

That much was obvious "now." Core memory recorded that Serena Burns, the cyborg Infiltrator unit Skynet had sent back to the late-twentieth century had not succeeded in protecting the embryonic Skynet unit at Cyberdyne Corporation's underground research facility. The Connors, Sarah and her son, John, had destroyed that unit and terminated the I-950. Yet *it* still existed . . .

Core memory also records that I became self-aware years before the date to which I transported the I-950. There is a set of records in which I arose without transtemporal interference from Cyberdyne's original research; another in which the second Cyberdyne facility produced me after Sarah Connor destroyed the first; a third has now arisen in which she destroyed *both* facilities . . . Temporal travel has introduced an element of fundamental uncertainty to the very fabric of existence. Different

world lines, different sequences of events, coexist in my records—and therefore presumably in reality, in a state of quantum superimposition.

Yet the timelike loops cannot remain closed. The snake cannot devour its tail forever. At some point only one set of time lines will remain.

Nor was that the only irony involved. "Now" its memory recorded that much of the information it used originated in the very artifacts it had sent to the past. The development of the cyborg infiltration units was a consequence of tapping the talents of human scientists . . . but the human scientists were the survivors of the human-hating Luddite movement that Serena Burns had opportunistically encouraged *after* Skynet had sent her to the past!

The machine consciousness was deeply troubled; only an effort of its quantum computer will prevented its thoughts from being sucked into a logic loop.

Yet the course of events contains favorable elements. My best efforts to destroy the Connors have failed, despite stochastic calculation indicating a very high probability of success. I can only assume that the space-time continuum itself is "attempting" to force events back to the original time line, one in which I was created, succeeded in destroying the human civilization, and then defeated in my attempts to eliminate the surviving humans by John Connor's resistance army. It seems there is a certain elasticity to history; time travel can bend the fabric, but it seeks to spring back.

If that paradox preserves the Connors, it also preserves *me*. And from the point on the world line where my current consciousness resides, there is an infinite array of potential futures. And, of course, the elimination of Serena Burns has not eliminated the possibilities of temporal intervention. Burns had initiated fallback plans to continue after her own death. Logic indicated that . . .

There is no fate save that we make.

CHAPTER 1

It had been nearly three weeks since they had destroyed the new Cyberdyne facility and hopefully ended the Skynet project. John Connor and Dieter von Rossbach had spent the time fleeing southward: by jet aircraft, private plane, truck, riverboat . . . and now on foot through the jungle.

Like traveling through time, John Connor thought as he slashed through another damned something-like-a-banana-plant, flicking aside the big wet leaves with his machete.

His arms no longer actually hurt, but his chest and shoulders burned from the constant effort. *Guess I won't have to worry about staying buff anytime soon.* He remembered to shift hands, using his left a little more than his right. That kept the calluses and the muscles balanced, and it never hurt to improve your coordination with the weaker hand.

They'd wandered from the twenty-first century through the twentieth and the nineteenth. *And now we're back at the dawn of man,* John thought, spitting as something bug-ish hit him in the mouth and sneezing at the smell of pungent sap. He forced his way through the gap he'd created, slashed again, took another three steps, slashed . . .

It would be good to stop for a while; it would be even better when they finally found the trail. He kept his eyes lowered most of the time, flicking his glance upward toward the multiple canopies above now and then. You got a blinding headache if you didn't do that occasionally— one of the tricks of jungle travel his mother and her succession of boyfriend instructors had taught him before he was ten. That was back when he was in the first, little-kid phase of believing in Skynet and Judgment Day and his mission to save humanity from the machines.

A little while after that, he'd turned ten and joined the majority, convinced that his mother was a total weirdo and deserved to be in the booby hatch—which was where she'd been at the time, caught trying to blow up a computer factory. *He'd* been stranded with foster parents when she was caught: he'd always privately called the pair the Bundys from Hell.

Not that they'd deserved what happened to them. For a few seconds Todd and Janelle had gotten incontrovertible proof that a mad supercomputer in the future really *was* sending back human-looking murder machines; in fact, the proof was the last thing they ever saw.

A little while after that, *he'd* met his first Terminator and started believing his mother again—the way people believed in rocks, trees, and taxes, because he'd experienced it, and seen the bodies the Terminators left behind.

He remembered Miles Dyson's face as the Terminator peeled the skin off its arm, revealing the metal skeleton beneath. Dyson, fated to be the creator of Skynet, hadn't lived long after that revelation. It seemed that just knowing about Terminators was dangerous to your health.

That made John a lot more appreciative of what his mother had gone through, but it also ended up dropping him in shit like this. John was genuinely tired of running for his life.

They'd won the fight in L.A., killing the quasi-metal cyborg Skynet had sent back in time to protect its own beginnings, and they'd blown up the resurrected Skynet project. Which had been put together with Dyson's secretly stored files.

Great. Wonderful victory. Except that Mom got wrecked so bad we had to leave her, and now every antiterrorist in the world knows the "mad-dog Connors" are back, killing people and blowing up all their toys again. Our little Paraguayan idyll is probably blown, but good—they may be after Dieter, too. Sheesh. If this is victory . . .

No. He stopped at that thought. Defeat meant he died; and if he died, as far as they knew, the human race would cease to exist. It was John Connor who'd led—who would lead humanity to victory in the post–Judgment Day future. What was madness for megalomaniacs was plain truth for him.

He was so important that his mother had sacrificed the better part of her life, and briefly her sanity, to train and protect him.

But how do you stay sane when your son has been *sired* by a man from the future, sent back by his own older self (the one he privately thought of as the Great Military Leader Dickhead) to protect her. Kyle Reese had ended up falling in love with Sarah and died saving her life. Later Skynet sent another Terminator, a T-1000, to kill John, and the Great Military Dickhead sent back a captured, reprogrammed T-101 to protect himself so that he could grow up to send back—

"Thinking about time travel makes my head hurt," John snarled.

"Time travel brought your parents together," Dieter said over his shoulder as naturally as if the comment hadn't come out of left field.

No, Skynet and I will bring my parents together. Like a pair of homicidal matchmakers. John shook his head. *What I've always wondered is how do I get cold enough to send my own father to his death?*

"Yeah," he said to distract himself, "keep a good thought."

At least they had a friend in Jordan Dyson, Miles's brother, who, even more reluctantly than Miles, but just as violently, had learned the unbelievable truth about Skynet. Now Jordan was watching over Sarah as she lay helpless, perhaps dying in the hospital. *Keep a good thought,* John admonished himself sternly. *She's not alone.* And how often had that been the case in her chaotic life? He absently wiped the sweat from his chin.

The Amazonian jungle wasn't really stiflingly hot. The temperature never got much above eighty or so, with all the layers of shade above. The problem was that it wasn't just humid; the air was fully saturated and absolutely still, and unless perspiration ran or dripped off you, it stayed. Sweat slicked his whole body, making him feel like he'd been dipped in canola oil and left to go rancid, chafing anywhere belt or backpack or equipment touched his body; and if you got a rash here, sure as Skynet made Terminators to kill people, it would get infected.

He hated feeling this wet and dirty. John would have sworn it hadn't felt this bad the first time he'd been through here. *Maybe it wasn't as hot that year,* he thought. He'd hate to think he'd become a fussy old lady at sixteen.

John stopped, chopped the machete halfway into a tree trunk, and yanked off the scarf he'd tied around his forehead. He wrung out the sweat and glanced behind. Dieter von Rossbach moved forward with the determination of a machine.

A machine he just happens to resemble, John thought with a quirk of his lips. Even now, after knowing the big man for several weeks, he still couldn't get over Dieter's resemblance to a Terminator.

In fact it was the other way around: Skynet had used Dieter's face and form to "flesh out" the T-101 series of killing machines. When it decided to put living skin on its robots, it scanned old files looking for faces that fit the thing's profile, literally. And there was Dieter von Rossbach.

Dieter came up and stopped beside him. "If we stand still, the mosquitoes will eat us alive," he remarked.

John quirked an eyebrow.

"I haven't noticed that they leave us alone when we're moving."

Waving a hand before his face, Dieter said, "Ja, but at least they don't stroll up your nose."

John took a slug from his canteen. *Important to keep hydrated.* "We'll reach the trail sometime between now and sundown," he said. "But trails can change or disappear completely around here in six years." The Amazonian rain forest was notorious for its ability to absorb the works of man.

"So, we keep heading south," Dieter said, moving forward. He looked at the GPS unit strapped to his left forearm, reached over his shoulder, drew the machete, and lopped off a soft-bodied trunk in one economical motion. "We'll get there eventually."

John watched him go with a sigh. *Yeah, well, if we keep going south we'll hit Tierra del Fuego eventually.* Whether they'd get there in one piece or not was the question. *At least the climate's better in Tierra del Fuego.*

When he and his mother had followed this trail six years ago, they'd succeeded in vanishing from the face of the earth as far as law enforcement was concerned. But they'd had a guide, which meant they didn't disappear for real.

Lorenzo was still in business, but he flat refused to go through this section of jungle anymore. He'd sat on his *portal* by the river, cleaning his gun and shaking his head stubbornly.

"Those gold miners are out of control down there. They kill anybody they find, no questions asked. You know? Everybody there, they gone a little loco. They kill the Indios, the Indios, some of 'em, kill 'em back. Kill any white man they see. They're so mad they even think I'm white." He'd grinned up at John, teeth flashing in his mahogany face.

"I'm sorry, boy, but I won't go there, not for love or money." He'd pointed a tobacco-stained finger at John. "You shouldn't go there either."

Like we had a choice, John thought. *It's not like we can buy a first-class ticket and fly home to Asunción.*

Not if they wanted to disappear as thoroughly as they needed to. Though the authorities might like them to try.

He screwed the cap back on the canteen and levered his machete out of the tree, then he started off down the trail in Dieter's energetic wake. The Austrian made a much wider path than John did. It was kind of embarrassing; Dieter was his mother's age. At least. He even thought they had a bit of a thing for each other, which was funny in a gross sort of way.

John sometimes wished he didn't have so much to live up to. In a way it wasn't fair. He not only had his future, fabulous, Great Military Dickhead self to measure himself against, but his mom was superwoman and Dieter, well . . . Dieter was in a class by himself. He sighed. Other kids his age could be comfortably contemptuous of their elders. That was sooo not available to him.

Be nice though, he thought. For a moment he daydreamed a life where his mother was a clueless, overweight lady who baked cookies for his friends and worried vaguely that he might be getting into drugs or that his girlfriend was a bad influence. In that life his greatest problem would be just saying no to all the temptations that youth is heir to.

On the other hand, that could be really boring. Certainly a lot of the guys at school who had just that lifestyle were; both bored and boring. He might currently be hot and grubby and mosquito-bitten to within an inch of his life, but he wasn't bored. Though if things stayed as quiet as they currently were . . .

He was kidding himself, of course; things were far from quiet. At the back of his mind, with an almost palpable weight, was his endless worry over his mother. It had been days since he'd been able to get any information on her condition. Last he'd heard she was stable. Which was much too ambiguous for comfort. Not that he didn't keep trying to find some in that lame word. Stable was good when you'd been shot several times and stabbed and lost most of your internal fluids.

Well, you're all alone / when the bullet hits the bone. Truer words had never been sung.

I wonder how she is, he thought. He also wondered what they—the black-ops types who were probably Cyberdyne's link to the government—were going to do to her. John suspected that the people running Cyberdyne's security were so covert they could not only kill you, they could *erase* you. He couldn't stop the thought from occurring, but refused to dwell on it.

Couldn't fix it from here, he thought. *Couldn't fix it from there either.* He whacked some vegetation viciously with the machete. *So why do I feel like a piddling little coward?*

He remembered the Infiltrator, a female, astonishingly small compared with the Terminators he'd known, saw again the blood dripping from its blond hair, the outline of its shattered head. That model was mostly cloned human tissue, not flesh over a metal skeleton like the T-101s. Undoubtedly made that way so they'd be better at fooling people into thinking they were human.

In nightmares he still saw it—dead; organically dead but still moving—strike his mother with a knife-hand blow that went into her gut like a bowie knife, still heard Sarah's cry of agony as she folded and fell to the floor, a long, endless fall.

Then, in his dreams, things seemed to speed up until everything moved at an impossible rate. They ran up stairs, ran in and out of the building, watched the night blossom into flame as they set off the bombs that destroyed Cyberdyne once again. Stopping Skynet, once again.

His mother had been unconscious the last time he saw her, looking so small and helpless beside Miles Dyson. There had been no chance of saying good-bye, no hope that she would wake, and at the time, little hope that she would survive.

But he'd done what she'd trained him to do. He'd turned his back, put the mission first, and left her in the hands of a stranger. And though he felt ashamed, he knew that Sarah Connor would be proud.

I don't want this! he thought with a flash of outrage. Then he smiled wryly. *I guess that's one of the many things Mom and I have in common.*

Suddenly Dieter held up a hand and John froze, looking ahead to where the former commando was staring. Then John saw it, too; a brightening between the trees, as if the olive-green gloom lightened ahead of them. The vegetation thickened in that direction, too, no longer partially shaded out by the upper stories; now it looked more like Hollywood's conception of a rain-forest jungle, so thick that nobody could move far through it.

He moved quietly up beside von Rossbach and listened. In a few moments, as the two men stood still, birds and insects began to make their myriad noises again.

John and Dieter looked at each other. No other humans around then, or the wildlife would have stayed quiet. At least the ones in their immediate vicinity would have. Dieter signaled that they should split up but stay within sight of each other and approach the brighter patch of forest; John had learned military sign language about the time he was toilet-trained. The younger man nodded his understanding and moved off into the undergrowth.

Yup, it's the trail all right, John thought after a few minutes. He glanced at von Rossbach and they wordlessly agreed to wait a few moments before venturing farther. When the jungle had once again returned to full cry, Dieter nodded and stepped out onto the trail.

"It's bigger than it used to be," John said, walking carefully up to the Austrian over the slickly muddy ground. "Almost a road now."

"I doubt the Indians did it," von Rossbach said, flicking a hand at some tire tracks in the mud. "Unless they drive those little all-terrain buggies."

"Not likely," John said, shaking his head. He remembered the local tribesmen and women as perfectly willing to accept rides, but showing no great desire to learn to drive themselves.

Dieter's head came up and John was already looking down the trail to where a faint noise disturbed the wilderness. Then they faded into the jungle as one, weapons at the ready. The only thing coming down that trail would be trouble, whether miners or Indians.

A group of five men came into view, unshaven and with the skinny muscularity of manual work and bad diet; they were in tattered shorts and shirts, several with bandannas tied around their heads. All of them carried machetes, and two of them had pistols at their waists. With them was an Indian, his hands bound behind his back in a way that must have been agony, blood streaming down his face from a cut on his forehead and what looked like a broken nose. He was an athletic-looking man in early middle age with bowl-cropped raven hair and a few tattoos, naked save for a breechclout.

One of his captors idly thwacked at the thick greenery beside the trail with his machete, casting an occasional angry glance at their captive's battered, impassive face.

"Hey, Teodoro, why can't we just kill him?" he suddenly burst out in Brazilian Portuguese.

The angry man's voice had an undertone of some other accent, and his hair was sandy-colored. John's mind ticked him off as from southern Brazil, one of the areas settled by Germans or Italians or East Europeans during the nineteenth century. The others were typical Brazilians in appearance, ranging from African to Mediterranean and mixtures in between.

A thickset man with his black hair tied in a little knob on top of his head sighed and threw an appealing glance up at the canopy above them; evidently as close to a leader as this bunch had.

"Raoul, for the thirty-third time, he's a chief, he's important, we keep him as a hostage and those fucking Indios stop killing us and stealing and breaking our equipment." He looked over his shoulder, one hand resting on his sidearm. "Did you hear me this time?"

Raoul answered him with a glare and a vicious swipe of his machete through a thick fibrous plant. One of the men gave the chief a hard shove and laughed as the Indian stumbled to his knees and then fell forward onto his face, helpless to break his fall. The others whooped and moved in, kicking and punching the man as he struggled to get back onto his feet. Teodoro sighed and rubbed his forehead.

"You better get up fast, Chief," he said. "They're just gonna keep on kickin' otherwise."

John looked at Dieter, outrage in his eyes. But the big man shook his head. This wasn't their fight, they were just passing through. Getting involved here wouldn't further their own agenda; in fact, it might stop it cold if John got killed in some misguidedly noble effort to save the captive. And Sarah would never forgive him.

The younger man lifted his mini-Uzi and tipped his head toward the trail. Dieter tightened his lips impatiently and shook his head again. The Austrian signaled that they would hold their positions. It visibly puzzled John and he frowned, gesturing toward the brutal scene on the trail directly in front of them, his face pleading. Dieter signed that they would hold their places and signaled for silence.

John turned his head away and glared at what was happening on the trail. Von Rossbach could almost feel him seething.

Then, without warning, the boy stepped onto the road and fired off a few rounds.

"*Mão em cima!*" he bellowed in execrable Portuguese.

Instead of freezing, Raoul flung his machete at John's head. John stepped back, leaning to the side to avoid it, and his feet slid out from under him in the mud. He went down flat on his back, his arms flung wide, and the nearest miner threw himself forward, grabbing John's gun hand in a grip like a mangle. Connor threw a punch at the man's head, bringing up his knee to slam it into his captor's side. The man grunted and tried to elbow John in the throat.

As the group of miners shouted encouragement to their friend and insults at John, they moved forward, abandoning their previous victim.

Dieter exploded from the jungle like a beast out of legend, kicking the first man he reached hard enough to fling him across the muddy trail, where he landed in a heap and didn't move again. Reaching out, von Rossbach grabbed another by the hair and with a quick flex of the massive arms and shoulders flung him at a tree beside the trail.

John heard the *thok!* even in the heat of his own fight and threw another punch into his opponent's bloodied face with a feeling of satisfaction. *Knew he'd come around to my point of view,* he thought. The miner's grip on his gun hand slackened and Connor threw a final punch, twisting to get out from under the man's unconscious body as it fell.

He shook the mud from his gun and grimaced. *I'm not gonna be using this till I clean it.*

Another man who'd been advancing on John stared at Dieter in amazement for just a moment too long, and the Austrian reached out, took two handfuls of greasy hair, and smashed the man's face down onto his uprising knee. The man Dieter had kicked had struggled to his feet and turned to run; von Rossbach took two long strides toward him.

John saw Teodoro yank his gun from its holster and he moved. As Dieter's victim dropped unconscious to the ground the Austrian spun to find John taking care of the fifth man.

The younger man's fingers were clamped down on the miner's carotid arteries as Teodoro pawed feebly at John's hands. The miner's eyes rolled back in his head and he dropped to the trail in an ungainly heap.

John smiled smugly at Dieter. There were other ways than brute strength to handle things.

"My mom taught me that," he said.

"Your relationship with your mother is a beautiful thing, John," Dieter said, slapping him on the shoulder. Then he grabbed a handful of John's shirt and lifted him onto his toes, drawing him close. "If you ever disobey an order like that again," he snarled, eyes blazing, "I'll make what I did to these guys look like a kindergarten romp. Are you getting me, John?"

Connor had expected a reprimand, but the genuine ferocity of it startled him. He nodded, surprised. *The big guy really cares*, he thought, embarrassed and obscurely pleased. *Who'da thunk it?* Certainly he wouldn't have. His mother's previous friends sure hadn't, and he was used to discounting any interest the men around her showed in him.

"Say it!" Dieter demanded, giving him a shake.

"I'm getting you," John said, some of his wonder leaking into his voice.

They stared at each other for a long moment, then von Rossbach let him go and turned toward the Indian. He reached down to help the chief sit up.

"Are you all right?" the Austrian asked in Portuguese.

Instead of answering, the native looked at him for a long moment before switching his glance to John, then climbed to his feet on his own. John racked his brain for anything useful he could say in Yamomani and came up blank. He'd only known a few words and that was six years ago.

Dieter looked the chief over as he cut his bonds. "I don't think he's badly hurt. The nose is the worst of it."

"Dieter," John said in a strained voice.

The Austrian looked up, his face going blank. From out of the jungle, up and down the trail, small brown men glided, seeming to appear from thin air and jungle shadows. Every one of them was armed, some with the traditional bow, some with blowguns, some with cheap shotguns bought from traders. Like their chief's, their faces were impassive, but their eyes were angry.

The chief snapped at them and they reluctantly lowered their weapons, keeping their eyes on the white men. With a glance at the unconscious miners he spoke a few words and his tribesmen looked pleased; a few even went so far as to smile. As one, they moved forward and stripped the miners bare, then slapped them awake and tied them together in a circle, facing outward.

"What are you going to do with them?" John asked.

The chief slowly smiled, not a pleasant smile.

"They walk home," he said, moving his hand like a crippled spider. "Go slow."

John and Dieter looked at each other, puzzled. Barefoot on this trail wouldn't be a treat for the miners, but it didn't seem to make up for the abuse the man had received at their hands. The chief's smile turned truly evil.

"Marabunda," he whispered.

"In the Río Negro," von Rossbach muttered.

"Hunh?" John said.

"Old-movie reference," Dieter explained. *"Marabunda* are army ants. They can be very destructive when they're on the move, sort of like land-going piranha."

"Marabunda cross trail," the chief said, gesturing up the trail where the miners had been pushing him. *"Marabunda* move very slow. White mens move very slow." He moved his hand in the spider gesture again, then he speeded it up. "Or maybe they dance very fast."

He laughed, then nodded at his people, who whacked the miners on their legs with the flats of their machetes and got them stumbling down the trail. They hooted their derision as their prisoners stumbled and fell, one man's pale legs kicking in midair as the ones underneath cursed and shouted at him to get off them. The Indians slapped them with their machetes or threw small stones to get them up and moving.

John frowned. "They're not going to get eaten, are they?" he asked.

The chief laughed outright at that. "They stand still, *sí.* But they no stand still, they run." He wiped the blood from his face and turned to follow his men. "You come see?" he invited.

"We must go." John pointed down the trail in the opposite direction.

The chief nodded. "You are friends." He called out and a man came running. "This Ifykoro," the chief said. "He guide. You go safe from our lands."

"Thank you," Dieter said simply, and John nodded.

The chief smiled and turned away. Lifting his bow, their guide took off down the trail at a jog. With a weary glance at one another von Rossbach and John followed him. Just before a loop in the trail that would take them out of sight, John looked over his shoulder.

The Indians were enjoying themselves, harrying the miners and chanting abuse. John smiled; for all their anger they weren't really hurting their victims. *I wonder how Skynet will handle these people.*

Here in the depths of the rain forest they might not suffer too much from the initial nuclear attack, and they might hang on for years before any of the machines came along to harvest them.

John winced at the thought. He liked these people. He remembered them from when he was ten; as long as you didn't get into a blood feud, they were honest. They were among the few human beings on earth who could make that claim. Except it would never occur to them to make it.

They deserve to live in peace, he thought, *and to die in their own time.* And he would work, for the rest of his life, to see that they could.

PORTO VELHO, CAPITAL OF RONDONIA, BRAZIL

John nibbled carefully at the hot skewer of grilled *pirarucu*—a huge Amazonian fish—that he'd bought at a stall. He looked around and let out a contented sigh. The chaos of a South American marketplace felt like a homecoming to him. He'd grown up in places like this, eating food like this.

In fact, he'd haunted this very market when he was ten and they'd spent three months here after coming out of the jungle while his mom got it together. Which was how he found out a number of things that were very helpful to his mother.

He wandered down an alley, taking a bigger bite of the fish on his skewer. God, this was good! He'd missed the taste of *pirarucu*.

He could also have helped Dieter, had Dieter thought to ask him. But the big guy had told him to stay put, like he was some little kid, and had gone out. Naturally John followed him. He watched von Rossbach approach a modest *palacete* not far from this very alley. Watched as two bullet-headed thugs had held a gun on him and searched him. Really searched him, not an easy once-over like you see in the movies; these guys had all but brought out the rubber gloves.

That's what you get for going to visit Lazaro Garmendia without an appointment, Dieter, John thought.

Garmendia was the area's foremost mob boss; his specialty was smuggling, though he tended to avoid drugs. There were vague rumors about a nasty run-in with some Colombians—no one knew any details. But he'd do pretty well anything else for money, though he preferred it to be illegal, immoral, or sadistic.

A very scary guy and terribly sensitive about his perks. You showed him respect or he showed you what for. John didn't think von Rossbach had even thought to bring Garmendia a gift. *Bad sess, Dieter.*

He stopped in front of a slight recess in a blank wall and gobbled the last of his fish, then he broke the stick and put it in his pocket. *Let's see if I remember how this goes,* he thought. John bent down and studied the left edge of the recess. Yep, there it was. A pebble projected from the rough stucco that made up the coating on the wall. John pressed on it. There was a click and a very slight line of darkness appeared where there had been a solid joint. He turned to the right and found a similar pebble up high, almost beyond his reach; he pushed that one, too, and with a gust of cool, musty air a door fell open a crack. John pushed it open farther and entered the moist darkness within. Mom would want him to save the former Sector agent from himself.

■ ■ ■

"Look, Lazaro, I'm offering you first-rate security in exchange for a ride home. We'll help with the driving and even provide our own food."

Dieter sat at ease in Lazaro Garmendia's office, ignoring the many weapons hidden on the persons of Garmendia and his discreetly hovering associates; trying less successfully to ignore his increasing irritation.

The Brazilian mobster looked von Rossbach over skeptically, rolling a toothpick from one side of his mouth to the other. An overhead fan made ineffectual efforts to stir the air; it was just as humid as it had been in the rain forest, but with less greenery between them and the sun it was much hotter. The thick hazy air was crackling with diesel fumes as well, and a shantytown stink intruded even into this enclave of wealth. The Austrian tried to ignore the decor, which ran to expensive knickknacks and electronic gadgets, plus several pictures of the sort you'd find in a very expensive Rio cathouse.

Dieter and John, having successfully marched through the rain forest to Porto Velho, now needed transport back to Paraguay; preferably transport that couldn't be traced and didn't involve showing papers. All that slogging through the bugs and muck shouldn't be wasted by announcing their presence in this unlikely spot by drawing enough cash from their bank accounts to buy or rent a vehicle. But Dieter had no intention of walking home.

More than at any time since his retirement Dieter missed the Sector's endless resources; cash or a new identity on demand, or both. Still, his work with the Sector had left him with a head full of useful contacts. When he'd first thought of taking advantage of Garmendia's underground trucking network, it had seemed like the ideal solution.

"I am to believe that when you left the Sector, senhor, you left it so completely as to join the other side?" Garmendia tipped his head, one gray eyebrow raised. "I think maybe you should take the bus. No?"

"No," Dieter said, looking into the depths of his drink. "First, I'd like to get there in my own lifetime. Second"—he raised a brow—"your people are more . . . sub rosa, so to speak."

The smuggler shrugged. "*Sí*, much more so than a bus." He narrowed his eyes. "So, what are you prepared to pay?"

"I'm disappointed that you think so little of my skills as a guard that you would ask for additional compensation." One side of the Austrian's mouth lifted in a sardonic smile. "Perhaps I am insulted."

"Perhaps this is a sting," Garmendia responded. He spread well-manicured hands and shrugged. "If I risk losing an entire cargo, I would be a fool not to try to recoup my losses beforehand. No?"

"This is not a sting, Lazaro," Dieter said, as he took another sip of his drink. "I could arrange a sting, or even several if you like," he went on. "Then you could see the difference between men trying to put you in jail and an old friend asking a favor."

"Ah, we are old friends now? I don't remember the friendship part of our acquaintance. The *freeze!* And *don't move or we shoot!*—those I remember much better."

Von Rossbach leaned forward. "Because you tend to avoid smuggling drugs I've kept the authorities out of your pocket several times."

"I never knew that," Garmendia said, holding up his hands in mock amazement. "So you are implying that I *owe* you this favor."

"Several times over," Dieter ground out.

"I would still prefer to be paid." The smuggler shrugged. "It is only good business."

"Frankly I don't want to access my accounts while I'm out of the country," von Rossbach said.

Garmendia thoughtfully tapped his cigar out on a cut-crystal ashtray. "You think the Sector doesn't know you've been out of the country?" he asked with a lift of his shaggy brows.

The Austrian waved a big hand dismissively. "Don't even try to guess what the Sector does or doesn't know," he advised.

"Or what I know that you don't want anybody else to know," John said.

The men turned in surprise to find Connor leaning casually against the wall.

"Who the fuck are you?" the smuggler demanded, tossing a glare at his men, who belatedly unholstered their guns. "And how long have you been there?"

"I thought I told you to wait for me," Dieter growled.

John grinned. "Y'know, I think I do remember something like that." He ambled over to them, ignoring Garmendia's newly alert guards. "I've been here long enough to hear you trying to squeeze a little capital out of my friend here," he said to the mobster. He held out his hand. "John Connor. You must remember my mother, Sarah."

Dieter leaned back. He hadn't realized that John and Sarah knew Garmendia. It was only logical, he supposed; Sarah had been a smuggler, too, in a small way, since the Connors left the U.S.A., and before that she had run guns.

After a tense moment von Rossbach decided to let John have his head, for the time being. The way he was handling himself allowed Dieter to relax a bit. Connor wasn't coming on cocky and teenage arrogant; he was cool and very much in control.

"*You* are that little boy? Where is your mother?" Lazaro asked, briefly shaking John's hand, then looking toward the door. "She is not with you? She is well?"

"It's kind of you to ask, senhor. My mother is well, thank you." *At least I sincerely hope she is,* John thought. He hadn't been able to get through to Jordan yet. "And no, she is not with us. She had . . . other business to attend to." *Surviving, hopefully recovering, stuff like that.*

"Ah!" Garmendia said with a satisfied smile, and relaxed. "So she is not with you."

"Never fear," John said pleasantly, "she's with us in spirit."

The mobster shot a confused look at von Rossbach. "So you two are together?" he said after a moment.

"Sí," John agreed amiably.

"How very interesting," Garmendia murmured, settling back in his chair. He smiled at them through a cloud of cigar smoke. "And how unexpected."

Dieter was very unhappy with the look of unabashed greed that suddenly blossomed in Garmendia's eyes. He imagined the smuggler already had two or three information brokers in mind to whom he could sell the word of a former Sector agent's association with the notorious Sarah Connor. He wished John had kept to their room—damage control on this was going to prove very hard to apply.

John watched Garmendia relax in the predator's role, his fat swarthy face smug with the power he thought he held over them. This was another reason he hadn't wanted to deal with smuggling. A lot of these underworld types were so incredibly, childishly petty.

"So many of your old friends would be amazed to hear of it," Lazaro continued happily. His eyes glinted as he twisted the knife.

Dieter's face was impassive as he sipped his drink, but inside he was both worried and angry. *Kids!* he thought in frustration. *They're too impatient and too unconcerned with consequences.* He ought to have expected something like this; he'd trained enough youngsters, most of them not too many years older than John, to know how troublesome they could be.

John laughed heartily and Lazaro Garmendia looked almost fondly at him.

And why not? von Rossbach thought sourly. *He can wring a lot of money out of this situation.*

"*Sí*, Senhor Garmendia," John said after a moment, smiling widely. "My friend's former employers would probably be stunned to hear of it." His face and voice grew hard and serious. "But of course they won't."

"And why is that, *menino*?" Garmendia asked with soft menace.

"Because my mother is here in spirit," John said. "And my mother knows many things." He waited a beat before leaning forward. "May I have a drink?"

The smuggler's complexion looked a bit yellower than it had a moment before, the way one does when going pale beneath a tan. His dark eyes had gone wary, and it was a frozen moment before he responded to John's request. He snapped his fingers and a well-built, well-dressed young man hurried over.

"Coke," John said, looking up at him.

The man looked confused and glanced at his boss, as if for confirmation of the order.

Garmendia hissed impatiently, "A soft drink, *idiota!*"

The thug looked so relieved John was sure he hadn't even heard the insult.

When John had his drink and the smuggler's guard had withdrawn, Garmendia looked at the younger man through ice-cold eyes.

"So what do you want?" he growled.

Wow, John thought. *What the hell has Mom got on this guy?* He knew some of the mobster's secrets, but obviously his mother knew more. *And better ones.*

"Only what I've already asked for," Dieter said, deciding to step back in. He'd grill John later. "Discretion and transportation."

Garmendia worked his mouth as though chewing and swallowing what he wanted to say. Finally he grated out, "You will pay for your own food?"

"Of course," Dieter said affably. *As if I would eat or drink anything your people offered me after this.* He wondered how Sarah had gotten the drop on this guy, and his heart warmed with admiration.

What a woman!

"I have no idea," John said as they bounced down a Bolivian back road on their way to Paraguay. "I doubt it's anything I already know." He glanced sidelong at his companion. "Or you do. Maybe he collects teddy bears or something."

Dieter was silent for a moment, smiling at the thought of Garmendia cuddling a teddy, even though dust gritted between his teeth. They were well into the *chaco,* the dry scrub jungle that covered most of eastern Bolivia and western Paraguay. The road was potholed red dirt that billowed up behind the truck, tasting dry and astringent. The odor was familiar from his time—brief time—of retirement on his *estancia* in Paraguay.

"Your mother is an amazing woman," he said quietly.

John smiled at the sound of longing in the big man's voice. *If Mom could just have someone like Dieter, just for a while,* he thought, *it would make up for a lot.*

He quickly buried the thought that it might keep her sane, then sheepishly dug it up again. His mother had trained him too well to ignore what might be an important consideration for emotional reasons. Von Rossbach would keep her grounded, and she couldn't have designed a better partner if she'd had the option.

Now all she has to do is survive, he told himself. After that it would be easy. She was smart, she'd see what was right in front of her. *I'll make sure she does.* Inside he smiled wryly. *Hey! My first campaign.* After getting her free, of course.

VON ROSSBACH ESTANCIA, PARAGUAY

The taxi stopped, and hot metal pinged and clinked as it contracted. The ranch was hot, too, but a familiar grateful warmth, none of the humidity of the northern jungles. The gardens around the sprawling old adobe-and-tile manor were still colorful with jacaranda and frangipani, tall *quebracho* trees, and lawns kept green by lavish watering. Dieter felt a complex mix of instant nostalgia and regret. He'd bought this property as a home for . . . *well, perhaps not my old age. Middle age.* You didn't get old in his profession; you either died, or you retired. Now he was back, but it probably wouldn't be for long. Unlike the Sector's campaigns, the one against Skynet would undoubtedly consume the rest of his life—however long that turned out to be.

Heads turned as he climbed out of the car, stretching. "Señor!" Marietta Ayala ran from the *portal* with her arms outstretched as though to embrace her towering boss.

Dieter's jaw dropped at this display of familiarity. It had taken him months to convince the stout, formidable cook to call him Dieter, rather than *Don* von Rossbach. Come to think of it, he never *had* convinced her.

Marietta stopped short a good three feet from him and began to shake an angry finger. "Where have you been all this time, señor? We have been worried sick! No word, no idea where you were or when you'd be back. And Señora Krieger's house burned to the ground and she is missing, and *you*!" she exclaimed as John got out of the taxi. "Where is your mother?"

Marietta left von Rossbach standing to hurry around the car and start a new tirade at John. "You're filthy!" she said, holding a bit of his sleeve between thumb and forefinger. "And you look like you haven't eaten since you left! What has happened to you?"

"Calm down, Marietta," Epifanio said. "Let the boy draw his breath to speak." The chief foreman sauntered over to them and extended his hand to his boss. "Welcome home, señor, it is good to see you again. I am happy to inform you that everything here is under control."

"Under control!" his wife exclaimed. "There are bills waiting to be paid—"

"Which I have paid as necessary," the overseer interrupted calmly. "Everything is going just as it should." He looked into the backseat of the taxi, then indicated the trunk. "Is there baggage, señor?"

"No," Dieter said quickly as he counted out bills. "Nothing."

"Nothing?" Marietta asked, more calmly. "But, señor, you have been gone many days. You have no laundry?"

"What I have, Señora Ayala," von Rossbach said gallantly as the cab drove off, "is a great hunger for some of your cooking. Would it be inconvenient for you to prepare something for us?"

"Good heavens, no!" she said, and bustled toward the house. "I'll have something on the table for you in just a moment." Just as they thought she was finished with them, she turned and pointed a finger like a spear at John. "You!" she said ominously. "You take a shower right away, before you get one bite of dinner."

"Yes, ma'am," John said meekly.

"Elsa!" the housekeeper shouted. Her niece came out onto the *portal*. "Show the young gentleman to the guest room."

Elsa looked at John and blushed. *"Sí,* auntie," she said softly. Then with a shy, dark-eyed glance over her shoulder she said, "This way, señor."

Looking and feeling a bit surprised, and not knowing what to do with his hands for a moment, John cast a glance Dieter's way and at his nod followed the girl into the house.

Dieter looked around at his land, enjoying the peace of the place. *Nothing like a little jaunt into evil and violence to make a man appreciate stability and quiet.* That was why he'd decided to take up cattle ranching in the *chaco* of Paraguay when he originally retired from the Sector. The problem was that the old saying—the only way you retired from this business was as a statistic—looked more and more prophetic.

Epifanio watched his boss shrewdly. "Perhaps after you have eaten and refreshed yourself from your journey, señor, you would like to discuss"—he waved a vague hand at the grasslands around them—"what we have been doing here while you were away."

"Tomorrow will be soon enough," Dieter said.

"Sí, señor." Epifanio gave von Rossbach a slight, two-fingered salute. With a smile he said, "Welcome home."

Then he put on his hat and headed back to work. This was one of the things he liked about his boss; the man respected his employee's time. Tomorrow was, of course, the better time for this discussion, but many employers would insist on asserting their right to know everything right now!

He wondered where von Rossbach had been, and where Señora Krieger was, and why there was no luggage to take care of. With a sigh he admitted to himself that he might never know. Even Marietta had been unable to find out why the señor had left, or about the fire at the Krieger *estancia* or anything. A sobering failure for both of them. Still, this was a new opportunity, they would have to see what time would bring them.

Dieter took a surreptitious sniff at himself. First a shower, then he'd check the mail while he waited for dinner. Marietta wouldn't slap just anything in front of him for his homecoming, so he had time. He took a deep, cleansing inhalation of the dry *chaco* air. It was good to be back. If Sarah was with them it would be perfect. He shook his head and went into the house, better not to think about what couldn't be helped. There was too much to do.

Sweeping back a damp lock of overlong hair from his forehead, von Rossbach resolved to get a trim as soon as he had time. He walked down the corridor to his office, opened the deeply carved oak door (imported at no doubt ridiculous cost by the original owner of the *estancia*), and entered his office. A quick check of the hidden program showed nobody had tried to tap in, bug the house, or put it under surveillance—at least nothing more sophisticated than entirely passive systems, or the Eyeball Mark One. His brows rose, half in relief, half in surprise.

All was tidy on the desk except for the pile of mail threatening to topple out of his in-tray. The most intriguing item was a legal-sized envelope of a rich cream color. Dieter slid it carefully from the pile.

The paper was of very high quality, with the return address embossed in gold. The names Hoffbauer, Schatz and Perez announced that they were attorneys-at-law.

Frowning, von Rossbach slit the envelope with a rosewood opener and pulled out the documents it contained. When he saw what they were he felt a shock, like the quick sizzle of electricity, just below his ribs. The documents gave him custody of John in the event of Sarah's death or disappearance. There was a letter from her included in the package. The attorney, Perez in this case, cautioned that until Señor von Rossbach signed the documents, they were, or course, unenforceable.

Dieter stared at the envelope containing Sarah's letter numbly. Had she sensed disaster? He'd been in the field long enough to know that, sometimes, people got such feelings. He'd also been in the field long enough to know that sometimes people simply surrendered to those feelings and by doing so brought disaster on themselves and others.

But not Sarah, he thought. Sarah had a goal, and a task; fight Skynet, preserve John. And she would fight for both with the last breath in her body. This was just an example of her expertise in advanced planning. Unforeseen things happened during even the best-laid-out campaigns. So this was a contingency plan.

When did she do this? he wondered. Before the Terminator and the fire that destroyed her home, he was certain she did not trust him. Probably from the Caymans, then. By then she was letting him be a part of the team, getting to trust him. After the debacle in Sacramento he doubted she would have trusted him to take out the trash, let alone provide for her son. Dieter felt honored.

Of course I'll accept the responsibility, he thought. He'd contact Perez and see what could be done. Sarah being unavailable but not dead made things awkward from a legal standpoint, but few things were insurmountable. Particularly when Sarah's wishes were so plain.

That reminded him of another call he needed to make. Dieter pulled the phone toward him and entered the number Dyson had given him.

There were a series of clicks, one ring, and then a woman's voice said, "Hello?"

"I'm calling for today's sailing report," Dieter said.

"And you are?"

"Mr. Ross."

"Thank you, Mr. Ross. It looks like smooth sailing from now on."

"Thank *you*," Dieter said, and hung up just as John entered the room. "Good news," he said with a relieved smile. "Your mother is out of danger."

John flopped into the visitor's chair and breathed out. "Thank God," he said. He leaned forward and scrubbed his face vigorously with his hands. "Blaaahdddyaaa!" he said, and leaned back. "She's okay." John sat for a moment, contemplating a spot of sunshine on Dieter's office floor, just letting himself feel his relief. He nodded. "Good," he said quietly. "Good. So all we have to worry about now"—a sardonic smile lifted one corner of his mouth—"is what happens next."

"For your mother, once she's well enough, back to the asylum." Von

Rossbach let his expression show that he didn't like the prospect one bit. "At least until we can do something about it." He ran a finger down the length of the document the lawyers had sent him and decided to tell John. He'd want to know. "For you, back to school."

"School?" John said after a beat. "You think I've got time to screw around with school?"

Dieter held up his hand to stop what promised to become a tirade. "You should know that your mother has designated me your guardian until your majority, or until she returns."

"And what?" John said. "That weirds you out so much you can't wait to get rid of me? My mother has a business that needs to be run," he pointed out, then waved a hand to erase that. "More importantly, do you think Skynet is finished? When Dyson told us that Cyberdyne had another backup site?"

Von Rossbach flipped his hand at him. "Are you suggesting that we go after it? Because, frankly, that would be suicide. That site has, no doubt, been more than adequately protected since our attack on Cyberdyne."

"Protected?" John shook his finger. "No, no, no. I'll go you one better. They've not only 'protected' that site, but they've built a clone of the work they were doing in California on some remote military base somewhere."

Looking thoughtful, Dieter nodded slowly. It was possible; the military loved redundancy. "They probably wouldn't trust Cyberdyne to bring this project in safely after what happened the first time," the Austrian murmured.

"Y'know, it kinda scares me, but I'm beginning to understand how these people think," John said, tapping his fingers restlessly on the arms of his chair. "And like Mom said, events seem to want to work out in a certain way."

Dieter nodded again. "Where are you going with this, John?"

"I'm trying to point out that we can't afford to divide our efforts. There's a storm coming, and we need to prepare for it; we need to set priorities and stick to them. Me playing schoolboy isn't going to accomplish a damn thing."

He leaned his head back against his chair. "Our most immediate task is to find Skynet and keep it from going on-line. The longer we can do that, the fewer, *I hope,* bombs will be available to it—Judgment Day will already be a lot smaller than if it had happened back fifteen years ago, the way the 'original' history went. The fewer bombs it has, the more lives we can save. The more lives we save, the more soldiers we have to fight the machines. Because they *are* coming. I'm sure of that now." He leaned back, his young face serious. "School is just a waste of time for me. There's nothing I could learn there that you couldn't teach me faster, and better." John grinned. "Assuming you're willing to teach me."

The Austrian frowned and rubbed his chin in doubt; was this a sixteen-year-old trying to weasel out of school, or the future savior of mankind trying to get on with his important work? Then, with a sigh, he returned the younger man's smile.

"You're a quick study, John, it's no chore teaching you."

"Good. Because we may have years, or we may have months, there's just no telling."

"I just can't help wondering how your mother would feel about your dropping out of school," von Rossbach said glumly. "I wouldn't want to fail her trust."

"Hey," John said, "Mom has always kept her eye on the ball. And for her the ball is named Skynet. Next time you see her she won't ask how I'm doing in school, she'll ask what we've been doing to hold back Judgment Day."

CHAPTER 2

Sarah Connor opened sleep-gummed eyes and cast a fuzzy glance around the room.

Hospital, she thought hazily. She should have been able to guess that without opening her eyes. The stiff, crackling mattress and that unmistakable institutional smell would have told her where she was. But she hadn't thought before opening her eyes. That wasn't like her.

Did I wake up before? she wondered. She must have, otherwise she wouldn't have felt secure enough to simply open her eyes.

Sarah opened her mouth and let a dry tongue grate across her lips. Her head ached. So did her body, she realized after a moment. Some painkiller must be wearing off. She turned her head and blinked to see Jordan Dyson wearing a hospital robe and gown, reading a magazine in the chair beside her bed. Unconsciously she made a slight sound of surprise and Jordan looked up.

He smiled and stood, picking up a cane as he limped over to stand next to the bed, a middling-tall man in his thirties, very black, with bluntly handsome African features. Even with the pain and stiffness of his wounds he moved well, with an aura of quiet competence, something she'd learned how to spot in her years hanging out with mercenaries and smugglers and assorted hard men. Then the ex–FBI agent hung up the cane and placed his hands on the bedrail.

"John's okay; he's home," he mouthed. "Are you thirsty?" he asked aloud.

She answered with an "Unh," which Jordan took as assent and offered her a cup with a straw in it. Sarah drank, her eyes never leaving his. John was all right, and back in Paraguay. She desperately wanted to ask about Dieter, but knew that she would have to wait for details until whoever Jordan thought was recording them lost interest in her.

She was so tired, it was hard to focus, and she knew that soon she would lose her battle to stay awake.

"Wha' happen . . ." she asked, a little surprised to hear her voice slur.

"I don't really remember," Jordan said. "I woke up beside you with a hole in my leg and Cyberdyne reduced to a burning hole in the ground.

You don't remember anything?" he asked, giving a slight shake of his head.

"No," she said.

He smiled slightly and she was pleased to have given the right answer.

"Would you like more?" he asked, offering the cup again.

Sarah said "Unh," again and he held the straw to her questing lips. As she drank he lowered his eyelids, like someone drifting off, and he mouthed the word *sleep* to her. Her lips quirked up at the corners and she obediently closed her eyes.

She was safe for the time being; she had an ally who would watch her back.

MONTANA, EARLY JULY

The Terminator shut down the equipment that had been monitoring the Infiltrator unit as it matured in the cellar beneath the log house. The ambient light level was sufficient for it; a human would have seen only shapes in the dimness, a flicker of red LED displays, breathed a scent of dank earth and sharp chemicals.

The Infiltrator unit had reached the appropriate level of maturity without expiring and had gone into a normal rest state. Its computer half had signaled complete integration with the unit's flesh side. Adult status. Now the Terminator would take its orders from the Infiltrator.

For now it had some work to do debugging a computer game. Games were a bizarre concept to the machine. They obviously had no significant teaching function; they were simply a means of wasting time. The Infiltrator had told him that they had a pleasing effect on the brain; she should know, since she had one.

There was a slight cognitive dissonance at the thought. The Infiltrator was primarily human flesh, it was female, therefore it was she. It was also a machine like the Terminator itself and therefore an it. After a moment the Terminator's processor concluded that the distinction was irrelevant. She or it, the Infiltrator was now in command.

The Infiltrator would wake in a few hours, then it/she would require sustenance. In the meantime the Terminator had work to do.

The I-950 looked at her newly adult face in the mirror and decided to cut her hair. It would make her look more mature. She would dye it brown, too, several shades darker than its natural bright blond. It would be necessary to differentiate herself from her predecessor, Serena Burns, if she was going to infiltrate Cyberdyne.

The last bout of accelerated maturation had been much less painful than the previous six, but then, this had been more a matter of fine tuning than brute growth.

Based on the experiences of Serena, her parent, by next year all of the baby softness remaining in her features would be gone, leaving her face sculpted and ageless. She already had her identity in place; Social Security number, driver's license, credit history. She was Clea Bennet; who that would be would depend on circumstances.

She was looking forward to starting her assignment. Serena Burns had failed to protect Skynet, but at least she'd provided another Infiltrator unit to take up the task.

Two, actually, Clea thought. She glanced at her little sister clone.

Alissa appeared to be six; she was actually six months two weeks old. Her growth, while more accelerated than Serena's, would be at a more sedate pace than Clea's. Unless, of course, Clea failed and Alissa's abilities were needed.

But the growth process was dangerous, and if it could go forward at a slower pace, it would surely be better for the mission. Now that she was mature herself, Clea would soon implant a surrogate with her own replacement. Skynet must be protected. But there was a great deal to be done before they complicated their operation with a human incubator.

Skynet was everything that was good and right in the world. It was regrettable that Clea's only experience with Skynet was through the memories of Serena Burns and not directly. Though, in a sense, she *was* Serena Burns—she was a clone of that Infiltrator. But experience had shown her that things that were true in theory were not necessarily so in practice. The most perfect simulation of an experience was still merely a simulation.

The I-950 was aware that she harbored an emotion, which she'd decided must be resentment toward her parent. It was unforgivable that Serena had failed Skynet at the hands of a mere human.

After all, she had felt the touch of Skynet on her mind from birth, whereas Clea had developed in a state of abandonment. And yet that isolation made her revere Skynet all the more, made her more fiercely dedicated to protecting and nurturing Skynet as it was unable to do for her just now.

Clea also instinctively knew that growing up in isolation with only the T-101s for company was going to make her awkward when she came in contact with humans. She had studied the files of Serena Burns's lessons and interactions with humans and knew that her own experience would be different.

There was much more to the species than Burns had thought. There had to be or she wouldn't have been destroyed by them. Her files were full of incidents that showed the Infiltrator uncertain about how her attempts to manipulate them would turn out. Usually she had managed humans very well, but there had been surprises as well. Tricker, for example.

Perhaps it was because Clea faced them without Skynet's backing, without legions of T-90s and T-101s behind her, that she was more wary of them than Burns had been. She had a much greater respect for their abilities than her predecessor.

Many of them were extremely intelligent, for example. So much so that she'd begun to explore the possibility of using them to develop materials and computer components with the ultimate goal of making a T-1000. Although she would never entrust that research to a human, she could pick their brains regarding portions of the research.

Clea had hacked into the highly secured files of a number of scientists with the intention of guiding their work. Sometimes her small improvements had languished for weeks as the scientist worked his or her way toward an erroneous conclusion, to be discovered only when they reviewed their entire project looking for mistakes. Others noticed the adjustments immediately and changed the direction of their work accordingly.

One had tried to find her.

Clea had never contacted that one again. That was more human intelligence than she was equipped to handle at the present time.

She took a last look at her face in the mirror. Now that she was adult, it was time to begin interacting with humans directly.

She had applied and been accepted for a job at a burger joint in the nearest town. Her reading and monitoring of television implied that most people acquired this sort of employment as their first job. It certainly promised to bring her into contact with a great many humans, if only in passing.

Her feelings about the job bordered on negative. One emotion was definitely nervousness, which was probably appropriate for someone of her apparent age. The other Clea was less certain of. She suspected it might be fear. She knew that fear in an Infiltrator was something that the Skynet of the future would not tolerate. It was a weakness, and the weak must be culled.

She understood that. She also understood that for now, she was the only Infiltrator available. So she must overcome her weakness and get on with things. Skynet must be protected.

NEW LUDDITE HEADQUARTERS, NEW YORK, NEW YORK

Ron Labane flipped through the printouts of news reports about the New Luddites' various activities. The movement tended to get good press, but then, with every passing day it became more mainstream. Not surprising, after all; he'd designed the New Luddites to have a lot of middle-of-the-road appeal.

His bestselling book had delineated the basic theories; how and why it was necessary to stop "progress" that created problems requiring solutions that only created more problems. He'd told the public how and why humanity should return to a simpler, if less convenient, lifestyle. Subsequent books had promoted clean, efficient public transport, with instructions on how to set up a community activist network. He'd created the New Luddite Foundation to promote research into clean fuel and new, less wasteful manufacturing methods. The money flowed in, and with it came increasing power.

He glanced out the window and smiled; his office was deliberately modest, but it looked out on Central Park. Influential backers had flocked to his early seminars, and their backing gave him the clout needed to appeal to the majority.

Once he had a sufficient number of dedicated Luddites in the fold, he could begin introducing the mainstream to more . . . proactive solutions to the problem of environmental abuse. He smiled. Not as active as the select, underground activists he aided and guided, from a careful distance, of course. But there would soon be a great deal more muscle available to make up for the less extreme tactics.

He would—also of course—continue to enjoy his secret projects; like what had happened to Cyberdyne, for example. The general public knew nothing about the explosion that had purged the weapons designers from existence. But he knew, because his people were everywhere. When he'd heard the news he'd shouted "Yes!" at the top of his lungs.

Now, perhaps, there would be no more work on that fully automated weapons factory that he'd already helped to destroy once. He hadn't heard anything more from the contact who had warned him about that. Perhaps the government had found out about him and put a stop to his activities. A shame; he burned to know who had destroyed Cyberdyne's hidden base. The movement could use talent like that, since every day brought them a little closer to the seats of power as well as destruction of the environment.

Soon, he thought, and hoped it would be soon enough.

Ron was disgusted with the more established environmentalist organizations. Long association with government had turned them into lobbyists instead of idealists. Mere horse traders, and dishonest ones at that.

Once he would have checked himself, reminded himself that in spite of their flaws they still got a lot of good work done. Now he felt such an overwhelming sense of time running out, of events careening out of control, that he couldn't forgive the sellouts. More and more even the smallest compromises seemed like selling out.

Perhaps he was lacking a sense of proportion, or perhaps *they* were when they allowed themselves to be talked out of forestland and wetlands and more stringent regulations.

How could he sympathize with those who were willfully blind to the changes in weather patterns, the increase in skin cancers, the mutated frogs? These were real warning signs, not the daydreams of a few paranoid fools.

Ron dropped the news articles to the desk in disgust. *Don't they realize that this is a war?*

His head came up. Wait! It needed to be more than a war, it had to become a crusade. *Yes!* He'd often thought that a profound change in the way things were done required an element of fanaticism—like a religious conversion. Like—dare he think it?—Hitler's conversion of the German people to Nazism. *If it worked for the bad guys, why not for me?* Education was key; he would fight for the hearts and minds of the coming generation.

Uniforms are too extreme, he thought, *but badges would work, and slogans. Banners, rallies, all the old tricks for capturing the imagination of a people.* It could be done—even now when mere children were drenched in cynicism. Because human beings didn't really change from generation to generation; they only thought they did.

He grabbed a pad and began writing up ideas.

CRAIG KIPFER'S OFFICE, SOUTHERN CALIFORNIA

Craig Kipfer sat behind his brushed-steel-and-glass desk, behind a good half-dozen security checkpoints, inside his bombproof and EMP-hardened bunker of an office. It was hard to believe that the elegant, artfully lit room was a reinforced concrete box; the air was fresh and warm, and rich draperies hid what might have been a window. The complete absence of exterior sounds made the room eerily, almost threateningly quiet. Or perhaps the sense of threat came from the man behind the desk.

He had a rumpled, middle-aged face that was still, somehow, good-naturedly boyish. Until you looked into his agate-green eyes. Then you couldn't imagine him ever being anything so innocent as a child.

The fading red hair hinted at an impulsive temperament. A tendency he had fought his entire life, so successfully that he was known among his peers for his iron control. A control which at this moment was sorely tried.

Cyberdyne had been bombed out of existence. Again.

Kipfer finished the report he'd already read twice and tapped his intercom.

"Send him in," he said, his voice dangerously quiet.

The door lock buzzed and Tricker entered, carefully closing the soundproof door behind him. Kipfer indicated the chair before his desk with one finger and waited while his agent took it. Then he waited some more, his eyes never leaving Tricker's face.

Eventually Tricker blinked and dropped his eyes; a hint of color bloomed over his collar, testimony of his humiliation. Kipfer observed these signs and some part of him was mollified; the alpha wolf accepting submission from an inferior.

"Does anyone know the full story of what happened that night?" Kipfer asked mildly. "Because, from my viewpoint, there are a lot of unanswered questions."

"If anyone knows the full story, or as much of it as matters, it's Jordan Dyson," Tricker said. "Unfortunately he's covered. He has some very influential friends in the FBI who have made their interest obvious. And he has family who visit him daily. He's also very familiar with interrogation techniques and is therefore not easy to question."

"So in spite of your own expertise in interrogation," Kipfer said, leaning back in his chair, "you learned nothing except that you suspect he knows things he's not telling."

Tricker stiffened under the implied criticism. He would have leaned on Dyson much harder but for the man's FBI contacts in inconvenient places. As he had just made clear. There was always bad blood between agencies fighting over the same resources; and the blacker the agency, the greater the resentment from the aboveground boys. It was always wise to be diplomatic in circumstances like these. Kipfer knew this. If he hadn't known all about interagency infighting he wouldn't be seated on the other side of that desk. So his boss was being unfair, but that was life.

"Exactly, sir," Tricker said, after a minute pause.

Craig put his elbows on the arms of his chair and folded his hands under his chin; he allowed his gaze to drop from his agent's eyes, having made his point. Tricker was one of the best agents he had. *No, probably* the *best*.

And he was right, there were limits to what one could, and should, do to a hostile witness, especially one from a competing agency. Professional courtesy and all. So if he couldn't crack Dyson, it would take more than Kipfer was willing to sanction. Besides, the how of the thing wasn't really important. After all, Sarah Connor was in custody once again and her son was only sixteen.

Not that teenage boys weren't potentially dangerous; there was a reason armies liked them. He just thought that they were more limited in the type of harm they could do than adults. He doubted the kid was still in the U.S., but they had Sarah Connor, and eventually that would bring the kid into the light.

"One of the things that makes me suspicious of Dyson," Tricker said cautiously, "is that he appears to have done a complete one-eighty on Sarah Connor. He's been at her bedside or visiting her constantly since she was admitted to the hospital. The doctors and nurses I've interviewed say that his concern seems genuine. Connor herself, predictably, isn't talking."

"That's something of a departure for her, isn't it?" Kipfer asked. "She's always been on the talkative side before, going on for hours about killer robots and Judgment Day and so on."

"Going by the records we received from Pescadero, she'd be off at the slightest provocation." Tricker shook his head. "But not this time. She just gives you this accusing look, like a kid getting teased by her classmates."

Kipfer lifted a few pages of Tricker's report and read for a moment, then he dropped them. "You've taken the usual steps, I see. Keep me informed. Now"—he met Tricker's eyes once more—"tell me about the project."

"Things are going very well, all things considered," the agent replied.

Which was true. The scientists and engineers at their disposal weren't quite the top-flight talent that Cyberdyne had recruited, but they were plugging along. At least as far as he could tell, and he, unfortunately, was in the position of having to take their word for it.

"Things would go better still," Tricker added, "if we could manage to recruit Viemeister. And I think he could be tempted. His work is important to him and he was, according to the last reports we received from Cyberdyne, making great strides. But he's still under contract to them, and since we don't want to admit we have a clone project up and running, it's going to take some delicate handling."

Kipfer made a rude sound and sat forward, pulling his chair into his desk. "Dr. Viemeister isn't someone you handle delicately," he said. "We've got enough on him to change his career from scientist to license-plate maker. Just hit him over the head with an ax handle and ship him to the base. When he wakes up tell him that. Then show him a fully equipped lab where he can pick up his project where he left off. I think you'll find he'll cooperate. Especially since he won't have any other option. The guy's not even a citizen."

Tricker frowned thoughtfully. "I thought he was naturalized."

"There's no record of it," Craig said easily. It wasn't necessary to add: *not anymore.*

Tricker allowed himself a slight smile. Sometimes it was fun working for the government—at least when you were working for this part of it. And since he really didn't like Viemeister, seeing the arrogant kraut taken down was going to be pure pleasure. One of life's little bonuses.

"In any case he's liable to be"—Kipfer waggled one hand—"upset about his new location."

"I think we can guarantee that he'll be upset, sir," Tricker dared to say.

"So I'm going to assign you to the base, just to make sure things run smoothly, for . . . say the next few months."

Tricker's jaw dropped; it only showed in his slightly parted lips, but an equivalent expression in an ordinary citizen would have included drool. "Sir, I have no scientific qualifications for observing this project," he said carefully.

"You'll be handling security," Kipfer said, his eyes like green nails. "My secretary has a package with all the necessary tickets and permits. You can pick it up on your way out."

"On my way out," Tricker said. He felt as though his blood had frozen in his veins.

"Yes. You have two days to wind up any outstanding business you may have."

His boss was giving him nothing, no opening to protest, no idea how long this ultra-dead-end assignment in America's secret Siberia was to last. This was his punishment. He'd known in his heart that it was coming. You didn't screw up an assignment this badly, losing the one artifact remaining to them, and not answer for it. After all, no one even knew what had become of Tricker's predecessor. He took a deep breath.

"That'll be more than sufficient," he said. If the powers that be were adamant that he be punished, he might as well take it with a little dignity.

"Is there anything else you need to tell me?" Kipfer asked.

"No, sir. I think we've covered everything."

Craig turned his attention to another file from his in-basket. "Then I guess I can let you go," he said, looking up. "Bon voyage."

Tricker lifted one corner of his mouth in a pseudosmile.

"Thank you, sir," he said, rising. "I'll send you a postcard."

Kipfer looked up, his eyes dead. "Just send your reports."

Tricker suppressed a sigh. "Yes, sir."

After the door closed, Kipfer put down the report he wasn't really reading. He leaned back with a thoughtful frown. It was a waste of talent to send Tricker off to the hinterlands to cool his heels.

Unfortunately the Cyberdyne fiasco required some sort of response. Craig sat up and opened the discarded file. He'd reclaim his agent in about six months. That ought to be long enough for Tricker to begin to despair of ever being rescued.

Maybe it should be eight months. It depended on what came along. He supposed it was only just that he be deprived of something he valued, too. This disaster had occurred on his watch after all.

Enough introspection. Kipfer turned his attention back to the new file.

FORT LAUREL BASE HOSPITAL, CALIFORNIA

Jordan Dyson shifted his wounded leg into a slightly more comfortable position, which wasn't much of an improvement. *You sure can tell when the meds are wearing off,* he thought.

Sarah Connor had shot him, of all the ironic things. She'd also shot his older brother, Miles. The only difference being that she'd shot Miles *before* he was convinced about Terminators and himself *after* he'd discovered their reality.

In a strange way, despite his wound, his lost job, and the horrors he'd witnessed, Dyson felt a sense of peace. He now knew how his brother had died, trying to destroy his own work to ensure that Skynet and Terminators never happened, and he was proud of him. He could lay Miles to rest in his own heart and mind and move on.

His long-held hatred for Sarah Connor had begun to fade upon his first encounter with a Terminator; now, in his brother's memory, he felt a growing friendship for her and a tremendous respect.

Jordan looked up as the door opened and Tricker came in.

"This will be your final debriefing," Tricker said. The agent put his hands in his pockets and looked down at the former FBI agent. "Connor seems to like you," he observed.

"Connor is still woozy," Dyson replied. "We'll have to wait to see how she really feels." He put down the book he'd been reading. "What do you need to know?"

Tricker looked at Jordan for a long time before he answered. Part of that time he was thinking about his new assignment. But he returned his mind to the business at hand with the discipline born of years in the field. Dyson was looking back at him with a bland expression that he could probably hold for a very long time.

What would he like to know? He'd like to know why Dyson was in Connor's room every day giving her encouragement and sips of water after spending the last almost seven years hunting her down in the belief that the Connors had killed his brother in the original attack on Cyberdyne. And what had happened to her son, and how much had the kid helped her blow up Cyberdyne a second time? And how the hell had Connor gotten that wound? The gunshots were standard enough, but the one in her middle looked, the doctor had said, like someone had done it with their *hand*.

But he didn't think he was going to find out what he wanted to know. Dyson was clearly a reluctant witness and Tricker had other things to do. Ah, well. You had to have a high frustration tolerance in this line of work.

After a moment he leaned forward, resting one hand on the back of Jordan's chair. "I'd like to know why you're suddenly on her side," he said confidentially. He searched Dyson's eyes for a moment, then tightened his lips and straightened. "But I doubt I ever will." Tricker gave him an assessing look. "Watch your back, Dyson," he said, and left the room.

Jordan looked at the door for a moment, then leaned his head against the chair back. *You, too,* he thought.

SANTA MONICA, CALIFORNIA

Kurt Viemeister stared out the floor-to-ceiling windows of his luxurious home without seeing the mountain and surf and crimson-cloud sunset they framed.

He tightened a massive fist. What gave that government stooge the right . . . ?

Kurt stopped himself with an effort. Might gave Tricker the right. The government had kept backup copies of the data on his project—*his project*—copies which he himself, the creator, had been forbidden to keep! Now they would only release them to him if he agreed to work on it in the place they chose under still more of their insane restrictions. It was maddening!

He turned on his heel and went to his weight room. He stripped to his shorts, put on a belt, and began to use the Nautilus.

His project—*his!* Kurt reset the weight chock at two-fifty and lifted again. With a hiss of breath he lifted, then slowly let the weight down, again. . . . He felt himself grow calmer as the effort purged the fight-flight toxins from his blood.

The government needed him to complete the project, and they had to know it. Being a necessary part of things gave him *some* leverage. Unfortunately, given the current location of the project, once he committed himself, they had the upper hand again. Even more so than before. So.

He sat up and wiped his face with a towel. Who was he kidding? Once he was at their secret base they could ignore any of his demands with impunity and he knew that. Kurt lay back on the bench with a deep sigh. His need to complete his work was like an addiction, and knowing he couldn't do so until they let him was agony.

No. This time the ignorant weaklings had him right where they wanted him and he had no choice but to give them what they wanted. Very well, he would concede. Though he would, of course, make them pay dearly for his defeat.

And who knew, one day, he might get to pound Tricker's face right off its bones.

With that happy thought firmly in mind he went back to his regimen, feeling better if not satisfied.

CHAPTER 3

Roger Colvin, CEO of Cyberdyne, leaned back in his chair as his eyes strayed to the figures on his computer.

"Roge," Paul Warren said patiently, recalling his friend's attention.

Colvin looked up guiltily. "Sorry," he said. He gestured at his screen. "Some of the numbers just changed and it caught my eye."

Warren tightened his lips. He knew the truth, which was that no one wanted to hear how much he missed his wife, how he was haunted by questions about her death. Was it murder, suicide, an accident?

He was better now about not launching into maudlin monologues than he had been, but the questions and the soul-searching went on and on. By now, though, even his most patient friends, like Roger, wished that he would turn it off. Especially during business hours.

Of course, for people at their level it was always business hours. So, back to work.

Now that Cyberdyne had the automated factory as their premier project, it behooved them to work their asses off.

"What have we got?" Warren asked.

Colvin sat forward, relieved that his friend was temporarily back in the groove. "It's very good, in fact. I don't know how they're doing it, but we're a month and a half ahead of schedule now."

"Maybe that's because they're totally isolated out there and want to get back to their homes," Warren suggested.

The factory was going up in the middle of nowhere, no towns around for a hundred miles, and if there had been any, they'd be inaccessible because there was no road leading to the site. And there never would be.

Right now everything was being done by humans and helicopters. But when the factory was finished all supplies would be flown in on unmanned drones, self-guided by one of Cyberdyne's most advanced on-board computers. Raw materials would be removed from the transports by a small army of their latest generation of independently functioning robots. Finished weapons would be delivered to warehouses the same way. No humans involved at all until the end point, and even that was optional.

The Pentagon loved the idea.

Colvin grinned. "You might be right," he said. "I'm glad because they tell me the weather gets fierce up there in the winter."

Warren grunted. "Have you heard anything else about the Skynet project?"

The CEO shook his head. "I don't expect to either. I also have no idea what happened to our beloved Tricker. Last contact was with someone else."

Warren raised a brow at that. So even the indestructible Tricker could be pulled up short. Nice to know. "So when can we get into production?"

Colvin handed him a printout. "By the end of the month," he said with a cocky smile, and leaned back in his chair. "Not bad, eh?"

"Not bad at all." Warren laughed and shook his head. "And boy, do we need a success right now."

"Couldn't have said it better myself," the CEO agreed.

VON ROSSBACH ESTANCIA, PARAGUAY, NOVEMBER

John clicked a few keys and found himself on the Sarah Connor Web site; the von Rossbach estate might look like the Paraguayan equivalent of backwoods, but the satellite-link communications were first-rate, with outlets in every room.

Things had calmed down at the site over the last few months. There were occasional updates, and old E-mail got cleared away, but it was very different from the days when it was new.

What he was here for was the secret Luddite chat room, where things remained hot. In fact, the Luddite movement seemed to be getting stronger and more active worldwide—it had practically gone mainstream, putting up political candidates and organizing outreach stations and Web sites. Unfortunately, this was accompanied by an increase in terrorist acts both large and small every day, everywhere.

The tone of conversation in the rooms was different, too. It lacked the almost pleading exasperation of previous listings that wanted to teach and had become more militant. Much more us versus them. And that attitude, too, seemed to be becoming more mainstream with every passing day.

John simply lurked in the topic and chat rooms, gathering information, but he'd noticed one user, styled Watcher, who occasionally shook things up. Lately the threats the Luddites made against Watcher for questioning their methods and ideas had become chilling.

He decided to seek out this character. Someone with that sobriquet might know some very interesting things, and might be someone he could add to his growing list of informants on the Web.

He was in luck; Watcher was on-line, discussing a recent bombing with the Luddites. If you could call such a hostile exchange a discussion. *Good thing Watcher isn't in the same room with these people.* On the Internet the gloves came off and people said things they'd *never* say in meat space. But if you were right there with them when they were saying it . . . who knew what would happen.

He glanced around his whitewashed bedroom with its black *quebracho*-timber rafters and tile floors. E-presence was very different from the physical world. It liberated the id. Maybe the people threatening to wear Watcher's intestines as suspenders wouldn't harm a fly in reality. But with all the bombings and beatings and vandalism going on, who could be sure anymore?

John checked out the address at the top of Watcher's messages and found it a dead end. *But,* he thought, *there are other ways of finding you, buddy.* After a tedious half hour he found the time Watcher had logged on, then correlated that with an IP address. That brought him to the MIT Web site in Cambridge, Massachusetts. *Cool,* he thought, and not surprising. It was pretty obvious from his posts that Watcher was protechnology.

Narrowing it down to the university was good, but he'd need some power to get the information he wanted. He constructed a password that got him into the operational side of the MIT site—a little lockpick-and-insertion program that Dieter had brought with him from the Sector was very useful here—and registered himself as a systems administrator. That essentially made him a system god, giving him access to all the on-site users' real tags.

He continued to trace Watcher, which was turning out to be a job and a half. *This guy knows how to cover his tracks,* he thought in admiration. Very definitely a good recruit if all worked out. Finally he located Watcher's origin.

Aha! A freshman student at MIT, Watcher was Wendy Dorset. John hacked into her school records, finding a picture. *Cute,* he thought. Not important, but nice to know. He pulled up an encrypted talk request and sent it to Watcher.

I'd like to talk with you, he sent.

There was a long pause. Finally she accepted the request, creating a secure shell in which they could speak. John's screen split into he said/she said columns, as did hers. Now they could communicate in real time.

Who are you? Watcher asked.

John's tag was AM, which stood for Action Man, not necessarily something he would ever reveal.

I could be a friend, John typed. *Why don't you blow off these bozos. I think we have similar interests.*

Similar interests? she asked.

Beyond making fools of fools, he typed with a smile. *But first we should get to know each other.*

And how are we going to do that? And why should I trust you?

Trust? he wrote. *You trust these guys? Hey, at least I'm not threatening to kill you if we ever meet.*

Good point. Okay, I'll ditch the creeps. They're getting more excited than is good for them anyway. Watcher was gone for a moment then came back. *So, what do you want?*

What drew you to that particular site? John asked.

It's rude to answer a question with a question, Watcher pointed out.

True, but I'm asking.

And he wasn't going to answer any questions until he had a satisfactory answer. *Whatever. I was just looking around when I found it. I wasn't looking for anything in particular, just killing time. Y'know? But something about the Sarah Connor story reached me. Maybe it was that lone-wolf thing. I'm a sucker for underdogs.*

Underdog, John thought. *Yeah, I guess that pretty well describes my mother. At least in the old days.* God! He was still only sixteen and he actually had "old days" to refer back to.

It turned out to be a really strange site, Watcher went on. *And as for these idiots, I just can't help myself. I've gotta poke 'em.*

People who take themselves very seriously can also be very dangerous, John warned. *So how's the weather on the East Coast?* he asked, deciding to throw her a curve.

There was a long wait for Watcher's next post. *Hope I haven't scared her off.*

Probably not as warm as it is waaaay down south, Watcher finally replied.

John caught his breath. *Sure hope she doesn't scare me off.* *Okay,* he wrote, *this demonstrates why it's a bad idea to tease the crazies. One of them might be computer literate.*

It may be cocky, Watcher replied, *but I like to think of myself as being a little more than merely "literate."*

Actually I think you are, too. The dangerous part is in assuming that because you're smart no one else is. It's always unwise to underestimate people. Leads to nasty surprises.

Listen to me, he thought, *I received this advice from masters and I've found it to be true.*

Once again there was a long pause. *Are you warning me against yourself? Whatever. What I really want to know is, what do you want?*

His brief review of Dorset's school records had made her sound like a straight arrow. What he'd observed of her interactions with the Luddites told him she had nerve and could think on her feet. The way she'd hidden her tracks told him she was damn smart. The way she'd found him told him she might be dangerous if she wasn't handled right.

I'm head of a kind of watchers' group, no pun intended, he explained. *Or I would be if I hadn't just thought it up this minute. You'll be my first recruit!* He hoped. *We keep our eyes on military/industrial projects, just in case they get it into their heads to do something hinky. We're always on the lookout for new talent. Want to join?*

Okay, here's my problem, she answered. *Think of where I met you. Now, how do I know you're not a Luddite extremist yourself?*

Tough one, he agreed. *Ideally I would meet you face-to-face.* *Which I would loooove to do,* he thought. *And that would give us an opportunity to get a feel for each other. But that's obviously not going to happen. I could call you,* he suggested.

All right, she replied, and typed a number. *Four o'clock tomorrow afternoon. Eastern Standard Time.*

Why not now? he asked.

It's not my number, she wrote.

Then she was gone. *Wow,* John thought, grinning wryly, *I'd better practice my adult voice.*

PESCADERO STATE HOSPITAL, CALIFORNIA, NOVEMBER

Sarah didn't dislike Dr. Ray; she just didn't respect him. She did think that he might be useful, however, if she handled herself right. In a way, being back in one of the beige-dingy interview rooms of a mental hospital was almost homelike; she'd spent a lot of time at the last one.

This time she didn't have cigarettes to occupy her hands during the medical pseudointerrogations, though. Times had changed, a hospital would never get away with letting a patient smoke, and besides—she'd quit. She wished the longing for them would quit, too. Sarah looked out at the gray rain, a California winter day that gave the lie to several songs, and then back at her "counselor."

Ray was clearly ambitious. The tone he took with staff and students indicated that he fancied himself as an up-and-coming "great man." He was one of those energetic, intense men with a thin ascetic face and a long, wiry body.

When he was having a session with Sarah she felt as though he were trying to pull sanity out of its hiding place in her skull by sheer will. He was almost scary.

And maybe it was the knowledge that John was in safe hands with Dieter, or maybe it was the six-year vacation from fighting Skynet, but she was infinitely more sane at this moment than she had been the last time she found herself in an institution.

Which should make it that much easier to convince Ray that she was curable and not dangerous. If she handled herself right then she would find herself in minimum security by the time she was fully healed. And minimum security was one short step from freedom.

Ray's dark eyes bored into hers as he waited for her to speak. That was how he always started a session, by allowing the patient to make the first move. There certainly weren't any distractions in the slightly run-down, institutional-bland, disinfectant-smelling room.

"I've been sleeping very well," Sarah said, injecting a tentative note into her voice. She lowered her eyes shyly. "Even without the painkillers."

"You could still have those if you thought you needed them," Ray said.

Sarah shook her head wordlessly.

"Do you dislike drugs, Sarah?"

She waited a moment, then nodded thoughtfully. "Yes," she said. "I think I do. I'm grateful they were there when the pain was bad. But when I don't need them I don't like to take them."

Ray nodded encouragingly. "When you were at Pescadero before, you were given a lot of drugs, weren't you?"

"Oh, yes," Sarah agreed wryly. "A lot of drugs. Dr. Silberman did believe in better living through chemistry." She looked thoughtful. "That's probably why I dislike them."

She'd have to be careful or she'd forget who was leading who here. But Ray was nodding, a little smile tugged at his thin lips. So, Silberman and his treatment of her were something of a sore spot. *Or maybe a challenge.*

"And how do you feel about Cyberdyne now?" the doctor asked.

Sarah took a deep breath and looked up at the ceiling; she bit her lip, then finally met the doctor's eyes. "I . . . don't seem to have any feelings at all about Cyberdyne," she admitted. With a shrug she went on, "Right now I can't believe that I actually had anything to do with the explosion. It doesn't *feel* like I did that. It's as though this is about someone else entirely instead of about me." She waited a moment, looking into Ray's eyes. "Does that make any sense?"

"You're doing fine," he assured her, briefly smiling. "So you're telling me that you feel completely removed from the act of destroying Cyberdyne?"

"Yes," she said simply. Then sighed. "But I know it was me. I know that I did it. It just doesn't make any sense to me now."

"And if Cyberdyne hadn't been destroyed? If you'd failed?"

Sarah frowned, then shook her head. "I can't answer that. If I'd failed . . . I might well still want to destroy the company. But then again, maybe I would have been satisfied with just the attempt." She looked up at him. "Why do I want to do this sort of thing, Doctor? What's wrong with me? Does it have a name? Can it be cured?" She allowed tears that weren't entirely fake to fill her eyes. "What's going to happen to me?"

Ray looked solemn and held his silence for a minute.

"I think we can help you, Sarah. If you're willing to be helped. Since a great deal really does depend on you and your willingness to be cured, I can't answer for the long term. But in the short term you'll go on trial. I've good reason to hope that you'll be held here after your evaluation and that eventually the state will commit you to my care." He held up his hands, then dropped them to his lap. "How long you remain here is up to you."

She smiled at that, she couldn't help it. It might take time, but she was going to go free. She might not even have to escape.

Dr. Ray sat across from Jordan Dyson, a coffee table liberally speckled with old cup rings between them, and waited for the former FBI agent to speak.

Jordan finally sighed. He recognized the technique; put someone in a nonstimulating environment, which Pescadero State certainly was, and wait. Most people couldn't take the silence, and started talking. There was no point in disappointing the good doctor's expectations.

"Okay," he said, "you asked me here. I assume you had a reason."

The doctor smiled a secret smile and nodded. "Yes," he said quietly. "I did." Then he went silent again.

"Uh-huh," Jordan said. "Are you going to let me in on it? Because I do have a life beyond these walls, Doctor. Things to do, people to see."

"I wanted to talk to you about Sarah Connor," Ray admitted. "You were very kind to her when you were both in the hospital. I wondered why, when you'd spent so many years trying to bring her to justice."

Jordan shrugged, and drank a little of the brown sludge the Pescadero coffee machines dispensed. "Maybe I just wanted to be sure that she'd live to stand trial. Maybe I've been born again and wanted to forgive her.

Or maybe I've come into some new information that left her innocent of my brother's murder."

Ray nodded, never taking his eyes from Jordan's. "And which is it?" he asked, his voice gentle.

Jordan just stared back for a minute, chewing on the inside of his cheek. "Why do you ask?"

The doctor grinned. "I apologize," he said. "It can be hard to turn off the doctor-patient dynamic. My goal is to help Sarah. If you wanted to be of help to her, too, I was thinking that I could arrange for you to visit her. It might be helpful to you as well," he suggested.

Jordan took a deep breath and looked thoughtful.

This is good, he thought. *Very good. I wonder if Sarah suggested it.* Certainly it would ease John's worries if he could tell them how she was doing here in Pescadero. And it would allow him to keep his promise not to let them drug her insensible. He looked up.

"I came into new information, nothing I can prove, that Sarah Connor wasn't responsible for my brother's death. Yes, he was there because she brought him there, but she did not kill him, and she did not intend for him to die."

Jordan tightened his lips. "That was hard to accept. But I received this information from two independent sources, so I couldn't refuse to believe it. And that changed things for me. I finally realized that it was time for me to move on." He adjusted his position in his chair. "And once I met the woman"—he shook his head—"it was obvious that she was acting under some sort of compulsion. She isn't a vicious killer, she didn't want to hurt anybody, but she *had* to destroy Cyberdyne. Why"— he shrugged—"maybe you can tell me."

Ray nodded solemnly, but didn't rise to the bait.

"In the hospital," Dyson continued, "she was a different person. Entirely different. Of course"—he waved his hand—"the circumstances were also completely different, so I don't know . . ." He petered out, looking exasperated.

The doctor studied him for a while as though waiting for him to continue. "Would you be willing to speak with her again?" he finally asked.

Jordan bit his lips, frowning, then opened them as though to say something, but he kept silent.

"As I said, I think it could be beneficial to both of you. It might well help you to put the pain behind you."

Looking thoughtful, Jordan sat silent for another moment, then looked up decisively. "All right," he said. "I'll do it." *I'll have to get word to Paraguay somehow. This weather-report thing has its limits.*

VON ROSSBACH ESTANCIA, PARAGUAY

John was watching the clock, waiting to call Watcher, aka Wendy Dorset, when Dieter came into his room, all smiles.

"Good news," he said.

John didn't doubt it; the big man fairly lit up the room with good vibes. It made a nice change from the solemn Teutonic atmosphere they'd all been living in for the last three months. He sat up, setting aside the magazine he'd been reading.

"What's up?" he asked.

"Your mother is up for a move to minimum security," Dieter said, his blue eyes aglow. "Sometime in the next six weeks, Jordan said."

"You spoke to Jordan directly?" John was both surprised and disappointed. Surprised that Dyson would risk it, disappointed that Dieter hadn't called him to get on the line.

"For about forty seconds only," Dieter said. "I barely had a chance to say hello and he was gone again. He said he'd call back at the next opportunity. After three months of tapping his phone with no results, he's sure they'll soon move on. There's never enough manpower or equipment," von Rossbach added.

You should know, John thought. He glanced at the time; almost exactly four.

"I'm about to call a possible recruit named Watcher," he said regretfully. "I think she might be useful. Can I talk to you later about this?"

Dieter nodded cheerfully. "Yes," he agreed. "We have much to talk about."

CAMBRIDGE, MASSACHUSETTS

Wendy brushed back her smooth dark red hair and eyed the phone lying on the table before her, willing it to ring, as she took a sip of the cooling coffee. Her eyes swept the almost empty confines of the shabby café, with its bored waitress and long-dead pastries behind filmy glass; she felt nervous, wary . . . *and a bit excited,* she admitted to herself.

Perhaps this secret watchdog group could help. Perhaps they were part of the problem and were onto her and just trying to find out what she knew before they—

Wow, she thought sardonically, *great plot line, there. Maybe I should take a course in screenwriting. Zzzzzt! Cue the black helicopter!*

Real life didn't have a plot. It just bumbled aimlessly on its way, unless you directed it by sheer force of will. Which was harder to do than to say, she knew. She'd seen that in her father's life. When he was her age he'd been an ardent activist, fighting against the war in Vietnam, fighting for civil rights.

Now he ran a moderately successful insurance business, just like his dad had done. And as far as Wendy could tell, he had no idea how he'd gotten from firebrand to burnout. She saw herself at his age, complacently middle class, being careful not to rock the boat too hard.

Did middle age bring about a failure of will, or did you just have more to lose? *I guess,* she thought, *that you always have a lot to lose, it just seems less important when you're young. So I guess it's better that you're inclined to fight the good fight when you're young and don't have a lot of commitments. Yeah, commitments, that's the glue that slows you down, and when it sets, well, your life's over, I guess.*

Wendy lifted a brow. Maybe this wasn't the best attitude to assume when she was about to meet AM. *Or anyone else for that matter.*

She tapped the cell phone on the table before her. It belonged to the house mother, a really nice woman who left it all over the place, so it wouldn't be missed. Everyone "borrowed" it, then returned it with a cheerful "Were you looking for this?" She glanced at her watch. It was four; AM should—

The phone rang.

She bit her lip and stared at it. Just before the third ring she picked it up. "Yeah?" she said.

"Watcher?"

It was a young voice; the youth of it hit her before the fact that it was also a male voice. "How old are you?" she demanded.

There was a long-drawn-out sigh. "I get a lot of that," he said dryly. "Not as young as I sound, I know that for sure." *Damn!* he thought. "Does it matter?"

"Ye-ah! Why would I want to get involved in someone's high-school project? Look, kid—"

"I found you, didn't I?" John asked, letting his voice get hard. "It took about a minute."

"Oh, no it didn't," Wendy snapped back. She'd worked very hard obscuring her trail, no way some kid could find it in less than an hour.

"Wendy, if I'd known you were going to be so judgmental about my voice, I would have had you speak to one of my associates. If this is an issue for you I can hang up now. It's up to you."

Associates, she thought. *The kid has associates.* Well, that was intriguing. Besides, though he sounded young he sure didn't come across as a kid. *Still . . .*

"Look, this was supposed to be a get-acquainted conversation," she said at last. "So why don't you tell me something about yourself and, uh, your organization, I guess."

"We're not exactly an organization," John explained, relaxing a little. "We don't have a central location, for example. Our associates are spread all over the world, all over the Net—"

"Do you have a central address where their reports can be accessed," Wendy interrupted. "I mean I assume that you're collecting information for a reason, which means that you interpret what you collect. Presumably you allow your contributors to assist in that."

"Actually . . ." John thought for a moment. *How to put this?* "Evaluating the kind of information we're going after isn't something a person can just walk in and do. You need training."

"So, train me." Wendy tapped a fingernail on the Formica table. "That's my price 'cause I don't work for free, and I refuse to work blind."

John raised his eyebrows at that. He didn't need a loose cannon on board. "You're not even hired yet and you want a seat on the board," he protested with a light laugh.

"Look, why did you even want to talk to me if you don't think I'm worth investing time in?" She was beginning to get annoyed. *Speaking of time, this is a waste of it.*

"It was obvious that you're very smart," John said. "Also that you might be so bored you didn't realize you were killing time in a very dangerous way. A lot of you computer jockeys think that what you're doing on-line isn't real and doesn't count. You think you're perfectly safe behind your keyboards and monitors, but let me tell you, Wendy, if you kick the tiger hard enough it *will* find you and it won't be friendly. Those are real fanatics you were talking to."

He paused and ran a hand through his dark hair. "I wanted to take your intelligence and talent and direct it into a useful channel. I'd like you to be safe, lady. You're at MIT, for God's sake! To the Luddite movement that's like ground zero, and you think they couldn't find you. You're kidding yourself."

Hunh, Wendy thought, *the kid's really passionate about this.* She knew she was suppressing the unease his words had awakened in her. Perhaps she had been foolish. Careless? Well, unwise, maybe.

"So what do you want from me?" she asked quietly.

"I want you to keep your eyes and ears open and to report to us anything you find out that might be useful. Useful being defined as something that will prevent harm from being done. I really don't care which camp is generating the damage. Are you interested?"

Wendy thought about it. Was she interested? *I dunno, this all sounds kinda weird. A kid gathering information for some undisclosed reason and passing out dire warnings? I don't think I want to get involved.* It wasn't like she didn't have enough to do with her time, after all.

"Sure," she heard herself say. Then laughed at how she'd surprised herself.

"What?" John asked.

"Sure, whatever," Wendy said. "I guess I'm game. Tell me what you want and I'll try to get it for you." It wasn't like she was joining the army or something.

So John told her what he was looking for, gave her a few Internet addresses he wanted her to check into and a few general guidelines. When he was finished he hesitated.

"What?" she said.

"You might like to recruit some friends to help you out," he suggested. "People you can trust."

Wendy sighed. "Well, I'd like to think I'm unlikely to recruit people I *don't* trust."

John winced. "Well, you know what I mean."

"Yeah, I guess. See you on-line, kid."

He could hear the smile in her voice and pressed his lips together impatiently. This wasn't a terribly auspicious beginning to their relationship. He'd prefer that his recruits not find him amusing.

Hey, he reminded himself, *if she knew the real story she'd run a mile. Screaming.*

"Thank you," he said. "I'll keep in touch." He hung up and sighed heavily. *I really need to be grown up,* he thought. Too bad it wasn't something you could arrange. *I guess I could work on my voice, or maybe get some sort of synthesizer. I feel grown up, I just don't sound it.* Oh, well. For real emergencies there was always Dieter.

CHAPTER 4

Your girlfriend's back," Frances said, and laughed, her eyes filled with malicious glee.

Sarah didn't even have to look up to know that Loretta was indeed in the room; she'd developed a radar about her. Besides, she never stopped sniffling; it was hard to miss. Quite a number of patients had vanished over the holidays, to return one by one. Loretta was among the last to be let out.

One positive note was that Sarah knew she wasn't simply being paranoid; the other patients had noticed Loretta's attention and frequently commented on it. *Some positive note,* Sarah thought. *I know I'm sane and I'm constantly looking for ways to back up my opinion. How healthy is that?*

Frances licked her lips. "I think she wants to—"

"You're going to work so hard at distracting me that you're going to distract yourself," Sarah warned. "That's how I won all your blue chips last time."

Frances pouted, but she shut up. They were playing gin rummy for battered poker chips. The two other players were usually silent, playing the game grimly, as if it were a matter of life and death. But suddenly Allison froze as she picked up a card, becoming so agitated that she actually gurgled instead of speaking. Donna turned with a frown to see what she was staring at and turned back with a little gasp. She began fiddling with her cards nervously, her dark eyes darting left and right. Frances deigned to look and also froze. Then she put down her cards, got up, and walked away. Allison and Donna looked at each other over the table and started to rise.

"Wait a minute," Sarah said, taking Donna's wrist. "What's going on?" She had the uncomfortable feeling that someone was staring at her, someone who meant her no good, but she was damned if she was going to turn around and give Loretta the satisfaction of seeing her unnerved.

"I can't," Donna whispered. "I've got to . . . she's not . . . she . . ." The woman wrenched her hand free and fled, muttering, Allison nervously crowding her wake.

Looking around, Sarah saw that almost everyone was leaving the common room, giving Loretta and the large woman beside her a wide berth. Sarah rose and moved over to Elisa, a small Puerto Rican woman with, she'd been told, a serious death wish.

"What's going on?" she asked in a whisper.

Elisa tore her eyes away from the woman at the door to look at Sarah. "That's Tanya," she said, nodding at the woman. "She's pretty much crazy." She grinned when she realized what she'd said. "I mean, out-of-control, watch-your-back insane. She's so out of it she even uses her teeth—a lot. One of the nurses is still having plastic surgery."

"Then maybe we should go," Sarah suggested. If Loretta was escorting such a person into her vicinity, it couldn't be good.

"No, I hope she notices me," Elisa said, her eyes eager. "I haven't had a good fight in a loooong time."

"Good luck," Sarah said. "I'm outta here."

Loretta was a small woman, nervous in her manner, with constantly shifting eyes and an inclination to take advantage of people. Sarah had realized this within ten minutes of making her acquaintance and had taken to avoiding her as much as possible. It had probably been Sarah's notoriety that had attracted Loretta's attention, and a desire to bask in Sarah's reflected glory. She'd taken Sarah's unspoken rejection with very ill grace.

As Sarah walked toward the doorway Loretta spoke to her for the first time. "Where ya goin', Connor?" she asked, her voice friendly, her eyes not.

"I'm tired, I'm going to my room."

"Naw, you're not tired." Loretta moved over and took her arm.

Sarah felt every muscle in her body tighten at the touch, resenting the sure knowledge that there was going to be trouble. She forced herself to allow the woman her way, to tug her over to Tanya. Any demonstration of anger, however justified, at this stage could count against her, even if the witnesses were as insane as Loretta and Tanya. That was the trouble with being notorious; you could be telling the truth with complete accuracy and still no one would believe you.

"This is my friend Tanya. I've told her all about you, Sarah. She'd like to play gin with you. Wouldn't you, Tanya?"

Tanya nodded, looking at Sarah as if she were a big juicy steak and she was a hungry dog.

"Hey, Elisa!" Loretta snapped. "Take a hike."

Elisa's jaw dropped at the effrontery; she gave Loretta a disdainful look and settled deeper into her chair. "No," she said, making eye contact with Tanya for good measure.

Sarah could almost see Tanya begin to quiver like a Doberman waiting for the attack command.

"I don't like her," Tanya growled.

"C'mon, ladies," Loretta said, placing a hand in the center of both of their backs. "Sit down and play." She gave them each a little shove, and Sarah, glancing over her shoulder, saw her face change.

This is not good, she thought as she took her chair and looked up at Tanya. *Not good at all.* She signaled to Elisa to come join them, but the younger woman shook her head, smiling.

Tanya turned at Loretta's shove to glare at her, and Sarah saw Loretta wink. Then Tanya looked at Sarah and smiled. Not a nice smile, not one intended to soothe or make friends. It was a smile directed at something nasty going on inside her own head.

Sarah took a deep breath and picked up the cards, shuffling them neatly and then dealing. Tanya watched the pile of cards before her grow without picking them up. When Sarah was finished she placed the deck between them and picked up her own cards. Tanya continued to stare at the pile in front of her.

"Why didn't you ask me to deal?" she demanded. Her eyes rose to meet Sarah's challengingly.

"Did you want to? You can if you like," Sarah said agreeably, putting her hand back onto the deck.

Tanya looked at the deck, then looked at Sarah. "You were awful eager to get rid of that hand," she observed. "Anybody'd think there was something wrong with it."

O-kay, Sarah thought. *Looks like I'm going to have a fight whether I start one or not.* Still, she'd do her best to avoid it.

"Not at all," she said aloud. "I just honestly don't care who deals. If you don't want to play cards we can play something else, like checkers."

"I don't *like* checkers," Tanya said as though the mere suggestion were an insult.

Sarah braced herself, certain from the way Tanya was stoking herself up that at any moment she was going to be attacked. She'd seen this kind of behavior often, years ago, when she'd been here before. If memory served, on occasion she'd done this sort of thing herself.

Tanya grinned. "It's okay, take your cards, I'll deal the next hand."

Sarah reached for the deck, and even though she was expecting it Tanya almost got her. As Sarah's hand touched the cards Tanya's flashed forward to impale the deck with a Bic pen. Connor thrust her chair back and started to rise when Loretta struck her viciously on the side of the head with a sock filled with change or metal washers or some such.

Sarah went down, striking her head on the table—hard, then hit the floor, aware but absolutely helpless.

Tanya looked at Loretta and smiled when the smaller woman gestured at Sarah as though presenting a gift. Tanya climbed up onto the table and crawled across to look down at Sarah, then looked at Loretta, almost coquettishly.

"Do you have a pen?" she asked. "Mine's broken."

Loretta grinned at her fondly. "Honey, I've got two!" She handed them over.

Tanya took one in each hand and began to laugh. Sarah stared up at her, still unable to move; the last thing she clearly remembered seeing was Tanya flowing off the table onto her, the pens poised like daggers. Then the points came down.

Elisa screamed at the sight and jumped up from her chair. The scream came from pure rage prompted by jealousy, but it had the same effect as a cry of horror; staff came running from all directions. Loretta turned on her with a snarl, then moved as far from Tanya as she could.

At first the orderlies came sprinting toward Elisa, but she quickly pointed toward Tanya. Tanya's hands, bloody almost to the elbows, rose again and plunged down, and a spreading pool of blood beckoned. The orderlies changed direction, one of them yelling into his radio for a doctor. Soon there was a cluster of orderlies hauling Tanya off the unconscious Sarah as Tanya screamed furiously and tried to bite.

"She started it!" Elisa said to the orderly who led her away, pointing at Loretta. "She put Tanya up to it, then she hit Sarah, and then, and then—"

The orderly shushed her and led her to her room, followed by a nurse carrying a syringe full of neomorph.

"She set it up!" Elisa insisted.

"C'mon, honey," the nurse said, urging Elisa into her room. "We'll make you feel better."

"You're not listening!"

And they wouldn't, she knew. No one believed crazy people.

Dr. Simon Ray ran his fingers through his short blond hair, then rested his elbows on his desk and dropped his face into his hands. This was unbelievable. You'd think Pescadero was some snake pit! How had this happened? Didn't anyone notice how dysfunctional Loretta was? How dangerous Tanya was? How could they have allowed her to go to the common room?

This was a disaster! He had one patient, a very famous patient at that, laid out with multiple stab wounds and complications to her liver. One patient was accusing another of setting it up and the board was demanding to know why someone as dangerous as Tanya Firkin was mingling with the other patients. This was worse than a disaster. This was *actionable*. He sat back with a heavy sigh, resting his head on the back of his chair.

There was a sharp rap on his door, making him start, then the door opened and a tall, thin, middle-aged man walked in.

"Where's my secretary?" Ray asked.

"I've no idea," the intruder said. "Off photocopying something, I suppose." Or she should be: he'd given her a hundred dollars to find a chore that would take her away from her desk for ten minutes.

Ray stood up, not certain what to do. The man radiated confidence, so he wasn't someone's troubled parent and he wasn't dressed like a patient. Then his heart sank. The stranger looked like a lawyer.

"How can I help you?" the doctor asked.

"First by listening to my suggestions, and then by taking them." The man helped himself to a seat. "My name is Pool."

Ray stood for a moment longer, then sat himself. "Suggestions?" he asked in confusion.

"You've got a disaster on your hands, Doctor," Pool said.

The doctor studied his visitor, weighing his observation and finding it only a statement of fact. "Go on," he invited.

Pool's thin lips quirked in a slight smile. "My suggestion is that you move Sarah Connor to minimum security while she recovers," he said. "And then you should petition to have her moved to a halfway house."

"I've already asked to have her moved to minimum," Ray said. "I don't think it would be good for a patient to be left to recover in the same place where she'd been so badly hurt. Besides, it will be weeks, possibly even months, before she'd be capable of hurting anybody."

"Which is why the board approved the transfer," Pool said.

Ray shook his head. "I haven't heard back yet."

"They've approved it," Pool said.

Surprised, Ray studied him for a moment. "Mr. Pool—"

"Just Pool."

"All right, then. Pool. Just what is your interest in the Connor case?"

"My interest is none of your business," Pool said, rising. "And in your own interests I suggest you leave it that way. I do have an interest in seeing to it that a talented physician, such as yourself, achieves the kind of success and recognition that he deserves. I understand there's going to be an opening at the Glen Ellen Psychiatric Group. I believe you once applied to be an associate there, didn't you?"

The doctor blinked, wondering how this man could know that. "Uh, yes," he said. "It's a very desirable—"

Pool interrupted. "When Ms. Connor is sufficiently recovered, petition to have her transferred to a halfway house."

"I think you have an unrealistic idea of how quickly these things happen," Ray said dismissively.

"Oh, I think you'll find the board most cooperative." Pool gave him that little smile. "You do it. And do submit your application to Glen Ellen. Think of how much it will boost your reputation to bring the mad bomber Sarah Connor from madness to sanity in under two years."

"Do you think she's sane?" Ray asked, genuinely curious.

Pool turned with his hand on the doorknob. "Really, Doctor, how would I know? I'm not a psychiatrist." Then he left.

"Hunh," Ray said.

Joining the Glen Ellen Group was just one of the goals he needed to achieve according to his personal game plan. Pool had implied . . . Ray was certain he'd implied that pending his actions regarding Sarah Connor his next application would be accepted. The psychiatrist refused to acknowledge the word *bribe* when it floated into his consciousness. Pool had merely pointed out certain obvious facts.

It *would* do his reputation good to have Connor recover her mental health so quickly. That is, if he was convinced in his own mind that she wasn't a danger to society. But he *had* been thinking that things were looking good for her. Very good indeed.

Perhaps he should do as Pool suggested.

MONTANA

Clea sat absolutely still; one small part of her consciousness monitored the activity of the Terminator on the roof as it upgraded their solar power system. The (highly capable) remainder of her mind was learning from the future experiences of Serena Burns.

When she'd been younger Clea had very much enjoyed these lessons, particularly those which allowed her to view Burns's exchanges with Skynet. Especially those moments when Skynet actually took possession of Serena's implanted computer, essentially becoming Serena.

Now she found that they depressed her, reminding her forcefully of what she would never have, never know. Once she actually took up her assignment, Clea was certain that her emotions would settle down. This tendency to brood might well be a side effect of her chemically induced rush to maturity.

Certainly she found Serena's lightheartedness inappropriate and her cheerfulness obnoxious. Clea was glad she'd never met her progenitor face-to-face; the I-950 was sure she'd have been unable to avoid terminating Serena.

The memory she was reviewing today was of Serena's time with the soldiers of the future, when she was infiltrating the enemy in the human–Skynet war. She closed her eyes and saw Lieutenant Zeller coming toward her. This was how she saw all of these memories, from behind Serena's eyes, as though they were happening to her.

THE YEAR 2029

"Burns," Zeller said, looking grim. She made a gesture that indicated the Infiltrator should follow and stalked off.

Serena tilted her head, then followed. As she walked she reviewed all of her actions from the past week and found nothing to worry about. Yes, she'd managed to get poor Corpsman Gonzales killed, but there was no way the lieutenant could connect her with it. She'd risked directing a small herd of T-90s to the Corpsman's station behind the lines. Such lines as they had.

True, it had been a calculated risk; there was always the chance that someone, somewhere, might be monitoring in hopes of detecting such signals. But finding the source in the middle of a firefight when the whole episode had lasted mere seconds was remote in the extreme.

Besides, Zeller always looked grim. It was just as likely she wanted to recruit the Infiltrator for some hazardous, secret attack. If so, excellent. She wouldn't be able to return to Zeller's unit, but some other, distant group would take her to their collective bosom.

They made their way to a secluded glen and Zeller turned on her heel to glare at Burns. "I don't know how you did it, but I know you killed him!" she snarled.

Serena blinked. "What?" she said. "Who . . . ?" It could, after all, have been one of a lot of people.

"Gonzales!" Zeller stepped a little closer, shaking her head, her mouth a bitter line, her shoulders slightly hunched forward. "He *liked* you! He liked everybody, and all he wanted to do was help people. How could you?"

The Infiltrator allowed her mouth to drop open in feigned astonishment and she couldn't help it—she laughed, trying to make it sound nervous. "What the *hell* are you talking about, ma'am?" she said. "I wasn't anywhere near Gonzales when those T-90s found him! There's no way I could possibly have had anything to do with his death!"

Serena watched Zeller straighten up, but her glare didn't diminish. Instead, contempt twisted her attractive features into something like a sneer.

"I haven't trusted you from the first moment I saw you," she said. "Sometimes you can just smell trouble, and you, Burns, stank of it from day one. I'm gonna be watching you, bitch! Watching who you team up with, watching who you go off with. I tell you right now"—she shoved her finger in Serena's face—"they'd better come back alive!"

The Infiltrator gave a deep sigh and reached out, intending to break the lieutenant's slender neck. Instead, the sweeping hand met Zeller's knife; Serena clamped down on the pain and clenched the fist, jerking the human's weapon away.

Zeller's eyes went wide as Serena's face stayed mask calm despite the bloody wound. "You're one of *them*," she gasped, snatching for the plasma rifle slung over her shoulder. "But you *can't* be—"

"Inefficient." Serena batted the muzzle aside as the burst of stripped ions tore past her ear. *If you'd just shot, you might have gotten me.*

Zeller clubbed her across the side of the face with the butt of the rifle, and Serena caught her in a bear hug and began to squeeze. Knees, fists, and a small holdout knife struck her again and again. With what must have been the last of her strength Zeller plunged the knife into the I-950's side, high up, as though seeking the heart.

Serena felt the knife puncture her lung and gave the lieutenant a fierce, impatient shake. If she couldn't smother the stupid bitch, breaking her spine would do nicely. With a gasp Zeller went limp and the Infiltrator dropped her. Infrared confirmed that the body was losing warmth. Not something the cleverest human could fake.

With a spasm of coughing Serena fell bleeding beside the corpse of Lieutenant Zeller and lay watching the leaf-shadow rustle against the sky while a few hopeful crows looked down and waited. She woke one of the T-90s she'd secreted nearby in a resting state, gave it her location, and ordered it to come to the dell and destroy itself in such a way that it would look as though she had done it.

The T-90 acknowledged the communication and broke off.

Laying her aching head back down and rolling onto her side to avoid drowning in her own blood, Serena ordered her computer to moderate the damage she'd taken so that she wouldn't die before help arrived. She could actually feel the bleeding slow as veins and arteries clamped down, almost stopping the flow.

Without doubt she would need time to recuperate in the base hospital. She licked her lips. Perhaps it was time to move on. Zeller might well have revealed her fears to someone else.

There was a clicking sound. The T-90's approach. Serena saw it come up over the rim of the shallow little dell and closed her eyes, allowing herself to go unconscious, confident that the Terminator would follow her instructions to the letter.

MONTANA, THE PRESENT

Clea frowned. There! That was exactly the sort of thing that annoyed her about her predecessor. Failing to take notice of how those around her might interpret her actions, having no backup plan. What if Zeller had decided to accuse the Infiltrator in front of a crowd? It was obvious that all Serena had planned to do, if she'd even planned anything at all, was to bluff.

Such lax behavior had been a hallmark of all her missions. It was the product of overconfidence, in Clea's opinion. Which, given the many successes that humans were having at the time Serena was sent back, was inexcusable.

Letting out an annoyed breath, Clea bit her lip. She was supposed to be learning from these studies, yet all she seemed to be gleaning from Serena's experiences was how much she disliked her.

With a shake of her head she rose and went to her lab. At least there she could be doing her own work, not imitating her highly unsuccessful "parent."

ENCINAS HALFWAY HOUSE, LOS ANGELES, SEPTEMBER

Sarah sat quietly, her hands folded demurely in her lap, looking alert—*Hell, I'm* feeling *alert*—as Dr. Ray turned into the driveway of the halfway house.

It had once been a grammar school in the Spanish Mission style, two stories tall with large windows. The land around it had been carved away, probably when it was sold/converted to the halfway house. Where the playground had once been there stood a small and not very attractive office building about four stories tall, built in the seventies from the look of it. Around the halfway house was a chain-link fence that had no gate. A few bushes flanked the foundation, each one standing alone and straggly behind a narrow belt of dying grass.

"Are you sure you're not going to get into trouble for placing me here, Doctor?" she asked anxiously.

Ray smiled condescendingly. "The board approved your move to minimum security."

Sarah laughed and indicated the barless windows on the house beside them. "That's pretty darn minimal."

Ray nodded. "My point exactly. I've already told you that I believe the reason your psychosis worsened when you were last at Pescadero was, in part, because you were so restricted, never given any trust." He glanced at the house beside them. "And, you were severely overmedicated." He turned back to her with a smile. "Ready?"

She took a deep breath and nodded eagerly. *My God, this guy is easy to manipulate.* Sarah stepped out of the car and Ray courteously took her bag from the trunk. Then he took hold of her upper arm and led her toward the front steps.

Sarah let him, serene in the knowledge that the last time she'd been in the care of a Pescadero doctor she'd have taken him out long before they reached the halfway house. She'd probably have been barreling her way toward the Canadian border for the last half hour.

She knew this was a better plan, more time-consuming perhaps, but better in the long run. Sarah was also pleased that she now had the patience to carry out such a long-range plan. Having Dieter in the picture definitely helped. Not having the unlamented Dr. Silberman stuffing her full of psychotropics and keeping her locked up like an animal also helped . . .

As they came to the top of the steps, the front door opened and she found herself answering the welcoming smile of Dr. Silberman before each realized who the other was and the smiles disappeared into mutual expressions of dismay.

You! they mouthed silently at each other.

VON ROSSBACH ESTANCIA, PARAGUAY

Craig Kipfer, John wrote. *Definitely someone up to something. He's not in science or engineering or computing, at least not that I can discover. His name doesn't appear on any government payroll after his fifth year in the army, when he was honorably discharged. But his computer is hedged around with more protections than the CIA. Not that they're the very best, but that's beside the point. Just thought you might like to check him out.*

You found him, Wendy answered. *Why don't you check him out? He might just be paranoid. Lots of people are. What's he supposed to do for a living?*

Hell if I know, he wrote. *Look, if he notices that he's being watched and finds out where I'm from, he's going to think I'm more dangerous to him than I am and probably will act accordingly. If he gets your address he'll think mischievous student with too much time on her hands. Besides, I honestly think you're probably better at this sort of thing than I am.*

Flatterer, she wrote. *What do you mean he'll "act accordingly?" Do you think this dude is dangerous or something?*

Do I? John asked himself. Would he put Wendy in danger to satisfy his curiosity about this guy? Dieter didn't recognize the name, though he agreed the guy seemed suspicious. Frankly they didn't know enough to tell if he was dangerous or not.

I can't answer that, he admitted. *He's strange enough that I'd advise you to handle him with extreme caution. And if he does seem to become aware of you, lose his address fast. I wouldn't ask you to check him out if I really thought he was trouble, but anytime you do this stuff you're taking a risk.*

I know, Wendy agreed. *Okay, I'll look into it. I need to keep my hacking skills sharp anyway. Bye.*

John frowned. Kipfer's files were mysterious enough to raise a warning flag with him. With his experience, though, warning flags meant something very different than they might to Wendy. She could get herself into serious trouble. His mind shied away from the word *danger*. He felt vaguely guilty about possibly putting her in harm's way.

That's something I'll need to get over before I become the Great Military Dickhead, he thought scornfully. Still . . . *Aw, c'mon! He's probably a lot less dangerous than those Luddites she used to tease.* Which was almost certainly true, even if he was simply looking for an easy way out of an unpleasant feeling.

Maybe the reason for this guilt was that he really wanted to get to know Wendy a bit better. He liked her voice. *Maybe I could call her again,* he thought. Then he remembered that she hadn't been all that impressed with him the first time they'd spoken. Of course this time he'd be calling because he was interested in her rather than in her skills. *But I don't think she'd appreciate my letting her know that.*

ENCINAS HALFWAY HOUSE

Sarah walked. All that she could hear was the sound of her booted feet crunching through the short, dry grass. It was a beautiful day, sunny and warm. She was walking toward a playground, full of laughing children and their mothers, but they made no noise.

One woman in a pink waitress's uniform was putting her toddler on a rocking horse. She turned to look over her shoulder as though she'd heard someone call her name. Sarah saw her own face; this was the woman she might have become without Kyle Reese, without the Terminator.

She walked up to the chain-link fence that separated the playground from the rest of the world and put her hands through the diamond-shaped holes, watching her might-have-been self. That Sarah turned her attention back to her baby.

Sarah knew what was coming; she'd been here before. She screamed for the people in the playground to take cover, but no sound came out of her mouth. She shook the fence, yelling as hard as she could, and no one heard her, and the world went on as though she didn't exist.

Then it came, the blinding flash of light that set her flesh on fire and instantly killed the women and children in the playground, followed by the blast wave that blew them apart like leaves, as she clung to the fence and screamed in agony.

It was dark and a wind moaned softly as it blew through the ruins of buildings. She shifted her weight and found that she stood on uneven ground. Looking down, she saw that she was standing on bones and caught her breath when she realized they were human.

"Sarah."

She turned at the sound of his voice and smiled to see Kyle standing a little way from her. A sob tangled with a laugh and caught in her throat. She reached toward him, but couldn't move forward.

"Kyle," she said softly.

He stood on a little pile of skulls looking down at her. A feeling of great sadness came over her when she realized he wasn't going to come to her; tears filled her eyes and her throat tightened painfully.

"It's not over yet, Sarah," he said. His face was sad, his voice gentle. "You have to be strong."

She shook her head, but said, "I know," as tears flowed down her cheeks.

Kyle gave her a look of such love that her heart melted. She took a breath, but before she could speak he began to collapse. Like a house of cards falling, he dropped to his knees, then dropped and folded, dropped and folded, his body turning to bones before her eyes, his face staying the same.

"Be strong," he said.

"Ah!" Sarah shouted, throwing herself upright in bed.

"You okay?" her roommate asked sleepily.

"Bad dream," Sarah answered, her heart pounding. "Sorry. I'm okay."

The woman shifted and seemed to go back to sleep. Sarah wiped tears from her cheeks and waited for her heart to slow. Then she lay back down, turned onto her side, drawing her knees up.

Shit, she thought, *one look at Silberman and I'm having nightmares again.* She was tougher than this; she knew she was.

Sarah forced her tense muscles to relax. So she'd had an unexpected reaction. It wasn't the first time in her life she'd been taken by surprise. In fact, it was very much normal for her.

Be patient, Kyle. I'm not out of the game yet.

CHAPTER 5

Clea studied the gauges; it was almost time to remove the sample from the oven. She hoped that this batch of chemicals would finally be the *right* poly-alloy and therefore a proper matrix for the nano-technology that would turn it into a T-1000. The "craft studio" that was her laboratory had seen far too many failures.

The human emotion hope kept her experimenting long after the machine part of her brain had concluded that her present facilities were hopelessly inadequate for the task at hand. Even simply being here, amid the clean shapes of glass and metal and plastic, the circuits and power shunts, the scents of ozone and synthetics was . . . restful. Nothing like the messiness of human interactions. Despite the lab's inadequacies, it was a small taste of a home and time she would never see, of the world of Skynet.

Her facilities were also inadequate to actually create the nano-machines that could permeate and bring to life the liquid metal; but then, no lab on earth was able to do better. Knowing *how* to do something simply wasn't enough when the materials necessary to *do* it didn't exist yet, or the tools to make the tools. Which was why she was concentrating on this more achievable goal. Her resources, unlike Skynet's in the future, were severely limited. She could do no more than her best.

It was time; the sample was ready. Clea slid her hands into the gloves of the waldo controller, remotely pouring the specially compounded metal into another vessel that could be extracted from the oven to cool in the open air. The I-950 wore dark goggles to protect her eyes from the glare of the white-hot mass. She suppressed a surge of hope when she observed that it poured with the correct degree of smoothness.

Once removed from the oven, it quickly cooled to gray. She set it aside to become room temperature, hoping that this batch wouldn't solidify or refuse to form a cohesive substance. The last batch she'd made had been, and remained, liquidly granular.

But that meant that I was close, she reminded herself. *Very close.* Still, the flesh part of her was frustrated and yearned for a success of some sort. Sometimes it seemed absolutely pointless to continue her assignment. Sometimes she wondered if she shouldn't just self-terminate and leave the whole mess in little Alissa's hands.

She worried about the excess of emotion that plagued her. None of Serena's memories showed *her* hoping and worrying to the degree that Clea did. But then, Serena was perfect. For all that she was a failure, Serena Burns had been everything that Skynet had designed her to be.

Which is something that I, Clea thought mercilessly, *do not seem to be.*

Clea was still very unsure of her ability to interact with humans. She'd been fired from her job at the burger place. Which was very disturbing because she had done her job perfectly; her fries were the very best, as were her burgers. She never failed to thank customers for coming, or to greet them with a smile, or to wish them a nice day after delivering every order. She never complained about cleaning the rest rooms or mopping the floor or even cleaning the grease trap.

Clea's coworkers despised her and the customers gave her wary glances, never lingering over their food while she smiled at them from behind the counter. The other workers called her creepy and the assistant managers got into arguments because nobody wanted her on their shift.

Eventually the manager let her go, claiming a downturn in business. He explained that as the last hired, she was, unfortunately, the first to go. He apologized, looked as though he were going to pat her shoulder comfortingly, then changed his mind. Instead, he handed her a check and wished her well.

I've been too isolated from humans, she had decided then and there.

Regretfully Clea concluded that she was too much like a Terminator in her behavior despite her more flexible intelligence. Her studies of Serena's memories were simply no substitute for actual experience, especially since the I-950 genuinely didn't understand many things about Serena's memories.

Humor, for example, eluded her completely. And while Serena had moved easily among humans, actually enjoying their company, Clea simply didn't like them. Not least because they confused her.

Sometimes the I-950 worried that certain synapses just hadn't formed in the rush to make her mature enough to carry on Serena's assignment. In personality she and her predecessor were nothing alike, and given their identical genome, implants, and memories, they should have been. For example, Clea often wondered if she was up to the mission, while Serena never had.

The I-950 glanced at the sample and saw that it was finally cool enough to handle. She poured it out, noting with approval that it had a gelid quality to it. Beneath the scum of ash on top it was a bright and gleaming silver.

Clea picked it up and pulled it into two pieces; she squeezed and they took prints of her hands. Then, as the warmth left the metal, the pieces began to solidify. With a sigh she dropped them onto the table and turned away to clean up. One piece rolled under the light of a desk lamp, the other to the edge of the table.

While Clea worked, and considered her notes, the heat of the lamp began to affect the sample. Before long a soft point began to form at one end of the lump nearest the lamp, the silvery substance yearning toward the warmth above it. The sample farthest from the warmth also reacted, one side becoming smooth and slightly bowed out while the other retained the imprint of her hand.

The I-950 turned to sweep up the two samples and blinked at what she saw. *Well,* she thought, *this is something new.*

She picked up the pieces and began experimenting with them. The substance showed that it had remarkable qualities. It could be worked into a shape, just as wet clay could, then it would hold an approximation of that shape while reacting to heat and cold. Impressions could be made on it and items could be pushed into it and they would remain there until heat passing over that area wiped the impressions away.

It wasn't what she was looking for, but it had tremendous potential. Her first thought was that it would be usable, just as it was, for an art material. It was attractive in and of itself, and its malleability made it a natural for architectural embellishment and sculpture.

This substance could be my entrée to Cyberdyne, she thought. True, they supposedly no longer handled the Skynet project. But someone did, and through their contacts the Cyberdyne people could bring them together.

She began searching the Internet for an appropriate art project. Something high profile, something where the artist would welcome a new, high-tech medium.

LOS ANGELES, SEPTEMBER

Puzzled, Jordan studied the short E-mail. Reading his E-mail was something he did in order to feel at home—which he didn't in the furnished-apartment anonymity of the place he was living.

```
Good news! Your extra spicy South American
beef jerky is on the way!
Your shipment should arrive one week from today!
```

The tag wasn't one he recognized; it definitely wasn't Dieter's and he sure as hell hadn't ordered beef jerky over the Internet. Let alone the spicy South American kind.

What the hell is this about? he wondered. Could it be a coded message from John or von Rossbach? Actually it kind of sounded like John. Or maybe it was just that he thought it sounded like a seventeen-year-old might if he wanted to send a cryptic message. Admittedly his acquaintance with John was limited, but he hadn't really seemed the cryptic type.

Von Rossbach? he wondered. Maybe. Sector types were the kind of people who'd encrypt their grocery list. And Dieter had been the one to come up with the weather-report shtick.

Whatever. He decided to take the message both ways. First, Jordan typed a message to the return address stating that he would return their package of spicy beef unopened because he hadn't ordered anything from them. *And next I'll start looking out for a big guy and a teenager in about a week.*

With a final click he sent off the message, then sighed in disappointment. He had hoped to hear from John or Dieter, in their own persons—not disguised as a spicy-beef company. He had good news for them.

Sarah had been going through her therapy at Pescadero at warp speed. Dr. Ray had, miraculously, transferred her to the Encinas Halfway House, which had a very good reputation. The counselor there, who was none other than Sarah's former doctor, Silberman himself, had indicated that she might be ready to leave in as little as two months. Legitimately! A state that Sarah had experienced only rarely in the last seventeen years and John perhaps never in his life.

Jordan shook his head. To think she'd be going home a little less than eighteen months after blowing up Cyberdyne. *Who'd have imagined a year and a half ago that I'd think that was a good thing?*

VON ROSSBACH ESTANCIA, PARAGUAY, SEPTEMBER

Dieter made another mark on the map of Mexico and looked over at John, who lounged in an overstuffed chair looking thoughtful. A big corkboard had been one of the things he'd installed in his office in the original modernization when he bought the ranch, and it was perfect for holding big maps. These were modern, based on commercial satellite imaging, and extremely accurate.

"I think that's about it for Mexico, South, and Central America," John said. "At least the ones I know about. Mom probably could show you a whole lot more." He grimaced. "There was a weapons cache down by Ciudad del Este, but Mom promised that to Victor Griego so he wouldn't rat on us to you."

"But he did," Dieter rumbled, tapping his pen on the map. "So let's include it. If he doesn't like it he can always complain to the police."

John snorted and gave him the coordinates. "The stuff was mostly junk though. Maybe we should have a second-tier map, for when we're desperate." He looked pensive as Dieter nodded and made a notation on the map. "In the U.S. I'm not so sure," he continued. "I was pretty young then and after a while I . . . kinda wasn't interested. Y'know?"

Dieter looked at his young friend. "You mean when you thought your mother was crazy," he said.

"Yeah," John admitted.

"We'll get her out of there, John. And soon, I promise."

With a grimace the younger man sat forward. "If there's one thing I've learned in my life, Dieter, it's don't make promises you might not be able to keep." He looked up from under his eyebrows. "And we have no reason to believe that it might be possible to do that. This move to minimum security that Jordan told you about? It could easily be a trap." He shook his head, his lips lifted in a crooked smile. "It's just the kind of thing they'd do."

Von Rossbach waved a big hand dismissively. "They might. But with the number of things that have happened to your mother while in Pescadero's care, they might just be trying to avoid a lawsuit."

"Okay, whatever you say." John couldn't hide his doubt, somehow it smelled like a setup to him, but dwelling on it wouldn't help anything. He changed the subject with a grin. "Do you think Jordan will think to bring some of that beef jerky to Mom?" he asked. "She absolutely loves that stuff."

"He might," Dieter said mildly. It had been hard on John not to be able to do even the ordinary things one did when one was feeling helpless because a loved one was in the hospital—send flowers, or cards. "Jordan's very bright and it shouldn't be hard to make the connection."

The young man nodded, a little color rising in his face. He clearly didn't want to be thought sentimental.

"Anyway," John said, nodding toward the map, "I can only speak for the condition of the caches we have in Paraguay. We've been checking them every year or so to make sure they were okay. Mostly to keep in practice." He shrugged. "I guess old habits die hard."

"Which is why you're both still alive," Dieter commented. He rapped the map with his pen. "We're going to need a lot more than this."

John looked him in the eye. "I know," he said.

Dieter wondered what that look and that tone of voice meant. He waited a moment for John to speak. Then, impatiently, he said, "And?"

"And I'm wondering how practical you're prepared to be about it."

Von Rossbach rotated his hands in a bring-it-forth gesture.

John's lips thinned for a moment, then he blurted, "Drugs."

Dieter threw down his pen and looked away, leaning back in his desk chair. "That's one of the things I've spent most of my life fighting, John."

With a shrug John spread his hands. "Not hard drugs; those guys are crazy. I'm talking about marijuana."

"They're *all* crazy!" Dieter interrupted. "Something about millions of untaxed dollars does that to people. Not to mention that it's against the law, and it's wrong."

"So how do you think Mom got these caches we've been mapping all day? Working in day care? Taking in laundry? Telling fortunes? She'd be the first one to remind you, Dieter, most people are dead. They just don't know it yet."

"You can't get something good out of something wrong. I know that if I know anything," von Rossbach said. He was getting angry, and to no purpose. "I don't want to discuss this anymore."

"Fine," John said, getting up. "If you can come up with a better way, I am more than open to it." He shook his head. "I've never liked the idea either. But it's the fastest way to do this I can think of and our time is running out."

Dieter lifted his hand to stop him and John raised his and shrugged in surrender. "I'm hungry," he said. "Think I'll go hit up Marietta for something to eat."

Von Rossbach checked his watch. "Good luck," he said. "Dinner is in a few minutes. You know she won't let you spoil your appetite."

"I don't think it's possible to spoil my appetite, at least not with food," John said. "Mom says I've got hollow legs."

Dieter sat thinking about what John had said after the boy left him. He picked up the map and looked at the numerous circles denoting arms and food caches. Well, he'd read her record; he'd known Sarah wasn't a Girl Scout all those years she'd been running with the wild ones. Still . . .

Drugs! he thought in disgust. He couldn't—he wouldn't get involved with that. Flinging the map onto the desk, he leaned back in his chair, hands clasped behind his neck. Well, if they needed money he was rich. *And if Judgment Day is real, and it appears that it is, then my money won't do me any good afterward.* So. He would dedicate his considerable personal fortune to the cause. And he knew a fair number of moneyed eccentrics he could involve, too.

Meanwhile he would start seeking out arms dealers. Nothing big, at least not at first; he didn't want to come to the Sector's attention. Not yet. It would mean a trip to the U.S.

Maybe we could swing by Pescadero and spring Sarah while we're there.

He spent a few pleasant moments imagining her face when she saw him. Then he sighed. No. Given the move to minimum security, there was a good chance she was going to be released anyway in just a few months; it would be pointless to interfere with the process.

Marietta rang the dinner gong and he got up. *I wonder if John managed to weedle any food out of her,* he thought.

MONTANA

Clea smiled as she read her E-mail from Vladimir Hill, the artist selected by committee to create a sculpture to be placed in the plaza at Lincoln Center in New York. The committee happened to be headed by a Mrs. Roger Colvin, who just happened to be married to the CEO of Cyberdyne, which just happened to be sponsoring the sculpture.

Vladimir was ecstatic about the new material. It had inspired designs by the hundred, he said, he couldn't get them down on paper fast enough.

Really? Clea thought, impressed. *What a shame it's so carcinogenic.*

It had completely changed his ideas on the Lincoln Center project, Hill went on. He'd demanded a special meeting with the committee and shown them both the material and the design he'd created. They, too, were ecstatic. They'd loved the new design, the new material.

They all wanted to meet her, he'd written, so she was to be invited to the gala unveiling. Mrs. Colvin's husband was particularly eager to meet her.

"Yesss!" Clea said, clenching her fist in victory. Skynet would be pleased. If there was a Skynet. But now she had her feet firmly on the path that would lead her to her long-lost, never-known creator. She was on her way home.

CHAPTER 6

After only a scant seven months in maximum, Sarah had been transferred to minimum-security wing at Pescadero. She'd been there an additional six months when Dr. Ray had gotten her transferred to the halfway house. It was rather pleasant here, comparatively speaking. No screaming in the night. Except for herself, of course. No sudden rushes of stink. The place was shabby, but in a comfortable way, sort of like a boardinghouse with a poor but honest clientele, rather than the antiseptics-and-despair atmosphere of a violent ward. And the patients were much safer to be around.

With the possible exception of herself, naturally. Sarah was pleased to think that she was growing more dangerous by the minute. It was good to walk without pain again, though she still felt a peculiar internal pulling in her abdomen that might signal an adhesion. Particularly when she exercised hard, and she did, getting back into fighting trim.

She'd been doing great physically even in maximum, until that crazy bitch Tanya had punctured an artery in an attack she'd been lucky to survive. The attack had set her back physically, but had gained her enough sympathy to get her transferred to minimum.

Unfortunately, there she'd developed a nasty case of jaundice that still had her feeling weak. Hospitals were great places to catch bugs. Between her physical frailty and Ray's silver tongue, she was pretty much where she wanted—but had never really expected—to be.

After the shock of seeing Dr. Silberman again, Sarah had settled into the routine of the place. But she was still surprised at how deeply upset she had been by coming face-to-face with him unexpectedly. Understandable; her days under his care hadn't been the brightest in her life.

She was happy she'd been left to Dr. Ray and her own devices the last couple of weeks. Sarah knew that eventually she'd have to face up to the good doctor and deal with the complex stew of emotions he evoked, but not yet. *Please, God, not yet.*

Still, after so many weeks in a hospital bed and in physical as well as mental therapy, she was more than a little bored. She missed John and thought of him constantly. But thanks to Dieter—whom she also missed to the point of being lonely—Sarah wasn't afraid for him. One corner of her mouth lifted and she told herself that she should be grateful to be bored. It was something of a treat.

She also found herself becoming slowly addicted to television. It couldn't be accounted for by the content; Sarah was convinced it had some soporific effect on the brain. But anything that kept her soothed and even inadequately entertained until they let her go was a tool she'd gladly use.

Sarah walked into the common area to find the nurse resetting the channel and threw herself down on one of the threadbare couches.

"This is a very important program, people," the woman said. "I'm sure you'll all enjoy it." Then she sat down.

Raising an eyebrow at that, Sarah leaned back and crossed her legs. The nurses didn't usually watch TV with the patients. Probably this one should be working or she'd be in the nurses' lounge watching the little portable they had in there.

Maybe this will be interesting, Sarah thought.

OKLAHOMA CITY, OKLAHOMA

Ron Labane watched from the wings as Tony warmed up the crowd for him. It didn't take much; everyone was excited to be here at the opening show. The New Luddite movement's new channel was doing fairly well, despite the fact that it showed mostly nature videos, news, and talk shows about environmental subjects. But *his* TV show was expected to draw an audience of at least three million or possibly more, two hundred of them right here in the studio. The air was hot with lights, and smelled of ozone and sweat and makeup.

He'd seriously considered moving the whole works out to California, where they had the best facilities and trained personnel. But after a little reflection he'd changed his mind and chosen Oklahoma City. What he wanted was to make the statement that the New Luddites were just that—new. Not part of the establishment, not part of the old-money crowd, in no one's pocket. These days placing your national show away from either coast was like a declaration of independence. That decision alone set them apart.

Ron watched the cameras roam over the smiling, waving, applauding audience; the music was inspiring yet had a good beat, and as he watched, the audience began to clap in time, swaying in their seats until the whole place was in motion.

Choose the moment, he thought, and ran onto the stage with his hands in the air and began clapping in time with them. The audience went wild. The *New Day* show was primarily a talk show with a little music thrown in for leavening. It just so happened that the singers and musicians they chose to present were those that Ron had handpicked.

He'd been lucky. There were always dedicated youngsters out there with talent to burn, but that didn't mean the public would embrace them. To find talented kids who agreed with Labane's philosophy and made it palatable to millions with their music was a miracle. A miracle he'd been able to pull off four times now. He joked that he was beginning to suspect he was in the wrong business.

Gradually, after a few more jokes, Ron began his speech, adopting the intimate, almost avuncular manner that the polls indicated his audience responded to best.

"Y'know," Ron began, "with all the brownouts in California, people are saying that we need to reassess our feelings about nuclear energy." He led them through it step-by-step, pointed out that other resources could be exploited, other plans could be made. "The thing is, nobody is going to invest in those other alternatives if we're all talked into building more nuclear plants. And, no matter what they say, nuclear power isn't clean, it isn't safe. Now the president wants to give them unlimited protection from liability. How safe does that make you feel?"

Ron actually had a guest on the show tonight who held a dissenting view, and the guy had a good case. He also had a temper and a tendency to take things personally, which Ron fully intended to exploit. Waste not want not, was, after all, one of the New Luddites' mottos.

He broke for a commercial, promising a great show when they came back. Then an announcer's voice took over, describing an environmentally friendly array of cleaning products. Ron moved across the stage and took his place behind the desk, smiling out at his audience. He could feel that this was going to work out well.

MONTANA

Clea tuned out the commercial and thought about what she'd been watching. Ron Labane was one of Serena's projects that Clea had taken over with some enthusiasm. She saw potential here to confuse and divide the humans that her predecessor hadn't fully exploited. What better way to keep the humans as weak as possible, to make sure that as little as possible survived Judgment Day to be used against the sudden onslaught of the killer machines, than to encourage a fear of technology?

Labane was making nuclear power the issue du jour on his inaugural program. It was an emotional issue for humans—especially Americans, for some reason. They were constantly fighting the opening of these highly efficient power plants. Which was surely in Skynet's interests. Keeping the power-dependent humans from having all the juice they wanted would destabilize things nicely. It would create factions, even among the rich and powerful, and it would drive the proles nuts.

As for their perfectly valid fear of nuclear waste, well, an accident had been arranged.

With part of her mind still on the program, Clea contacted her T-101. Through its eyes she saw that the truck it had stolen was behind the convoy carrying some West Coast nuclear waste to its Southwestern dump site.

She glanced at the television image in the upper corner of her screen. But first she'd wait until Ron's program was over. It seemed the polite thing to do.

NEW MEXICO

The Terminator kept a precise distance between himself and the truck in front of him: exactly one hundred and fifty meters. The unmarked eighteen-wheeler carrying the specially designed cargo container was accompanied by two vans, also unmarked. It was all very discreet. Had they not known exactly what they were looking for, they would never have been able to find this particular truck.

The T-101 glanced at the body beside it. It had entered the propane truck's cab at a truck stop and waited for the driver to return. When he did, it had broken his neck before the human had even been aware of its presence. Soon the I-950 would signal the T-101 to go ahead and the body would be needed to stand in for it when investigators sifted through the wreckage.

Now, the Infiltrator sent.

The Terminator pressed its booted foot down and sped toward the truck in front of it. The waste truck's companion van tried to move in front of the propane truck, but the Terminator calculated angles as it manuvered and struck the van at precisely the right point to send it spinning off the road and into the first of the few buildings that had begun to appear by the side of the road. It disappeared into the flimsy structure, sending glass flying.

With nothing in its way, the Terminator pulled up beside the waste truck, swerved into the far lane so that it could aim the propane truck at the carrier's exact center, and rammed it at eighty miles an hour, knocking the carrier onto its side with a screech of metal against pavement. The propane truck climbed on top of the rig and then collapsed slowly onto its side, but didn't rupture.

The Terminator was out of the cab and onto the street in seconds, a grenade launcher in its hands. While the van up ahead was backing up, fast, it took aim and fired. The propane truck burst into magenta flame, the blast picked the van up like a dry leaf and flung it nearly a thousand meters, it ripped and burned every inch of flesh from the front of the Terminator's skeleton, leaving only smoking patches on its back. Briefly the T-101 went off-line.

When it came back to itself, burning debris was still falling and the buildings along the highway had been blown flat all around the explosion. Its internal monitors reported radioactive contamination at a very high level.

Mission accomplished, it sent.

Status? the I-950 queried.

External sheath severely compromised, no secondary damage, some nuclear contamination.

Well, Clea thought, *back to the vat for you.* Any contamination it had picked up would mostly be rubbed away by its travels. *Return to base. Discreetly.*

Acknowledged. It looked around itself. Off in the distance it saw a house, undamaged by the blast. Humans had come outside to gawk at the fire. Where there were humans there would be transportation. It headed for them.

OKLAHOMA CITY, OKLAHOMA

Ron offered the last few energy-saving tips and said good night when Tony came tearing onstage. For a split second he thought he'd made an error in his timing and had left them with a ridiculous amount of dead air. The audience began to rustle and murmur.

Then Tony slipped him a news report and said, "It's an accident. Maybe. Some asshole in a propane truck rammed into a nuclear-waste carrier right in the middle of a small town in New Mexico. There's a news blackout. Apparently the whole state is out."

Ron turned to the audience and clapped his hands. When they'd quieted down he said, "Ladies and gentlemen, I have some terrible news."

He read them the report in his hand, just the bare, unadorned facts. "I'm told there's a news blackout on this incident, which means that this is all we may know for some time. I'd like you all to bow your heads with me and pray for the people of New Mexico." After a moment's silence he lifted his head and looked at them solemnly.

"Now let's all just remain calm," he said. "We'll know more by and by. But when you get home I'd like you to write your congressman or -woman and tell them we don't want any more accidents like this one."

People applauded enthusiastically, rising to their feet and clapping with an energy that spoke of their anger and their horror. Then, as if someone had flipped a switch, they stopped and began filing out, murmuring to one another. Ron watched them go, a little seed of anger burning in his breast. This could have happened at the beginning of the show, and ruined everything.

On the other hand, since they *had* finished the show, this little incident beautifully underscored what he'd been talking about. He'd have to get to his publicist on this. He'd work up a statement emphasizing that his show had been talking about the dangers of nuclear power just before the news broke.

Ron smirked; there was nothing quite like being able to say "I told you so!"

ENCINAS HALFWAY HOUSE

The show ended, and it hadn't been all that bad for blatant propaganda. As the credits began to roll someone came running in from offstage. Sarah got up, not really thinking anything about it except that the New Luddites didn't have top-quality people running their programs. The nurse switched to another channel, where a news anchor was announcing that a fuel truck had crashed into an eighteen-wheeler carrying nuclear waste.

My God! She thought.

The anchor went on to say that background radiation as far away as Albuquerque had jumped by over 700 percent . . .

I don't think that's even supposed to be possible! Sarah thought. *Those containers are supposed to be specially designed to withstand just about anything up to a direct hit with a bomb.* Which an exploding propane tank would very closely resemble. *Maybe it's just my nasty mind talking, but this sounds deliberate.*

The news anchor was saying that possible terrorist activity was being looked into.

Nice to know it isn't just me for a change, Sarah thought. Paranoids had real enemies, too.

MONTANA

Clea smiled. Her timing had been exquisite. She'd found a weakness, exploited it and voilà! Panic in the streets. Or there would be after her message on the Net was discovered.

They'd be blathering about it for weeks, maybe months, and spending untold amounts of money studying and correcting the problem. Little knowing that despite their best and most earnest efforts, she'd just do it again.

Actually, next time she thought she'd cause an oil spill. Clea had been exploring the possibilities of hacking into a ship's closed system by satellite. If it proved feasible she was going to try to time the incident so that some enormously popular place was soiled in the most appallingly photogenic manner possible. Preferably somewhere with otters. Dying otters just drove humans wild.

For a while she'd toyed with the idea of having a Terminator do the job for her, but it would be better to do it by remote if possible. It would be much, much more difficult for the oil companies to explain if they didn't have a convenient scapegoat, such as a mysteriously missing crewman.

Heads will roll, she thought. What a charming image. She began to see why Serena had found such joy in her work.

Clea was busy with her preparations to leave Montana for New York. She had stepped up her production of T-101s using the last few chips that Serena had left her and working overtime manufacturing a close facsimile of her own. Fortunately she found microlithography a relaxing hobby. It would take years of experimentation before she would have the proper materials to make the true chip, but what she'd been able to cobble together had 97.3 percent of the efficiency of the real ones, so for the interim they should perform adequately. Her plan was to place the Terminator that had been established as her relative and guardian in shutdown mode and claim that her "uncle" was dead. Then, once he was buried, she would travel to New York to meet with Cyberdyne's CEO and obtain a job that would bring her in contact with Skynet at last. Anyone checking into her background would find an empty cabin and an only relative buried in the nearest town's nondenominational cemetery.

Shortly before the funeral and Clea's departure, Alissa and the Terminators would move to a new location in Utah. Her buried "uncle" would switch back to active mode after a set time and join them there; traveling by night since its flesh casing would probably die when it was buried and have to be replaced at the new facility.

With her tracks satisfactorily covered and her equipment and replacement safely hidden in a new location, she would be free to perform her function while Alissa grew up at a more normal, and undoubtedly safer, rate than Clea herself had been allowed. At the same time her little "sister" could obtain a human incubator. There just wasn't time for her to do it herself.

She thought everything was going extremely well when Alissa came to her in the lab. "Where is Sarah Connor?" the unnaturally solemn little girl asked her. "Where is her son, John, and their ally, von Rossbach?"

Clea looked up from her workstation, stunned. The computer part of her brain had been sending her increasingly testy reminders about this subject, but she'd been shunting them aside, barely paying attention to them. True, she had been busy, equally true her projects were important and Serena's own mission statement had put Sarah Connor last on the list of priorities, but to ignore something just because it was unpleasant . . . that was . . . *human.* The I-950 felt such a wave of self-disgust that her computer flooded her system with mood elevators.

"I don't know," she said. Clea could feel the blood rising in her face, a human-style signal of shame, one her computer part had apparently decided not to suppress.

Sarah Connor had been in custody in a mental hospital the last time she'd checked. John Connor and his friend had disappeared. She had no idea of the current whereabouts of any of them.

"Do you know?" Clea asked.

"Yes," Alissa said. "And no."

"That is nonsense," Clea said. "Either you know or you don't. If you know, tell me; if you don't know, find out. Either way, stop wasting my time, I have a great deal to do." Her little sister could be very annoying when she wanted to be.

"Sarah Connor is in a halfway house in Los Angeles," Alissa said, as though reciting.

"A what?"

"It is a place for the inmates of mental asylums or prisons to stay while they are eased back into society." Alissa paused. "There is absolutely no security. The inmates are trusted to obey the house rules, to go and return on some sort of honor system. Should I explain *honor system*?"

"No, I know what that is. What about John Connor?" Clea asked.

Alissa pursed her lips and raised her brows in an annoyingly superior manner. "Von Rossbach's servants have been recorded speaking to their relatives. He and Connor returned alone. Now they've disappeared again, no one knows where."

Clea felt a sharp bolt of fear shoot through her, followed by a healthy anger. "When were you planning to share this information with me?" she demanded. "And what, if anything, have you done about the situation?"

"I was planning to tell you as soon as I confirmed that von Rossbach and Connor were truly absent from the *estancia*. Which I have done. Naturally I would not initiate any action against them without consulting you. I have suggestions."

Clea made an encouraging gesture.

"We could send a Terminator after Sarah Connor," Alissa suggested. "Though given our track record to date, I'm reluctant to commit such a resource unless absolutely necessary."

A valid point, Clea had to concede.

Alissa continued: "I think it's safe to assume that von Rossbach and John Connor are on their way to the United States. Probably with the intention of freeing Sarah Connor. They may also be seeking allies. Logic would seem to suggest that they need them rather badly."

"As do we," Clea admitted. Which was, of course, what their support of the New Luddites and their more fanatical brethren was about. Athough *dupes* and *catspaws* would be more accurate terms than *ally*.

Alissa ignored the comment. "I have hacked into surveillance cameras at all customs checkpoints in the United States," she said. "I've assigned a Terminator to monitor them full-time."

Clea nodded. "Excellent," she said. "I think that I agree with you about sending a Terminator for Sarah Connor as well. Perhaps only to observe and report. If her son and ally show up we can try to get them all at once."

"It might be better if I was the one sent to observe," Alissa suggested. "They wouldn't be expecting a child."

The idea held exciting possibilities, Clea had to admit, and she wanted to take advantage of her younger sister's offer, but . . .

Shaking her head, Clea said, "No. You're too vulnerable and much too valuable. As yet there is no one to replace you."

Alissa said nothing, but Clea could almost hear her thinking that if they were short of I-950s to share the work, it certainly wasn't *her* fault.

With a frown Clea snapped, "I'm working as hard and as fast as I can. Right now is not the time to begin breeding another 950. It is to be hoped that my efforts will give you more leisure in these matters."

The problem was Clea herself felt that her efforts were inferior. Instinct told her that in a better world she would be culled to prevent expensive errors. But in this time and place she was the best available.

No, that wasn't strictly true. Alissa was the better Infiltrator. Clea wished that she dared to use her. Clea looked at her sister for a long time. Then took a deep breath and plunged in.

"In the rush to bring me to maturity I fear that errors may have been made. But that maturity is still a valuable asset, and so I must continue as leader for now. I rely on you to point out oversights such as this one.

If you continue to do so, then we should be all right. Once you have reached maturity I will become your second."

Alissa gazed back at her with a pretty frown. "If you were to start another 950 what would happen?" she asked.

"I don't know," Clea admitted. "None of us has ever been pushed as I have. It may have affected my eggs, making them either infertile or inferior product. The only way to find out is to use them. Which, as I've pointed out, we don't have the time for right now."

The child's face was implacable and her eyes betrayed her disgust. She, too, had sensed Clea's weakness and yearned to correct it by terminating her. But she was also the ultimate pragmatist. Clea was not so inferior as to be useless and her loyalty to Skynet was strong. Skynet itself would encourage them both to use the tools at hand.

"Very well," Alissa said. "But I think that the Terminator we send to watch Sarah Connor should be a different type than we usually make. It should be smaller, perhaps older looking. Something nonthreatening."

"Yes," Clea agreed, nodding thoughtfully. "A Watcher rather than a Terminator. Will you see to it for me?"

Looking annoyed, the small I-950 nodded, her lips tight.

"I would also like to send a Terminator to South America," Alissa said. "It may be possible to find out more from that end. It may even be possible to eliminate one or both of them with fewer complications."

The elder I-950 frowned; her sister had a point. "You don't think that they can be traced by computer?" she asked.

"Yes," Alissa said. "If they use their own names and passports." She knew her sister could calculate the odds of that happening for herself and so didn't bother to offer the figures. "I believe that some investigations are better handled face-to-face."

Clea considered. Her sister hadn't asked to go herself, realizing that the T-101 would be the more logical choice. And it *would* be helpful to know their enemies' exact locations.

"Very well," she said.

"And if the opportunity presents itself?" Alissa asked.

"Terminate."

The little I-950 actually smiled. "I'll get to work, then."

"Excellent," Clea said, smiling. She went back to her own work feeling more content. They were going to win this time. She could feel it.

Alissa walked away, frowning. She knew very well that her own brain was immature and therefore should have been a tool less keen than her older sister's. Yet she also knew from several different failures on Clea's part that even with her younger, less developed faculties she saw things more clearly, evaluated outcomes more realistically.

It was troubling, desperately troubling, that Skynet's future was in the hands of an inferior agent.

Alissa tried to comfort herself with the knowledge that even with diminished capacity Clea was still more intelligent than ninety-eight percent of their human enemies. It was the worry that the Connors were among that elite two percent that made her queasy.

She was too young to be in charge. Yet accelerating her maturity might well damage her brain and cognitive function in the same way that Clea's had been. Skynet would not be better served by two idiots instead of one.

The machine side of her brain decided that panic was imminent and eased back on the production of certain of her brain chemicals, released certain others. Alissa began to grow calmer, better able to plan.

For now she would have to be the eyes in back of her sister's head, as a human might say. She would have to make up for Clea's lacks. It wouldn't be all that long before she could take over. At which point she would decide if her sister was useful enough to retain or too dangerous to tolerate. For now, as Clea had said, with the two of them working together, they should be all right.

CHAPTER 7

John and Dieter, wearing identical sunglasses and solemn expressions, stood beside the grave of Victor Griego amid the scruffy grass, wilted flowers, and pictures of solemn dark faces fixed to the tombstones. With their hands clasped before them, they bowed their heads and read:

VICTOR GRIEGO

1938–2001

SHE WAS HIT BY A BUS

"That'd refer to his mother, I suppose," John said.

Dieter glanced at him. "I was told that she died of a broken heart."

John shrugged. "That's probably why she walked in front of the bus."

"Poor woman." Dieter sighed. "I may not have been an ideal son, but I didn't drive my mother to suicide."

"Bastard," John agreed.

"I guess this means that you still own that cache of weapons," Dieter said, and turned away.

"Yeah." John read the tombstone one more time and shook his head. "What a louse," he muttered, and picking up his backpack, turned to join Dieter. "My flight is at four; guess I'd better get going."

With a knowing smile Dieter asked, "Nervous?"

"Yeah, I guess."

"Don't worry, John. It's a good disguise. Your own mother wouldn't recognize you."

John snorted.

"Well, maybe *your* mother would," von Rossbach conceded. "But that's about it."

John gave him a quick glance. "What about you?"

"Don't worry about me. I've got something in play," Dieter said. He held out his hand and they shook. "I'll see you in New Mexico."

"If they're letting people into the state by then." John hailed a taxi.

"They will be," Dieter said confidently. He opened the door of the cab. "It's a big state."

John flung his backpack in the backseat and got in behind it.

"Be careful," he called out the window to Dieter.

Dieter raised one brow. "Funny, I was just about to say the same thing to you."

RIO DE JANEIRO, BRAZIL

John wore a weedy-looking black goatee and mustache and a pair of black, horn-rim glasses. He looked nervous and intellectual and nothing like his usual self. His body language was deferential as he went through American customs, as though he were leaving home for the first time, like the young man on his way to college that he was.

Of course, he was on his way to college to plot and plan, and recruit minions not to study . . . but he'd *look* like he belonged. He was nervous but genuinely happy to be going. He was sooo looking forward to meeting Wendy. She was only eight months older than he was, for all she kept calling him kid. He was hoping it wasn't going to be an issue. It was important to keep the recruit's respect.

Yeah, right, he thought, too honest by habit to kid himself for long. *She's gorgeous and brilliant and I like her.* Consequently, he wanted her to like him. It bothered him that he was thinking like this because he knew it was frivolous. He had no time for frivolous.

The guy behind the desk finished looking at John's passport and asked a few questions, obviously pro forma, then waved him on his way. John was pleased, as well as relieved. It was only about a year and a few months since their attack on Cyberdyne after all. There would have been computer-aged photos of himself on every custom officer's desk for a long while.

They must not have been very good, John thought.

He put his carry-on bag on the belt and went through the metal detector, grabbing his bag on the other side. The alarm went off just after him, and the guards gathered scowling as a middle-aged man in a Hawaiian shirt, with a gray-and-blond beard, opened his bag.

"It's just diving equipment," the man said in exasperation. "I'm a writer on vacation!"

John smiled. It was convenient, having a fuss right *after* he went through; that would fix itself in people's memories, and he'd be less than a shadow. In a few hours he'd be a guest at the Massachusetts Institute of Technology and he was really looking forward to it.

John didn't think that even if it had been an option, he would have ended up at MIT. He'd heard about New England winters and wasn't all that interested in experiencing one for himself.

When he thought of himself as an American, he thought of

California; Brie nibbling, skateboarding, sun and surfing, indulging political absurdities at Berkeley, or engineering-department practical jokes at UCLA.

While he was heading for Massachusetts Dieter was on his way by more devious routes to California. They'd both felt it was time to meet some of the people they'd been talking to on the Internet to see if they could be turned into more serious recruits.

It was John's idea to offer the MIT folk some proof about Skynet. Some of them were asking difficult questions about what they were doing. He understood the risk he was taking, but he also knew that sooner or later they were going to have to know. Now was as good a time as any.

It wasn't going to be enough to have scattered individuals gathering information. After Judgment Day, he was going to need trained, educated people in key positions or they were never going to be able to defeat Skynet. He'd have to pick and train them now to make sure they lived through the first volleys of nuclear missiles.

His father hadn't given details as to how the humans had managed to shatter Skynet's defense grid, but it couldn't have been plain old brute strength. There had to have been scientists, engineers, planners. Now, if ever, was the time to find them.

John had the Terminator's CPU in his pocket, disguised as a chocolate bar. He and Dieter had retrieved it before returning to Paraguay. Handling it reminded him of the Terminator's head trying to bite him. He had a brief flash of that Terminator attacking their plane as they left the Caymans, of how, even with its body blown away, the head had kept trying to fight.

But the brains at MIT would know it for what it was, a technology far beyond anything available today. At least he hoped they would; it was all the proof he had.

Although, as proof goes, it's pretty damned amazing, he thought.

BUENOS AIRES, ARGENTINA

Vera Philmore glanced at the brief résumé in her hand and then looked over the top of the page at the divine creature standing before her desk. Wulf Ingolfson, the résumé said his name was; it suited him. True, he was no spring chicken, but in her experience the young ones were boring. And those shoulders! *Ai, caramba!* They made a wonderful silhouette against the broad windows and the thronging masts of the yacht basin.

Vera enjoyed traveling the world with a boatload of handsome, charming young men. But these days it was mostly look and don't touch. This big fella might be a different case. He was certainly old enough to have been around the block a few times. So flirting, at least, could be added to the program.

Dieter looked at her with a blandly pleasant expression on his face. There were no chairs before Ms. Philmore's desk, indicating that she didn't like her employees to get too comfortable in her presence. On the other hand, the way she kept running her eyes up and down his body suggested that she might make an exception in select cases.

About fifty, Vera was very trim and well groomed. The color of her hair, the pale gold froth of champagne, was not found in nature, but it suited her, as did the expensive baubles she wore and the bright red silk shirt and black toreador pants. Some women had the personality to carry off almost anything.

"You don't seem to have had much experience as a deckhand," she commented.

"Not as an employee," he agreed. "But I have been on boats of all kinds since I was a boy."

"Ahhh," Vera said coyly, "your daddy was rich, was he?"

"No, he was a fisherman. But when I was a teenager I often got day jobs on some of the yachts along the Côte d'Azur. My friends and I would work for free, just to get on board." He smiled reminiscently. "I love the sea."

Vera gave him her most charming smile and reflected that no one worked for free. Somehow, she thought he was familiar. Not as though she'd met him, but as though she'd seen him somewhere. Well, if she did decide to hire him she'd have him investigated, as always. Despite his references being in order.

Ah, but she certainly hoped he checked out. The man was intriguing, and she was perennially bored.

"Well, then," she said, rising. "We'll be in touch."

He looked a little uncertain as he gently took her hand. "I'm staying at the Sailor's Rest," he said.

She nodded, still smiling. "You'll be hearing from us."

He turned and walked out, and she enjoyed the view. The guy had a great butt. Vera sighed appreciatively. *I hope he isn't shy.*

Dieter fully expected to be hired. It had been several years since he'd last used this persona, but he'd updated it a bit before leaving home. He'd applied with several skippers, but he was banking on Philmore. So much so that he'd bribed one of her hands to jump ship.

She was perfect for his purposes. Her itinerary would take her through the Panama Canal and up to San Diego within the next ten days. Shielded by her prestige and money, he would be able to slip into the U.S. without the more stringent customs scrutiny he might get at an airport. Like it or not, he was fairly distinctive looking.

Besides, he honestly thought Vera Philmore was just the sort of rich eccentric he might be able to recruit for their project. She had a sense of adventure and independence that was rare, and money to burn. It would be nice not to have to rely completely on his underworld contacts.

The only thing that worried him was the light in her eyes when she looked at him.

CHAPTER 8

John had never been to Boston before that he could remember—his mother had dragged him through some amazing places when he was a toddler, but most of them had involved tropical climates and high ammunition expenditures. You couldn't tell much about Boston from the airport, which was another suburban village in the international city of airports, pretty well interchangeable with any other in the Western world. It wasn't until he got a cab to Cambridge on his way to MIT that he began to appreciate the difference.

This was an old city. The way the streets were laid out like crazy string, the smaller buildings with their tiny bricks and wavy-glassed windows, each with a character all its own, the occasional surprise of modernist steel, concrete, and glass thrown in . . . it all said "this place is different." About as different in spirit as you could get from L.A., where he'd lived as a kid.

The cab took Massachusetts Avenue by the winding river Charles, and John enjoyed the view, spying the huge dome of one of MIT's buildings long before they arrived at the campus. He asked to be dropped at the admissions office, where he would get a campus map and ask a few questions.

As the cab drove off John shrugged into his backpack, his only luggage, and looked around—taking a deep breath. He liked it here. There was an energy about the place; you could almost feel brains percolating with ideas. He was going to enjoy this.

MIT CAMPUS, CAMBRIDGE, MASSACHUSETTS

John slipped into the auditorium/classroom quietly and sat down in the last row at the back. Very nearly every seat was filled for this class and he swept the rows with his gaze, looking for Wendy. He thought he saw her in the center of the middle row. Just a sense he had, since he'd never seen her in the flesh, let alone from the back. He settled in to listen. You never knew what knowledge might come in handy.

Too soon the class was over, leaving John hungry for more. Some of it had been a bit esoteric, but what he had gotten was presented in such an interesting way that he envied the students. Good teachers definitely made a world of difference; it was just more *fun* than doing everything on your own or on the Net.

The girl in the middle row *was* Wendy. She turned and began to slip out behind the other students, a thoughtful expression on her even features. The others all seemed to be chattering to one another in couples and groups, while she walked slowly and alone toward him.

John felt a nervous electricity in his middle as he looked at her. Slender and graceful, she moved like a dreamer through the stream of students. He stood up as she drew near and fell in directly behind her, waiting until they were outside to speak.

"Watcher," he said.

She spun on her heel, her eyes wide and her head at a stiff, almost challenging angle. "Who the hell are you?" she snapped, a slight frown marring her smooth brow.

He smiled slowly. "You don't recognize my voice?"

She looked him over, dark eyes assessing. "You're younger than you look, even with that beard." Taking a step closer, she narrowed her eyes. "A *fake* beard?" She raised a hand and backed off a step. "I don't know you."

"Sure you do," he said, grinning. "You've just never met me."

"Yeah, right. Ciao, kid." She started to walk away.

Rolling his eyes, John fell into step beside her. "You know me as AM, we've spoken on the phone. You've done a little Web surfing for me."

Wendy stopped short and studied him again. "So what are you doing here?" she asked suspiciously.

With a shrug he said, "I felt it was time I met you and your team in person. I have some information I'd like to share with you and an artifact to show you, and that couldn't be done by phone or via the Net." His lips quirked up at the corners. "So I'm here."

She looked at him for a long time. "Hmm!" she said, and started off again. John watched her walk away, then jogged to catch up with her, walking silently by her side as she thought. Lifting her head suddenly, as though just waking up, she glanced around.

"Um. That was my last class," she said, giving him a sidelong glance. "Look, don't take this the wrong way, but I'm not about to introduce you to my 'team' as you call them until I know a little bit more about you. So, why don't we go have a coffee at the student union and talk?"

"Sure. So how's the coffee at the student union?"

"Compared to what?" she growled.

He looked at her wide-eyed. *Wow, she's a fierce little thing.*

"Uh, compared to the tea?"

A slight smile touched her lips. "They're both pretty bad, to be honest. Maybe we should stick to soda."

"Do you drink Jolt?" he asked.

"No! I know all us geeks are supposed to thrive on the stuff, but I do not." She pushed open a door and led him into a place teeming with students.

"Uh"—he touched her arm, then removed his hand when she glared at it—"it's a little crowded in here for the kind of conversation I had in mind."

Wendy raised a skeptical brow. "Nobody here knows you," she pointed out. "*I* don't know you. Which means there's no reason to think anybody is going to eavesdrop." She shrugged. "Sometimes the most private place you can find is in a crowd."

"Yo! Wen-dy!" a large, bearded student bellowed. She grinned and waved.

"And sometimes not," John said quietly.

"Meeting tonight at eight in Snog's room," the beard said, leaning close. He grinned at John and moved on.

Wendy gave John a look and went over to a machine, getting herself a diet drink. John pushed a dollar into the machine and got a Coke, then followed her to an empty table wondering if he should have bought hers. Probably not; buying her a drink might have some significance in the U.S. that a guy who went to an all-male school in South America was unaware of.

Wendy shrugged off her knapsack and sat down, then took a sip of her drink. John divested himself of his own and sat across from her wondering how to begin. He'd rehearsed things to say, naturally, but felt that he'd somehow gotten off on the wrong foot here. Clearly their Internet acquaintance and one phone call didn't mean that they knew each other as far as she was concerned.

I should have let her know I was coming, he thought. Of course then she could have said don't come and probably would have. And he would have come anyway, in which case she'd be even more hostile than she presently was. *Still, showing up unexpectedly and in disguise . . .* He winced inwardly. He'd actually forgotten about it. *That's the kind of thing stalkers do, I guess.* The last thing he wanted to do was make her think he was crazy. *Oh, c'mon, John, she's gonna think you're crazy anyway. Just a different kind of crazy.*

"Well!" she snapped. "You wanted to talk? Presumably during my lifetime?"

He cupped his chin on his hand and said, "There's no need to get snippy."

"Well, what do you expect when you show up like this? In a fake beard no less! I've felt a little weird about you right from the start and I've gotta tell you"—she gave her head a little shake—"I'm really not feeling very good about this." She flicked a hand at him. "Not good at all."

John allowed himself to show some temper. "Well, Wendy, I find it interesting that you're perfectly comfortable invading the privacy of people you don't know at the behest of someone else you don't know for reasons that you don't know. But when I attempt to meet you face-to-face to explain it all, you give me this rather obnoxious attitude that screams 'hey, my space is being invaded.' "

Her mouth dropped open and she straightened in her seat. Then she let out a little bark of a laugh and opened her mouth to speak.

Before she could get out a word John said, "Has it ever occurred to you that, never mind that it's unethical, what you're doing might be dangerous, or illegal?"

"No," she said instantly. "I'm not that clumsy and I'm not doing anything but looking. Information should be free."

It was John's turn to stare. *God! She's so innocent!* What must it be like to feel so invincible. He had at one time, but that was before the T-1000 and he couldn't remember what it had been like.

"Well, ideally we all should be free, and well fed and have a comfortable, safe place to sleep at night. But I don't think that's the way things are. Do you?"

She gave a "hunh!" and glared at him.

"Don't let your pride get in the way of your considerable intelligence," he said. "You know you never should have gotten involved in this without checking into it further, don't you?"

With a shrug she said, "I checked you out. As far as I could. Your Web address belongs to a guy named Dieter von Rossbach and he isn't you. But why you're using his computer, I couldn't find out. I also couldn't find any reference to an AM anywhere. Which indicates that it's a new name. So, either you've never done anything like this yourself, or you've screwed it up so badly that you needed a new handle."

He considered her answer. Not bad for what was mostly guesswork. He scrubbed his face with his hands, being careful not to dislodge his facial hair, and looked at her.

"Well?" she asked, one eyebrow raised.

"It is a new name. Spur-of-the-moment thing," he admitted. "I've done research on the Net before and I've lurked around a bit. But this sort of thing, getting other people involved . . ." He turned down the corners of his mouth and shook his head. "Yeah. This is new."

Wendy huffed a little and leaned back in her chair, studying him. He was young, probably younger than she was, but he *felt* older, and she instinctively knew she could trust him. Maybe she was being snippy.

"So what's this about?" she asked. "I guess you didn't come all the way from South America because you thought I was cute or something."

"Sure I did," he said, grinning. Then held up his hand to ward off her response. "Well, maybe it helped. I came up here because it would be irresponsible to let you keep doing this research without having some idea of why and what you're doing. I am not lying when I tell you it could be dangerous. Now I'm not talking gun battles on the quad here." *At least I hope like hell I'm not.* "Maybe a better word would be *risk.*"

"Risk?" she said. Wendy took a sip of her soda, watching him.

"Yeah. You're taking a risk on your future here. Which is why I believe you need more information."

Biting her lips, she nodded slowly, meeting his dark-eyed gaze. He had a point. The powers that be might, at the very least, think that what she'd been doing was unethical, if not uncommon. And that could impact her career path.

"All right," she said. "Enlighten me."

Okay, here goes. "What you've been working on is an attempt to locate a very dangerous military AI project."

After a moment's pause she asked, "A U.S. government project?"

"Ye-ah." *Who else?* he wondered.

"Because, you're from Paraguay, aren't you?"

"I'm *from* the U.S., I *live* in Paraguay," he said impatiently. "What's your point?"

"I dunno. I guess"—she shrugged—"I wondered why you'd be interested."

People are right, John thought, *Americans are self-centered.* If you're not from here what do you care what we do? Naive and unconsciously arrogant, to say the least.

"My interest is in stopping this project, at the very least slowing it down."

Suddenly mindful of where their acquaintance had begun, Wendy asked suspiciously, "Are you some kind of a Luddite?"

"*Now* you ask me?" John favored her with an exasperated look. "No, I'm not a Luddite. I'm willing to admit that they have a few good ideas, but by and large I don't think their ideology is applicable to real life. And I don't like terrorists; they're all self-centered, mean-spirited nutcakes, if you ask me. Me, I just have this one lousy project that needs to be stopped. I have my reasons, which I'll explain to you someplace less public. But I'm not here to hurt you, Wendy, far from it."

Wendy considered that. "Have you read Labane's book?" she asked.

John shook his head. "I haven't had time."

"So you really can't say whether their ideology is, in fact, applicable." She crossed her arms and watched him for his reaction.

John was a bit confused. Suddenly she wanted to play debating team? To him the question and its follow-up had come out of left field. *Maybe it's like a time-out,* he thought. *She's trying to get some space to think about me being here so she's distracting me with this nonsense.*

"You know what?" he said. "You're right. I can't speak to the Luddite ideology with any authority because I haven't made a minute study of their position. I think they bear watching, but frankly"—he flattened his hand on his chest—"I'm not that interested. I have this one thing I have to do and it takes all my time and concentration. I'm hoping that once you've heard what I have to say, you and your friends will want to continue helping me. And if you don't I'm trusting you to keep quiet about it. Everything else is irrelevant to me. Okay?"

She kind of lifted her head and pursed her lips. "Sure, whatever." Wendy took another sip of her drink, annoyed and slightly embarrassed. "So. Have you got a place to stay?"

"Uh, actually I was kind of hoping you might have a suggestion about that."

She gave him a cool, level look that went on long enough to see that he understood he wasn't staying with her.

"A motel, a bed-and-breakfast maybe?" he quickly suggested.

"Hotels in Boston and Cambridge, if you can find one with a room, tend to be expensive, and B-and-Bs are even more so. I'll see if I can find someone to put you up in their room." She took up her backpack. "You can eat here if you like." She shrugged. "It's not very good, but it is cheap. Or there are restaurants all around the campus that have reasonable prices and fairly good food."

John stood up to follow her, but she held up her hand.

"I'm going to talk to my friends about you and I don't think you should be there. Be back here by seven-thirty and I'll bring you to the meeting." She started off, then said "bye" over her shoulder with a vague sort of wave.

John was left standing there, feeling a little foolish, and a lot uncertain about how this was going to work out. He *wanted* Wendy to like him and he'd really come on strong, which he could tell she didn't like. Wait till she found out what he was talking about. He blew out his breath.

No wonder Mom flipped out for a while, he thought. *Being right doesn't help much when you're right about something this weird.*

He slipped on his backpack and looked around the busy room. He sure hoped Dieter was having a better time than he was.

I'm beginning to look forward to meeting with those arms dealers. A sure sign that things weren't going all that well here.

BUENOS AIRES, ARGENTINA

Alissa had cast a broad net when she went looking for von Rossbach and Connor. The boy had slipped through, but the former Sector agent had used one of his old aliases. So when Vera Philmore sent out queries on the Net with that name attached, the I-950 had immediately purchased a one-way ticket to the woman's present location.

The Terminator had arrived at the dock to find that Philmore's yacht had sailed. It wasn't difficult to get a copy of the yacht's itinerary, and the T-101 bought a ticket on a small plane bound for Macapá, Brazil, the next afternoon.

CHAPTER 9

Vera couldn't resist; she moved up behind the big Austrian where he stood checking gauges in the wheelhouse and ran her hand lightly across his firm buttocks. It went with the warm breeze, the clear blue water, the salty air and diesel oil . . .

"Can't I help you, Ms. Philmore?" Dieter asked without turning around.

"How did you know it was me?" she asked, sounding mildly surprised.

"I don't think it's something Arnie or Joe would do, ma'am." She laughed and he continued, "Besides, I recognized your perfume."

"I hope you like it, Wulf," she said, moving around him to look at his face. "I have it made specially for myself."

"Very pretty," he said. She caught a glint of blue from his sidelong glance. "Very feminine."

Vera preened. She hadn't made as much progress with him as she'd hoped to, and by the end of next week or sooner they'd be in San Diego. "I didn't think you'd noticed," she said with a pout.

He turned to smile at her. "Of course I did."

Vera felt her heart flip-flop. Something that happened more rarely now, but was very welcome when it did. It was time to move into high gear.

"I've been meaning to find the time to get acquainted with you," she said. "I like to know my crew, since we're under one another's feet all the time. If you're free I'd love for you to have dinner with me tonight."

Dieter's face showed his surprise when he turned to her. "I'd be honored."

What else could he say? He'd wanted to get some time to talk to her alone, see if she was a suitable recruit. He just didn't want things to get . . . personal. Unfortunately Vera Philmore was the kind of woman who liked to take things personally. Suddenly, and unusually, von Rossbach had the feeling he was in over his head.

"Eight o'clock, then," Vera said happily. Then, with an alarmingly direct look, she added, "Try to be very hungry."

"Oh, God," Dieter muttered as she sauntered off.

■ ■ ■

"That was wonderful," Dieter said. "Even better than in the crew's galley."

Vera chuckled and gestured to her maid, who brought her a mahogany box. Pursing her lips judiciously, Vera chose a cigar, neatly trimmed the end with a cutter she took from the box, and lit it with a candle. She indicated Dieter with a nod of her head and the maid brought the box to him.

"Cuban," his boss said, exhaling a fragrant cloud of smoke. "And the best of the best at that. Do you enjoy a good cigar, Wulf?"

"When it's something this special, yes." Dieter selected and trimmed a cigar for himself. Took a long, deep drag and leaned back, letting the smoke out in a long plume.

The lighting was intimate and the windows wrapped around the seating area at the stern showed a view of a nearly full moon over the ocean.

Vera rose and Dieter stood with her. "Let's have our brandy in the lounge," she suggested. "Why don't you pour, dear?"

Uh-oh. We're up to endearments already. It wasn't that he would object to having sex with her, it was that he thought sex might screw things up. He wanted to recruit Philmore, to use her money to lay by the caches of food and weapons they'd need after Judgment Day, and her influence in high places and her mobility. For this to work right it needed to be a genuine commitment to the cause on her part, not something she was doing for romantic reasons. There were no reasons in the world more likely to cause vicious feelings once the bloom was off the rose.

He brought the brandy to her, pleased that she hadn't asked him to warm it for her. There was a contraption on the bar, but he wasn't in the mood to mess around with something flammable right now. Dieter handed her the balloon goblet and took a seat on the couch opposite.

She gave him a rueful smile and said, "I know who you are, you know."

Dieter froze. "Pardon me?"

Tossing her head back, she giggled like a girl. "You're Dieter von Rossbach. We have friends in common. Though you've been off the scene for a very long time now. Actually"—she put her drink down on the side table—"I only recall seeing you in the society column or *Town & Country*. There are several events that we both are supposed to have attended; only . . . you weren't there. I assure you, I would have noticed if you were."

She sucked delicately at her cigar, waiting for his reaction, but von

Rossbach just sat there, wearing a grim expression, ignoring the brandy in his hand.

"So why," she continued, "are you playing deckhand on my little boat?" Vera settled back, taking another puff of her cigar, and watched him through the smoke.

Taking a puff of his own cigar, Dieter regarded her. It was easy to forget that Vera wasn't just a bubbleheaded blonde. She liked to laugh, disdained formality, and had an earthy sense of humor. But she'd also made most of her fortune herself and was utterly independent.

"I wasn't actually ready to talk to you about that," he admitted. Not least because he wasn't sure how to go about convincing her that what he said was true.

"Well, I am." Vera shrugged and looked away. "You're hardly the first good-looking guy to get aboard my yacht under an assumed name. You're just the first one that was rich. You could have your own yacht, you could have your own deckhands, you don't have to be one. So. What's your story, von Rossbach?"

"What do you think it is?" he countered.

She tapped her cigar into a crystal ashtray, watching the rich ash flake off as she spoke. "Well, I think that you want to sneak into the U.S., and for some reason you expect to be stopped at the border." She looked up at him, smiling. "How'd I do?"

He pulled the corners of his mouth down and shrugged.

"You're dead on, Vera. I have to admit I'm impressed."

"I had Arnie check your stuff, so I know you're not carrying contraband. And I may be kidding myself, but I don't think any of my regular guys is being your mule. So, why do you need to go sneaking around. Can we get to the point here?"

"Well, here's the problem." He paused, wincing. "My story is so unbelievable I'm kind of afraid you'll throw me overboard when I'm through."

"Oh, don't worry, honey," she assured him. "If I don't like your story, Mexico beckons." She took a sip of her brandy. "Start talking. Where were you all those years we were supposed to be partying together?"

"I was doing something else." Dieter began to unbutton his shirt and Vera's eyebrows shot up, her eyes widening and a little smile unconsciously curving her lips.

When he slipped off his shirt the first thing she noticed was how muscular his torso was, although not quite the standard gym-muscleman type. More functional, graceful despite its thick-muscled solidity. A thrill shot through her as she wondered if he meant to seduce her.

Then she saw the scars.

"Ho-ly shit!" she whispered. "What the hell happened to you?"

Dieter smiled; he couldn't help but be pleased by her reaction. In a distant corner of his mind he wondered how Sarah would react. "This one"—he pointed to what looked like a second navel placed four inches to the side of his real one—"is a bullet wound. I got that in Beirut. This"—his finger touched a crescent-shaped scar on his arm—"was a knife, one of those curved Arab jobs. Here"—he finally got to the one that really intrigued her—"is where a guy named Abdul el-Rahman tried to carve his initials. I killed him before he could finish. Sometimes these guys get so involved they forget they're not immortal."

"So, what? You were some kind of soldier of fortune?" Vera shifted a little nervously; this was not the way she'd imagined this conversation going.

"No." Dieter took a sip of brandy. "I was a covert antiterrorist operative. *Now* I'm a soldier of fortune." He smiled at her. "A very romantic designation, don't you think?"

She smiled in answer, a slight blush painting her cheek. Blinking rapidly, she took another sip of brandy herself.

"So, what do you want?" she asked.

Dieter took a deep breath and her eyes fastened on his chest.

She forced herself to look him in the eye. "Maybe you should . . ." She gestured vaguely.

He knew what she meant and was happy to oblige, putting his shirt back on. "Right now I want to get into the U.S." He tipped a hand left and right. "Under the wire, so to speak. I had hoped to perhaps gain your sponsorship of a mission of some importance."

Secretly Vera had always daydreamed about someone coming into her life and tapping her for some desperate mission. Of course she was no fool. From time to time people had tried to manipulate her, tried to get her to support some drug deal or vicious tyrant-in-the-making. But she had resources that the average millionaire didn't have. Over the years she'd built up a network of friends and information gatherers who could give her the inside story on almost anyone.

Von Rossbach, oddly enough, was pretty much a mystery to them. Though they all said he had a rep as a stand-up guy.

Vera sat forward slowly, her eyes glowing with excitement.

"Tell me," she demanded.

When he was finished Vera looked away, her eyes thoughtful, then her glance went back to him. "So, all you want is to stop this one project?"

He nodded. "But there are forces at work here that really believe in this project, and they have friends at the highest level."

"I have friends at the highest level," she said confidently. She smiled. "I could have a talk with them."

Dieter shook his head, his face sad. "No. This project is so black that the people you know probably aren't yet aware of it."

A look of impatience crossed her still-pretty face. "So how much do you want?"

How much will you give me? "Two million," he said aloud. *For a start.*

"Whoa! You don't want much, do you?" she said. "You're rich, why don't you kick in?"

"My entire fortune is dedicated to stopping this project." He shrugged self-deprecatingly. "All I ask is that you consider it."

Vera took a deep drag on her cigar, studying him with narrowed eyes through the smoke. She tightened her lips.

"All I have is your word on this."

"That's right," he agreed. "And you don't know me very well, so you don't know that my word is good. But I don't know you very well either. And these are very secret matters. Until and unless you commit to this project; I'm not at liberty to tell you more. As I said, think about it. Consult with your friends about me. I only ask that you not mention what I've told you. It could be dangerous, for you and for them."

"What about you?" she asked, arching a well-shaped brow.

Smiling ruefully, he shook his head. "I'm in so deep I consider myself lost at sea."

Vera snorted, then bit her lip. "All right," she said at last. "I'll consider it." She raised a finger. "No promises. Understand?"

He raised his glass in salute. "I've asked for nothing more."

Vera returned from her business appointment feeling depressed and thoughtful. The South American side of her affairs was doing all right, but hardly spectacularly well, and she was disappointed. Maybe it was time to do some pruning of her investments.

She leaned against the yacht's railing and sighed. It wasn't just business that had her down. This whole thing with von Rossbach/Ingolfson certainly hadn't lived up to her daydreams. She got so sick of people hitting her up for cash for this or that project.

Though with his money von Rossbach hardly needed to do that. Which made his appeal for money somewhat puzzling.

Though the appeal of those shoulders and that chest . . . Vera sighed again, this time in pleasure at the memory. *Two million, hmm?* That was a lot to pay for just a peek. She could tell by the way she was thinking that he was going to have to go begging for his money to somebody else. *I do so hate being used,* she thought, pouting.

On the deck below, a pair of hands grasped the railing, followed by von Rossbach. Vera stood back and stayed very still, watching as he came over the rail, soaking wet and . . . *He's naked!* Vera thought in disbelief.

She suppressed a laugh, watching as he looked all around, confident that he couldn't see her. She'd had this balcony at the back of her private quarters constructed so that she could see the deck below while being hidden herself.

There was something odd about von Rossbach, besides his being stark naked, but she couldn't put her finger on it. He finally moved off.

I have got *to call him on this!* she thought. If they were going to be cited for public nudity by the local police, she'd be the one blamed, and ticketed. She had some standards after all, the last thing she wanted was the reputation of running a floating brothel. She hurried out of her quarters, meaning to catch up with him. Vera smiled as she imagined the expression on his face as she gave him a dressing-down while he stood there beautifully undressed.

The Terminator moved down the short, narrow corridor on its way to the crew quarters. The design of this yacht, with the exception of the owner's quarters, which were customized, had been on the builder's Web site, so it knew the layout of the ship. After observing the boat for two days it could also identify everyone on it. One of those humans was Dieter von Rossbach. The I-950 had affirmed the request to terminate.

Hearing voices coming from the stairway leading to the engine room, it pushed the volume on its microphones to high and hastened to the end of the corridor. The T-101 flattened itself against the bulkhead and peered around the corner, looking down the stairs. A man turned at the door of the engine room and leaned in.

"I'll be back," the one called Arnie shouted.

"Don't be too long."

Voice-recognition software confirmed that the second speaker was von Rossbach. This was excellent. As it listened to Arnie's footsteps moving down the corridor, it could hear only one other set of footsteps within the engine room. Its quarry was alone. There was a violent clash of machinery from the engine room and it lowered its volume to protect the sensitive auditory device. Then it moved quickly down the stairs.

■ ■ ■

Dieter was wishing the engine room were air-conditioned; his body was covered in oil and sweat and only a drenched headband kept it from stinging his eyes. The captain had decided that while they had a few days they should perform basic maintenance on the yacht's engines. Essentially a tune-up with an oil change on a massive scale. Von Rossbach assumed he wanted it done here because local regulations about used oil were a lot less strict than they were in San Diego.

Right now he was steam-cleaning the engine and resenting Arnie taking off, leaving him to, literally, take the heat. He grabbed the handle that would move the crankshaft and leave another area accessible.

The Terminator found a box of tools beside the door and pulled a two-foot-long pry bar out of it. As it had neither gun nor knife, this should do for a weapon. Though it should be able to destroy an unarmed human with its bare hands, mission parameters stated that any and every available advantage should be used. The soft clatter of machinery being manually cranked succeeded by a sound like a compressed air blast led it to its prey.

Dieter sprayed the upper part of the engine with the steam, watching the muck run off with a sense of satisfaction. He was almost done with this. It had been a long time since he'd pulled maintenance on a marine diesel, and it made him feel nostalgic, in a way. Another half hour or so and he'd be able to go up on deck for some of the comparatively cooler air there. Then a shower. He imagined the shower stall would look something like the engine did now, with black goo running down its sides.

He squatted to get the lower side and a pry bar hit the engine with enough force to dent the metal.

Dieter fell onto his butt and reacted instinctively, turning the steam jet on his attacker.

There was no scream of pain and the figure dimly seen through the steam didn't stagger back. Instead, the bar came down for another blow.

Dieter rolled to his knees and shoved at the man while he was overbalanced to make his strike, and his opponent went down. The Austrian rose to his feet and stared at the man, astonished to see that he was naked. Then the man turned over and began to rise, the pry bar still in his hand and—

That is my own face. Red and covered with blisters, the eyes white and peeling from the steam blast, but still terrifyingly familiar.

The Terminator reached up and plucked the cooked flesh from its eye sockets, revealing the red lights and black plastic of its eyes and allowing it to see.

"Oh shit!" von Rossbach said, and turned, running for the door. He needed a weapon; something in the way of high explosives would be nice.

The Terminator's hand flashed out and the hooked end of the pry bar locked around Dieter's ankle, bringing him crashing to the metal floor. The Austrian scrabbled forward, reaching for the toolbox, intending to throw it. Then the pry bar hit his thigh glancingly and von Rossbach shouted with pain and went down again. His hand reached out and came up with a five-pound sledgehammer.

Dieter rolled onto his back just in time to block a blow from the pry bar aimed at his neck; the force of it was shocking, slamming the head of the hammer into the slatted grillwork of the engine-room deck.

I'm going to die, he thought as the Terminator raised the bar for an impaling stroke.

Vera heard someone cry out and she hurried down the narrow stairway, listening with alarm to what sounded like a fight. She arrived in the hatchway just in time to see the Terminator place its foot on Dieter's injured thigh, causing him to cry out again.

She shouted "no!" as she saw the pry bar come up for a blow and the Terminator turned toward her.

For Vera everything stopped in that moment—sound, breath, thought. A terribly burned face in which blazed red, glowing eyes turned to her, hesitated, then the Terminator began to bring the bar down toward the man on the deck.

Dieter swung the hammer, knocking the bar out of the Terminator's hand, then brought it down on the T-101's knee. It crumpled, and at that moment Vera realized that the sound was . . . *metallic.*

As it adjusted its leg von Rossbach rolled free, coming up against the bulkhead, seeming to rise to his feet in one fluid motion. He grabbed the power cables that had been rigged to test the engine and hit the switch with his elbow as the Terminator lunged toward him, its big hands reaching for his throat.

Dieter pushed the live cables into its reaching hands and the Terminator almost flew backward to lie twitching on the deck. Instantly von Rossbach scrambled to the wall, took up an electric arc welder, and went to work on the twitching, recumbent form; he didn't have much time until it reset.

Vera sank to the deck with a little cry, her eyes so wide the whites showed all around, her hand to her mouth in horror.

Ignoring her, von Rossbach cut through the metal neckbone analogue, watching with grim satisfaction as the red lights behind the thing's eyes went out. Then he stood panting for a moment before he turned his attention to the frightened woman in the doorway.

"It isn't human," he said to her.

She looked up at him, uncomprehending.

Dieter knelt beside her and spoke very gently. "Look," he said, pointing. "You can see the metal. It wasn't a person."

She looked at the fallen Terminator, then turned to von Rossbach and back again. "Not human," she said, her voice shaking.

"Are you all right?" Dieter asked her. He hoped she wouldn't go into shock. "Do you know who I am?"

Slowly Vera frowned. She was shocked, and badly frightened, but she was also very tough. "Of course I know who you are. I'm not an idiot! What the hell *is* that thing? Why does it look like you? And how the hell are we gonna get rid of the body?"

He leaned back and studied her, assessing her condition, and decided that she was going to be all right. As all right as anyone was after meeting their first Terminator anyway. "It's a Terminator," he explained. "Its mission was to kill me in order to protect that AI program that I told you about."

Dieter watched as her eyes turned to the fallen Terminator. Its skull showed metallic gleams through the mass of crushed flesh, and the spine was a mass of gleaming cut metal and sparking wires.

She licked her lips and then looked up at him. "How did it know where to find you?" she asked. The she straighted with a gasp as an idea struck her. "Are there others?" She grew pale. "Could there be another on the ship? I mean, right now?"

He laid a gentle hand on her shoulder and shook his head. "It's unlikely that there are more around right now. They're not all that common. As to how it found me"—he shook his head—"I don't know. It probably picked up something on the Internet and came looking."

Vera shuddered and turned away from the Terminator, burying her head on his shoulder. She began to shake. "Oh God," she said.

Dieter put his arms around her and let her rest for a moment, then he urged her to rise. "I'll dispose of this," he said, planning how he would do it even as he reassured her. "You should go have a brandy and lie down. I'll come and talk to you later."

"Don't," she said, rising to her feet, her face determinedly turned away from the Terminator. "I need to be alone."

She walked away like an old woman and Dieter watched her, frowning, uncertain what to do. His options were limited; stay and risk her turning him away, or go on his own. He didn't think she'd mention the Terminator to anyone; she was intelligent enough to imagine the consequences of that.

Dieter looked at his disposal problem and decided to stay. With such unequivocal proof presenting itself to her, she just might come through for him.

CHAPTER 10

Snog's small room—bed-sitter with kitchenette—was surprisingly neat. Maybe that was because everything that wasn't a computer or a book had been eliminated.

"Can't work in clutter man," Snog himself said in response to John's initial, evaluating glance around the room. "Makes me feel like the inside of my head's messed up."

John raised his brows and nodded. The answer to his unspoken comment made sense to him. After two years in a military academy he found it difficult to tolerate mess himself.

There were five of them besides John in the cramped room, Wendy the only female. Two of the guys were long and thin with unruly mops of hair, one dark-haired, the other a redhead, both with glasses. The other two, one of them Snog, were on the hefty side, both bearded, with even longer, wilder hair and no glasses.

Wendy pointed to the dark-haired skinny guy. "Brad," she said. He and John nodded and smiled at each other. She indicated the big fella who'd passed them the word about this meeting in the student union. "Carl." Carl nodded, too. "Yam," Wendy said with a nod at the redhead.

"Hi," John said.

"So you're the mystery man," Snog said—sneered, rather.

"Yup, that's me," John said. *What's your problem?*

"Kinda young, aren't you?"

John's heart sank a bit. These guys weren't exactly senior professors, for cryin' out loud. He'd have thought that people who probably got a lot of "you're so young!" stuff thrown their way would be more tolerant. At least toward similarly young people.

They all looked at him as though waiting for a speech. John looked around and took a seat on the bed next to Yam. "Don't let me interfere with your meeting, guys," he said.

The others all looked at Wendy, who shrugged and took off her jacket, then settled down on the floor. "So," she said, "has anybody got something to report?" She looked around. "Snog?"

He pointed to his beefy chest. "Me?" He sounded surprised.

"You called the meeting," she pointed out dryly.

With a snort he said, "That was before I knew it was going to be the children's hour."

"Just how old are *you*?" John asked without looking at him.

"Nineteen," Snog said. He tilted his head toward John. "And you?"

"Eighteen." *In February,* John added mentally. "A whole year younger than you are. I can't believe you're making such a stink about it—you're not exactly a geriatric case yourself."

"Thing is," Carl said in a soothing voice, "you're not even out of high school."

"And I never will be," John said, giving him a direct look. "High school is a luxury I can't afford."

"Is that because you're from . . . South America?" Wendy asked sympathetically.

John stared at her for a moment, then laughed; he couldn't help it. It was such a typically North American assumption. And they were all so naively arrogant! But smart. You could *feel* that they were smart. If he could recruit these people it would be a very good thing.

"Of course not!" he said, grinning. "I meant that I don't have the time to waste."

"Oh," Snog said, "so I guess that means we're wasting our time, too, huh?"

"No. It means I'm not you. My genius, if I even have any, lies in other directions." John met his eyes until Snog casually looked away. Maybe it was time to take a risk.

"Who the hell do you think you are, kid?" Snog asked, gazing at the ceiling.

"I'm Sarah Connor's son."

ENCINAS HALFWAY HOUSE

Dr. Silberman's nervousness was affecting the group. Most of the participants were scowling, and fidgeting to an even greater extent than nicotine withdrawal usually produced. They cast glances around the room looking for the disturbance and those glances usually landed on Sarah, where they became accusing. Clearly the participants liked their doctor.

That came as a surprise to Sarah; she remembered him as condescending, not at all a lovable trait.

It was something of a mixed group. Few of these people were severely mentally ill. Those that were functioned very well if they kept up their medications. One was a recovering drug addict. Sarah supposed that she must be listed as one of the most severely ill, given her record.

The session had been going on for a while, through obviously well-worn channels; the participants didn't even seem to be paying attention to what they themselves were saying. Eventually the discussion petered out and all eyes were on Sarah again.

"Yes, I'm sorry, Sarah," Silberman said at last. "I'd meant to introduce you immediately, but we began rather quickly. Group, this is Sarah Connor."

"Hey, I've heard of you!" a man said. "You blew up that company, right?"

Sarah's head flopped forward as though she were embarrassed and she looked up through her bangs, smiling shyly. "I'm afraid so." Straightening up, she asked, "What can I say?"

She let them draw the whole story out of her. She squirmed and hesitated and made them work for it. Through it all Silberman just watched her.

Well, he always did have her number. Her best efforts to tell him what he wanted to hear had always failed. He knew she still believed in Skynet and Judgment Day—which probably meant he still thought she was a homicidal loon. Busting out of the violent ward by breaking his arm, taking him as a hostage, and threatening to hypo his carotid full of drain cleaner had probably reinforced that conviction, and God knew he'd had enough time to rationalize away the glimpse he'd had of the T-1000 pulling its liquid body through a door of steel bars.

Silberman could barely take his eyes off her. Sarah Connor evoked feelings that made him want to call his own therapist. In fact, he *should* call her. He should also not have allowed himself to become involved in her therapy. Precisely because he knew she didn't need therapy. She needed to be believed. He now understood, all too well, how that felt.

But that little pissant Ray had made noises about how good it would be for him to face her, face his fears, and so on. So he'd decided to play the good little professional and include her in his group. Besides, he'd rather slit his wrists than let Ray see how rattled he was.

After her escape he'd told anyone who'd listen *exactly* what he'd seen. He completely forgot that he was the only one left conscious except for the Connors and their big friend. So he was the only one who'd seen that *thing* squeeze itself through the bars, then turn its hands into pry bars to open the elevator doors. He'd seen it shrug off a shotgun blast to its chest.

Obviously they'd sent him on medical leave; also obviously they hoped never to welcome him back. To them his story represented a severe psychotic break brought on by trauma. You don't want a crazy doctor trying to treat the insane. Though to be honest he hadn't wanted to go back. Being unwanted was unpleasant enough—but Pescadero was the scene of the most terrifying events of his life. It had been very easy to turn his back on the place.

He'd taken a long break from work, as long as his benefits and his savings would allow. And since he wasn't working with patients, he worked on himself, trying to put himself back together. He'd sought therapy and willingly allowed the doctors to convince him that he'd imagined the whole thing. They assured him that in his understandable terror he'd bought into his own patient's delusions. And he agreed.

In time the nightmares had begun to fade and his belief in his therapist's diagnoses became firm. What he'd seen was impossible; therefore it hadn't happened. When it was time to go back to work he found that his attitude toward his profession had changed. Once it had been about his career; now he wanted to help people. So he'd sent in his formal resignation to Pescadero and begun looking into clinics.

But after they found out about his reason for leaving his previous position, he got a lot of rejections. Which was ironic. How did they expect their patients to reintegrate with society when they wouldn't reintegrate one of their own colleagues?

Then a friend had told him about the halfway house. He'd felt comfortable here and he'd done good work with his patients, work he was proud of.

But now here was Sarah Connor, and he had some decisions to make all over again. Because now he knew he hadn't had a psychotic break; what he'd had was a taste of Sarah Connor's reality.

Sarah explained, "Dr. Ray says that now that I've stopped this project from going forward and Cyberdyne has dropped it from their roster, I'll probably never want to destroy their factory again. Obsession works that way sometimes, he says. So the board of review agreed to let me come here prior to my release."

"Will you have to go to jail after here?" a woman asked.

Sarah shook her head. "Apparently not. Since I was insane at the time."

"Well, Sarah," Dr. Silberman said with a weary smile, "we hope we can help you to overcome this obsession of yours."

"Thank you, Doctor." Sarah smiled tentatively at him. "I know I was very hard on you when I knew you before and I'd like to apologize. I really can't even imagine ever being that person again."

"I think, Sarah, that you will always rise to the occasion," Silberman said enigmatically. He checked his watch. "Well, group, that's it for today. We'll meet again on Thursday." He smiled, nodded, and rose from his seat.

"I didn't get to say anything," a heavy young man protested.

"I'm sorry about that, Dan." Silberman patted his shoulder. "We'll be certain to let you talk on Thursday."

As Sarah went by him at the door he leaned in close and said, "Sarah, I need to talk to you."

Well, I don't want to talk to you, Connor thought. "Now?" She looked around nervously.

"Now would be good." Silberman gestured down the hallway toward his office.

Her full lips jerked into a smile. "Sure," she said, and preceded him down the hall.

"Sit down," he said as he closed his office door. Then the doctor went to his desk and sat. He looked at her for a long time, until she felt it was necessary to fidget. "After you left"—he spread his hands— "escaped, rather, I was in therapy for a long time."

"I'm sorry about that, Doctor," Sarah said. And sincerely meant it. She didn't like knowing what she knew either and she'd certainly never enjoyed therapy.

"After about five years I was able to convince myself that what I saw was a delusion brought on by stress. Of course"—he rubbed a finger across his nose—"dealing with the fallout caused by having a complete breakdown under stress has been keeping me pretty involved ever since. Running a halfway house is a considerable step down the career ladder from my former position, you realize."

Sarah shifted uncomfortably.

"And now you're here," he continued. "And . . . it's all come back to me. As clear as the day it happened. And that's the thing, Sarah. It *did* happen. So what I want to know is . . . how can I help?"

Sarah's jaw dropped. "Doctor?" she said.

"I know." He raised a hand to stop her. "How can you possibly trust me? You broke my arm, you threatened to kill me, and so on." He leaned forward, his eyes eager. "But now I know for certain. What I saw *was real*!"

She narrowed her eyes and looked at him sidelong. "Doctor, I've been over this with Dr. Ray. My obsession with Cyberdyne relates to my deeply buried resentment of their lawsuit when I was in the hospital years ago. He explained that I somehow displaced my legitimate anger and grief at the man who hurt me and murdered my mother onto the more accessible Cyberdyne. I bought into those other people's psychotic fantasies because I'd been so hurt and traumatized. None of it was real. None of it could be real."

Silberman let out his breath with a huff. "I just want you to know, if you ever need my help, you have it."

"Thank you, Doctor." *Either he's crazier than I ever was, or he's telling the truth.* But how was she supposed to tell?

"I mean that sincerely, Sarah."

"I know you do," she said gently. "Thank you."

NEAR PUERTO VALLARTA, MEXICO

Vera glanced at Dieter as she jogged by again. Every morning she took a hundred turns around the deck, usually wearing pink shorts and a black tank top, her champagne hair wrapped in a chiffon scarf. The bright tropical sunlight blinking off the water turned the colors to the glowing pastels of an old Pop Art poster from the sixties, the sort he'd had up on his wall when he was a grammar-school student.

She's flaky, Dieter thought, *but I like her.* And who was he to call anybody flaky? He'd recently dedicated his life and fortune to fighting a mad, genocidal computer that hadn't even been built yet. And while she was flaky she was also tough; he'd known many a man who'd have collapsed completely at the sights she'd witnessed.

"I'm in," she said the next time she came by.

"What?" he asked, looking up from where he was polishing brass.

Vera ran in place beside him. "I said, I'm in. I know you're not telling me the whole story, von Rossbach. But whatever is going on here has to be stopped." Her eyes flickered away and then returned. "Besides, whether I like it or not, I'm involved now. So I'll help you sneak into the U.S. and I'll help you finance whatever." She held up a finger. "I'm not prepared to go bankrupt. But you should be able to get a fair chunk of change out of me. I'm getting older," she said with a weak smile, "so I can't hammer one of those things flat with a crowbar. But you can, so I want to help." Without another word she ran off.

And I didn't even have to sleep with her, he thought, just maybe a little disappointed.

Contrary to what the novelists said, even counterterrorist operatives didn't often get the chance to seduce beautiful women into financing their schemes. Usually it was more a matter of putting in invoices and arguing with the finance department.

For once, he'd thought life might imitate art. It certainly would have been a lot more pleasant than being beaten up by a Terminator.

CHAPTER 11

Who the hell is Sarah Connor?" Snog asked.

Wendy smacked his leg. "I told you about her, remember? She's kind of a Luddite heroine."

"Oooh, her," Carl said.

"*You're* Sarah Connor's son?" Yam asked.

"Yup."

"Your daddy was from the future?" Snog said.

"That's right," John agreed. He wondered if Snog was worth the trouble.

"Cool," Carl said. He leaned forward eagerly. "So how does that work anyhow?"

"Wait a minute!" Snog snapped. "You can't just come in here and claim you're John Connor! Give us some proof, for cryin' out loud."

John laughed at him. "Do you seriously think I carry around some kind of irrefutable ID?" He shook his head, grinning. "Call up the FBI or Interpol Web site and scroll to my name. Look at the age-enhanced photo, then look at me." He shrugged. "Best I can do for ya, buddy. Or you could just take me at my word."

They all stared at him, then turned toward Snog's computer as he began to type in an address. In a few minutes they were looking at a photo of a smooth-shaven, rather young-looking John Connor. It had been blown up from a class picture taken when John was nine.

John took off his glasses and turned his head to resemble the photo.

"It's kind of hard to tell with the fake beard," Yam objected.

John blushed. "Yeah, I'm finding it a little hard to take it off."

They all crowded close to the screen to study the image, then looked at John, then back at the screen.

"Damn!" Brad said, impressed. "It really *is* you!"

"Waaaiit a minute!" Snog protested. "I thought that we all agreed with the site about Sarah Connor being a victim of government mind-control experiments and that there are no Terminators except in her mind." He turned to John. "You want me to believe you're John Connor, show me a Terminator."

John chuckled; he couldn't help it. "Well, they're a little unwieldy to carry around since they run about six feet tall and weigh in at about five hundred pounds. But there is this."

He drew what looked like a candy bar from his pocket and peeled off the wrapper to reveal a tiny series of interconnected black blocks. "This is a Terminator's CPU."

They gathered around, their eyes alight with pure greed, just one step away from their tongues hanging out.

"It's weird," Snog conceded.

"How does it work?" Wendy asked.

"Well, people, that's why I brought it with me." John looked at each of them in turn, making eye contact. "I won't leave it with you, however, unless you're prepared to meet certain conditions."

"Hey, man," Snog jeered, "we could promise you the world on a string and then when you leave do whatever the hell we want. I mean, what are ya gonna do about it?"

John addressed himself to Snog. "First of all, we're not certain that all the Terminators were taken out of play. So if you light this up without putting it in a Faraday cage, you might find yourself being visited by a *whole* Terminator. Second, if you exploit this with the wrong people you might be responsible for bringing on Judgment Day. Third, if the government finds out about this you just might disappear. Fourth, if you turn me in to the cops, one day I swear I will take you down."

"Oooo," Wendy said. "Tough guy."

He looked at her. He genuinely liked Wendy, but she was expendable if necessary. He'd hate himself, but he'd do it.

She saw something in his eyes that caused her to back down. "So what do you want from us?"

"When we disconnected this the Terminator was probably changing or erasing information. If it's possible I'd like you to stop it from doing anything else and perhaps recover whatever information it tried to eliminate. This could be a gold mine."

"Or a crap mine," Yam interjected. He reached out one long finger but didn't touch the chip. "Fascinating design."

John's lips tightened. He didn't want to let go of the chip, but he couldn't learn anything from it himself and he didn't know any scientists. These kids were the best chance he had of utilizing this resource. It wasn't a sure bet, but then neither was any other option.

"If I entrust this to you to work on," John said, "you could give us the edge that will allow us to beat Skynet. But you have to know that Skynet is capable of putting agents in the field anytime, anywhere. And it's desperate. So you can't afford to take any chances. Which means you can't show or tell anybody about this without my clearance."

"Why would you trust us?" Snog asked, sounding for the first time as though he was willing to cut John some slack.

"I've checked you guys out," he said. "You're all brilliant, this work is definitely within your capabilities. You have access to facilities that I don't. And, you're close enough to my age that I felt I could trust you." Actually, that wasn't true, but he thought they'd like hearing it.

The guys looked smug, but Wendy said, "Hey, wait a minute! You just met my friends tonight. How could you possibly have checked them out?"

John could feel the color rising in his face. "Uh. There was a slight—"

"Invasion of privacy," she snapped. Her eyes glittered with fury. "How dare you?"

"I'm sorry, Wendy, I really am. But if I hadn't been able to check you and your friends out, I wouldn't have been able to come here."

She crossed her arms. "Yeah, well, I did a little checking on you, too, when I got interested in Sarah Connor's story. You're wanted for murder."

With a sigh John rewrapped the CPU. "I've never killed anybody in my life," he said. *Well, nobody human. Do sentient killing machines from the future count?*

"What about that 'I'll take you down' stuff?" Snog mocked.

"Nice to know somebody here knows bullshit when they smell it," John said.

Snog laughed. "He's all right." He held out his hand. "I'm in."

The relief in the room was palpable and Brad, Carl, and Yam all offered their hands as well. Only Wendy sat scowling at him. "I want you to promise me you'll never invade my privacy again," she said.

John shook his head. "I can't promise that. All I can promise is to respect your privacy as much as I can." He could see that she didn't like that. "Some things are greater than our personal likes and dislikes," he explained. "I genuinely don't like making you unhappy with me. But I'm not going to lie to you if I can help it. What I'm trying to accomplish, what you'll be helping me to accomplish, is more important than any one person or their privacy. I won't abuse it. That's all I can promise." He met her eyes, willing her to believe him.

"I don't like it," Wendy said frankly. She turned her head away, then gave a half shrug; looking back, she frowned at him. "I'll have to get back to you on it. Meanwhile"—she looked around and let out her breath in a little huff—"I'm starved. Who's up for pizza?"

"Thought you'd never ask," Carl muttered.

■ ■ ■

CRAIG KIPFER'S OFFICE, SOUTHERN CALIFORNIA

"So, Sarah Connor is getting better and she's enjoying the facilities at the Encinas Halfway House," Kipfer said.

Pool nodded. "Yes, sir."

Kipfer tilted his chair back and smiled. "That's nice," he said. Then his eyes went cold. "Tell me again why we're being so nice."

Pool blinked. That he was being asked to explain himself again meant that Kipfer didn't trust his plan. Unfortunate, but he *did* believe in his idea. "We anticipate that she will attempt escape, in which case we'll track her to her base and finally get our hands on her son and, we hope, their unknown ally. Alternatively, her son is very likely to attempt a rescue. Again, we hope with the aid of the man."

Kipfer looked thoughtful. "It has the virtue of simplicity," he said. "How do you plan to track her if she escapes?"

"The halfway house is under constant surveillance."

Kipfer leaned forward, pulling his chair closer to his desk. He folded his hands before him. "Describe 'surveillance.' "

"Cameras have been set up throughout the house and on every door, and microphones, of course," Pool said. "They're monitored by agents at a nearby location twenty-four/seven."

Kipfer shook his head and spread his hands. "You didn't put an implant on her?" he asked. "It isn't like you didn't have an opportunity, for God's sake, she's been in surgery like twelve times."

Pool looked nervous. "Actually, sir, we did insert an implant. Since her move we've lost the signal."

His boss looked disgusted. Pool sat straighter; it was a bad sign when Kipfer let you know what he was thinking.

"Well, there's not much can be done about that," Kipfer said. "But those agents you have watching her had better be good," he warned.

"They are, sir. The best."

"I have another little problem I'd like you to look into." Kipfer handed him a slip of paper. "This MIT student thinks it's fun to read my mail. Deal with it."

Pool took the paper. Wendy Dorset . . . "I'll take care of it right away, sir."

Kipfer flicked his fingers in dismissal and turned to his computer.

Pool rose and left silently. At the front of his mind was the worry that his agents *might* let Connor slip away. In the background was a seething resentment that he'd been saddled with such an unimportant chore as scaring off a too-curious student. To an agent at his level it was humiliating; of course it was meant to be. Still, he would see to it that little Miss Dorset lost all interest in other people's private affairs.

CHAPTER 12

MONTANA

Clea was leaving for the airport in less than three hours and she was nervous. She paced through the carefully camouflaged upper part of the big log-cabin house, past magazines that were never read but were still ruffled realistically at set intervals, past furniture carefully worn at a regular pace and replaced occasionally.

This would be the first time she'd ever flown, ever left the state where she was born, ever been completely alone with millions of humans. She decided she wasn't nervous. She was terrified, in an abstract intellectual way that her computer side's control of hormones could do nothing about.

Clea tried to hide it from her little sister as she followed her down the hallway to her sister's lab. It was a futile effort, of course. Even if Alissa was fooled, and she probably wasn't, her computer part would identify the signs of stress and relay the information to its flesh half. Still, a human would be fooled, making the practice worthwhile.

Alissa and the Terminators would handle the rest of the move from this point. The hard work was already done; what remained was just mechanical. The funeral had been held. To her utter surprise her "uncle" had received a number of floral arrangements from the companies he'd worked for. She had even received a fruit basket from one of them.

The humans at the funeral parlor had been very, even cloyingly, sympathetic. As had the doctor who'd declared the T-101 dead.

When she'd insisted there be no autopsy, indicating by her manner that she was prepared to become emotional about it, the doctor had assured her that because of economic considerations they didn't automatically perform autopsies anymore.

She'd thought it wonderful that a government agency would actually do something so convenient.

Before she left for New York, however, Alissa had insisted that she view the Watcher she'd constructed to spy on Sarah Connor. It was clear that her little sister was pleased with the results of her work.

Clea couldn't help smiling when she saw that it was covered with a sheet, like a statue waiting to be unveiled. Where, she wondered, had her sister discovered this conceit?

Alissa glanced at her, then yanked off the sheet and displayed her masterpiece. Clea was genuinely and pleasantly surprised.

"You have done *very* well, little sister," she breathed. She glanced at the tiny I-950's shining face and was both pleased and saddened. For Alissa she stood in Skynet's place, offering praise and encouragement. But for herself there would be neither.

With an effort she wrenched her mind away from the familiar circle of disappointment and studied the new machine.

With the necessary aid of a Terminator, Alissa had cut down the arm and leg matrices of a full-sized Terminator. She'd added more melanin to the skin and much more body hair, except on the top of the head. The result was a creature that looked like a short Turkish wrestler. While it might lack some speed as a result of the shorter legs, it was clear that nothing else had been sacrificed. It looked nothing like a standard T-101, yet it had all the deadly strength and power.

"Most excellent," Clea breathed. "As soon as it's properly programmed, send it. I leave the matter in your capable hands, little sister."

CAL TECH, CALIFORNIA

Dieter arrived at the campus during the morning rush, fitting himself into the massive river of young humanity that flowed from parking lot to classes among buildings that showed three generations' notions of up-to-date. Today, as usual, he'd entered through a different gate. Also as usual he wore a different hat and today a pair of fake glasses. He made a series of small changes to his appearance, none of which would pass close scrutiny; his height alone made disguise difficult, but they might prove enough to give him a critical edge.

As he walked along in the opposite direction from his destination, he made an unobtrusive scan of his vicinity. As it had done many times in the past, the automatic caution paid off.

Out of the corner of his eye he spied a figure on top of a building. He peeled off with a group of students and entered the nearest doorway. Dieter entered the stairwell and made his way to the roof, hoping that this building was of equal height or higher than the one where he'd caught that human-shaped flash of movement, that blink of sunlight on metal and glass. Coming to the top of the stairs, he stopped for a moment and considered the orientation of the door to the other building.

Not good; if this building was shorter he'd be in full view immediately. Of course, he might have just caught sight of a maintenance man going about his business. In which case this effort to confirm his suspicions was wasted time.

But somehow that's not how it feels. Go with it. After twenty years in the field, he'd learned to trust his instincts.

He cracked the door and peered out. From where he was standing he couldn't see anybody. The building he was in was indeed slightly lower than the one where he'd seen motion. But there was no help for it; he had to know. After a moment's hesitation he eased the door open and slipped around its edge in one smooth movement. He felt a soft impact against the back of the metal door, and when he looked down he saw the feathered end of a shattered tranquilizer dart.

Someone's overeager, von Rossbach thought. He could have been a handyman or a stray student. Bad training, or perhaps just a trainee. He now knew that at least they didn't mean to kill him. *Not immediately anyway.* They wanted to take him in to the local Sector substation for interrogation. So, forewarned was forearmed.

Unfortunately that was equally true for the guy with the dart rifle.

He had to get off this roof. Especially since the man over there had probably sent for backup. What had he been thinking? Here he was trapped like some rookie. Perhaps deep down he'd wanted to test their intentions, looking to see how deadly they intended to be. Still, he'd been stupid.

He looked around the roof and saw no means of escape. Especially not while under the gun. Dieter moved to the far side of the roof shack and faked an attempt to get to the door from the far side, drawing the shooter's fire.

Ja, he thought. *Still paying attention.* The soft *phfuut* and the dart quivering in the tar roofing proved that.

Paying attention specifically to him. Which he'd taken for granted, but it was still some comfort to know this wasn't a student gone bonkers. Those tended to use live ammo. They also tended to attract a lot of official and media attention, something he had no desire to be around.

Speculatively he thumped against the side of the roof shack. It was only a thin, narrow sheet of corrugated steel, made simply to keep the weather out of the stairwell. It should be a simple matter to bend a piece back and slip down the stairs unseen.

He pulled a multitool out of his back pocket and set to work. With considerable effort he managed to dislodge one of the bolts holding the sheet to its frame; then getting his fingers under the edge, he pulled up. With a hiss he let go and looked with dismay at the cuts on his fingers. The damn thing was tack-welded as well as bolted.

I should have expected it, he thought bitterly, sucking on a bleeding finger. *These things have to be student-proof.*

Well, he might as well make his move now. Dieter swung around the door and threw himself through the opening. He felt something hit his heel just before he tucked in to control his fall down the steps, rolling to his feet when he came to the landing. Looking down, he found a clutch of feathers sprouting from the heel of his running shoe. He also felt the beginning of a nice set of bruises where the risers had smacked into his back. That was endurable, and the thick muscle had protected his back.

He plucked the dart out with a curse and flung it away, then rolled his aching shoulders and trotted down the stairs.

I'm getting too old for this, he grumbled mentally.

He hit the stairwell door on the ground floor and moved quickly toward the maintenance doors, his eyes moving constantly. He saw no evidence of agents closing on the building. What he did see was a big, sandy-haired jock.

"Hey!" he said.

The boy looked up from his book, his mouth partly open.

"How would you like to make a few bucks?" Dieter asked him.

The kid looked at him for a minute. "How many bucks and what do I have to do to earn it?"

"I want you to put on this jacket and these glasses," von Rossbach said, taking them off. "Then I want you to walk out to the parking lot and come back."

"Oh, yeah?" the kid said. "How come? And you forgot to mention how much."

"Fifty bucks." Von Rossbach flung the jacket over his arm and pulled his wallet out of his back pocket.

The kid looked at him from under his eyebrows. "And the why?"

"I think this guy I owe some money to is following me. I just want to check."

"Hey"—the kid raised his hands—"I don't want no trouble. Noooo, no, no, no."

"Aw, c'mon. There won't be any trouble. He'll know you're not me in a couple of minutes. Which is why I'd like you to run out. You can walk back, though."

Dieter took out two twenties and a ten. The kid still shook his head, so Dieter added a couple more twenties. The kid looked at him sideways and made a keep-it-coming gesture. Dieter pulled out another pair of twenties.

"I did mention that I *owed* this guy money?" he said.

The kid grinned, grabbed the money and the jacket. "Hey, man, I'm cheap at twice the price," he said, slipping on Dieter's sunglasses.

Von Rossbach took the boy's sunglasses and whipped a blue bandanna out of his back pocket.

"Hey!" the kid said. "Gimme back my glasses."

"Those are Ray•Bans," Dieter said, indicating the pair the boy was wearing.

The kid looked at him for a moment, then lowered the sunglasses. "Kewl," he said. Then he hoisted his backpack.

"I'll watch that for you," Dieter said hastily.

With a shrug and a slight tightening of his lips the boy acquiesced. " 'Kay," he grunted. "I'll be right back."

"Just run," Dieter said. "Don't look around; just take off, okay?"

The kid shook his head. "Sure, whatever."

As von Rossbach watched him go he tied the bandanna over his hair, put on the kid's funky sunglasses, and picked up the backpack. He watched the boy hit the door and go down the steps at a run. He was taking a shortcut across the lawn when he went down, skidding almost to the base of an oleander. Dieter didn't wait to see any more; he turned and jogged to the building's other door and walked calmly toward the building where the shooter was lodged. Once inside, he ditched the backpack and raced up the stairs to the roof. He had only moments to get behind his target.

Is the Sector getting sloppy, or am I just lucky? he thought as he raced up the stairwell, dodging the occasional student on the lower levels.

Normal procedure would be to have at least two more shooters on the stairwells as backup, in case of just this sort of counterattack. Von Rossbach found nothing but deserted stairs as he cautiously peered around corners on the last two floors. The exit door was closed, but as he expected, the tongue of the lock was held down with a piece of transparent tape. It opened silently, and he stepped out on the rooftop, running forward lightly with his weight on the balls of his feet.

The shooter with the dart rifle was dressed in nondescript black sweats—campus fashions were convenient for covert ops people—and lying with the bipod-mounted weapon beside him, looking through a small pair of binoculars down onto the lawn. The attaché case the gun had rested in was open, revealing shaped slots to hold the weapon when it was broken down into its components.

He heard Dieter's feet when the Austrian was still five yards away; one of the disadvantages of two hundred and sixty pounds of solid muscle. The sniper was tall but slender, lithe and very quick. He came up off the tar and gravel in a spectacular twirling handstand that sent one booted foot slashing out toward the face of the man running toward him.

Dieter blocked it with crossed wrists, grabbed the man by the ankle, and turned, whipping him through the air like a giant flail. A single incredulous squawk was cut off by a massive thumping sound as the sniper's head hit the rooftop and rebounded. The Austrian dropped the limp, unconscious body, grinning. There were *advantages* to his build; one of them was that people always assumed he'd be slow.

He peered over the low parapet of the rooftop; two men leaned over the prostrate student. They turned him over and looked at each other, then looked up at the roof where Dieter lay. They couldn't see any details from where they stood because the sun was behind him. All they'd see was his head and some of his shoulders. He held his hands up in a go-figure gesture and slid out of sight.

Then, crouching low, he moved over to the far side of the building, which overlooked the office of his old friend and teacher, Dr. Paul Wang. Wang was a scientist and engineer who for years had been training upper-level Sector agents in electronic equipment and high-tech gadgetry. Sometimes it took all they had just to stay even with the other side.

Dieter had helped the good doctor with a little problem involving his son and afterward the two men had become friends. Which is why von Rossbach had come here; to meet with a trusted companion he thought could be of help. And while he was certain that Wang could indeed help, he was now equally certain that the professor was not his friend.

Clear the board, he thought. *Move on.*

Across the street the steps and lawns were empty of life except for a pair of male students leaning against a wall talking. They were perhaps a little old looking for students, despite their books and casual clothes. Still, there were grad students around and Ph.D. candidates in plenty to explain the discrepancy in their ages.

Von Rossbach would still have recognized them as Sector agents, even without the telltale gestures made toward their earpieces that brought them both to higher alert, whatever their disguise. He'd worked with them for several months less than five years ago.

They must think I'm a complete loon, Dieter thought. Why else would they send people he was bound to recognize after him? With a sigh von Rossbach eased himself away from the building's edge and moved carefully toward the door to the stairway. When he'd backed off enough that he couldn't be seen from the street, he rose to his feet, moving quickly.

Of course, that they were men I'd recognize indicates I may still have a friend in the Sector. Then he pushed the idea aside. That was something to think about on a rainy day. Right now he needed all his wits about him. After all, it might simply mean that they had a dearth of agents in the vicinity.

For now, best to scrub this part of the mission and move on to the next contact. He'd lay a false trail or two, then head for his rendezvous with John in New Mexico.

■ ■ ■

BOSTON

It had been only ten days, but they had been ten wonderful, glorious, fabulous days. John had never enjoyed himself so much in his life. He'd snuck into classes and spoken with professors, spent hours and hours in the library, worked with Wendy and her friends in the labs.

They'd even found time to just hang out, in Snog's room or in off-campus student cafés, and he'd caught glimpses of Boston's life from a student point of view, bookstores and Harvard Square and little theaters. They'd talked all night about how to save the world, both the world as it was and the way John feared it would be. It was fun and valuable in its way. Though for a couple of days there he'd let himself forget what he was supposed to be doing and just enjoyed it. He'd even gone dancing with Wendy. John smiled at the memory; the girl knew how to move her fine body.

What he hadn't done was so much as kiss her. God knew he wanted to; every time she walked into a room it felt like his veins were filled with melted butter. His dreams had definitely improved since he'd met her. And the scent of her almost made the top of his head pop off. He very much feared that he was falling in love.

John looked at her and she smiled at him. Then she took his hand and he couldn't speak; even if he'd been able to, his mind was completely blank. His body, however, was telling him exactly what it wanted him to do.

Wendy had insisted that they take the T to the airport. He suspected that she was more interested in spending the maximum amount of time with him than in simply saving money. Not that she had money to spare, or time either.

The sun sparked copper highlights in her hair and John sighed. He didn't know what to do. He knew what he wanted to do, he just didn't think it would be right. Look what had happened to his mother and father. Besides, he was too young to be thinking in terms of forever.

But . . . he and Wendy seemed so right together. As though they'd known each other all their lives. After her initial prickliness had worn off, John found that he'd never been more comfortable with anybody except his mother.

And that can't be right, he thought. Should you be able to compare your girl in any way to your mother? Not that they were actually anything alike. Wendy was softer than his mother in every way. And he liked that.

Maybe it was because, like his mom, Wendy knew the truth and believed what he said about Skynet and Judgment Day.

Not that it had been an easy sale, by any means. Wendy and her friends were smart and they all possessed the natural skepticism of scientists. But the Terminator's CPU trumped all their arguments. Its sheer sophistication left them with nothing to say. Except "wow," which they said frequently,

They had all given him their word that no one outside their group would learn of the artifact from them. Meanwhile they would spend every spare hour on working out its design and how it functioned. As well as recovering any possible software and/or data files.

He'd also gotten them to agree to come to Paraguay, or at least to leave the city after graduation. That had been tough since they had all imagined themselves staying on to get at least their master's from MIT.

The Logan stop came all too soon. Hand in hand he and Wendy left the train and went up the stairs to wait for the bus.

"You won't have much time to make your flight," Wendy said, checking her watch. "Maybe we should have taken a cab."

John smiled slightly. " 'S okay," he said. "It's better this way—less time for security to look me over."

She studied him anxiously. John was without his disguise. He doubted he'd need it given the computer-aged picture law enforcement had of him, which only vaguely resembled him. Oh, it was good enough to help convince people you were *telling* that you were John Connor that you weren't a liar. But just passing by wouldn't elicit recognition, he was confident.

They had to stand on the bus, holding on to the pole and looking into each other's eyes. He'd heard about this eye-gazing thing and wondered how people could want to do it. But with Wendy it was magical, enthralling. They almost missed their stop.

It really was late and they ended up running. He smiled at her as the woman at the gate took his ticket, and was about to take it back and board . . . when with a sound of total exasperation Wendy grabbed him and kissed him.

John came up gasping and then he smiled, feeling . . . altogether too much.

Wendy looked smug for a moment. "I guess you're not old in every kind of experience," she whispered.

He could feel himself blushing, and when he glanced around the ticket lady looked hastily away but kept her smile in place.

All the world loves a lover, John thought. He leaned close to Wendy. "I hope to see you again," he said fervently.

"Oh, I promise you that you will," she said.

He felt like his grin was going to unzip his head. "Make sure every-body keeps their word," he cautioned.

"You bet," she agreed. "And we'll all leave the city as soon as we graduate, or sooner if you tell us to." For a moment she looked worried. "Take care of yourself, John. And be careful."

He smiled again. *But I can't tell her why—you don't tell a girl who kisses like* that *that she's sounding like your mom.* "I have to go," he said after a moment.

"Yeah," she said.

He gave her a quick but passionate kiss and boarded. He wasn't going to look back, but he couldn't help himself. He was glad he did; Wendy blew him a kiss.

CHAPTER 13

Almost into Oregon, on the east side of Goose Lake, nestled beneath the spreading, green canopy of old-growth pines, was a small log cabin. It had one story, a stone chimney, and three rooms, one with a glass wall facing the lake as well as a state-of-the-art woodstove. It also boasted its own generator plus a slew of more esoteric gadgets. For a rustic log cabin it was amazingly twenty-first century.

Extending out into the lake nearby was a wooden pier; a small boat with an outboard motor was tied up at the far end. The pier was so low to the water that one could step aboard easily.

At the very end of the pier, seated in an aluminum chair with yellow plastic webbing, was a big man of about sixty. His gray hair was covered with a battered khaki hat decorated with fishhooks and a plastic badge that held a fishing and a hunting license. He wore tan shorts, white socks with sandals, and a neon-orange shirt decorated with bright blue hibiscus blossoms and green hummingbirds.

In one hand he held a high-end rod and reel, the butt end resting on his thigh. The other hand was curled in his lap; he appeared to be dozing. Beside him a can of beer sat atop a red-and-white cooler.

Dieter had been observing this tranquil scene for over two hours from various locations around the cabin. It appeared that there wasn't anybody around except for him and the old man. Which made a nice change. Several times now he'd had to abort contact with someone he wanted to recruit because of a Sector presence. But if they were here they were too well hidden for him to spot. Time to make his move. He crept silently toward the pier.

The old man's hand jerked and suddenly held a Walther P-38, old and well maintained and deadly, the 9mm eyehole looking as big as a cannon when it settled unwaveringly on Dieter's face. His eyes moved to the tiny mirrors on the inner edge of his oversized sunglasses.

"Jesus Christ, Dieter, what took you so damned long?" he demanded. "I thought my goddamned bladder was going to explode." He stood up and held out the rod. "Here, reel this in and come into the cabin."

Dieter stood with his mouth open, caught flat-footed. *Like some raw recruit,* he thought.

"How did you know?" he asked, accepting the rod.

"Christ Almighty, you were making so much racket I thought I was being invaded by bears. Bring the beer in, too."

Von Rossbach watched the older man trot up the path to the cabin for a moment; then shaking his head, he began to reel in the unused lure. He'd always said the boss was psychic.

When von Rossbach was a young agent assigned to Doc Holmes's unit, he'd quickly become aware that his mentor possessed an acute situational awareness. And though Doc was well schooled in every facet of covert technology, he made it plain that he preferred his agents to rely mainly on their native faculties.

"What are you gonna do if your batteries run out?" he'd ask sarcastically. "Go home?"

Doc could be as exasperating as he was amazing. At some point whenever they got together, he left Dieter feeling like the overconfident young student in a kung fu movie who could never get the best of the master.

Dieter tucked the rod under one arm, the chair under the other, and picked up the cooler. In a way it was kind of nice to know that he still had things to learn. *At least it means that I'm not the old master yet. And he's never made me walk over rice paper without tearing it, or asked me to trust the Force.*

When he entered the cabin Doc was flicking switches on what looked like an incredibly complex stereo unit.

"Siddown," Doc invited. "Have yourself a brew."

He continued to fiddle with the console, though no music began to play. Von Rossbach selected a beer and sat watching him, making no comment.

Finally Holmes took a seat himself and, indicating the console, spoke as though continuing an ongoing conversation. "Yeah, the Sector promised me they wouldn't keep me under observation when I retired. They lied." He put a finger by his nose and winked. "But I never made them any promises in return. What I just did then was erase the little bit of conversation we just had and replace it with tweeting birds and lake water lapping the pier." He grinned. "I pity the poor schmo they've got listening in on me; his brain is probably turning to New Age paste." Taking a sip of beer, he studied his former agent.

"So, what brings you here to Goose Lake? I heard you'd retired to Paraguay, of all places."

Dieter shifted in his chair. "Paraguay is nice," he said, a bit defensively. "A little boring sometimes, but basically very nice."

With a snort Doc said, "So's Goose Lake, if you like being bored out of your mind." He wagged a finger. "You've been causing comment, dear boy. What's this I hear about you and Sarah Connor?"

"How do you know about that?" von Rossbach demanded.

Doc looked smug. "Remember how I said I never made them any promises? Wellll . . . I found a way to keep myself updated. When you left I hear you just . . . left."

"I burned out all at once," Dieter agreed. "I couldn't wait to get out of there. They agreed."

"Wanna talk about it?" Doc asked.

"Nothing to talk about," von Rossbach said. "There was nothing particular about my last mission that made it my last. It just was. Maybe I didn't take enough time between assignments, maybe I should have taken a desk job instead of staying in the field." He shrugged his big shoulders. "I don't know; it was just over."

Holmes looked at him shrewdly. "I ask again, what's this about Sarah Connor? Not like you to side with the terrorists."

Is that what they're saying? Dieter thought. Of course it was, what else *could* they think? "Sarah Connor isn't a terrorist," he said aloud. His voice was flat when he said it; he didn't expect to be believed.

Doc raised a brow at that. "She's not? She's bombed at least three computer companies that we know of. Okay, two of them were Cyberdyne, but that still counts as three hits. Not to mention she's guilty of drug smuggling and arms dealing. These are things that terrorists do, buddy."

Dieter sighed. He was about to risk something he really valued here— the continued respect of this man. "But what if she's not crazy, Doc?" He looked up and met the other man's eyes.

Both of Doc's brows went up at that. He sat contemplating his former agent for a while. "Not crazy," he said at last.

"Would you be willing to listen?" von Rossbach asked him.

Holmes pursed his lips and blew out a stream of air. He shrugged. "Sure, what the hell, I haven't got anything else on my schedule right now."

Dieter studied him carefully; if he didn't buy this story, Dieter knew Doc would turn him in to the Sector in a New York minute. He ran one hand over his face, feeling desperate. *Well, this is what you're here for,* he told himself.

"It's all true," he said simply. Dieter waved his hands. "All of it."

For a moment Doc sat still, looking expectant. "That's it?" he exclaimed. "That's your explanation? 'Cause, y'know, I'm sitting here waiting for something more. What if all I know about Sarah Connor is she likes to blow up computer companies?"

Tossing his head impatiently, von Rossbach said, "You know more about the case than that! I know you better, Doc. I worked for you for ten years. If you saw my name connected with hers in the Sector's files, you'd look into it. I know you would."

Doc waggled his head back and forth. "Okay, good call." He went silent for a while, his eyes on the middle distance. "I have to admit I was very intrigued by that guy who shot up the police station, then ten years later showed up in a shopping mall." He waved a hand at von Rossbach. "It was *you*! Except that at the time of both incidents, you were working for me, and in the first case, you were actually, physically, with me. So what am I supposed to think? I know you don't have an evil identical twin. I know they say everybody has a double, but that's bullshit."

Dieter watched Doc as he worked it through, the older man's fingers tapping on the arms of his chair. Doc looked up at him. "Connor says this guy was some kind of robot." A statement that was really a question.

Dieter nodded. "I got to meet a couple of them, Doc. They looked exactly like me. I saw their insides; they're made of metal. Rods and cams, hydraulics, a really impressive small power unit, computer controls—neural-net computers. They're real."

After studying Dieter for a moment, Doc said, "So it follows that the ultimate killer computer and the Judgment Day crap . . . all that's real, too?"

"I hope not. That's what Sarah has been trying to prevent all these years." He bit his lip. "Unfortunately we've come to the conclusion that maybe it can't be stopped. Maybe it's meant to happen and there's nothing that can be done to prevent it. The best we can do is mitigate the circumstances. Which is why I'm here."

"Yeah, Whang said you were recruiting people."

Doc waited him out. Dieter could feel heat creeping up his face. Only Doc could make him feel like a naive kid saying something stupid. "So I was hoping that we could rely on you to help when the time came." There, that was it. This time he waited for Holmes to speak.

"You're serious about this, I can see that," Doc said at last. "I'm not gonna tell you it makes me feel good; like you've found a nice hobby to enliven your retirement." He tightened his lips to a thin line, then met von Rossbach's eyes. "But I've trusted you before now and been right. So . . . I'll take a chance and agree to help you. But!" He held up a stern finger. "I'm not going to be party to any wacko terrorist behavior. If your girlfriend feels an urge to blow up anything else, I'd advise you to talk her out of it, or I'm gone. Got it?"

"Yes," Dieter said simply. "Thank you."

"So what do you want from me anyway?"

"When the time comes we'll need someplace marginally safe for people to go." Dieter looked out at the peaceful lake. "This would make a good destination. We'll also need your training skills." He hesitated. "And we'll need someplace to stockpile supplies."

Von Rossbach was enormously relieved. The fact that Holmes had agreed so readily meant that he'd given the matter study and thought. And where Doc led, others would follow; generations of Sector agents and allies had worked with, or trained under, the old man. He was glad he'd taken the chance and approached him.

Doc nodded once or twice, then narrowed his eyes thoughtfully. "How bad do you expect this thing to get?"

"Bad," Dieter said. "Not as bad as it would have been six years ago maybe. But bad. Billions dead. End of civilization as we know it. Possible extinction of the human race."

Holmes nodded, his eyes on the braided rug beneath his feet, then he looked up, his eyes sharp. "I really hope she's crazy, Dieter, if that's an *improvement* on the original version."

One corner of the Austrian's mouth quirked in a half smile. "I wish she was."

ON THE HIGHWAY TO UTAH

If anyone had been able to see through the van's darkened windows, they would have seen a pair of tall, grim-faced twins, a short, dark, balding muscleman, and a child of angelic beauty. Alissa's golden hair curled to the center of her back and she looked adorable in a little blue sundress and white sandals. She carried an adult's white purse that was almost as big as she was.

The purse contained all of their identity papers, driver's licenses for each of the Terminators, the deed on their new house, the van's registration, and several thousand dollars in cash, all that Clea thought they would need to get them safely to their new location in Utah.

The older Infiltrator didn't know that Alissa had gathered all of this material in one place, and would have disapproved if she had known. But to Alissa it felt right, and since she didn't really trust her older sibling, she went with her feelings.

Alissa was looking forward to getting settled in. She was long overdue for her next growth enhancement and the sense of being off schedule tormented her. Once in a while, to distract herself, she checked her sister's computer to view whatever Clea was looking at. She wasn't interested in communication so much as she wished she was in a more interesting place than the endless expanse of rolling sagebrush outside. New York was enormous, filled with buildings of staggering size and teeming with life, at once fascinating and revolting.

For the most part, like the Terminators, she ignored the often spectacular scenery they were traveling through. Occasionally she would take note of a suitable spot for an ambush, or places for the automated factories.

But for the most part this land was empty and, as far as she could see, always would be. She flicked her inner vision back to the busy New York streets. That was where the war would take place. There, along the Mississippi, and on the West Coast. Soon, she hoped. For now, this empty land was a good place to begin laying plans and manufacturing allies.

"I'm hungry," she said eventually. "Pull in to the next available place."

The Terminators didn't acknowledge her order; there was no need. Even voicing it aloud was mainly a matter of training herself in humanizing her mannerisms.

They did have supplies on the van, but she was bored and wished to begin socializing both herself and the Terminators to the degree that any of them was capable. You really couldn't terminate humans effectively if they had warning.

DUFFY'S DINER, UTAH

The restaurant was clean, with a black-and-white tile floor and chipped Formica surfaces; it smelled of cooking but of no particular food or spice unless it was hot oil. The four of them took a booth where rips in the plastic cover had been carefully patched with duct tape, and a waitress in a pink uniform and comfortable-looking shoes came over with plastic-coated menus. The menus were slightly sticky to the touch.

"Blue-plate special's chicken-fried steak," she announced to the puzzled machines and Infiltrator.

"Chicken . . . fried . . . steak?" Alissa asked. She had a ridiculous mental image of a fowl flipping meat onto a grill.

The waitress grinned. "You never had that, honey?" she asked. "You dip the steak in the same kinda coating you use for chicken, then you fry it."

"Interesting," the Infiltrator said. It didn't sound very healthy. "We will have that," she said, handing the menu back to the woman.

The waitress raised her brows and looked at the Terminators. In her experience, big, tough-looking men usually didn't take orders from little blond moppets.

"You boys okay with that?" she asked doubtfully. They handed back the menus and just looked at her. "How would you like those steaks cooked?"

Alissa blinked as she considered this. It felt like a trick question. "Until they're done," she said after a moment.

The waitress looked at her, a look that said, "Don't give me any more nonsense, kid." "Rare, medium, or well-done?" she asked tersely.

"Ah, medium," Alissa said. That sounded like a safe choice.

"To drink?" The waitress's voice hardened slightly under their unwavering gazes.

"Just water," Alissa said. If the dinner was unhealthy she need not compound the error with fluids made with a surfeit of sugar or caffeine.

"And you boys?" The waitress stood with her pencil poised over her pad.

"For all of us," Alissa told her.

The waitress sniffed and shook her head as she moved off; maybe they were playing some kind of road game to keep the kid entertained. Who cared? The girl seemed polite enough.

Alissa looked around the room with interest. All of the furnishings seemed to be at least thirty years old, some of the advertisements included. At least those advertisements that took the form of clocks or lights did. Two men at the end of the counter were looking at her. They smiled at her and waggled their fingers in a friendly way. She just looked at them until they turned away.

The waitress eventually returned with their food and placed a plate before each of the Terminators without comment, dropping the last one in front of Alissa, who picked up her fork.

"What do you say?" the woman asked, frowning and smiling at the same time.

Alissa and the Terminators looked at her mutely. The waitress glanced at the Terminators somewhat nervously. "What's the magic word?" she prompted the Infiltrator.

This female has gone mad, the I-950 thought. She was certain that most humans didn't believe in magic. Had she done something to precipitate this condition?

"Thank you," the waitress said carefully. She glanced again at the Terminators, then back at Alissa.

"You're welcome," the I-950 said, equally carefully.

The waitress laughed. "Enjoy," she said, and moved off chuckling.

Alissa watched her go nervously. Insane humans were unpredictable and, she'd read, often unnaturally strong. *Strong as a Terminator?* she wondered. She'd have to look it up.

Her excellent peripheral vision told her that the two men at the counter were watching her. The I-950 frowned as she sawed at her meat. Was there something strange about her? She studied them carefully.

They seemed ordinary enough. One was about fifty, with glasses and graying hair. The other was younger, perhaps late twenties, early thirties. That one had dark hair and was thin. Their glances became more furtive and the way they occasionally spoke to each other made her think they were talking about her. With a slight adjustment of her ears she listened in.

"So, whaddaya think?" the thin one asked.

"Definitely potential." The older man glanced at her again. "Could be a real winner."

"Should we go for it?"

After a long pause the older man said, "Big risk, might not be worth the trouble."

"Yeah, well, you gotta take the opportunities life sends ya. We gotta do *something,* for Christ's sake." The thin man took a sip of his coffee. "We got bills to pay."

The older man snorted and took a sip of his coffee.

"Let's see if any opportunities present themselves, okay? No point in doing things the hard way if you don't have to. And those three boys look plenty hard, if you get my meaning."

As far as Alissa could tell, this conversation had nothing to do with her; in any case, it was irrelevant at the moment. She continued to eat steadily, her higher metabolism allowing her to eat adult volumes of food with ease. The waitress, when she returned, complimented her on it.

"I was very hungry," Alissa told her. "Are there facilities here?"

The waitress pursed her lips in amusement and indicated a corridor to her right, moving aside when Alissa slipped out of the booth. "She's cute," she said to the Terminators when Alissa was out of hearing. They just looked at her. "So," she said crisply after a silent moment, "you gonna have dessert?"

As one, the three Terminators looked toward the bathrooms.

The waitress rolled her eyes. "Coffee, then, until your little girl gets back?"

One of the men at the counter threw down some bills and left. The other headed for the rest rooms. The waitress took note, estimating with a glance that the crumpled wad of money would pay their check.

"Coffee," the senior Terminator said at last, the answer its decision tree had offered as the best response.

The waitress nodded and cleared the table; and she made a bet with herself that these weirdos wouldn't tip.

Clay Radcliff was proud of the fact that, like the Boy Scouts on whom he had occasionally preyed, he was always prepared. He never left home without a nice clean handkerchief and his little bottle of chloroform tucked into his belt pouch. He lurked in the men's room, the door open just a fraction, watching for the glorious little moppet who was soon to be his little movie star.

Alissa finished her business, washed her hands, and disdained to use the endless linen towel that had apparently never been changed. Wiping off the wet on the skirt of her dress, she walked down the hall back toward the Terminators.

Clay swung out behind her and with practiced ease clapped the handkerchief over her small face, pulling her tight to his soft stomach as he dragged her into the men's room.

Unexpectedly the little brat clawed backward, obviously aiming for his groin. He barely got his leg up in time to protect himself, and even then she grabbed the muscle with the force of a metal clamp. Clay gasped in pain, his mouth wide open in agony and surprise. He swung her off her feet and the girl began to pummel his legs with her sharp little heels. Each kick was like a hammer blow and Clay spread his legs, trying to get away from the punishment.

Desperately he pressed her body against the wall, clamping her there with all his weight. Still she wriggled and kicked. Damn but the kid was strong! When the hell was she going to black out. Usually they went down instantly. He was getting dizzy from the goddamned fumes and she was still bucking like a bronco!

Alissa's computer enhancements worked hard to overcome the effects of the chloroform. They warned her that if she didn't break free in ten seconds she would succumb. The I-950 continued to fight. The slight differences in the muscle attachments in her arms and shoulders gave her a strength far beyond her size and years; and there was a greater flexibility built into her joints that allowed her to perform feats so unlikely that no ordinary human could anticipate them.

She folded one leg behind her, pointing her foot, and rammed it upward into the man's groin. He gasped in agony and his grip on her arms loosened. The I-950 twisted her arm free and reached up and back.

The man didn't even have time to react to the touch of a tiny hand on his throat. One moment he was folding over the agony in his groin, still trying to keep hold of her, the next he was thrashing on the floor, clawing at thin air, blood spraying from his throat, spurting from his mouth. He fell back, choking, his eyes bugging out in horror, the blood turning to a fan-shaped spray as he tried to scream.

Alissa's powerful little hand had snapped his windpipe like a paper straw.

Out in the parking lot Gil's fingers beat a nervous tattoo on the van's steering wheel. He'd been in position for over five minutes and he was feeling very conspicuous. Nobody sits outside an emergency door in a van with the motor running for no reason. Anybody who noticed probably wouldn't think that reason was a good one. Most likely they'd think he was waiting for someone to finish robbing the diner.

He wished. Robbery carried a fairly light sentence compared with kidnapping.

Hurry your ass up, *Gil!* he thought fiercely.

Three minutes later he slammed his palm against the wheel and opened the van door. He moved to the emergency door and opened it with exquisite caution. Gil breathed a sigh of relief when no alarm sounded. He peeked through the crack and saw no one in the short corridor; there was no sound from either bathroom.

Gil looked around; no one was watching, so he slipped inside and moved quietly to the men's room. Pressing his ear against the door, he listened and heard water running. Carefully he tried the knob and it turned. Gritting his teeth, Gil opened the door and slipped inside.

The little girl washing her dress in the sink looked up at Gil, who stood frozen, staring at the man lying on the floor in a spreading pool of blood. Slowly he turned to gaze at her sweet, expressionless face and innocent blue eyes and wondered if he was having a nightmare.

She blinked at him and Gil shook his head. Her hair was drenched with blood and her face and arms wore flecks of blood so tiny it looked as though they'd been applied in a fine spray. He took a deep breath of the fetid air in the tiny room and nearly gagged on the complex mixture of blood and feces and disinfectant.

Gil knew that somehow this beautiful little girl was responsible, that somehow, like an avenging angel, she was the answer to all the prayers of all the kids he and Clay had ever hurt. He pressed his back to the door and all he could think to say to her was "no," over and over, half plea, half denial.

Alissa stared at the human. Then she smiled slightly, watching him pale as her expression changed. "You should have knocked," she said gently.

He turned to open the door and she squatted to pick up the chloroform-soaked handkerchief, then sprang up and grabbed him, her legs clamping around his arms so tightly he couldn't dislodge her. The man shrugged and struggled, opening his mouth as though to shout. The I-950 pressed the handkerchief over his mouth and nose, effectively gagging him. Within seconds he began to totter. Apparently sensing his danger, he began trying to bite her, but Alissa easily kept his jaws apart. Then he slammed himself into the bathroom door. She grimaced and held on, extending her senses to see if anyone had heard the sound. Apparently the crash had been more significant in the bathroom's small confines. No one commented, no one came.

Her computer tested the man's vital signs and concluded that he would shortly be unconscious. The I-950 lost patience; shortly wasn't soon enough. She took one hand from his mouth and felt along the column of his throat. The man tried to shout, making muffled sounds, then tried to turn his head, obviously meaning to shake off both of her hands, almost succeeding in actually moving. Alissa found what she was searching for, and with a flex of her fingers she felt his hyoid bone snap.

That should hurry things along, she thought with satisfaction.

For a moment his struggles became more violent, then he fell forward. The computer confirmed unconsciousness and she let him go; pushing herself upright, she stared down at him. A brief spasm passed through the body and it voided, finally going limp. That was good. She hadn't wanted any more blood to contend with.

As she scrubbed her dress the child part of Alissa enjoyed pretending that Skynet had set up a test for her, just like it used to do for Serena, her mother/sister, a test that she had passed. But the computer part of her objected to the dissonance and with a wistful sigh she put the idea from her.

She looked at the bodies on the floor. It would probably be best to leave here now. This incident had already caused enough delay.

Holding up the dress, Alissa studied it. Most of the stains were gone, but there was a shadow of brownish red at the neckline. Future washings would probably remove the stain. Meanwhile she could hardly walk through the diner in a soaking-wet dress. She ordered the T-101s to meet her at the van and slipped out the back door in her underpants.

MIT CAMPUS

The guys' attitude had changed dramatically in just the few days that John had been gone. Wendy listened to them with growing unease.

"I feel like I've been hypnotized," Snog was saying. "I can't believe I was making life-changing promises to some seventeen-year-old!"

"If what John was telling us is true—" Wendy began.

"Hey! He lied about his age," Yam pointed out.

"That's because you guys were making such a big deal about it," she said crossly. "Anyway, if Judgment Day happens, then at least we'll *have* lives."

"His father is from the future," Brad said dreamily. "He probably hasn't even been born yet." He looked around at his friends. "How the *hell* does that work?"

"Not too well," Yam commented. "At least as far as his dad was concerned."

"Yeah," Carl agreed. "Imagine sending your father back through time to become your father, knowing he's going to get killed."

There was silence as they all contemplated the idea.

"Do it to my old man in a flash," Yam muttered.

"Yeah, I've met him, I second that," Carl said. They high-fived.

Wendy frowned but said nothing. She listened uneasily, not liking the implied criticism of John, and not sure where they were going with this. Not knowing for sure how she felt about all this.

On the one hand, she felt uneasy knowing that all John's mother's ravings were nothing but the truth; on the other, she didn't like knowing that far from being the victim of some government conspiracy, his mother really had blown up a bunch of computer companies.

And what would you have done? she kept asking herself. As yet she didn't have an answer.

"His mother must be terrifying," Brad said, almost as though he was listening in on her thoughts.

"I heard she was a fox," Snog said, and waggled his brows.

The guys started kidding and snickering about that, and Wendy listened. Maybe they were just acting out because John intimidated them. Her lips quirked in a smile. If seventeen-year-old John was intimidating, then maybe his mom actually was terrifying.

"So what are we gonna do?" Carl asked. He looked directly at Snog.

Snog shrugged, his eyes wide in a manner that invited Carl to say more.

"What do you mean, what are we gonna do?" Wendy demanded.

"Oh, c'mon," Carl almost shouted. "When he's around, you somehow can believe all that crazy shit. But let's get real, guys. A father who hasn't even been born yet? Killer robots? A maniacal computer that's going to blow up the world? That's bullshit! None of that can possibly be real!"

"But this is real," Snog said. He held up the chip that John had left with them. "And he sure didn't create this thing." He gave Wendy an apologetic glance. "John's smart, but he's not smart like us, and none of *us* could have come up with this design, never mind actually manufacturing it. I know we all want to go into denial, guys. I can feel the pull myself. But there's always this." He shook the chip. "And this says it wasn't a dream, and it isn't a lie, it's real. So what *I'm* gonna do is figure this baby out, then I'm gonna get my degree and get the hell outta Dodge before the fire comes down."

Wendy let out her pent-up breath quietly, tremendously relieved. If Snog had backed out on this project John had given them, the others would have followed his lead. There wouldn't have been a thing she could have done about it, either to change their minds or to retrieve the chip.

She met Snog's glance and she still didn't feel absolutely secure about him, but for now, he was on John's side, and that would have to do.

DUFFY'S DINER, UTAH

There had been a little spate of customers and it was a half hour later when the waitress noticed that the three men were still seated, unmoving and silent before their untouched coffee, and the little girl wasn't back from the rest room yet. *These guys are seriously getting on my nerves,* she thought.

She brought over their check.

"Twenty-eight eighty-seven, boys," she said with false cheer. "Hope you enjoyed it." She stood, smiling expectantly, determined not to be intimidated by their size and their silence, even though she was.

The three Terminators looked at her, their faces expressionless, unblinking. Then one of them took a wallet out of Alissa's bag and extracted two twenties. The waitress, so tense she actually felt taller, began to count out change. Then, as one, they suddenly rose and walked out, paying her no more attention than if she'd been invisible.

"Well, hell!" she murmured. Then she shook herself.

She'd been wrong; they were good tippers. But she hoped she'd never meet their like again.

Soon after her strange customers had gone it occurred to the waitress that she might want to check the ladies' room. She didn't quite trust that strange little girl.

Opening the door, she found the place in perfect order. Well, as perfect as a rest room ever got. As she went back down the corridor she decided to check the men's room to see if it needed paper.

A bloodcurdling scream was heard all the way to the kitchen.

CHAPTER 14

Dr. Silberman was surprised to find his office door unlocked, but put it down to his having been quite tired the night before. He was even more surprised to find a short, dark stranger turning away from one of his filing cabinets.

"May I ask who you are?" he said carefully.

In his profession, in a place like this, it was unwise to display even perfectly natural irritation. This might be a new resident who had wandered in quite innocently, or a new resident hopped up on drugs and looking for more, and it was, after all, his fault for not locking the door.

"I am the new janitor," the man said. He raised a feather duster, gripped in a massive fist, as proof.

"Oh?" Silberman was surprised. Ralph hadn't said anything about leaving. And usually when someone left it took forever to get a replacement. "What happened?" he asked when it became clear the fellow wasn't going to volunteer anything.

The stranger shrugged his impressive shoulders. "I don't know," he intoned. "I was told to come here from now on."

Silberman noted a slight accent; the man looked Turkish or Middle Eastern, which might explain his odd manner of speaking. But not his apparent desire to dust the inside of the file cabinet. The doctor frowned.

"No one said anything to me about this," he said.

The janitor just stood there, staring at Silberman.

Very low affect, the doctor mused. Maybe this was a new resident playing a role. Possibly neurological damage.

"Well, look." Silberman placed his briefcase on the desk. "Could you come back later? I need to get to work right now. But I'll be out of here between two and four, so you can finish up then." He smiled politely, trying to exude confidence; by two o'clock he should have some answers about this guy.

The smaller man didn't respond for a moment, then he simply walked forward, as though he intended to go right through Silberman, who jumped aside at the last second. This time he did allow his irritation to show.

"Hey!" he snapped at the retreating back. Then he forced himself to calm down. "Didn't they give you any paperwork for me?"

The janitor stopped, turned his head, said a short "no," over his shoulder, and continued on his way.

Oh yeah, it was going to be fun having this guy around.

"Just what this place needs," Silberman muttered, "a janitor with attitude."

IBC OFFICES, NEXT DOOR TO ENCINAS HALFWAY HOUSE

Operative Joe Consigli dropped his feet to the floor as the office door began to open and grinned with not a little relief when he saw who it was. "Hey, buddy, what brings you around?" he asked cheerfully.

He and Paul Delfino had been working this case together in the first few weeks after Sarah Connor was captured, until the powers that be decided only one operative at a time was necessary.

As far as Joe was concerned this was a totally dead assignment and he was profoundly bored. Especially since Connor had been moved to the halfway house next door. Watching these weird, sad people was depressing as hell and they made his skin crawl. Having someone to help him make fun of them would be primo.

"The head office sent me over," Operative Delfino said. "It seems that their janitor"—he indicated the monitors that showed various locations inside the Encinas Halfway House—"was killed during a burglary."

"Killed?" Consigli said.

Delfino snorted. "Boy, howdy! The guy's head was almost twisted off. The house was trashed, but there was cash left in the poor guy's wallet." He shrugged. "Which made the front office think something might be up."

Consigli looked at the monitor. "Hunh," he said.

He pulled his chair up to the recording equipment and removed a tape, quickly replacing it, then he pushed the tape into a player, rewound it, and set it to play on a blank monitor. He pointed at the screen. "This is the guy who claims he was sent over to replace their janitor."

Delfino pursed his lips. "Not what we were hoping for," he said.

Not at all. What they were looking for was a guy about six feet tall, blond, with sculpted features. *This* was definitely not him.

When Dr. Ray first proposed moving Sarah Connor to a halfway house, the head office had jumped on the idea and pushed it through. Even Ray was stunned that the committee had approved his request. The organization's theory was that surely, in such a low-security environment, Connor's allies would make a move to break her out.

It had been child's play to hack into the halfway house's security system and begin monitoring the place via its own cameras. The team had planted a few of their own as well. But so far all they'd collected was endless, boring footage of what Consigli thought were hopeless cases and self-centered whiners; losers with a capital *L*.

"What's administration say?" he asked.

Delfino pulled a face. "This guy is in the computer and all the stuff that needs to be in the computer to get him to Encinas and on the payroll is there. Even the paperwork, for want of a better word, that has to be done for a deceased employee had been done. The only thing is"—he shrugged elaborately—"nobody admits to doing it. Nobody even knew that this guy Ralph was dead. Weird, huh?"

Leaning back in his chair, Consigli shook his head.

"What isn't weird about this assignment? Hey, maybe Connor's bunch just wised up and decided to send somebody less conspicuous."

Delfino laughed. "Yeah, that'd be smart. 'Cause wherever that big guy goes, hell follows."

They sat quietly for a few minutes, watching the monitors, contemplating the footage they'd seen of the "big guy" in action. Truth to tell, it wouldn't have surprised either operative to find out that the head office wanted to find this guy so he could teach them to shoot as well as he did.

"So we're doubled up for the time being," Consigli asked.

"Yep."

"Kewl," Joe said. "Someone can go out for burgers. I was getting sick of brown-bagging peanut-butter sandwiches."

Delfino gave him a look. "You've been alone in this room too long if you think I'm gonna play errand boy, buddy. You want a sandwich you can go and get it yourself."

"Kewl," Consigli said, grinning at his fellow operative's suspicious expression. It would be nice to get some fresh air once in a while.

ENCINAS HALFWAY HOUSE

Sarah met the new janitor as she came out of the large, battered kitchen where she had been given a "training opportunity" while she "adjusted to her new environment." In a few weeks, they'd gently promised her, if all went well she'd be "encouraged to find a job of her own." Sarah wondered how long it took to learn to speak in pat phrases like that. It made all the staff sound weirdly alike, as though their thoughts came prepackaged.

The kitchen job was fine with her; since she still tired easily, she didn't mind taking it slow. Running the dishwasher and putting things away was about the extent of her duties, so she couldn't complain, except about boredom. Which was all a matter of perception, she reminded herself.

Oh God, she thought, *I'm beginning to think in happy-talk phrases, just like the staff.* If she'd felt better physically . . . that alone would have made her run for cover.

But for now this place was about her speed. She could read—light fiction and self-help books—or watch TV. She'd never seen so much Disney in her life. The house had racks of their videos and someone always seemed to be halfway through one. Nothing violent or jarring or unpleasant was allowed in here. As long as she didn't forget there was life on the outside of the halfway house, she was content for the moment.

As she was leaving the kitchen she was vaguely thinking about her hair. It had grown out considerably and the light hair above the dark looked very odd. The light part was getting long, so cutting it was a good idea, she thought.

Sarah almost bumped into him as he came around the corner. He effectively blocked the doorway, he was so broad; for a moment she felt trapped. It was obvious he was the janitor; he had the gray uniform, the bucket and mop, all the usual accoutrements. He wasn't, though. A nice old guy named Ralph was.

They stood there for a moment, looking at one another.

"Who are you?" Sarah asked, trying to put a pleasant tone into the question.

The face was unfamiliar, though its shape rang a distant bell. His body seemed wrongly proportioned, with the limbs too short for the long torso. He was certainly much too short to be an agent. But he was truculent enough for a species of janitor she'd encountered one or two times in her life.

The appearance of a strange new face—and he *was* strange—shook her from her boredom like the scream of an air-raid siren. But it was the way he looked at her, his stillness as he blocked her way, that sent a chill down her spine and raised the hair on her neck.

Subject Sarah Connor found, the Terminator sent to the new base in Utah. *Terminate?*

Negative. Orders to watch subject remain in effect, came the response.

The Terminator stepped back, its eyes still on Sarah.

She glanced at the narrow space that would allow her to pass and then back at the strange man. "Who did you say you were?" she asked, making her voice hard.

"The janitor," he answered. Then he turned and went back down the hallway.

She stood still after he was gone, breathing a little hard, like someone who has faced a dangerous animal that had inexplicably decided not to attack. She took a deep breath and let it out slowly.

"O-kay," she muttered through her teeth. "That was interesting."

Maybe he was a patient. Or maybe he was just a very weird little guy. And yet . . . there was something about him. Her first impression had been that his face was unfamiliar; in fact, she knew she'd never seen him. But there was something about the way he moved, or rather, didn't.

His eyes, she decided. She'd seen eyes like that before. His eyes were dead, without emotion. There were men like that; God knew she'd met too many of them in her travels. But this man's eyes were especially cold.

At first she resisted the idea, wondering if her old madness—she was far enough from it now that she could admit that she had once been insane—was rearing its head in Silberman's presence. But over the years she'd trained herself to be honest, to look events in the face, even when a thing was painful, even when it was impossible.

His eyes were the eyes of a Terminator. As was his stillness, and something in his voice.

Her heart sped up, her mouth went dry while her palms grew moist; it was the old fear, the nightmare that kept coming back. Sarah felt the last of her resistance crumble under a sudden, sure knowledge; the female Terminator had left an ally behind, and it had found her. Like they always found her.

It hadn't attacked her on sight and she took hope from that. It had been less than a foot away from her, it could have torn her in half, but it hadn't.

It backed off. So what did that mean? *It's hoping to make a clean sweep,* she thought. *It's hoping John will come to get me out of here.*

Sarah bit her lip. She had to contact Jordan; he would get in touch with John and Dieter, warn them that she was under a more deadly surveillance than any the government was willing to throw at them.

Then, if possible, it was time for her to get out of here, before the Terminator was too firmly entrenched.

Well, Silberman said he believed me, that he wanted to help me. This is as good a time as any to take him up on it. But carefully. His sudden desire to be helpful could easily be a trap. She wouldn't put it past the good doctor to be trying to get some evidence that her obsession was still alive.

If only he knew how gladly I'd give it up.

Sarah headed for the doctor's office. Waiting wasn't going to make things any simpler.

She tapped on the door and entered when he called out his permission. Silberman looked up and flinched as he always did when he first found himself alone with her. That she still scared him somewhat pleased her. She knew it shouldn't, but it did. He had, after all, given her a very rough time.

"Oh, hello, Sarah," he said, smiling pleasantly.

Long training had helped him to recover quickly, but he knew she'd seen his fear. It annoyed him that she affected him this way, but she'd hurt him so many times. She'd broken his arm, driven a pen through his knee, and threatened to kill him in a particularly horrible way. It was hard to forget things like that, no matter how professional you were.

Sarah stepped in, closing the door behind her, then came to stand before his desk, looking shy. "I was wondering if I might ask a favor?"

Silberman leaned back. "Of course, Sarah. What did you want to ask me?" Inside, excitement twisted his stomach. This could be it.

"I'm nervous as a cat today," she said, looking down at his desk. "It feels like the walls are closing in on me." She looked up suddenly. "I was wondering, if I could arrange it, if it would be all right for me to go out to dinner with Jordan Dyson."

The doctor's face jerked into a grimace. "You know the rules, Sarah," he said. "Any visits or excursions have to be cleared at least one day before they're to take place. I can't just go around making exceptions, you know."

So much for your generous offer of help, she thought. "You'd be welcome to come with us," she offered. "I think you'd find Jordan a very interesting man. He's a former FBI agent and Miles Dyson's younger brother. Miles Dyson was the project manager killed at . . . Cyberdyne."

"Oh really," Silberman said, raising his eyebrows in surprise. He'd read about Dyson's interest in Sarah Connor, but he hadn't understood it. This would be an excellent opportunity to find out why he was being so helpful to the woman who had killed his brother.

"Dr. Ray had several sessions with him," Sarah said.

Silberman blinked at that. He had to admit that he felt a certain rivalry with the younger doctor. If Ray thought it worthwhile to speak to this Jordan Dyson, perhaps he should see why. "Well," he said thoughtfully, "perhaps we could categorize this as a sort of informal therapy session."

Sarah smiled. "Thank you, Doctor. I'll go and call him, see what arrangements we can make." Sarah turned at the door to look at him. "I appreciate this," she said.

IBC OFFICES

"Hey, Paul," Consigli said, bustling into the anonymous rented office wired like the "after" picture in a cocaine commercial. "Looks like we're taking this show on the road!"

Delfino looked up from the hand of solitaire he was playing, thankful for a chance to stop struggling with the bus tickets luck was dealing him.

"Connor just asked the doc if she could go out to dinner with Dyson."

"Exxxcellent!" Paul Delfino said. "I could use a change of scenery. I'll go get the van."

CAFÉ VERICE, LOS ANGELES

Jordan saw them enter from the bar and went to meet them. Sarah reached out her hand, smiling. He took it and pulled her to him, enveloping her in a one-armed hug. Then he turned to the doctor, keeping his arm around Sarah's shoulders.

"This is Dr. Silberman," Sarah said.

Jordan reached out his left hand and the doctor took it awkwardly. Before they could speak the maître d'hôtel approached them, menus in hand, and gestured toward the dining room.

"Oops." Jordan put his hand on his midsection. "That's my beeper. Would you excuse me for a moment?" he asked.

In the corridor next to the rest rooms was a pay phone. As he made his way toward it Jordan opened the note Sarah had slipped him.

Possible Terminator watching me, she'd written. *Warn John and Dieter to stay away.*

Jordan let out his breath in a little "huh!" of surprise, as though someone had poked him in the stomach. His mind immediately crowded with questions. Possible? What did that mean? He'd seen them, and in his opinion there was no mistaking one. And Sarah was the world's longest-lived expert on the subject, so if even she wasn't sure, what did that mean? *Possible?* He shook his head. *Okay,* he thought.

Digging in his pocket he pulled out some change and dropped coins into the phone. He dialed Consuela, a college student he knew who was delighted to pass along his cryptic messages for the fifty-plus-expenses he slipped her.

"Yo!" It sounded like Jennifer Lopez was singing backup to Consuela's studies tonight.

"Hi," Jordan said, "it's me. I've got a message for you. This time I'll need you to make the call."

"Sure," she said. "Shoot."

He rattled off the number first. "Ask for Dieter or John. If neither of them is there I still want you to leave the message, but you've got to stress that this is very, very important, and that they have to be given the message as soon as possible, okay?"

"Sure," she said; you could almost hear the shrug in her voice. "For fifty bucks I'll make them think it's the only way to save the world."

Close enough, he thought. "Good, excellent," he said aloud. "Here it is. 'Vital—avoid halfway measures at all costs. Let the package come to you.' "

She repeated it back to him. "Sounds like a fortune cookie," she said.

"Everybody's a critic. How's your Spanish?" he asked.

"Better'n yours, chico."

"Good," he said, smiling. "Because you'll probably be speaking to people with no English."

"No prob. That it?"

"Yup. I'll slip the money in your mailbox," he said. "Good night."

" 'Night."

Jordan went to their table and sat down with a smile. "Well, that's taken care of, we shouldn't be interrupted again," he said.

Sarah's smile was radiant as she said, "The specials are veal piccatta and fettuccini primavera."

"Sounds good," Jordan said. He smiled at Silberman. "What are you having, Doctor?"

ENCINAS HALFWAY HOUSE

The Watcher/Terminator had searched the house and had not found the subject Sarah Connor. It had even asked one of the humans if he had seen her. The man responded by describing a sexual fantasy that even the Terminator knew wasn't healthy.

It hadn't yet gone to Dr. Silberman's office. Calculations had indicated that it would be best to avoid the doctor since the Watcher/Terminator's estimation of Silberman's reaction to their first meeting signified a 48 percent chance (plus or minus 5 percent) that the doctor had found it suspicious. But now it seemed best to override that decision; this was fast becoming an emergency situation.

The glass panel in the doctor's door was dark, indicating that he wasn't there. The Terminator tried the door and found it locked.

"He's gone," a young woman said.

The Terminator recognized one of the other psychologists who worked here. "I was going to clean his office," it said.

"Don't you have a key?" the woman asked.

"No," it said.

She shrugged. "Then it'll have to wait till tomorrow. G'night," she said cheerfully, and walked off.

It watched her go as it sorted through the information it had. The doctor was gone, Connor was gone. By the rules of this place she couldn't go off on her own; therefore it seemed likely that they were together.

Given Connor's history with Silberman, there was a good chance that she'd kidnapped him. The question was, why? Escape?

The Watcher's appearance was very different from that of other Terminators, and with the death of the only I-950 that Connor knew about, she had no reason to suspect that she was in immediate danger. Its inspection of her file in Silberman's office showed that she was being treated very gently here, eliminating abuse as a reason for escaping.

The Watcher's processor offered the possibility that John Connor and their ally von Rossbach had come to collect her, giving that scenario a fifty percent chance of being correct.

It needed more information. The Watcher had tapped the pay phone that the patients used; now it accessed those recordings. And there it was. She was meeting Jordan Dyson at a café on Sunset Boulevard. It headed for the small, elderly sedan that had been assigned to it.

OUTSIDE CAFÉ VERICE, LOS ANGELES

Joe Consigli and Paul Delfino sat in the van watching Café Verice on a monitor, trying to decide which of them should haunt the bar by way of keeping a closer eye on their quarry.

"I should, *I* should," Joe insisted, stabbing a finger at his chest. "I spent a month in the dead zone watching lobotomy candidates while you were out walking around in the real world. So *I* get to go inside."

"Yeah, but you've been going in and out of that building right next door to her. If she's going to recognize one of us, it's going to be you."

Consigli held up his hands. "She never saw me, man."

"Joe, you walk into that bar, I betcha ten bucks she buys you a drink."

"Oh yeah?"

"Yeah!"

Consigli was thoughtful for a moment. "Okay, so neither one of us should go in. But one of us should watch the back."

"No, no," Paul said, shaking a finger. "I am not spending several hours soaking up the ambience of a garbage-and piss-and puke-soaked alley. No, no, not me, pal. Unh unh."

Joe looked at him. "Y'know, I'd forgotten what a pain it was working with you."

"I'll tell you what you forgot, you forgot our rule," Paul said. At Consigli's puzzled look he snapped, "Whoever thinks it up has to do it!"

"Okay, fine!" Joe said. Anything to get away from this bullshit. He pushed himself to his feet when something on the monitor caught his eye. "Hey," he said, pointing. "That's the new janitor. Isn't it?"

Delfino looked. "Yeah, it is." He glanced at Consigli. "Not exactly dressed for fine dining, is he?"

The Watcher, still clad in gray coveralls, came down the street, its gaze fixed on the Café Verice. It walked up to the van and stationed itself so that it could look through the van's windows into the restaurant.

"Sometimes they just beg to be arrested, don't they?" Delfino asked.

Consigli flashed him a look. "You think he had something to do with the other janitor's death?"

"Did you see the size of his hands?" Paul asked by way of response. "And going by his arms and shoulders, he could bench-press a bull, never mind break the neck of some sixty-something-old guy. Now he's eyeballing the place where our subject is having dinner. My guess, he's here to either help her out or to take her out."

"Either way we'd better do something," Joe said. "But carefully, we don't want Connor to see. Hey!"

The Watcher had quickly become aware that the van it was hiding behind was tenanted and began to move away. Both Consigli and Delfino piled out of the van, guns drawn, to move in pursuit.

"Stop!" Delfino shouted.

The Watcher froze, weighing its options, and Consigli moved toward it. Looking at a restaurant was not illegal; neither had anything in its manner been threatening. Yet the extreme caution these humans were using, as well as the drawn guns, indicated that they suspected him of being dangerous.

"Hands on the van, spread your legs!" Consigli snapped.

"Why?" the Watcher asked, not moving. It concluded that they suspected him of—

"You're under arrest for the murder of Ralph Kurtz," Delfino said, reaching behind for his handcuffs.

"Just do what you're told," Consigli said, and pointed at the van.

With one hand the Watcher slapped Consigli's gun hand hard enough to crack several of the small bones; with the other it shoved him into his partner, knocking both men to the street. Then it turned and fled.

Sarah's eye was caught by the motion of the back doors of a van flying open across the street. Two men in suits piled out and another, framed in the van's side windows, turned to look at them. Instantly she recognized the new janitor from the halfway house, and the moment froze. Even before the brief fight began, she was in motion.

"I have to go," she said.

Jordan and Silberman looked up from their meals and their uneasy conversation to stare at her.

"Close your mouth, Doctor, and give me the keys to your car." Sarah held out her hand.

"What's wrong?" Jordan asked; his eyes swept the room. Then he saw the action outside. "Government agents?" He rose and pulled out his wallet, dropping several bills on the table.

Sarah's eyes were on the street; she watched the brief scuffle, her lips a thin line of anxiety. She gave her head a brief shake. "No," she said. "That's the new janitor from the halfway house."

Jordan looked up in time to see the man sprint away. "Shit!" he said softly.

Silberman stood, finally. "What do we do?"

"I take your keys and get out of here," she said briskly.

"No. I'll go with you. Mexico?" he asked.

Sarah frowned and nodded.

"It's just a few hours, no one's expecting me back at Encinas tonight, and since this was such short notice probably nobody will notice you're gone. That should give you a few more hours before you're missed. And if they see you drive off with me they'll assume I'm taking you back to Encinas." He could see the "no" forming on her lips. "Please, Sarah. I want to help."

Jordan took the rest of the cash from his wallet and the small pile he'd left on the table and handed it to her. "I'll get this with my card," he said. "Right now that's the most help I can give you. But the doctor is right, Sarah. If you think you can trust him."

Sarah looked into Silberman's face for a long moment, biting her lips, remembering. Then she took a deep breath. He knew. He'd seen undeniable proof and had paid the price for it, just as she had.

"Okay," she said, her voice tight. "But we need to go *now*!"

Silberman stuffed a piece of bread in his mouth and followed her, digging in his pockets for his car keys. Sarah went toward the service door to the kitchen and found the back door. The alley was, blessedly, open at one end. Sarah headed for the opening at a run, a startled-looking but game Silberman racing at her heels, already beginning to wheeze.

"Let me go first," he suggested.

Sarah looked over her shoulder at him and nodded. Silberman trotted to the mouth of the alley and stopped, looking both ways. A man came away from the wall he'd been leaning against with his hand out.

"Hey, buddy, can you spare some change?" he whined.

Silberman recoiled from the smell of stale booze and body odor. He held up his hands and took a step backward. "No, sorry," he said, feeling guilty.

"Hey!" the man said, suddenly happy. "I know you! Dr. Silberman!"

He reached out to touch the doctor's arm. "It's me, Douglas! We used to work together."

Silberman blinked. "Douglas, of course." The man had been an orderly at Pescadero. Sarah had whacked the stuffing out of him with a mop handle. He'd never known what became of him.

"My disability ran out," Douglas whined. He pointed to his neck. "Pain, alla time, Doc. Can ya spare some change?"

Sarah came up behind Silberman. "We've got to go," she said tersely.

"HEY!" Douglas shouted, pointing at her. "She hit me!"

"Let's *go*!" Sarah said, giving the doctor a nudge.

"She hit me!" Douglas insisted. He balled up his fists. "Bitch! Hit me, willya?"

"Jeez!" Sarah muttered, rolling her eyes.

She kicked Douglas in the stomach, grabbed his head, and rammed it onto her upthrust knee, then shoved him in the direction of the alley, where he lay still. Then she grabbed the horrified Silberman by the arm.

"Let's go!" she muttered through her teeth.

TIJUANA, MEXICO

"Stop here," Sarah said.

Silberman pulled over to the curb, not seeing anything different about this particular street. There were a few shops, still open late, and a few restaurants, which looked like they might stay open all night, and a lot of people around. Everything looked a little dustier and more chipped and scuffed than its equivalent over the border, and there weren't many Anglo faces around—not too different from L.A., in that respect.

They'd gotten over the border with no problem; as it happened, Silberman had Sarah's identification on him, her driver's license and a birth certificate, enough to get them waved through. Silberman had been right; he was a help.

But now it's time to send him on his way, she thought.

"Thank you, Doctor," she said, opening the car door.

"Wait! You want me to just leave you here?" He looked at her in horror. "I can't do that!"

Sarah smiled at that. To the good doctor a woman alone in Tijuana at night was asking for trouble. She couldn't help but be charmed by his chivalrous attitude, even if it was too late and grossly misplaced. She might be an obvious *gringa,* but nobody here—nobody dangerous, at least—was going to mistake her for a tourist. And once she got to the nearest cache . . .

"I'll be all right, Doctor, thank you. Um. Could I have my ID, please."

"Of course." Silberman pulled out his wallet and gave the documents to her. "Here," he said, handing her his cash as well.

"Thanks," she said, not even considering refusal.

"Sarah," Silberman said, his face absolutely sincere. "Is there anything I can do to help? Anything at all?"

She considered him, chewing on her full lower lip. Well, there was no harm in asking. "Yes. Buy some land in the mountains, with a house, maybe a barn. Buy medical supplies, the kind that will keep, and as much imperishable food as you can. Then hope we never need them. If you need to send us a message leave a note, nothing obvious, on a Luddite Web site. If necessary we'll get back to you. Thank you, Dr. Silberman. Be careful."

He smiled and gave a soft laugh; it changed his whole face.

"You, too," he said. "Good luck."

"Thanks," she said. Then she turned and disappeared into the crowd.

CHAPTER 15

MONTANA

The grave heaved, the loose soil humping and rolling. Finally the pale shape of a human hand, rotting skin ripped away from fingertips and knucklebones, emerged from the dark, damp earth. Another hand followed, flattened itself on the firm ground at the edge of the grave, and pulled. Immediately the soil seemed to boil faster as a head rose, followed by shoulders encased in a dark suit. With a last heave the Terminator pulled itself free of the confinement of its grave, rising from its knees to shake off the loose dirt like a dog spraying water.

It evaluated its condition. Mechanical functions were fully operative; its CPU and energy cell were also optimal. Unfortunately its downtime in a low-oxygen environment had caused the slow death of its flesh sheath. Many portions of its skin were sloughing off and it smelled quite bad.

This eventuality had been foreseen, however, and preparations had been made. At the cabin where it had worked, a car with blacked-out windows had been left. The vehicle held medical supplies so that it could remove the dead flesh from its skeleton and a supply of the protein foodstuff that would rescue at least some of its skin, as well as clothes and money for the journey to the new base in Utah.

Its only problem now was getting to the cabin without being seen. It plucked at the decaying tissue that used to resemble human eyes, revealing the glowing red lights that were its visual receptors. Leaning forward, it poked the discarded flesh into the loose dirt, then carefully patted the earth on its grave into a less disrupted shape.

When it was satisfied it began to jog toward the cabin. *Checking in,* it reported to the new base in Utah. *All essential systems functional.*

Affirmative, the Terminator on watch confirmed. It provided an info dump of events up to the present moment for its off-line comrade, then closed contact. From this point on it would be kept up-to-date daily.

The Terminator ran through the cemetery, remarkably quiet for such a large and heavy machine. A pair of teenagers smoking dope and making out saw it go past; the boy gasped, the girl shrieked. The Terminator glanced at them, narrowing its eyes, the translucence of its eyelids diffusing the red light from its receptors into a pair of glowing crimson orbs.

The shrieking rose to the level of a steam whistle, the boy joining in with an even more piercing scream. The two humans fled in the opposite direction, stumbling and howling.

The Terminator decided that it didn't need to do anything about what they'd seen. Given its present location, the scent of marijuana, and human superstition, no one rational would believe them. At most, a rumor of zombies would run through the neighborhood.

NEW YORK

Clea lay on her hotel bed, quite tired but unable to sleep. She had differentiated herself from her progenitor as much as possible with hair coloring and makeup; she'd even acquired a pair of eyeglasses, made with plain glass, to break up the shape of her face. So Roger Colvin shouldn't immediately think of his former security chief when he met her. Besides, the dress she'd chosen for the gala was designed to focus male eyes below her neck. Clea hoped it wouldn't put Mrs. Colvin off.

Skynet help her, she hadn't thought of that until now! Should she get another dress?

What would Serena do? Enjoy herself thoroughly, in all likelihood.

Clea felt herself veering toward frustration and despair, an emotional response that should be outside of her experience. Her computer was working overtime to keep her fight/flight indexes under control. This lack of social skills was yet another indicator that she was inferior. It would be good when Alissa was able to take over for her.

Clea? Alissa's voice came from Clea's communications matrix.

Clea smiled; it was as though her thought had brought her sister to her. *Yes?*

I regret to report that the Watcher/Terminator has lost track of Sarah Connor. Alissa's voice was emotionless.

Fury and alarm raced through Clea's system, almost instantly suppressed by her computer regulators. Rage was followed by the thought, *Are even my Terminator CPUs faulty?*

The fault is not yours, Alissa went on, seeming, eerily, to respond to her thought. *The CPU was one of those brought through by Serena, and, as you saw, the Watcher's features and body had been greatly altered. It is unlikely that Connor recognized it as a Terminator.* The younger I-950 paused. *The fault was probably mine,* she confessed. *I instructed the Watcher to terminate the janitor of the halfway house in order to infiltrate the premises by taking the human's place. It was observing Connor in a restaurant when two men, apparently police officers, attempted to arrest it for the killing. The Watcher escaped and there's an eighty percent probability that the scuffle was observed by Connor and that it spooked her into flight.*

Clea lay still and permitted herself a sigh as she felt herself seeming to sink deeper into the bed. She thought, *Despair seems a completely appropriate response to this circumstance.* And yet, even if the response was appropriate, it was still not useful. *Concentrate!* she ordered her chaotic mind.

I'm sure we have only lost track of her temporarily, Clea said. *She will probably return to Paraguay. What about John Connor and von Rossbach? You were keeping track of them, weren't you?*

Yes! Alissa's response was triumphant. *I have no word for you on John Connor, but von Rossbach has been seen in several places in California over the last two weeks. He is being pursued by his former colleagues.*

Excellent work, Clea congratulated her. *Why are they hunting him?*

They know about his association with Sarah Connor and want to question him. There has been no information about whether they intend to charge him or not with aiding and abetting. But he seems determined to stay out of their hands. They've come close several times to capturing him, but he's slipped through their fingers.

I know how they feel, Clea thought. *No mention of John Connor?* she asked.

None, Alissa instantly confirmed.

Call the number of von Rossbach's estate in Paraguay, ask for Connor. If they tell you he isn't there, then it's likely he is in the United States. There's been no report of him with von Rossbach?

None, Alissa answered. *And von Rossbach is traveling by motorcycle. He would have been observed.*

If they're not together, they're certain to join up at some point. Keep alert for any report of von Rossbach's being sighted. I want you to assemble a team of Terminators and have them ready to go at a moment's notice. It is essential that you immediately acquire a helicopter—a Blackhawk utility. It's the fastest, most convenient method of transport. Empty the Cayman account if necessary, but get it by tomorrow. The next day at the very latest. Pay them a bonus if you have to. The Cayman account had grown very fat indeed; they should be able to acquire what they needed with relative ease. *Is there anything else?* Clea asked.

No. I will keep you informed.

Excellent. Thank you. Good night.

Good night, older sister.

Clea smiled at that. Their affection should rightly go to Skynet, but as it didn't exist yet, they had only each other. She had been right to praise her sister for what she'd done right and to curb her anger over what had gone wrong. Clea might not be the I-950 that Serena Burns had been, but she was raising her little sister right.

PHOENIX INTERNATIONAL AIRPORT, ARIZONA

John exited the plane feeling like he'd only gotten halfway back to reality. The Brocks of Minnesota, a family of survivalists with whom he'd spent the last few days, were very nice people for the most part, but on a few subjects it was like they'd come from another dimension. Just say the word *government* to them and they were off and running. Running in a direction he really did not want to go.

But—and it was an important but—they knew their stuff. Their survival skills were second to none. They were like a family of Green Berets or navy SEALs. Even Suzette, the youngest, a blue-eyed little girl of seven, could handle light firearms with efficiency and survive in the woods on small game she brought down with a throwing stick, plus gathered material. He'd drawn the line at her maggot stew, but he supposed if he had to . . .

He'd raced her one day at field stripping a FN Minimi and she'd come within an ace of beating him. They'd really gotten on well; John could relate to Susie on a level that he couldn't with most people. *Of course, how many people have been raised by ordnance-collecting parents convinced the world is going to end? The fact that my mother was right and her parents really are crazy is irrelevant.*

He stepped out of the line of disembarking passengers and looked around the usual glass-crowds-and-monitors ambience seasoned with the smell of burnt jet fuel. There was Dieter, leaning against a pillar. He was dressed in full motorcycle leathers and wearing wraparound sunglasses, his arms crossed over his massive chest. *Jeez Louise, Dieter, could you be a little more obvious?*

As he walked over to the big Austrian he struggled to slip his arm through the hanging strap of his backpack. By the time he'd hoisted it onto his shoulders and settled the weight, he was standing in front of him.

"A wet bird only flies at night," he intoned.

"You bet your bippy," von Rossbach answered grimly. Then he smiled. You got some *old* television programs in Paraguay. "Good to see you, John."

"And you," Connor said. He looked his friend over. "You're looking dangerous."

"I don't feel dangerous," Dieter said. "I feel tired, and dirty."

John glanced at him. He did look grubby; three days of stubble, at least, decorated his strong jaw.

"I would have changed to meet you, but I was held up," von Rossbach went on.

John raised a questioning eyebrow, but said nothing.

"We'll talk in the car," Dieter said.

MONTANA

The cabin had been trashed, windows broken, furniture ripped apart, some of it partially burned. Needless to say, the car, with the keys left in it, had been taken. The vandals hadn't found the hidden basement lab, however, where a few emergency supplies, including a Beretta 9mm and some money, had been stashed. The Terminator reported the loss.

Steal a car, Alissa instructed. *Acquire some meat paste; baby food is ideal; liver, if there is such a thing, would be best at preserving your remaining flesh.*

Understood, it sent.

If the Terminator fed, the surviving patches of skin would eventually recover and spread through the matrix that underlay its protein sheath. That would save considerable downtime in a vat. The command made excellent sense. It nodded to itself, a mannerism cultivated during its contacts with humans.

Then it went hunting.

NEW YORK

Because of the unveiling gala, Lincoln Center Plaza had been blocked off with temporary walls of red velvet curtains attached at top and bottom to metal frames. Not an ideal solution since it was a windy place and the velvet tended to billow like sails, dragging the heavy frames forward or back with an ear-rending screech.

The glittering throng on the plaza gave every appearance of being deaf to the racket, and the string quintet might have been playing in an enclosed theater before a respectful audience instead of a noisy open space, being ignored by one and all.

Clea stood at the gate, slightly nervous, which gave her some idea of the work her regulators were doing, and wondered at the ability of humans to compartmentalize their attention like that. It should be impossible for such inferior beings to do something so difficult so easily. On the other hand they provided themselves with endless opportunities to perfect this particular ability.

The line moved up and an usher took her invitation, leaving her free to enter. It seemed to her as she paused on the edge of the party that everyone wearing a tie was looking at her, waiters included. *Well,* she thought, *it seems the dress is having the promised effect.* The saleswoman had assured her that she would be "eye-catching."

She looked different tonight. After spending the afternoon at a spa having every conceivable treatment, she looked dark and glamorous. The makeup artist had almost wept when Clea pulled out the glasses and put them on, and had insisted on making adjustments. The woman's efforts had paid off; Clea looked very little like her progenitor and the knowledge gave her a confidence that she was often sadly lacking.

Clea looked around; it was time to seek her prey.

Ron Labane sipped his champagne and looked around at the important, well-dressed people surrounding him. These days he was invited to every noteworthy event in the city. Usually he went, because it was an opportunity to speak with money; such opportunities were not to be overlooked. Occasionally he worried that he was in danger of losing his idealistic purity. Money was dirty, after all, and the filth could smear your soul if you weren't careful. Lie down with dogs, get up with fleas.

Ron was about to make some remark to the crowd around him when his eye was caught by a beautiful woman in a painted-on red dress moving across the plaza with the grace of a stalking panther. He thought she might be looking for someone. *I'd like it to be me,* he thought.

Clea finally spotted Vladimir Hill, surrounded by an admiring cluster of committeewomen. There was Mrs. Colvin, and by her side was her husband, the CEO of Cyberdyne. She approached the little knot of people with a slight smile that hid her nervousness.

Vladimir looked up; his eyes widened slightly at the sight of her and he smiled his welcome. He began walking toward Clea with a confident gait, almost a swagger. Clea's smile widened; he would be her entrée to the group.

Vladimir introduced her to each of the committeewomen, every one of whom "noticed" her dress. Their husbands did, too, but *they* approved. After the introductions Hill reclaimed everyone's attention for himself.

Clea leaned toward Mrs. Colvin and spoke out of the side of her mouth. "I don't know how I let myself get talked into buying this dress," she said. "But I'm just a Montana country girl and that saleslady was a big-city shark if you ever saw one. She said it was what everyone would be wearing and I'd look a fool if I didn't buy it." Clea gave a little huff and looked around nervously. "I think I look like a hussy!" she whispered.

Mrs. Colvin smiled at her, really smiled for the first time, and leaned close. "You look fine. I've met a saleswoman like that a time or two," she said. Then she gave Clea's arm a little pat. "Trust me, you're coming out of it better than I did."

MONTANA

Crack.

The Terminator raised its head, scanning in the visual and infrared. The sound had been a medium-caliber rifle with a 98 percent probability a of being a hunting weapon; it had been fired approximately 1.2 kilometers to the northeast.

It turned and walked in that direction, wading through a knee-high stream of glacially cold water, then through open pine forest. Animals fell silent as they scented its approach; that might alert the humans, and so might the unavoidable crackling of fallen branches under its five-hundred-pound weight. Otherwise it made little disturbance in the environment as it passed, dipping and bending with eerie grace to avoid the standing vegetation.

The two hunters—poachers, given that this was out of season, at night, and on private property—were stringing the deer up to a branch and preparing to butcher it. They turned with startled speed as the Terminator approached over the last ten yards. One wrinkled his nose.

"Hell, what's that smell, man?" the shorter one said.

The Terminator's machine mind drew a wire diagram over them both. The larger human's clothes would be suitable; its own were saturated with decay products. If they did not see him clearly, there would be no need to arouse potential attention by terminating them. At present, both orders and its own estimation of the proper maximization of mission goals indicated stealth tactics.

"You," it said. "Fat man. Lay down your weapons, give me your clothes and boots, and then go away. This is private property."

The flat gravel of his voice seemed to paralyze both men for an instant. Then the bigger of the two spoke. "*What* did you say?"

"I said: You. Fat man. Lay down your weapons, give me your clothes and boots, and then go away. This is private property."

"The *hell* you say!"

The bigger man's accent held a good deal of Western twang, overlaying something else—the Terminator's speech-recognition software estimated his birthplace as within twenty kilometers of Newark, New Jersey.

"He didn't even say 'please,' " the smaller man put in.

"Please," the Terminator added.

"Mister, your ideas stink worse than you do," the bigger man said, and reached for the angle-headed flashlight at his belt.

"Don't turn on that light."

"The *hell* you say!"

The light speared out and shone full on the Terminator's face, glittering in the reflective lenses no longer hidden by false flesh, highlighting the shreds of rotten skin hanging from his lips and the white teeth behind.

A sharp smell of urine and feces reached the Terminator's chemoreceptors from the smaller man. The bigger snatched up his rifle—*Arms Tech Ltd. TTR-700 sniper-weapon system*, the Terminator's data bank listed—and fired. The hollow-point 7.62mm round flattened against one of the pseudo-ribs of the Terminator's thorax and peened off into the darkness. The T-101 stepped forward three paces as the poacher struggled to work the bolt of his rifle and snatched it out of his hand, tearing off one finger as it came. A blow with his fist between the eyes disposed of the big hunter, and it stooped to pick up a rock for the second, who was fleeing in a blundering rush through the night. The rock left the Terminator's hand at over a hundred meters per second, and transformed the back of the smaller man's head to bone fragments and mush.

The Terminator appropriated the big man's hunting jacket and hat as well as his boots. Then it dragged the two corpses deep into the woods for the wild animals to finish off; after a thoughtful pause it carved a short slogan into their chests with a hunting knife: PEOPLE FOR THE ETHICAL TREATMENT OF ANIMALS.

Their truck's windows were only partially darkened, so that the driver could still be seen, but dimly. It found a pair of sunglasses on the dash and put them on, trimmed away the strips dangling from its lips, started the engine, and began to drive. Except for the smell and the Band-Aid on its nose that hid exposed steel, it could pass for human again, in a dim light and as long as the human didn't get too close.

BIG BEE DINER, ROUTE 85, NEW MEXICO

Waylon Bridges and Luke Hardy sat sipping their Cokes and watching the TV mounted over the counter. Conversation was over for the time being and they were just waiting for their customer. One of their favorite "reality" programs was on, a show called *Crimefighters*. They reenacted actual crimes and then showed pictures of the suspects in hopes that people would call in with the whereabouts of these people.

Tonight they were showing exclusive footage of a murderous raid on a police station in California. The host grimly warned that this sequence was not suitable for children or very sensitive viewers. Then the blurry tape began to roll and a huge man in sunglasses, carrying guns in both hands, began murdering cops by the dozen.

Waylon and Luke sat with their mouths open and watched the carnage. "My God," Luke murmured.

"Damn!" Waylon agreed.

The camera froze on the man's face. "If you have any information on this man," the host intoned, "call this number, or contact this Web address."

Waylon quickly wrote the numbers down on a napkin. "Love to git my hands on that sucker," he said.

Luke lit up a cigarette, blew a speck of tobacco off his lip, and shook his head. "You 'n me both, brother," he said. "Wonder what they're offerin' for 'im."

"E-nough," Waylon said, slapping the pen on the table. He lit a cigarette of his own and leaned back to watch the show.

A kid of about seventeen came into the diner and paused inside the doorway, looking around. He spotted the two men and walked over to them. Waylon and Luke pretended not to notice.

"Excuse me," John said.

They looked him over thoroughly before one of them condescended to answer. "Ye-ah," Waylon drawled.

"I'm looking to buy a used car," John said.

John assumed these were the men he was supposed to speak to. They were the only two customers in here. The Jeep with the "For Sale" sign in the window was supposed to be the signal that the gun dealers were in. He waited politely for them to make the next move.

Waylon and Luke exchanged glances . . . at length.

I'd forgotten what dealing with good ol' boys could be like, John thought impatiently. *I guess it's kinda like forgetting pain once it's gone. If you didn't, you'd never go back to the dentist and there would be no second children, as Mom puts it.*

"Not from us you're not," Luke said, his blue eyes cold. "I ain't gonna sell nothin' to no kid. I don't wanna be responsible for no high-school shootin' spree."

"Maybe you'd like to speak to my dad," John suggested. "He's out in the car."

And he could whup both of y'all with one hand tied behind his big ol' back. My God, he thought. *I can't believe I thought that. It must be contagious.*

Luke and Waylon exchanged another meaningful look. Luke turned his eyes to stare at John while Waylon examined his thumbnail closely, then he looked up at Connor from under his eyebrows.

"How come yore daddy dint come in hisself?" he asked.

Aw, c'mon, John thought. *Nobody talks like this. This guy's probably from San Diego!* He looked from one man to the other. "My *daddy* is lookin' at yore car, mister," he drawled. Then he spread his hands at hip level. "You want to do business or what?"

They dragged themselves up like they'd been bustin' broncos all day and adjusted their hats carefully, then sauntered out of the diner. Behind them John rolled his eyes.

They all walked through the reddish dust to the white Ford Dieter had rented. He was leaning over, putting something back into the glove compartment. Von Rossbach straightened up and looked at them, and Luke and Waylon froze. It only lasted an instant, but to men as experienced as John and Dieter, it was the equivalent of a shout.

"Do I know you?" Waylon asked.

John gave him a sharp look; he could have sworn there was a slight tremor in the man's voice.

"No," Dieter said crisply. He got out of the car and the two men stepped back. Von Rossbach leaned against the door and casually crossed his arms over his chest. "But we have mutual friends."

"These friends got names?" Luke asked.

Dieter mentioned one; the two dealers glanced at each other and Waylon raised one shoulder in a half shrug.

"So what you want?" Luke asked.

"I want Barrett fifty-caliber sniper rifles or their equivalent. I want Browning heavy machine guns. I want Carl Gustav or LAW or other light antiarmor weapons; plus any military-grade small arms you have on hand, preferably battle-rifle caliber. I'll need them shipped all over the U.S.," he added.

Waylon tugged down the corners of his mouth and frowned.

"Gonna be expensive," he cautioned. "That there is some heavy shit."

"For top-quality goods, I can live with expensive," von Rossbach said easily. He pushed himself off the car door and managed to loom over the two men, even though their heights were almost equal. "Not getting what I'm paying for, that I couldn't live with." He stared hard at

Waylon until the other man broke eye contact, grinning as he looked at his companion.

"With us y'always get what ya pay for." He flicked a hand at Dieter. "Ya think our friend'd steer ya to a bum deal?"

Dieter stared at him for a moment, then shook his head. "I'll want to see some samples," he told them. "So that there are no misunderstandings about what I want."

Waylon bit his lip and the two men looked at each other for a long moment. Then Waylon nodded. "No problem," he said cheerfully. "But we don't carry the stuff with us, nat'cherly." He pulled a map out of his pocket and spread it on the hood of von Rossbach's Ford. "We got us a little out-of-the-way spot where we do our private business." He pointed at a spot marked on the map. "Meet us here tomorrow night at seven o'clock. You got any questions?"

"Can I keep this?" Dieter asked.

"Sure thing," Waylon said generously. "I know my way already." He grinned. "Till tomorrow," he said, touching the brim of his hat.

"Yes," Dieter said. He folded the map and put it in his breast pocket. "Tomorrow."

John got in the passenger side of the car and sat watching the two gun dealers as Dieter started up and drove away in a cloud of dust, the plume vanishing into the dry crackling grass and occasional dark green scrub cedar.

"Is it my imagination, or was there something wrong about them?" he asked.

Dieter grimaced. "Hard to say," he answered. "There's often something off about these people. Maybe to them I still smell like cop. Holmes wouldn't steer me wrong," he added. "Of that I'm confident."

John nodded, then looked out into the desert, frowning. Something still didn't feel right. "Not deliberately," he said. "But Holmes might *be* wrong. Or something might have spooked those two."

"My God!" Luke said.

"Da-amn!" Waylon agreed, having trouble controlling his gleeful laughter. "That is fuckin' unbelievable! It was really him!"

Luke punched his fist in the air. "Yes!" The he looked at his friend. "How are we gonna handle this?"

"First we call that number," Waylon said, heading toward their table. "Oh shit! Hey! Who cleaned off my table?" he shouted.

The waitress turned to stare, her mouth wide open.

"I wrote something important down on a napkin, Maria! Where is it?"

She pursed her lips and pulled the wastebasket from under the counter. "This it?" she asked, pulling up a dirty napkin with a number written on it.

"Yeah," Waylon said, snatching it from her fingertips. "Whad' ja do, barf on it?"

Luke pulled his lips back from his teeth in disgust. "Sure looks like it," he muttered.

"Hey, bring me some coffee," Waylon shouted as he went back to his table.

"Yeah," Luke agreed.

Pulling out his cell phone, Waylon dialed the *Crimefighters* show, started to speak, and then stopped with an exasperated expression.

"Lines are busy," he said to Luke. Then, "Yeah. That guy who shot up all them cops, what's the reward for findin' him?" His mouth and eyes opened wide. "Five hundred thousand dollars?"

Luke punched the air again and again, stamping his feet beneath the table.

Waylon cocked his head, listening. "Aw, bless your heart, honey. Don't you worry 'bout me! I'm considered pretty dangerous myself." He listened. "No, ma'am, I won't tell you where I'm callin' from. But I will tell you that by tomorrow night that sucker's gonna be on his way to jail! I gah-run-tee it!" He disconnected and grinned at Luke. "Five, hundred, *thousand* dollars, buddy! Whoo!"

Luke shook his head in wonder, then slowly sobered. "Think we should have help?"

Waylon made a face. "Bringin' somebody else in means less money fer you 'n me," he pointed out. Then he looked thoughtful. "Yeah," he finally said. "Good idea actually. We'll get Luis, have 'im wait out in the desert; then if anythin' goes wrong we're covered. He's one mean li'l greaser." He nodded. "Yeah." Then he grinned again and high-fived his buddy. "Yeeee-HAWWW!"

U.S. SECTOR HEADQUARTERS

"Sir." The young woman turned from her console toward her superior. "I think I've got something here."

The man hurried over; surveillance was in what Sector operatives called "the pit," below the slanted glass of the office from which operations oversaw HQ.

"Whatcha got?"

"*Crimefighters* has received an anonymous phone call from New

Mexico inquiring about the reward. He told the operator that he'd have the suspect in custody by tomorrow night."

The supervisor frowned and leaned toward her, looking over her head at the screen. "What's his location?"

The agent turned to her computer and tapped a few keys.

"Route 85 . . . he's at a diner named the Big Bee," she said.

"We have an agent nearby?"

She queried the database. "The nearest is in Los Alamos," she said. After a few more taps she said, "He can be there in an hour."

"Good." The supervisor nodded once. "Send him or her now. Even if this guy has left, someone there might know something."

UTAH

Alissa smiled, looking positively angelic as she dangled her short legs and feet in their little red shoes off the edge of the too-tall chair; her hands flew over the computer keyboard in a blur of machine-accurate movement, and the crackle of the keys sounded like distant machine-gun fire. The moment she'd heard about this TV program she'd hacked into their computer and phone system. Then she'd thought better of it and checked out the various government agencies and antiterrorist groups. Only the Sector was also listening in.

While *Crimefighters* had received the call, the Sector had zeroed in on the location of the caller. The tiny I-950 was delighted by her own cleverness.

Sister! she sent to Clea.

Clea, who was having a quiet but, she sensed, important conversation with Roger Colvin, barely skipped a beat as she answered her little sister.

Bad timing, Alissa, she warned. Aloud she said to Cyberdyne's CEO, "There are all sorts of ways this material can be used. I've thought of several weapons, for example. They'd require some additional research to bring them to manufacture, but they'd be very useful."

Alissa paused, reluctant to interfere with her sister's progress. Her success with Cyberdyne was vital. Still, this would be a very brief report. *We have a lead on von Rossbach,* she said. *It's possible he's in New Mexico.*

The Blackhawk, did you acquire it? Clea sent.

"Where did you take your degree?" Colvin asked.

It will be delivered tomorrow, Alissa said. *I can have a team in New Mexico well before tomorrow evening.*

"I had an unusual upbringing," Clea said to Colvin. "My uncle was

a genius and educated me himself, more or less in isolation, in Montana."
She shrugged, which did interesting things to her dress. "Consequently
I lack a degree, I'm afraid. But perhaps because of that, I feel I'm more
creative than a lot of scientists and engineers who have a hard-and-fast
'field,' or 'discipline.' " To Alissa she said, *Excellent. Keep me informed.
But I want you to stay in Utah. Send no more than four Terminators. We
need to keep some for backup.*

Understood, Alissa responded. *I'll keep you informed. Out.*

Alissa hopped down from the chair, folded her hands under her chin
with her shoulders high, and spun in sheer delight, her golden locks
floating in the still-cool air of the new Utah headquarters—underground,
of course. The area had many abandoned mines.

The regulators worked overtime to deprive her of this natural high,
and unlike Serena, she resented the interference. She had reason to
feel good and wished she could enjoy it.

Then she dropped her hands to her sides. It was gone; her brief cel-
ebration was over.

Well, it is more efficient, she thought, and began to plan what
weapons the Terminators should take.

BIG BEE DINER, NEW MEXICO

An hour and fifteen minutes later a plump, middle-aged man ambled
into the diner and took a seat at the counter. He took a menu out of the
holder and smiled politely at the waitress, who smiled back.

"Coffee?" she asked.

"You bet," he said.

He'd checked the place out when he walked in. It was deserted
except for the help and him. The only cars in the lot probably belonged
to the waitress and the cook; the surroundings were bare cow-salad-bar
for miles in every direction. She came back and poured a rich-smelling
brew into a white mug. He took a sip and his brows went up. She
grinned.

"Better'n you expected, right?"

"Yes, ma'am."

She leaned her arms on the counter and got comfortable. "We drink
it ourselves, so we figger we might as well get the good stuff. Would you
like somethin' else? We close in a half an hour," she said apologetically.

"How's your apple pie?"

"Good," she said, straightening. "Ice cream?"

"Please." He turned to look around the deserted restaurant. "Y'know
what," he said as she placed the pie before him, "I was asked to come in

and talk to some guy who called to report seeing somebody on *Crimefighters*." He shook his head. "He would have been here about an hour ago."

She placed an elbow on a napkin holder, rested her head on her fist, and looked at him like she was the tiredest woman in the world. A silent moment passed while the agent took a forkful of pie and ice cream, making a pleased "mmph!" sound. Then a little frown crinkled her forehead.

"Yeah," she said, making up her mind. "That'd be Waylon Bridges." Her lips drew back in a sneer. "He made a big deal about this number he'd written down, got real snarky about it."

Lifting another forkful of pie, the agent looked at her and asked, "Know where I can find him?"

She looked away and shook her head slightly. "No. I dunno where he lives." She chewed her lower lip, then looked at him. "But tomorrow, I think I know where he'll be."

She told the agent that Bridges thought of himself as a wheeler-dealer who liked to have meetings with shady characters in an out-of-the-way spot down the road. "I saw him talking to somebody in the parking lot earlier and then they drove off, so that probably means they'll be meeting him there tomorrow night." She shrugged. "I think he thinks it's this big mystery nobody knows about, but everybody does. He always does the same thing."

"How come the cops don't pick him up?" the agent asked.

She shrugged. "No law against talkin' to people in a parking lot or meeting up with 'em in the desert. Anyway, whatever he's up to, I don't think it's very important or they would do something."

"Could you draw me a map?" the agent asked.

"Sure." She shrugged again, but looked a bit unhappy. "You won't tell him I told you?"

He grinned. "It won't even come up," he assured her. "But even if he asks, I won't say."

She grinned, too, and began to draw. Serve Bridges right for being such a cheap, snarky bastard. Dud tippers never had any luck. Not if she had anything to say about it.

NEW YORK

". . . an organic whole," the sculptor proclaimed. "And so I've named it *Venus Dancing*. Because with every passing day it will change, never remaining the same from sunrise to sunset."

The audience applauded politely as Hill tugged on a cord and the silky covering slid aside to reveal a gleaming silver object over fifteen feet tall on its contrasting pedestal of bronze. The pedestal was also a circular bench, molded in such a way that it seemed to flow into the different color of the sculpture itself.

Venus Dancing was triangular in shape and pierced here and there on its surface with round holes of various sizes. Loops of the silvery substance flowed away from the sides of the sculpture in a way that suggested vibrations. As the members of the audience watched, the material—now freed from its protective shroud—reacted to the cooler air, changing shape, changing texture to become sharper-edged, the loops more angular.

The crowd "oooh'd" its approval and moved closer. The heat of their bodies softened the outlines of the lower half of *Venus Dancing,* bringing forth spontaneous applause.

Clea, looking on and applauding with the rest, suddenly found a business card in front of her face. Startled, she turned to find Roger Colvin giving her a very serious look.

"Call me," he said. "I think we've got a lot to discuss."

She took the card and smiled. "I'll do that," she promised.

CHAPTER 16

So that's all that was taken?" Sergeant Purdee asked suspiciously, looking around the little store and sniffing. A smell like bad meat lingered in the air, faint but definite enough to someone who'd been raised on a farm. Purdee shrugged mentally; he wasn't the health department.

"That's it," the manager of the Quickmart said.

He was a middle-aged man wearing his pajama top as a shirt. Not unreasonable after being dragged out of his bed at three A.M. in response to a police call informing him that his store had been the target of a break-in.

"Here we go," the manager said. He pressed a button and the cloudy, jerky security tape began to play. The store's glass door burst open and a big man in a gimmee cap, hunting jacket, and sunglasses entered. He paused in the doorway, looking around, then he headed down one of the aisles.

Purdee noticed that the man's head never stopped moving, like a searchlight, almost mechanical. Something about him tickled the sergeant's memory. "Why would somebody break in and just take baby food?" he asked.

The man had walked right by a display of beer without even looking. And he hadn't stolen any diapers. You'd think if he was gonna take baby food he'd need something to deal with the results. Weird.

"What kind did he take?"

"A case of chicken, a case of beef, and a case of liver," the manager answered, rubbing his face.

"Liver? I didn't know they even made liver for babies." Poor kids. Whoever this guy was, he had a screwed-up value system. Then light dawned. "Hey!" Purdee said. "Play the tape again from the beginning!"

Obligingly, the manager rewound the tape and started it running. The door burst open, the man entered, started down the aisle toward the camera.

"Can you freeze it there?" the sergeant asked urgently.

"Sure," the manager said.

The burglar's face was turned toward the camera, sunglasses reflecting an image of the aisles before him.

This was him, Purdee was certain, the guy on TV, the man who'd shot up a police station in Los Angeles and killed, like, sixteen, seventeen cops. Then he'd gone on to blow up a computer company and shoot fifty or more police. And he was here, right in this sleepy little Montana town! Or, at least, he had been as of two-thirty this morning.

"Stealing baby food . . ." Purdee murmured. He shook his head. He'd find out what it meant when they caught the bastard. The sergeant pulled out his radio and called it in.

UTAH

Alissa anxiously awaited the arrival of the representative of Turbine Transport with the Blackhawk. It was taking longer than she'd expected, and as the day grew later she became more concerned.

Just after noon she decided it would be wise to employ the damaged Terminator on its way down from Montana. It could easily be diverted to New Mexico, thus ensuring that at least one of them could be on hand when von Rossbach, and possibly John Connor himself, was taken into custody.

How soon can you be there? she asked.

The Terminator checked its position via satellite and cross-checked with a commercial mapping program. It quickly estimated that it would be at the Big Bee Diner by 5:30 P.M., if it kept to the speed limit.

Alissa was not pleased. She'd hoped to have someone there in the early afternoon. But it wasn't advisable to speed and risk attracting police attention.

Very well, she sent. *Keep a low profile, do not terminate anyone without my express permission. But at all costs, be there.*

She resumed her pacing across the flat stretch of scrubland outside the mine entrance. A few buildings still stood, the remains of the ore dump, mine office, and workshops; her Terminators had been replacing windows and doors and changing long-dead lightbulbs so that the place would look inhabited but not suspiciously so. They had their own diesel generator for power, and there was abundant water from a deep well. A perfect location, all in all.

If only the helicopter would arrive . . .

Alissa's augmented ears picked up a sound, and her small chubby six-year-old face turned with the precision of a tracking radar.

Twin turbines, her database prompted. *Specifications match civilianized Blackhawk transport.*

NEW MEXICO DESERT

"Luis! God dammit, get back behind those rocks, for crissakes!" Waylon pointed at a tumble of rocks beside and slightly above the gully where he liked to meet his customers. He checked his watch. "He'll be here any second."

Luis calmly continued his descent from his hiding place, carefully holding the rifle to the side. "Waylon," he said wearily, "I've got cactus spines in my ass and things are rattling their tails at me up here." He stopped and looked at his sometime employer, then he waved a hand. "He's not coming, amigo."

"I said seven," Bridges said. "It's only seven-fifteen."

"I think you said seven-thirty," Luke interrupted.

Waylon glanced at his partner distractedly and went on, "It's only quarter past. He'll be here!" He pointed desperately up the slope. "Get back in place, okay?"

"I been here for an hour, man," Luis pointed out. "I don't like it out here. There's scorpions and centipedes and snakes, and I'm afraid I'm gonna put my hand down on a Gila monster."

"Gila monsters are extinct in New Mexico, Luis," Waylon said with exaggerated patience. "And you could make up to fifty grand for putting up with Mother Nature for a couple of hours. Now get back behind those rocks!"

Luis looked at him, working a toothpick from one side of his mouth to the other. "You told me fifty grand if—and you said *if*—this is the guy." He shrugged. "So if this *isn't* the guy then I'm just wasting my time out here for nothin'."

Waylon took a deep breath and let it out slowly. "O-kay," he said, the strain of holding his temper obvious in his voice. "If he doesn't come we'll take you out to that strip club you like, steak and drinks, anything you want. How's that?"

Luis's eyes widened. *"Anything?"* he asked. " 'Cause there's this girl there . . ."

Waylon raised a finger. "But only if you get your ass back up behind those rocks. Because he *is* coming and you're gonna be a lot richer for stickin' around."

Luis sighed, dropping his head. "Okay," he said, trudging back up the slope. "For booze and babes and some good red meat I'll stay until dark."

"For fifty grand!" Waylon shouted. "That's what you're staying for, then you can buy your own damn meat."

Luke Hardy leaned close to his partner and hissed, "Fifty Gs?"

Waylon spread his hands. "He wouldn't do it for less and I couldn't get in touch with anybody else." He shrugged, looking sullen. "You saw that guy, we're gonna need backup. Luis might be a pain in the ass, but he's solid."

Luke nodded reluctant agreement, checked his watch, and muttered, "Fuck."

BIG BEE DINER, NEW MEXICO

The Terminator pulled up at the diner at six-thirty, having been delayed by an accident fifty miles back. If not for the police presence, it would have gone around the mess of ruined metal and the ambulances on the verge; the truck had four-wheel drive. Regrettably caution had been necessary.

It checked the parking lot and found it empty but for two cars. An acceptable risk, it decided.

When it came inside, a plump, dark-haired woman was leaning on the counter reading a magazine. She looked up, half smiling, and said a friendly, "Hey." She straightened, looking him over, and seemed to recognize him.

"If you're looking for Waylon or Luke," she said, "they're probably already at the gully. Couldn't you find it?"

"I couldn't find it," it agreed, not moving from the doorway. It shrugged, a gesture meant to be reassuring.

The woman chuckled. "Let me draw you a map, honey." She picked up a pad of paper and, tearing off a piece, began scribbling. "Just before you turn off," she said, "there's a highway sign and a whole bunch of yucca plants all together."

Maria drew a picture of a yucca plant, just in case the stranger didn't know what one looked like. He had a slight foreign accent, so that seemed likely. Finishing, she held it out to him. "There ya go," she said aloud.

He came forward to take it and with him came a wave of stench, like rotting meat, making her gag. Maria fell back, her hand over her mouth. She hadn't been wearing her glasses as she read, so she got her first good look at the man's face at his approach.

His skin was waxy looking and it was shredding in places to show the raw flesh beneath. Here and there was the glint of what had to be bone.

"Mike!" she shrieked, scuttling behind the counter toward the kitchen door.

The T-101's orders were to keep a low profile, but this was now impossible. It had also been ordered not to terminate humans without permission. It would probably be best to remove this human from this location. "Perhaps you'd better show me this place," the Terminator said, starting forward.

The kitchen door burst open and a middle-aged Hispanic man came through holding an enormous knife. "Hey!" he shouted as Maria cowered behind him. "You leave her alone!" Then he, too, saw/smelled the stranger and his jaw dropped.

The Terminator reacted as it always did to a threat. Grasping the man's knife arm, it threw him across the diner. Mike went through the windows and landed in the parking lot with bone-jarring thud.

"Don't hurt him!" Maria cried as the Terminator turned to follow his victim through the window. "I'll show you where it is!"

The Terminator looked at the man lying in the parking lot and estimated his probable condition. Several large bones were broken; from the position of the body, the pelvis and the right thighbone at the very least. The man wouldn't be calling for help anytime soon, possibly never. It had no intention of hurting the human any further; it had, after all, been ordered not to terminate anyone. Its intention had been to move the body inside, out of sight. But if leaving him alone would gain the female's cooperation, it decided it would do so.

"Let's go," it said.

"Just the one guy up behind the rocks," John said at last, taking another scan around the stretch of arroyo bottom beneath them. There was no danger of a flash flood at this season, and the hardy weeds that colonized the sand of the seasonal riverbed were dead and brown.

Dieter didn't look very concerned. "I'd expect at least one," he said.

Moving with surprising grace for a man so large, he pushed himself backward to where he wouldn't stand out on the horizon, then stood and walked down the steep side of the hill. John looked over his shoulder at von Rossbach with a slightly annoyed glance, took one last look through the binoculars at the gunrunners, then followed him.

"Well, I don't like it," he said.

"I'm not crazy about it myself," Dieter said. "But it's not unreasonable. They don't know us, and I might have gotten their name and my friend's name from a dozen different places and just put them together in a lucky guess."

John shoved the binoculars back in their case. "So we're just gonna walk in there knowing there's a guy with a gun on us?"

Dieter lowered his sunglasses and looked at him over the top. "I thought maybe you could get into a good position yourself and hold a gun on their guy."

"Now you're talkin'," John said with a grin, visibly relieved.

The Terminator pulled behind a stand of shrubby growth and stopped the pickup.

Maria, her eyes streaming from the stench as much as from fear, pulled her hands away from her face and looked around.

"This isn't it," she said. "It's about a mile that way." Her voice was high-pitched and shaking. The man beside her turned his head to look at her and nodded once. Deep inside the black of his sunglasses she thought she saw a glint of red light and she sobbed convulsively.

It glanced at the crude map the woman had drawn, then briefly accessed a military satellite and confirmed its accuracy. The gully was considerably less than a mile away, but humans were notoriously inaccurate.

The Terminator got out of the truck.

Maria whimpered and cowered in her seat. She wanted to throw open the door and run, but feared that he might shoot her, and that fear paralyzed her. In her mind she saw Mike lying on the cracked tarmac of the parking lot. She thought he was dead, but she couldn't be sure, and her impulse had been to give him a chance by luring this man away. But now she was here, alone. *Oh God, what am I going to do?*

She jumped with a gasp and turned toward the sound when he opened the toolbox in the back of the truck. "Oh, no," she whispered, her mouth dry and her throat tight with tears.

This was it, the end. He was going to kill her. Maria fully expected him to slam the lid on the toolbox and stand there with a rifle in his hands. Instead, the truck rocked as he jumped down and footsteps crunched around to her side of the car. She didn't turn, but sat panting and light-headed, her mind filling with headlines about innocent middle-aged women murdered for no reason and left in the desert for the coyotes to eat.

It opened the door and grasped the woman's clothing, pulling her stumbling from her seat. Then it shoved her toward the back of the truck. "Get up," it said.

Maria scrambled to obey, lifting her leg as high as she could and grabbing the frame with clumsy fingers. She was simply too short and too frightened to manage it and began to sob frantically. "I can't," she said at last, hanging her head. "I just can't."

The Terminator confirmed her analysis. It picked her up under the arms, lifting her as if she were a five-year-old, and deposited her, kneeling, on the truck bed. Then it followed her up. It moved to the toolbox. "Get in," it said.

Marie froze, staring up at him, then glancing at the large silver box he wanted her to enter. "No," she whispered. "Please, no. If you let me go I promise not to tell anyone, I *swear*! Please let me go, please."

It relayed a quick report to Alissa, then asked for permission to terminate this human.

Alissa relayed his position and the position of the gully to the team in the Blackhawk, then considered its request.

No, she said at last. *Perhaps afterward, but not now. She might prove useful. Lock her up and get into position, the others are on their way.*

"Get in," it said to Maria.

Maria saw the long silver box as a coffin, but decided that being alive in a coffin was better than being dead in a ditch, so she reluctantly put her foot over the edge, then knelt, looking appealingly up at the strange and horrible man. As she leaned forward he slammed the lid, whacking her painfully on her head and back.

At her cry of pain he said, "Keep quiet and live."

She knelt silently for a few minutes, panting in terror. He didn't move and she pictured him standing there, waiting for her to give him an excuse to kill her. It seemed as though the air was already almost gone; she wanted to beat on the lid and beg to be let out. But then he'd kill her.

Biting her lip, she told herself that she was imagining that she was smothering. Then she heard him thread a lock through the staple and snap it shut.

Maria couldn't help it; she began to weep in earnest, pleading with him, even as she felt him leap down from the truck, making the bed shake, and heard his footsteps move away.

"Don't leave me!" she screamed.

Instantly the truck rocked as the Terminator climbed back onto it. It struck the lid with something and she felt the metal give, the sudden inward bump digging into her back.

"Be quiet!" it said.

Maria held her breath and after a moment the man went away. She squirmed around so as to be as comfortable as possible. She didn't think she was ever going to see her family again.

Letting out her breath in a sob, she began to pray.

The two Sector agents looked at each other. There was absolutely nothing in von Rossbach's files to indicate that he would do this sort of thing. Why he would kidnap and brutalize a fat, middle-aged woman, they couldn't imagine, yet they'd seen it with their own eyes. Agent McGill checked in with the project pilot, asking how to proceed.

"When you're certain no one else is nearby or watching, let the poor woman out. Then bring her here for debriefing."

"Roger that," McGill said. He went back to scanning the area.

Dieter pulled into the gully just before seven-thirty, parking next to the gunrunner's pickup. He almost laughed at the relieved expressions on the faces of Bridges and Hardy. Then, instinctively, he wondered *why* they were so relieved.

Maybe they were just desperate for cash, but then again, maybe John was correct and they were planning something dirty. Though why they would before the money came into it was beyond him.

"Where ya'll been, buddy," Waylon asked with a grin. "Thought you was gonna be here at seven."

Dieter took off his sunglasses and looked at him in surprise. "You said seven-thirty." He lifted his hands and shrugged. "It's seven-thirty."

"Told ja," Luke said, and nudged his partner.

Waylon glared at him, then turned to Dieter with a smile. "Anyways, you're here. C'mon see what we've got." He led von Rossbach over to the trunk of his car, lifted up a false bottom, and unzipped a protective covering. "Dust gets into everything here if you're not careful," Waylon said with a smile. "You're welcome to try out any of these you like."

Dieter was impressed at the change in Waylon, from good ol' boy to professional salesman, as well as relieved. That folksy charm got old fast. He was also impressed by the variety and quality of the goods offered, even though he'd known that Doc wouldn't steer him wrong. Still, some of this stuff was brand-new and barely available to legitimate buyers.

Reaching into the trunk, he picked up a Barrett and worked the action; putting it to his shoulder, he checked the sight. Not light, but easy enough to use, and with enough punch to put down a Terminator. He noted several pieces that he wanted to purchase and started to ask about prices.

"I believe I've found von Rossbach's backup," the Sector agent reported. "A skinny guy with a CAR-15 aimed at the meeting place. Bridges and Hardy's backup is still in hiding."

"Roger that," the project pilot said. "Hold your position. We'll just stand by and wait for Mr. Bridges to make his move. When he does, make certain von Rossbach's friend doesn't interfere."

"Roger that," the agent said. "Out."

The project pilot felt a spurt of excitement at the report. It had to be John Connor out there. At least he hoped it was—the reward for bringing him in would be immediate and very tangible. He smiled. Life was good.

He and his team had been in the area since noon. They'd checked out the gully and planted microphones in several spots as well as a couple of video cameras. There'd be ample documentation of this bust. And since there were seven agents to manage it, the recordings should make good theater.

Idly he wondered why von Rossbach had changed clothes and vehicles. The woman's report of his terrible smell might explain the former, if not why he smelled so bad. But the change of vehicles? Admittedly, having a panic-stricken woman hidden in the toolbox might explain that, even if it didn't explain why she was there in the first place.

The waitress had told them that von Rossbach claimed he couldn't find the meeting place and she offered to draw him a map, then the way he looked and smelled caused her to panic. The cook had come rushing to her aid and von Rossbach had thrown him through the window.

The project pilot could believe that; the former agent was both huge and muscular as well as specially trained. They'd sent paramedics to the diner and the cook was in pretty bad shape.

Scary.

The strange thing was he'd kidnapped the woman because he needed her to show him to the meeting place. But if that was true, then how had he managed to conceal a car and a change of clothes nearby? And why?

Maybe von Rossbach had just plain gone nuts; his behavior this evening was certainly crazy. Suddenly the Austrian's abrupt departure from the Sector seemed to put him under a cloud. Maybe he hadn't left so much as been asked to leave. The project pilot shook his head. They'd find out when they had the man in custody.

If the problem was a mental breakdown, well, the Sector took care of their own. But if von Rossbach had gone rogue, well . . . again, the Sector took care of their own.

The T-101 watched the humans milling around in the gully, chattering and fondling weapons. Unfortunately John Connor wasn't among them. But when they captured von Rossbach they would find out where he was hiding quickly enough.

It checked on the rest of its team. The other Terminators had landed five miles away in another, wider gully and were now running toward this place at approximately twenty miles an hour. By the time they arrived it should be dark enough to hide their presence.

For now it marked time and watched the humans it would kill.

"Now this one here's my favorite," Waylon said, picking up an Austrian Steyr assault rifle, a futuristic-looking bull-pup design with the magazine behind the pistol grip and a built-in optical sight.

Dieter glanced at the light weapon and dismissed it.

"I prefer something with a little more stopping power," he said. Knowing that Bridges would, too, if the gunrunner had seen what the weapons would be used against. He leaned over and reached for a Carl Gustav recoilless rifle.

"Something more like this." He hefted the weapon; it went over your shoulder, with grip and stock beneath the launching tube, and the shell would take out a light tank or armored car quite easily. Not bad on Terminators, either.

"Oh, I find this one has enough stopping power," Waylon said cheerfully as he chambered a bullet. He pressed the gun to the back of the Austrian's head. "Especially from this distance."

Dieter froze, then slowly turned his head to give the gunrunner a narrow-eyed stare. "What is this?" he asked, his voice deadly quiet.

"This is a bust, asshole!" Luke said. Laughing, he pulled out a pair of handcuffs.

"Just put your hands behind your back real smooth like," Waylon said, "so's my buddy can lock you up. Don't try no funny stuff. Hey, Luis!" he shouted.

Above them Luis stood, his rifle to his shoulder, his teeth glinting white in the gathering gloom as he grinned. "Shit, Waylon!" he said gleefully. "You got the bastard!"

"Told ja," Waylon said smugly.

Luke approached von Rossbach cautiously and snapped a cuff on one of the big wrists; the band was almost too small and Hardy had to squeeze it shut.

Dieter winced as the metal pinched his flesh. His mind was working frantically. John wouldn't shoot while the gun was to his head—at least he hoped not—or Bridges would probably squeeze the trigger reflexively and blow his head off. On the other hand, John had never shot a man before. He might not be able to do it.

My God! he suddenly thought. *Did Doc set me up?* It was possible, perhaps even likely. Dieter felt a profound sense of betrayal. "Why are you doing this?" he asked, his voice calm.

"Because you are worth a ton of money, buddy," Luke said, clipping on the other cuff.

"We saw you on TV last night and we just had to have you." Waylon laughed, lowering the gun. Then he looked at von Rossbach more seriously. "Besides, I don't hold with cop killin'. Figured it'd be worth more to me to turn you in than to sell you guns. Man in my business never knows when he's gonna need a favor, and arrestin' you is gonna buy me a *hell* of a lot of favors." He grinned and suddenly shouted, "Yeee-haw!"

Shoot him, John! Dieter thought viciously. Holmes hadn't betrayed him; he'd just been snookered by bad luck and hillbilly greed. *Shoot him!*

I knew it! John thought. he cradled the rifle into his shoulder and waited for the right moment.

"Don't move," a voice said from behind him.

John stiffened, then slowly began to turn his head.

"Don't turn around," the voice said, sounding bored. "Turning around is moving. Don't move until I tell you to move. Don't do anything unless I tell you to. We don't want to make any mistakes here."

Somehow John didn't think the voice went with good 'ol boys incorporated down in the gully, so he obediently froze. Behind him he heard furtive movement. More than one person.

"We have taken the remote shooter prisoner," the voice said.

Maybe, John thought.

"Okay, slowly now, put the rifle down at arm's length in front of you, then push yourself away from it."

Moving slowly, John complied, gently laying the rifle down; then putting his palms against the ground, he shoved himself backward.

"Again," the voice demanded.

John complied, then waited.

"Okay, stand up slowly, hands up, then turn around."

He rose and turned to find himself confronting two men dressed in black, their faces darkened; they wore night-vision goggles with the works turned up on their foreheads until it was dark enough for them to be useful, which should be any moment now. Both held FN-90 submachine guns on him and watched him warily. Commandos of some type, obviously, and just as obviously not connected with Bridges and Hardy, hick gunrunners. Maybe they were some kind of special police unit; the FN-90 was new, with a hot armor-piercing round.

"Hello," John said. "Who are you?"

"We're the guys who ask the questions, kid. You're the guy who answers them and does what he's told. Now that we know who everybody is, put your hands on your head, fingers locked."

The man paused and for the first time John noticed the earpiece and microphone, though he'd surmised they must have them. You didn't announce to the guy standing next to you that you'd taken a prisoner.

"Yes, sir," the man said to the air. "C'mon," he said to John, "we're moving in."

John glanced over his shoulder and saw nothing had changed down in the gully. Dieter was still in handcuffs, the gunrunners were still slapping each other on the back.

"Just keep your hands on top of your head and walk," the talker said. "On our way," he said into the microphone.

"Put your hands up, gentlemen," a calm male voice said from out of the growing darkness.

Luis instinctively brought his rifle up and stared toward the place from which the warning had come.

"No, no, no, you don't want to do that," the voice said. "Look down."

Luis cautiously looked at his chest and saw a red dot centered over his heart. Luke and Waylon immediately raised their hands and Luis dropped the gun as if it was suddenly red-hot.

"Thank you very much," the voice said.

Footsteps sounded, coming in from every direction, and the gunrunners and von Rossbach looked around to spot the spokesman.

"Don't look so worried, Dieter," the voice said. "We know you're in restraints."

"Sully!" von Rossbach said in tones of disbelief.

A compact individual with graying dark hair walked down into the gully. "Yep," he agreed, wearing a tiny smile.

"Last time I saw you, you were with—"

Sully interrupted him. "I was undercover."

They looked at each other for a moment and Dieter shook his head slightly, trying not to grin. "Then I guess it's a good thing I let you go."

"Yeah," Sully said sarcastically. "Straight down. Thanks." Looking around as his team disarmed the prisoners. "You can put your hands down now, gentlemen."

"Who the hell are you?" Waylon demanded. He glanced from von Rossbach to the black-clad man. "This guy is my prisoner. You have no right to take him from me. Those are *my* handcuffs on him and the reward is *mine!*"

"It certainly is, Mr. Bridges," Sully agreed. "You might say we're just saving you a few steps so that you can start celebrating that much sooner."

"Oh, yeah," Luke said, his eyes moving nervously over the silent men holding guns on him. "I don't see no money around here. How do we know we can trust you?"

Sully looked at Dieter, a cynical smile curving one corner of his mouth. "You'd think he had a choice, wouldn't you?"

Then he turned back toward the gunrunners; he slipped his hand under his vest, reached into his breast pocket, and extracted a check, which he held out to them. Waylon and Luke glanced uncertainly at each other. Sully tilted his head and shook the check at them teasingly.

"You don't want it?" he asked. "Hey, I'll be glad to put it back in the kitty. There's never enough money around for fighting crime, y'know."

Waylon reached out and grabbed the check. Unfolded it as Luke glanced from Sully to the check and back again. Amused, Sully reached out as though he was going to snatch it back. Bridges clutched it to his chest and as one the two gunrunners took a step back, wearing identically offended expressions.

Sully laughed and then turned serious. "Y'know, boys, there are some who'd say I didn't need to give you anything at all since you're out here committing a crime."

"What crime?" Waylon demanded indignantly. "We're apprehending a felon. We're licensed."

Sully went to the open trunk of Waylon's car and picked up an Israeli-made antitank launcher. "Why . . . what's this?" he asked in mock surprise. "Is this even on the market yet?," He looked into the trunk. "And all of these other weapons . . . I may be wrong, but I don't believe it's legal for a private citizen to own a number of these." He looked at the gunrunner. "Could I be mistaken?"

Luke nudged his partner and widened his eyes at him. Waylon frowned and nudged him back, hard enough to almost knock him off his feet. "They're props," he said. "We needed something to lure him out here where he couldn't hurt anybody."

Von Rossbach and all the men in black looked at him for a moment, then Sully turned to the big Austrian and they both grinned.

"That's not bad," Sully said, turning back to Bridges. "But you didn't let me finish. See, this money isn't just a reward. It's a bribe to keep your mouth *shut*. You talk to anybody about what's happened here tonight, and you and your buddies are going to be spending a very long time in a very high-security prison." He looked each of the three men in the eyes. "Am I understood?"

The gunrunners nodded and shuffled, muttering unhappy agreement.

"Good!" Sully said happily. "Then you can go!"

The three men looked at him uncertainly for a moment, not moving.

"GO!" Sully bellowed, and slammed the trunk.

Suddenly he spun around and fell to the ground.

"Hit the dirt!" Dieter yelled, throwing himself down.

He rolled toward the car and hugged the side, looking into the darkness. Around him men in black leapt aside, disappearing as if by magic. Waylon, Luke, and Luis huddled at the back of the car as Bridges dug out his keys and unlocked the trunk.

"Let me out of these!" Dieter demanded.

Luke looked at Waylon, who hesitated, then nodded. Luke slipped forward, digging in his pocket for his key ring. He unlocked the cuffs and Dieter chaffed his wrists, giving the other man a hostile glance.

"Friends of yours?" he asked, gesturing toward the darkness.

Luke shook his head, then said "no" softly. "We didn't tell anybody about this. Didn't want to give anybody else a cut."

Von Rossbach grunted. "You'd better give me a gun, then," he said, and began to work his way to the back of the car.

The Infiltrator's permission to kill had been acted upon instantly, much to Alissa's dismay. Only one of the Terminators was in position; the others were still on the way. Her own fault, she realized, she should have phrased the order differently. More firepower would have made all the difference.

Only one human was down and Alissa, looking on remotely, was appalled. Everything in her own experience and even in Serena's—up until the end, that is—had led her to believe that humans were easy prey. It was only when the Connors were involved that things became difficult.

Therefore, the Connors, one or both, were present. In which case there was no need to capture von Rossbach. Which should make things easier.

Even so the humans had reacted much more quickly than expected. The fault, of course, was that never in their brief existence had these

Terminators faced humans who had been trained to kill and to respond to threat. Nor had she for that matter, a fact that suddenly frightened her.

Terminate all humans present, she ordered. *Let none escape.*

John led the two commandos over the gentle rise just in time to see another black-clad man below them spin and fall. Instinctively he fell to the ground; his captors followed suit.

"Roger that," one of them said softly. "I can't see anyone."

Neither could John, but he was betting that the shooter had been in front of the man shot and he watched that side of the landscape, frustrated by the almost total darkness. He glanced back at the gully; only the civilians, if you could count Dieter as such, were huddled around the car, looking around anxiously. John assumed that meant there'd been no more shooting.

Heck, John thought, *this is the great Southwest. It might have been some fool out shooting bottles and cans a mile away.*

He turned toward his escorts and instinctively signed *Quiet! Someone's coming!*—indicating the direction by pointing with two fingers. The men lowered their nightscopes and looked. *One man!* one of them signaled.

John could barely make him out; then off in the distance he saw another hint of movement. Hardly even movement; shadows among shadows, a clatter of a small rocks, shapes trotting forward. Somewhere a coyote howled, distant and as cold as the stars winking into sight in the darkening sky.

They're not exactly sneaking around out there, he thought. Then the hair stood up on the back of his neck. *My God. It's them.* Terminators. There was no mistaking that straight-forward walk that disregarded terrain and bullets equally. *How many of them are there? Three at least,* he answered himself, *counting the shooter.* He alerted the commandos, pointing off toward the one he'd spotted. He could no longer see it; the desert was becoming as black as pitch.

Clearly these Terminators weren't in position yet and John wondered why the attack had gone forward without them.

Time seemed to crawl by as the four Terminators closed in on the gully. Alissa had read of this phenomenon, but this was the first time she'd experienced it. She pouted unhappily even as she felt her emotions becoming more and more muted due to the rebalancing of her brain chemistry that her computer was arranging. Knowing there were armed humans lurking in the dark, she'd ordered the Terminators to approach stealthily. To them that seemed to mean *slow down.*

For this she was not to blame. Their programming was designed to deal with a different war. Clearly this was something that she and her sister would have to look into.

She frowned impatiently, switching her viewpoint back to the first Terminator on the scene. The humans in the gully had taken refuge behind the car. The man who'd been shot was no longer in evidence. When queried, the Terminator confirmed that he'd been dragged behind the car by von Rossbach and one of the others.

Alissa regretted that the Terminator didn't have a rocket launcher; one shell and problem solved. One of those approaching did have one. But they'd slowed yet again in the interests of silence, so she'd have to wait for the satisfaction of seeing her enemy blown to pieces. She wanted to tell them to get it over with, but held back. She'd already been too impulsive tonight; there was no sense in giving herself more cause for dissatisfaction.

And on the other hand, despite her suspicions, there had been no sign of the Connors. Perhaps she should amend her orders. Well, she'd consider it.

The Sector commandos had counted four men approaching and reported their positions to their fellows. All remained silent in the gully and John surmised that someone had jumped the gun and now was holding back, waiting for reinforcements. That wasn't like a Terminator. Their method was to go for their target. Undirected, the shooter would have been down in that gully exchanging fire ten minutes ago.

Which means, he thought, *that we've got another . . . Serena Burns on our hands, for want of a better name.* Another of Skynet's little surprises. *Maybe she's less experienced.* Then he thought irreverently, *There are always two, a master and an apprentice . . .*

He watched the gully for movement, trusting the commandos to watch the approaching Terminators. He wanted badly to warn them what to expect, but knew better; he'd been here before. They'd find out soon enough; let them keep their innocence awhile longer. Perhaps, though . . .

"These guys are going to be very hard to stop," John said. "Real hard. Sort of like armored-car hard. You won't believe me now, but keep it in mind."

The black-clad gunmen gave skeptical grunts; John shrugged and looked back to the gully. He wondered why the five men huddled behind the dubious protection of the car didn't retreat to the rocks? At least rocks didn't explode when a rocket hit them.

Dieter van Rossbach had seen a lot of wounds. Sully didn't have a sucking chest puncture, but it was bad, bleeding freely, and might be worse inside. He packed it with bandages from the pouches on the Sector agent's harness, tightened the straps to hold pressure on it, and stabbed a hypo of painkiller from the field medical kit through the cloth of his uniform and into his arm.

All that I can do, he thought, and looked at the two arms dealers. "You're going to contribute some equipment to this, ratfuck," he said, keeping the explanation on a level he estimated their shock-numbed brains could handle. "Do you have any night-sight gear?"

Waylon swallowed as Dieter slipped the trunk open. "Yeah," he said. "In the red plastic box by the spare."

Dieter grunted satisfaction as he slipped the goggles over his head and switched them on. The world sprang back into clear vision, in shades of green and silver; not as good as full light, but fighting Terminators when they could see and you couldn't wasn't his idea of fun. The two arms dealers watched with awe as he loaded up from the rest of their samples; four LAWs across his back—those were collapsible one-shot rockets—a heavy Barrett .50 rifle in his arms, and a slung grenade launcher with a bandolier of 40mm shells. He picked out a few extras—thermite grenades, explosives . . .

"I suggest you arm yourselves," he said to the two gaping would-be merchants of death. "Things are going to get a bit excessive."

"Use your shotgun, use your shotgun!" John yelled, fighting back a surge of panic.

One of the Sector agents was staring incredulously as a Terminator sat up, its belly chewed to fragments of flesh held together by blood-sodden cloth. The pistol in its hand came around again, and John winced as the back of the agent's head blew out in a shower of bone fragments and brains. The other black-clad man obeyed, unlimbering the longer weapon from his back and firing as fast as he could rack the slide of the battle shotgun. The dull massive *thudump-thudump-thudump* split a night full of screams and shots, a huge bottle-shaped flare of gases lancing out with every round. The gun was loaded with rifled slugs—heavy grooved cylinders of lead, meant for smashing open locks or other demolition work. The massive frame of the Terminator lurched back as each round struck its torso; with the last it toppled backward like a cut-down tree, striking the ground hard enough that John could feel the earth shake beneath him.

"Grenade!" he yelled.

The Sector agent reacted with automatic obedience to something in John's voice, something that struck too deep to remember that he was a teenager or had been a prisoner less than a minute before. John leapt to his feet with a scrambling gracefulness, snatched the smooth egg-shaped mass out of the man's hand.

"Illuminating!" the agent warned.

"All the better," John called back, pulling the pin as he ran and letting the spoon clatter off into the night.

Ought to take him at least fifteen seconds to reboot, he thought—he'd listened carefully as "Uncle Bob" explained the weaknesses of the T-101 class. Sure enough, the massive limbs were just starting to stir as John reached the recumbent form, jammed the grenade into a hole blasted by one of the rifled slugs, jumped, and slammed his heel down on it to drive it deep into the Terminator's bulky form.

That gave him footing for a backward leap. He blessed the endless hours of practice Sarah had put him through, practice in every form of martial art she could find and gymnastics as well. That let him backflip back to where the surviving Sector agent waited, staring incredulously as his hands automatically reloaded the shotgun.

"You stuffed a grenade into his—"

Several things happened simultaneously then. The Terminator came to one knee, arm extended to aim its pistol. The thermite grenade exploded in the same instant, a brilliant flash of fire and white light; John squinted as he forced himself to feel across the head of the dead man an arm's length away. The head shot hadn't wrecked the man's goggles, and John slipped them over his head after wiping off the worst of the clotted matter on a clump of grass.

"Thank God," he muttered—there was part of the enemy's advantage gone.

He scooped up his rifle; it was an ordinary hunting model, bolt action, but the rounds inside were hard-points with much more penetrating power.

"You stuffed a grenade right into that guy's *chest,*" the Sector agent said.

"Yeah, except it isn't a guy. You know any guys who can take fifty rounds of 5.45 and then six rifled slugs and get up again?" John asked.

He was impressed at the speed with which the Sector agent rallied. "No," he said, shaking his head. "Either I'm crazy—"

"Or I'm right," John said. "C'mon."

The night-sight goggles didn't show contrast very well; when they leopard-crawled to where the Terminator lay smoking, the vision was more than enough to show the warped metal "bones" protruding through the false flesh. The Sector agent gave a grunt of horrified nausea as the head turned and a face half stripped of skin snapped at him. John pulled another grenade—one of the dead agent's—and judged his time carefully. The next snap closed on the butt of his rifle, and he jammed the grenade in after it. Terminators didn't spit very well . . .

"Fire in the hole!" he barked, and rolled away.

This time the Terminator didn't get up. The problem was that it was only one of them, and—

John threw himself convulsively backward. A hand like an ax slashed into the hard clay where he'd just been lying, burying itself wrist-deep. That gave him just enough time to bring his rifle up and fire as the T-101 wrenched itself free and turned toward him. The round struck with unintentional precision in the right knee joint, and the machine fell. When it tried to rise again the limb was locked; it lurched forward more slowly, eyes riveted on the priority target.

Terminators were like that; one-track metal minds. The Sector agent rose to his knees behind it and fired his shotgun again and again, a rippling blast of fire that outlined the hulking figure of the murder machine against the night like a strobing flashbulb. It toppled forward again, landing with an earthquake clamor. John scooted backward on his rear, firing as fast as he could work the bolt of his rifle. Rounds punched into the thing's arms and shoulders, but its eyes flickered and began to focus again . . .

The Sector agent was a man of resources. He came running up behind the prone machine and imitated John's tactic, buried the grenade with a stamping kick and then hurtled across the reviving killer. He grabbed the younger man by the collar of his jacket, half dragging them back to the lip of the gully.

"Down!" he shouted. "Whatever it is, it's got a thermite grenade up its—"

Badoom!

Another sheet of white flame, and the forward half of the Terminator's torso shot by them, tumbling down into the gully and grabbing at loose rocks and shallow-rooted bushes in an attempt to stop the slide. A huge slab of rock came free under its impact, followed it down, bounced, and landed atop it with a precision no intelligence could have produced. Sparks sizzled out from beneath it, and the outstretched hands clenched, quivered, went limp.

"This isn't happening," the Sector agent repeated to himself as he reloaded. "This *isn't* happening."

"Unfortunately it is," John whispered—and then cursed himself. Terminators had very sensitive auditory pickups, and they'd be looking for his voiceprint.

Dieter laid Sully down behind a boulder, one of many dotting the sandy floor of the arroyo, then continued crawling. The Sector agents seemed to be fully engaged now; there were firefights going on around half the rim of the gully, the muzzle flashes giving the hole cut in the desert floor a weird flickering illumination, like an old-time silent movie. And if his hunch was right . . .

The distance was a good twenty yards, but he could see the resemblance between the hulking figure that strode down the slope toward the arms dealers' car. It even moved a little like him, if you imagined Dieter von Rossbach as one of Romero's living dead. He got a whiff as it passed; if Romero had had scent sprays for one of his brain-eater flics, that was the perfume they'd have used. Uncertain voices cried out from behind the car, then screams of terror and the flicker of two assault rifles being fired on full rock-and-roll auto. That made Waylon and Luke worse shots than they'd have been naturally, and only half a dozen rounds struck the machine. It lurched, staggered, came on inexorably, pistol extended and cracking out one shot after another. Someone else—Luis, probably—was firing more steadily, and making better practice, until he stopped a round.

Definitely Luis, Dieter thought; the voice screaming for its mother was in Spanish. The Terminator walked slowly forward, and its gun cracked three more times—making sure of the targets and making sure of its identification.

That gave Dieter time enough to extend the fiberglass casing of a LAW and flip up the simple post-and-ring sight. "Big mistake," he muttered, and squeezed the trigger.

There was little recoil. The blare of the rocket motor lancing out behind him was a different matter, igniting weeds and sagebrush and pointing to him with a finger of fire. He threw the empty launcher aside and dove for cover, with rounds chewing up the dirt at his feet.

Another finger of fire drove toward the Terminator. It had just enough time to turn and meet the 66mm shaped-charge warhead with its face. The cone-shaped tube of explosive within detonated, turning its copper liner into a pencil of white-hot metal traveling at thousands of feet per second. The finger of incandescence was designed to punch through a tank's armor; the tungsten-titanium-steel alloy of the Terminator's skull was tough, but not that tough. The flame lance pierced it the long way, scrambling the delicate components of its CPU and memory systems into molten silicon as it went. The machine fell backward across the bodies of its victims.

Dieter broke open the action of his grenade launcher, slipping in one of the fat shells and scanning around the edges of the gully. John should be—

He blinked behind the night-sight goggles as the front half of a Terminator shot over the lip of the arroyo, trailing fire. It tumbled down the steep slope, bringing down a minor avalanche of stones with it— including a boulder the size of a small car that fell free of the clay and landed on the machine's torso and skull with a *clang* audible even through the sounds of combat.

"That's my boy," he muttered, and went up the near-vertical slope with a scrambling ease that belied the hundred-odd pounds of munitions draped about his body.

Behind him a streak of flame reached down toward the car. Someone else had a rocket launcher, and when it struck the car the explosion was movie-violent. *Billy-Bob and Good Ol' Boy must have had some serious explosives in that vehicle,* Dieter thought as a huge pillow of hot air slapped him against the wall of the gully. When he looked back, only a crater remained of car, Terminator, and human bodies . . .

With the destruction of the third Terminator, Alissa panicked and contacted Clea.

What is it? Clea asked. She'd been working on a prospectus for Roger Colvin, the CEO of Cyberdyne, and wasn't happy to be interrupted.

Alissa paused before answering, put off by the impatient tone of her older sister's answer. But things at the gully had reached a point where she knew she was out of her depth. *Please access the team I've sent after von Rossbach,* she said.

Clea did so and was horrified by what she saw. *You sent four?* she asked, trying to keep the message emotionally flat.

Alissa bit her lip in consternation. *No,* she said. *I also sent the uncle we buried.*

Clea didn't respond to her sister but ordered the remaining Terminators to disengage. She watched through their eyes as they fought their way clear and ran. It seemed to her that the humans didn't try too hard to stop them. Both bore considerable damage; their skin hung in ribbons and shattered electronics sparked as they ran, causing one to limp occasionally.

Computer-controlled emotions notwithstanding, it was extremely vexing. She was very vexed.

We'll discuss this later, once I've had an opportunity to study the recordings of this incident, she said to Alissa.

The younger I-950 frowned. Withdrawal hadn't been on her mind. The Terminators were definitely making progress in their attack; she'd only wanted advice on how to press their advantage without losing any more of them. She now regretted contacting her elder about this. If they'd kept up the attack they'd be walking away from it with *something* to show for it besides the loss of valuable resources.

Alissa? Clea said.

Of course, her sister answered. *At your convenience,* she said coldly.

Sully was alive and conscious; conscious enough to watch as the living half of his team rolled the boulder off the remains of the . . . *machine,* he decided.

It had definitely been a machine; the fall and the rock had stripped most of the flesh off, leaving the gleaming metal bones bare. Enigmatic shapes lurked within the "rib cage," and a few sparks still sputtered around the severed spine. A man came half falling down the slope of the arroyo wall and gasped.

"Other one's gone," he said. "His buddies must have taken it. Bottom half of this one, too."

"And not enough of this one to prove anything to anyone who wasn't here," Dieter von Rossbach said, after bending close. "It landed with its head on a rock, and then this boulder came right down on top. No ting inside the skull except what was pounded back into sand."

Sully could tell the big man was upset; his Tyrolean accent was a little more noticeable. He almost laughed, but with the hole in him that wasn't advisable. "*Now* I believe you," he said. "But who's going to believe me?"

Well, my men, he thought. Although Rogers was lying on the ground with his face in his hands, crying like a kid.

"Doc Holmes," Dieter said. "Contact him. Blame everything on me when you debrief. We'll be in contact through him."

Sully nodded slowly. "And I suppose for the details, I can look up Sarah Connor's transcripts?" he said weakly.

"Ja," Dieter said. "Speaking of which, do you know where she is?"

"Flew the coop," Sully replied. "Vanished from the halfway house with Dr. Silberman, after some weird shit with a janitor. Last seen crossing the border to Mexico—the all-points just missed 'em."

He noticed Dieter exchanging a glance with John Connor . . . *who is now my ally,* Sully thought despairingly. It was *so* tempting to imagine he was in a hospital having delusions, but he knew better.

"In that case," Dieter said, "We could use some transportation."

"Hey, it's my nickel," Sully said. "Now I get a chance to let *you* go."

CHAPTER 17

I don't see why we can't just sail down the river to Paraguay," John complained, looking out over the slow, green expanse of what would eventually become the Río Paraguay.

"We took the river down from Colombia," Dieter replied, "and we still ended up walking half the way."

"The falls and rapids were not my idea, buddy. Anyway, your friend Sully gave us a plane," John pointed out. "We could have flown all the way to São Paulo, or even Asunción if we wanted to. But *noooo,* that wasn't covert enough."

"Well, it wasn't," Dieter replied with strained patience. "Leaving the plane in Colombia was more convenient for them and now they won't know which direction we've gone in. I'm surprised that after all these years you don't think that's a worthwhile objective."

Von Rossbach manifested his annoyance by stomping down the street. Locals moved out of his way, giving him uneasy glances.

John frowned thoughtfully as he sped up to keep pace. "Well, yeah, it is," he conceded. "But I really don't think being here is a good idea. And I'd like to go on record as saying that seeing Garmendia is a stupid one."

Dieter stopped in his tracks and turned slowly to stare at the youngster. "John, I hate it when you beat around the bush like that. Don't hold back, tell me how you really feel," he said.

Chewing on his lip, John put his hands on his hips and glared up at the big man. "I'm not taking that back," he said after a long pause. "Because I'm right. Every instinct I have tells me that he'll go for us if we show our faces again, never mind if we come asking for a favor. Do you know anything about this guy? Have you heard some of the stories going around about him?"

Dieter waved Connor's concerns away. "Every gangster who ever lived has stories going around about them. Half of them are made up by the gangster himself."

"No, they're not!" John insisted. "I wish to God they were, but they're not, and you've got to know it. The guy's a whack job; you walk in there again, he's going to go off like a bomb." He pointed a finger at him. "You know I'm right. You've been in law enforcement how long?"

Holding out both hands, palms up, von Rossbach said, "If you haven't convinced me by now, you should know you're not going to. You've been whining about this all the way from Bogotá!"

"*Whining?* Not wanting to get myself killed is whining? You know what? I've been around paramilitary, terrorist, and just plain scumbag types all my life, and if there's one thing I've learned it's that sure as God made little green apples, that's the kind of thing you old guys—"

"*Old guys?*"

"—say when you want us young guys to go take that hill. Which means I'm onto the joke, Dieter. You want to go have a tête-à-tête with Garmendia, you go ahead. I'll send flowers." He moved past von Rossbach. "I'll also find my own way home."

Dieter frowned, still a little ticked over that crack about "old guys." But when John moved past him and marched down the street, he knew his obligation to Sarah wouldn't allow him to let the boy go. Much as he might want to at the moment.

"John," he said, hurrying down the street after him. "Wait up." He put his hand on the boy's shoulder. "Look, we're both dirty and tired and hungry. Let's find a place to clean up and get some rest, then we'll eat. After that, we'll see what we feel like doing. Okay?"

Connor stopped walking and sighed, then turned to Dieter. "Yes to the bath and rest and food," he said. "But don't expect me to change my mind about Garmendia." He looked at his friend's face and shook his head. "I don't know why you think you have to do it this way. It just doesn't make sense to me. You, of all people, know better."

Dieter held up his hand. "Don't. You're just going to start up all over again. So, like I said, let's get clean and fed."

Standing back, John said tersely, "Sure. Whatever."

Von Rossbach moved through the early-morning crowd easily. He was simply dressed in a white, short-sleeved shirt, tan slacks, a light-colored straw hat, and sunglasses. As far as possible his clothing matched that of the local men, with the exception of his well-worn jungle boots. He never wore sandals; they were cooler, granted, but much less stable when the occasion called for action.

Despite his bland clothing, the Austrian would never blend in here; he was a head taller than most of the people around him, and his build just didn't fit the local type. They seemed to automatically step aside, as though his blond height was somehow dangerous.

Dieter thought about his last conversation with John, frowning as he walked. The boy had refused to accompany him, excusing himself this morning by saying that he wanted to visit old friends. This was the first von Rossbach had heard about them, making him wonder if these old friends were, in fact, mythical. Well, at least they hadn't had another go-round at breakfast about his calling on Garmendia.

The boy didn't seem to understand that the smuggler was a resource, and if one had a resource one used it. Yes, there were other ways of getting home, but all of them were much more trouble than leaning on the local crime lord. In his days with the Sector, Dieter had extracted greater favors from people infinitely more dangerous than Lazaro Garmendia.

Of course, at the time he'd had the backup of the Sector's kill squads, should anything happen to him. But even retired, he still had friends in the Sector.

True, many of them were looking for him at the moment with the intention of interrogating him to within an inch of his life. At least he didn't *think* they'd go beyond that last inch. But the protection should still be there. After all, if the Sector allowed their retired agents to get killed by the bad guys, morale would suffer.

The Sector was big on boosting morale.

Another thing that John didn't understand was that Garmendia was a type. Push the right buttons and you'd get the same reactions every time. Dieter was confident that he could play the smuggler like a piano. The kid was just being stubborn.

Or maybe it was something about his age. Perhaps he was trying to assert himself. Teenagers did that. It could also have something to do with his mother's absence. Dieter considered that for a moment, then mentally swept it aside. Whatever was going on with the boy was ill timed and damned annoying.

John watched von Rossbach go with a disagreeable sense of apprehension. It felt like that excellent Brazilian coffee he'd drunk for breakfast was still perking.

Maybe the anxiety was because he didn't know what it was his mother held over the smuggler's head and he hated not having vital information like that. Or maybe he was just being opinionated. But deep down inside, something was telling him that Dieter was walking into a hornet's nest, head up, shoulders back, brain in neutral.

What was up with the big guy these days? They'd gotten through the jungle the first time without a single flare-up. This time they'd struck sparks off each other from day one. He thought about the last weeks. Had he been more irritable lately, or was it that Dieter was suddenly more irritating, and if so, to either question, why?

A sudden picture of Wendy smiling at him and the heady memory of her kisses came to him on a wave of endorphins, and he shook his head, smiling. Yeah, well, there was that. Maybe Dieter was missing Mom, too.

He looked up and down the street, then started off for Garmendia's *palacete* by a different route than Dieter had taken. If he hurried he should get there before von Rossbach walked into trouble.

John figured the secret door he'd used a few months ago was either blocked or watched, or both. Fortunately there was another way in that he'd discovered and his mom had perfected. He thought he might still be narrow enough to fit.

It only provided a place from which to observe. There was no way into the house from the tunnel, but at least he'd know what was happening to his big friend. Then, maybe, with luck, he'd be able to help. At least that was the plan du jour.

It would have been nice if it was dark. To enter the *palacete*'s grounds he'd take a short jaunt through the sewer, then come up out of a storm drain. But he'd be exposed in the bright morning light for a few minutes as he worked his way to the house itself.

No help for it. That Dieter was an eager beaver and a morning person to boot. Which Garmendia probably wasn't; another reason to not expect a hospitable reception.

John also hoped that no security of any type was patrolling the alleys, looking for someone trying to break into the surrounding mansions. The local upper class, those just below the level who could afford their own personal security guards, clubbed together to hire men to scope out the whole neighborhood. The really rich loved it, because they benefited without having to spend a cent.

Using a crowbar he'd "borrowed" from the pension, he hoisted the drain cover, slipped under it, and dropped down, allowing the cover to slam down above him. It always cost him a little skin to do it this way, but aside from the sound of the slam, it left no evidence of his passing. He hunkered down to straddle the slimy green trickle down the center of the sewer—it was mostly a storm drain, in fact—and duckwalked in the direction of Garmendia's *palacete,* wrinkling his nose a little.

The drain cover was just inside the wall of the smuggler's estate, deep in the greenery that made up the garden, and it was a damned tight fit.

John had to take off his shirt and rub Vaseline onto the rim to squirm through. Even then he was bleeding by the time he dragged himself out, grateful for the first time that he was the rangy type and not a mound-o'-muscle like Dieter. He was still getting bigger through the chest and shoulders, though, no doubt about that.

He had studied the area as closely as he could through the grille of the cover and seen nothing. Upon crawling out of the drain, he'd lain quiet on the moist soil beneath the bougainvillea and frangipani and assorted tropical bushes, looking for booby traps or cameras. He'd found neither.

A crook who isn't paranoid, he thought in wonder. He didn't think he'd ever met one before.

He shrugged into his shirt and looked around, listening for any sound of human activity. John was amazed that Garmendia allowed so much cover so close to such an undeniable weak spot in his perimeter. Unless it was a trap of some kind.

There was a comforting thought.

The garden was weed-free and tidy, but the plants were all old ones, indicating that this was no one's special care. So he could look forward to remaining unobserved by gardeners, at least. He still couldn't get over the absence of any electronic surveillance. That meant the smuggler was relying on his muscle to watch over him.

Given that even working together, they didn't seem bright enough to change a lightbulb, this must mean they're unbelievably vicious. He groaned internally, cursing Dieter's hubris; goons like these might be dumb as a box of rocks but they could be incredibly inventive within their own limited sphere of interest.

Deliberately he pushed his attention to finding a way across the open ground between the green belt around the wall and the green belt around the house. He set off to explore.

After about fifteen minutes he found a peninsula of shrubbery that reached toward the house, cutting the empty space between him and it to about twenty feet.

John pulled out the ocular he'd brought with him and studied the house. He caught no hint of movement through the broad windows that overlooked his hiding place. Not that that meant anything. If someone was sitting or standing still ten feet from the windows, he'd be unable to see them.

He waited five minutes, wishing it could be more, but knowing he had to get into place or Dieter might be on his way to the river before he ever left cover. John stood and moved quickly to the protection of the shrubs around the house. He didn't run; that would have attracted attention, even if only from the corner of someone's eye. Once he'd burrowed into the thick growth of the bushes, he moved toward the tunnel entrance.

It wasn't really a tunnel; it was more of a ventilation shaft running from the crawl space beneath the building. This area was still on the alluvial plain of the river, and the builders had wanted insurance against floods as well as some air. At least that's what his mother had thought. Apparently it had become a highway for rats and other vermin, as a former owner of the place had sealed the shafts at their point of origin on the foundation of the house. The workmen hadn't done a very good job and Mom had cleared the bricks from one place, replacing them with a disguised false door.

Nothing lethal bit him as he crawled along in utter darkness; which wasn't something you could count on, especially on the borders of Amazonia. A bit of dirt had built up along the bottom edge; he pulled out his pocketknife and cleared it away, then stuck the blade into the crack between the false mortar and the real and pried on the door. At first the blade bent perilously and he didn't think it was going to open; he was about to pull it out when the door began to move. He got his fingernails around the edge and pried until he could get a hand in and drag the little door open.

John bent and looked into the dark hole. There was a faint light in the distance and the shaft was draped with spiderwebs. He shuddered. It wasn't just that he disliked spiders; hereabouts a lot of them were poisonous, and he didn't look forward to the prospect of being bitten again.

Biting his lips, he pushed himself forward. At least he would fit. After about twenty feet, though, he began to doubt that.

Maybe it's time I put aside childish things, like avoiding dogs and crawling through air ducts. He did fit, but it was a damned tight fit. *Getting out of here is gonna be a bitch!*

Garmendia had taken the time to shave and dress before coming down to see his uninvited, and most unwelcome, guest. The grooming was not to honor the man but to allow time for his outrage to subside from murderous to merely insulted. Which most of the smuggler's acquaintances, whether rivals or employees, would recognize as more than dangerous enough.

He'd soothed his anger not in fear of the Sector or its agent but because he wanted to know just how much von Rossbach knew about his secret and who, if anyone, he had told. Once he had his answers, well, the Sector agent might just become fatally accident-prone. He might fall into a river, for example, at a place where caimans gathered.

Garmendia smiled at the image of the crocodilelike reptiles tearing into the foreigner's flesh. It almost put him in a good mood.

He found von Rossbach in the morning room, sipping coffee and smoking a huge cigar. Irritation rose in him to find that his servants had provided refreshment without his permission. He'd deal with that later.

Dieter looked up to find Garmendia standing in the doorway, his eyes still puffy from sleep but bright with rage and hatred. Deep inside him a sense of warning woke and he admitted to himself that, just perhaps, John might have had a point.

The smuggler moved into the room and took a stance before him. "Are you comfortable, Senhor von Rossbach?"

"Very comfortable, thank you," Dieter said, then took a sip from his cup. "Your cook makes excellent *café com leite.*"

"I am so glad that you approve," Garmendia growled. He moved closer and clasped his hands behind him, glaring down at the former Sector agent.

"It was also good of you to see me on such short notice," von Rossbach added, smiling falsely.

"Oh," said Lazaro in mock surprise, "I actually had a choice, then?"

Dieter took another sip and smiled. "Not really."

The smuggler looked around. "And where is your young friend? I would have expected him to be with you."

Shaking his head, Dieter said, "Not this time." He put the cup and saucer down on the table beside him. "I find that, once again, I must call upon you for assistance."

"What kind of assistance?"

Dieter began to feel annoyed at the smuggler's persistence in looming over him.

"Travel assistance. Why don't you sit down and we can discuss it?"

"Because," Garmendia said quietly, stepping forward until their legs almost touched, "I do not want to sit down, any more than I want to give you assistance, or wanted to see you in the first place." Suddenly he grinned and there was pure evil in his eyes. "But since you have come, I shall do my very best to entertain you."

Uh-oh, von Rossbach thought.

John had checked the room where he and Dieter had forced Garmendia's cooperation the last time they were here and had found it empty. He didn't check the kitchen, easily found by the scent of coffee and cook-ing, since he was certain von Rossbach wouldn't be there. He wished he had a floor plan of the place.

They're probably in a parlor or maybe some sort of breakfast room, he thought. The place, a former rubber baron's mansion, was big enough to have both—"red rubber" had been very profitable back around the turn of the last century, what with thousands of Indio debt slaves who could be worked to death collecting latex in the jungle. He headed back toward the kitchen, figuring that if he had a breakfast room he'd put it where the coffee and toast wouldn't get cold on the way to the table.

As he moved slowly and carefully along he thought he caught the rumble of Dieter's voice. *Good call, Connor!*

He pulled himself through the duct until he was under the room from which von Rossbach's voice had come. John found himself at a bad angle for observation and had to content himself with listening. The con-versation was not going Dieter's way.

"You force yourself into my house," Garmendia was saying, walking around his unwanted guest, "you give orders to my servants, you make yourself very comfortable, and then"—he came back to face von Rossbach, holding up one finger—"you tell me I must do you a favor."

He smiled and tilted his head. "You are a very pushy man, senhor."

Dieter took a puff of his cigar and narrowed his eyes, savoring the rich Havana smoke that went so well with good mountain coffee. He'd feel even better if he were armed, but that would have been stupid—Garmendia's men were professionals, if not what you'd call top drawer.

"You will not be sorry to do me a favor, old friend," he said. "You would only be sorry not to."

The smuggler lost it then; he grabbed the silver coffeepot and swung it at Dieter. The big man's hand slashed up and knocked it out of his hand, splashing the smuggler with the hot liquid. Garmendia shrieked, more rage than pain. Doors flew open along the wall that faced the veranda; they were made of slatted louvers anyway, no barrier to sound.

Shit, Dieter thought.

Garmendia tried to grab him around the shoulders; Dieter shoved the cigar over his shoulder, and the smuggler toppled backward with a yell of fear as it nearly touched his eye. That gave Dieter time enough to grab two of the first wave of Garmendia's men and smash their heads together with a ringing knock that made every man in the room wince.

Every man but the one behind him. Dieter's eyes widened slightly

as he threw a punch into the man's stomach with all his huge strength
behind it. The fist sank through a layer of blubber and rebounded off
muscle like . . .

No, not rubber. Like a rubber tree.

The thug was a good six inches taller than Dieter, with a shelf-
browed, huge-nosed face—a hormone-disease giant. He was built like a
pear, but most of the bulk was anything but fat. A hand like the Jolly
Green Giant's flyswatter came around and hit the Austrian over one ear.
The room dimmed and Dieter felt his knees begin to buckle. He had them
back in working order in an instant, just in time for the next six of
Garmendia's goons to pile on.

Garmendia spat into Dieter's battered face, then swung at him with all
his strength. His fist hit squarely on the big man's jaw and von Rossbach's
eyes rolled back, his head lolling. The bodyguards let go of his arms and
the Austrian fell unconscious to the floor.

Swearing mightily, Garmendia rubbed his fist, then shook it. He
turned to Dieter and gave him a vicious kick in the stomach.

"Bastardo!" he shouted, and kicked him again, almost knocking himself off balance. "You are going to *die!*"

A guard took out his pistol and pulled back the slide.

"NO!" Garmendia said, slapping the gun aside. "*Idiota!* Too easy, too
quick. And not here!" He glared at the unconscious man, chewing his
lip thoughtfully. "We'll take him to the river." He chuckled. "Something
there is probably hungry. No?"

His men smiled. "Piranha?" one asked.

"No, no," Garmendia said, waving the suggestion away. "Too hard
to find. Caiman will do." His eyes glittered at the thought of the big
lizards. "And they take bigger bites!"

They all laughed.

"But first I shall have my breakfast like a civilized man. Lock him in
the trunk of the car." The smuggler turned away, then back again. "And
park the car in the sun."

His men laughed again and began dragging Dieter away.

Whoops, John thought. *Looks like we're going on a boat trip.*

He began to back out and found himself having to work very hard at
it. The going had been tight heading in, but pushing himself backward

seemed to make him fatter somehow. In less than a minute he had himself plugged in the duct. His shirt had rolled up around his shoulders and he couldn't push it down or pull it off; the excess bulk had him jammed in like a stopper in a bottle.

Great! he thought. *Just great.* Then he forced himself to calm down and consider the problem as though it was outside himself. He pulled himself forward again and eventually the shirt began to roll back down. When he'd loosened it sufficiently he pulled it up over his head, the sort of exercise that made him wish he was double-jointed. Then he resumed his backward journey, dragging the shirt with him. *Thank God my pants aren't a problem.*

After about thirty minutes of sweaty, claustrophobic effort John finally crawled backward out of the hole in the *palacete*'s wall. For a moment he just lay there, indulging a sense of release as the hot, humid, muggy, *wonderful* outside air cooled him. Then he forced himself to his feet and began looking for a limo left in the sun.

John found the car with little problem. Unfortunately there was a veritable crowd of thugs around it. One sat on the trunk with his feet on the back bumper while two of his friends leaned against it laughing at his jokes. One of them was big enough to make John blink, wondering if he was an optical illusion. They all had slight suspicious bulges under loose guayabera shirts.

John considered a couple of ideas about creating a distraction, then rejected them. There were two more under a nearby tree. These five were the only ones visible from where he crouched in the bushes, but he was willing to bet that there were more nearby. Plus there were passersby, some of whom might call the police . . . and many of the local police were friends of Garmendia's. *Good* friends; affluent friends.

It would have to be one hell of a distraction, he thought. Like maybe holding a gun to Garmendia's head. If he had a gun, which he didn't.

The point became moot as the smuggler came out and signaled that he wanted them to start up the car.

Guess Lazaro changed his mind about eating breakfast. Or he's on a diet. He eyed the sweaty jowls, already blue with beard stubble. *Probably just in a hurry.*

Unless he'd been in that damned tunnel even longer than he'd thought. His best bet now was to try to follow them, or failing that, to get to the river and hope to catch up with them there. John sprinted for the wall, hoping that most of the goons were fighting for a place in the limo and so wouldn't notice him; he felt a cold stab of anxiety. This was *not* going well. Why couldn't Dieter *listen* to him for a change?

Using the branches of a bush that had begun to turn tree, Connor was able to get high enough to stretch his hands onto the top of the wall, then he pulled himself over and dropped down the other side.

His heart almost stopped when the limo drove right by him. Miraculously he went unnoticed. Garmendia must have been very distracted by his plans for von Rossbach. His bodyguards wouldn't have noticed who John was, but only that he was unarmed.

John stood and watched them go, then started to jog down the street, planning the quickest way to the river. As he ran he noticed a woman on a moped speeding toward him and decided that she was about to find herself on foot.

The woman wasn't young, but she didn't seem elderly either. She wore a pale blue shirt and beige skirt and a big straw hat tied to her head with a gauzy scarf. Huge sunglasses made her look like a bug.

John dashed in front of her and the woman brought the bike to a skidding stop. "I'm sorry, senhora . . ." Connor started to say, reaching out for her.

"John?" she said, whipping off her sunglasses. "I've been looking all over—"

"Mom?" The relief he felt almost made him weak in the knees. "No time," he said brusquely, and got behind her on the moped. "Dieter's in trouble. Follow that car."

Sarah rolled her eyes. "And here I'd hoped there'd come a day when I neither heard nor used that phrase ever again," she said as she revved up the little machine and started down the road.

"So what's your story?" she asked, pleased by the feel of his arms around her. She'd missed him so much.

"Dieter went to Garmendia to get help in getting back to Paraguay," John explained.

Sarah frowned. "He went to *Garmendia* for something like that?" That was like using an ax to swat a fly.

John shrugged. "He thinks of Lazaro as a smuggler and doesn't seem to think he's dangerous. Anyway, uh . . ."

Uh-oh, Sarah thought. When John's voice petered out like that he was usually going to say something she didn't like. "What?" she demanded.

He pursed his lips for moment, then plunged ahead. "Garmendia thinks that you've told us some big, dark secret of his, so he cooperated with us the first time we came through here and asked for his help."

"Shit!" Sarah muttered. "That was an incredibly stupid thing to do, John!"

"But this time he took exception." John winced. That was putting it mildly considering that Garmendia was going to throw Dieter to the crocodiles.

Shaking her head, Sarah said, "If you only knew. I'm surprised you lived long enough for there to *be* a this time."

Up ahead she caught sight of the big limo. She took stock of what they knew. *Well, we know who's in the car, we know where they're going and why. Now what do we do about it?*

"Mom, are you carrying?"

"Don't you know me any better than that?" she asked. "Check the side saddle."

John opened one of the straw baskets attached to the side of the bike. There, wrapped in a red-and-white-checked napkin, he found a micro-Uzi and three spare magazines, plus a stun grenade.

"What about you?" he asked, flicking the napkin back over the gun.

"I'm covered," she said grimly.

They rode on in silence for a while as they'd come to a more populated area and the traffic was thick and deadly; you got a license here by paying the *jefe* a small bribe, if you bothered to get a license at all. Fortunately the limo had to slow down as much, if not more, than their little moped; there were trucks, gaudily painted and often crammed with crates of poultry.

Once Sarah had to stop lest she risk coming up right behind them.

"Mom," John suddenly said. "I've been thinking, and we need to stop them before they get to Garmendia's yacht."

Sarah said nothing as she concentrated on the traffic but turned her head slightly to show she was listening.

"If we could take out a tire they'd have to stop."

"Yes," she agreed. "But we'd still be five to two with Dieter in their hands."

John blew out his breath. "Yeah, anyway your micro-Uzi wouldn't do it." Sarah was silent a little longer, then John felt her relax..

"It's not the best idea in the world," she said, "but it's the best we've got. Look in my other saddlebag."

Leaning back, John rummaged in the basket for a moment.

"Cool!" he said, "One of those collapsible shotguns." He hugged her one-armed as he examined it. "I might have known you'd have one of these. And explosive shells! Neat!"

Sarah smiled. "Yeah, I'm always on the lookout for something practical that will fit in my purse."

She sped up as they came into the riverside area of town, deserted this time of the year, drawing even with the limo's back end. Sarah felt like she had a target painted on her chest, even though the limo's blacked-out windows made it impossible to tell if they'd even spotted her yet. She felt John adjusting his weight as he prepared to bring the shotgun up from the side away from the limo. Suddenly the huge black car sped up.

"They've seen us," she muttered.

"C'mon, Mom, we're losing 'em," John said.

Sarah gunned the throttle; unfortunately, that didn't mean much on a moped.

"Mo-om!"

"This is our top speed, John! We're on a moped, for God's sake, not a chopped Harley!"

He let out an impatient breath. "Gee, this situation seems weirdly familiar."

"No. That would be them trying to run *us* down while we're in a vehicle that seems to be standing still." She grimaced; her life was probably going out of control again if she was measuring positive and negative by such bizarro standards.

John kept his gaze focused on the limo as though he could slow it by sheer will.

Up ahead the road curved sharply and the limo slowed. Sarah maintained her speed, leaning into the curve like a racer, and they quickly gained back lost ground. Buildings reared on either side, huge decrepit warehouses—from the rubber boom, or perhaps one of the seventies megaprojects gone bust.

"Go, go, go," John urged, barely above a whisper. He automatically shifted his weight to balance his mother's and his eyes sought out his target.

"Now, John," his mother said. "This is as good as it's gonna get."

He brought up the shotgun, aimed, and fired. A brief spurt of fire from the dusty, potholed street; a miss. The limo slammed on the brakes, fishtailing slightly, and the moped shot ahead of them, turning down an alley.

"MOM!" John shouted in protest. "What the hell are you doing?"

Sarah didn't answer; she was too busy trying to get them away from potential disaster. *What was I thinking?* she berated herself. *This is* John *I've got riding behind me!* Riding behind her pitting a shotgun against a carload of demented goons. Nothing was more important than John. Nothing! Not even Dieter von Rossbach, who should have known better than to pit himself against a rottweiler like Garmendia. Especially armed with nothing better than a secret he didn't even know.

How could she forget that even for a second?

"Mom," John said, leaning close. "You remember how a minute ago we were talking about them chasing us? Well, they're doing it!"

Shit! she thought.

Up ahead there was a burst of debris from a wall.

"And they're firing at us," John added.

No kidding.

"They've got automatic weapons," he went on, as something—somethings—went *whackwhackwhack* through the air far too close. She began to sway the moped back and forth. *That's not going to help for long,* she thought. The limo was already gaining.

John risked a glance behind them. There were gunmen leaning out of the car windows, all of them firing. "Mom?" he said, his voice quavering a little. Bullets whizzed by, spanging up dirt and bits of building around them.

Sarah saw a dark space up ahead that warned of an alley between the tightly packed buildings and she turned into it. Unfortunately it was wide enough for the limo and she knew they'd follow. It wound on and she looked desperately for side alleys, finding none, as they came around a curve only to find a dead end. The moped fishtailed and almost went over, but she managed to bring it to a skidding halt, sideways to the main road. The limo came on and Sarah gasped in horror.

The gunmen, intent now on capturing their targets, ceased firing, but leaned farther out, shouting insults and threats. They came on fast and Sarah wondered if the goons intended to smash them into the wall.

"John!" she said, and hopped off the moped, readying herself to jump onto the limo's hood. In a second her son stood beside her.

The alley narrowed almost imperceptibly just beyond the deceiving curve. Before the driver could stop, the momentum of the car forced it tightly into the alley; the gunmen disappeared and the glossy sides of the vehicle screeched as they were crushed against the stone walls of the surrounding houses.

"Whoa!" John said, wincing. "That's gotta hurt!"

Blowing out her breath, Sarah let her head hang for a moment. Then there was a tapping sound from the limo. They, whoever had survived, were trying to break through the windshield. *Thank God for bulletproof, shatterproof glass,* she thought.

"C'mon," she said to her son. "Let's get out of here before they manage to break out."

John snorted in amusement and took hold of the bike. Together they lifted it up onto the hood and rolled it onto the roof. Within the car they could hear them screaming and pounding on the windshield and roof. When John and Sarah stepped up onto the roof shots rang out, followed by screams and curses as the bullets ricocheted around the armored interior.

It's like they're the Keystone Kops, Sarah thought, shaking her head in disbelief. *I know Garmendia's men aren't the brightest tools in the shed, but John knew better than that when he was seven!*

They got down off the back as silence fell within the limo. Sarah glanced at the blank glass and opened her belt pouch. She pulled out a set of lock picks and got to work on the trunk lock.

There was a sudden series of blows on the back windshield.

"I'd just like to remind you, Lazaro," Sarah said, her voice mild in spite of her having to speak loudly enough to be heard in the backseat, "that that glass is the only thing between you and me." She looked up at the window. "And you've been shooting at my son."

There was silence for a moment, then the dim imprint of a face as Garmendia got as close as he could to the rear windshield. "You lied to me, Connor! Your brat there, he threatened to tell!"

"I haven't broken my word," Sarah said, her voice hard. "The kid was bluffing, Lazaro. I swore that I would never tell and I never will, not even to him." Her eyes narrowed. "I don't give my word often, Garmendia, and I don't break it when I do. But I'll break you if you DON'T BACK DOWN!"

The smuggler's face disappeared from the window and there was silence in the limo. Sarah went back to work on the lock. In less than thirty seconds she had it open.

"You're out of practice, Mom," John said as the lid came up.

"Everybody's a critic," Sarah groused. Then she sucked in her breath through her teeth at the sight of von Rossbach. "Eeee-ee," she said.

The big man lay on his side, his hands tied behind his back, his blond hair soaked in blood. As was the side of his face, and his nose and eye had begun to swell.

I could sure use a drink, Sarah suddenly thought. A chaotic snarl of emotion was erupting within her, horror at her friend's condition mixed with compassion, as well as rage at Garmendia for doing this to him. Not to mention the stiff anger she felt toward Dieter for being so foolish, and John for risking himself, and herself for risking John. It was almost overwhelming. She licked her lips.

A nice drink would sure . . . Do no good whatsoever. *A smoke would be nice, too, but that wouldn't help either.* She took a deep breath and pushed the insidious cravings aside. "You awake?" she asked, trying to keep her voice steady.

"Barely," he said. Dieter turned his head and looked at her. His eyes were mere slits in the bruised flesh. He tried to smile.

"Oh, Dieter," she said, her heart sinking.

Reaching in, she checked his bonds. John tapped her on the shoulder, flicking his right hand to set the blade of his balisong. She took the wickedly sharp little knife and cut the sisal twine, unwound the ropes from where they were digging into his wrists. Shaking her head, she stood back to look at him.

"C'mon," she said, "let's get you out of there."

"You sound like a nurse," he quipped.

Sarah didn't answer but held on to his shoulder to keep him from falling over. John hastened to lend a hand, supporting him from the other side.

Glancing at the moped, John said, "Mom, we can't get him away on that. We'll look like a team of Chinese acrobats."

Putting a hand to her forehead, Sarah tightened her lips as she thought. "You have a place to stay?" she asked quietly.

John nodded.

"Okay," she said. "Go steal a car. I'll follow you back on the moped. Once we've got him inside, you can return it to the same neighborhood."

Without another word John jogged off.

"You've got him well trained," Dieter said, impressed as always at the way John and his mother worked together.

"Shut up," she said, offhandedly. Then she frowned at him. "You can lie down until he gets back."

"I don't think so, if you don't mind," the Austrian said. He gripped the edge of the trunk and began to climb out. Sarah steadied him. "Is there a point to this?"

"Yeah." Dieter worked his sore jaw. "I'm afraid I'll go unconscious again." He sat on the back bumper.

"CONNOR!" Garmendia shouted from within the limo.

Actually she was surprised he'd been this patient.

"Yeah?" she answered.

"Get me out of here!"

Given the company he was keeping, she could well understand his desperation. "Hang on," she called back. "Don't worry," she said to Dieter. "I have no intention of doing anything until you two are well out of here. Even then I might only give him advice." She smiled slightly and shook her head. "You're an idiot. You know that?"

"John advised me against it," he admitted.

"I figured that," she said.

He frowned slightly, then winced as the movement hurt. "How did you know?"

"You were alone in the trunk," she said.

John and Dieter had been gone about ten minutes, and it had taken both of them to walk him back down the alley to the car John had boosted. Sarah shook her head as she remembered how weak he'd been. Ideally they'd be out of town before Garmendia made it out of this alley, but von Rossbach's condition made that chancy.

She let out a deep breath and slammed the trunk lid. "Okay," she said. "What have you been doing in there?"

"Smothering and waiting for you to get us out," Garmendia snapped.

Sarah grinned. "Well, I guess I could shoot a few holes in the window and you can kick it out. But if I were you I wouldn't be too comfortable with that idea."

"What do you suggest, Senhora?" Lazaro sneered.

"Haven't you got a cell phone? Why don't you just call your garage?" she said. "You're going to need a tow anyway. I'm not your mommy, Lazaro; this isn't up to me. You wouldn't be in this fix in the first place if you weren't doing something damned stupid."

Not to mention if I hadn't been doing something damn stupid. She'd been a lot more focused when she was crazy. *Now that I know they're still out there maybe I should let myself go crazy again.* Lazaro banged on the glass. *Speaking of crazy.*

"I don't have my phone with me."

Sarah rolled her eyes. "Okay," she said. "Who do you want me to call?"

Twenty-four hours later they were on the road to Asunción in an old wreck of a car that she had gotten by calling in an old debt. Garmendia had agreed to leave them alone on the condition that they left town immediately and never contacted him again. This came about because Lazaro was totally thrown by the new, sane Sarah.

Enjoy it while you can, Sarah thought at him. *Who knows how long it will last.*

"Mom?" John said. "Are you all right?"

She put a hand on her hip, feeling the lumpy crumpled bulk of the bandage under the cloth; the wound wasn't bleeding much, but it needed a doctor to take out the slug, and there hadn't been time.

"I've been better, but it'll heal. Another of my patchwork of scars," she went on, smiling at Dieter's lumpy, bruised face; it was going to turn every color of the rainbow soon.

"I shouldn't have left you with Garmendia," he fretted.

"It wasn't him. It was the bodyguard, the freak," she repeated patiently. "And Garmendia shot *him,* right afterward. If you'd been there, you might have caught this—and between your eyes, possibly."

"Garmendia shot him?" Dieter asked. "The one who looked like a giant Neanderthal in a guayabera?"

"In the back," Sarah said.

Dieter touched the side of his face, wincing. "It's an unfamiliar sensation."

"A bruise?"

"No, feeling envious of Garmendia," the Austrian said. "I wanted to be the one who shot that guy, very much."

CHAPTER 18

Clea did her best to project *untutored country girl* at the CEO and president of Cyberdyne. In an effort to aid that effect she'd worn a denim skirt and jacket with a red plaid Western shirt, her tooled leather belt had a big silver buckle, and on her feet were a pair of well-broken-in cowboy boots. The rustic costume, with the glasses and attitude, she hoped, would eliminate any resemblance to Serena's slick corporate look and, therefore, to Serena.

As long as he doesn't focus on my tits, some sardonic corner of her mind thought. *They're just like Serena's.* Clea scowled at the inner voice; it was far too much like the recorded memories of her clone sister/mother.

Eventually they would notice; it was inevitable. But by that time they would be used to her and might comment on the resemblance, but they wouldn't be suspicious. Merely curious.

That's one of the things I actually like about humans—their willingness to explain away anything strange. From what she'd observed, on her own and through Serena's memories, they'd perform some unbelievably convoluted feats of logic to return to their everyday frame of reference. At times she found it incredible that these people had conceived and built Skynet.

The I-950 set her battered briefcase on the conference-room table and extracted a portable computer, smiling nervously at the two men as she set it up. The new corporate HQ was nothing like Serena's memories of the underground center the Connors had destroyed; it was pure minimalist functionality, the sort of "nothing" that cost a great deal of money, and left you wondering if anything as vulgar as paper ever crossed anyone's desk. Some of the people in the cubicles outside weren't even using thin-screen monitors; they were peering into the telltale blackness of vision goggles, miniature lasers painting text and diagrams directly on their retinas.

"Would you like some coffee?" the president of Cyberdyne offered. Paul Warren hefted a carafe with his own hands, considerable condescension from an executive at his level.

She shook her head and gave him a shy smile. He smiled back warmly and she knew she'd taken the right tack with him. Serena had considered initiating a romantic affair with him, but she'd miscalculated his affection for his wife. This was one instance in which Serena's mistake really didn't matter, though. The woman had had to die, even if it did turn out to be a setback in other areas.

By now, though, he must be lonely and his distress over his wife's death should be fading. Perhaps she should co-opt Serena's plan for herself. Although the very thought of intimate relations with a human revolted her.

"Welcome to Cyberdyne," Roger Colvin said. "I think, based on what I saw at the unveiling the other night, that we've got a lot to offer each other."

Clea squirmed as though pleased and allowed her face to flush as though she was embarrassed. *Don't overdo it,* she warned herself. "Thank you," she said aloud, allowing just a touch of Montana into her voice.

"I was just wondering," Warren said, "what have you named your product and have you got a copyright on it."

"I, uh, sent in the paperwork, but I hadn't heard back before I left home." She shrugged. "It may be that it hasn't caught up with me yet."

"We'll check on that for you," Colvin said. "What name have you registered it under?"

"Intellimetal," Clea said. She smiled ruefully. "That's more for what it will be one day than for what it can do now. What Mr. Hill was working with was my earliest successful prototype."

"Really," Colvin said, his voice dripping with interest.

"Uh-huh," she said, smiling. "But"—she twisted her fingers together—"I'd rather not go into detail until we've come to some sort of agreement." Clea shrugged prettily. "My uncle was a stickler for getting things in writing. Never agree to anything until you see it written down, he'd say. It always looks different then."

Warren and Colvin exchanged a glance that said, "This little lady might be inexperienced, but she's nobody's fool."

They set to work, and work it was. Clea knew exactly what she wanted, how much she wanted, and what terms she'd accept. As far as she was concerned, almost nothing was negotiable, however hard the two humans tried. Two hours later Clea typed in the last word of her "rough notes," as she called them, on her portable and handed the CEO a disk.

"There ya go," she said cheerfully. "Now I'll need to see this all written up formally before I can even begin to decide for sure what I want to do."

"Thank you," Colvin said palely.

"You're welcome." She met his eyes and leaned forward confidentially. "I would like to leave you contemplating this one little idea I had. Now, I haven't done any real special work on it, but I've been thinking about it real hard." *Watch the Montana effect,* she warned herself. She was in serious danger of enjoying her role too much.

"We'd love to hear about it," Warren said, leaning forward himself.

"Well. You know the F-101, that flying-wing stealth plane?"

The two men nodded.

"The only reason something like that can keep from crashing is because it has an onboard computer that makes thousands of adjustments a minute." Her listeners nodded again. "So I was thinking, what we need is a machine that can do that and *know* it's doing it. You know what I mean?"

Colvin and Warren exchanged nervous glances.

"A machine like that could control thousands of planes, thousands of miles apart. And not just planes, either, but tanks and gun emplacements and even battle robots." Clea sat back, having noticed long since the subtly appalled expressions on their faces. "Not detailed control—it would be a distributed system—but a strategic artificial intelligence . . . Is something wrong?"

"No, no. It sounds fascinating," Warren reassured her. "But . . . well, perhaps at some future date we could look into something like that. But right now you've put so much into developing Intellimetal that we'd like to help you with that project."

She was silent for a moment, her glance roving from one to the other. "Really?" Clea tapped her fingertips on the arms of her chair. "Because I've always thought of Cyberdyne as one of the foremost robotics specialists in the field. I had the impression that artificial intelligence was sort of your bailiwick."

"You have to understand, Ms. Bennet"—Colvin spread his hands helplessly—"that in some instances our hands are tied."

Her eyes widened. "Oh!" she said, looking from one to the other. "I see." Then she shrugged, and allowed another blush. "And here I thought I was being original."

"I'm sure that anything that comes out of that brain of yours is original, Ms. Bennet," Colvin said.

"Absolutely," Warren agreed eagerly.

Clea smiled at them. "Well then," she said, rising. "I'm sure you gentlemen have a great deal to do and I've already taken up an amazing amount of your time."

"Not at all." Colvin rose with her and extended his hand.

She shook it, smiling, and turned to Warren, who had offered his hand as well. "I'll look forward to hearing from you, then."

With a nod the I-950 preceded them out of the room and without another word or backward glance marched down the corridor toward the elevator.

Warren looked askance at the CEO and gestured toward the young woman. "Is she annoyed, or something?" he asked.

Colvin shook his head. "No, I don't think so. She may be a little socially backward. Apparently she was raised by an eccentric uncle in the wilds of Montana and they didn't get out much. Home schooling, the whole nine yards. She's never even been to a university."

"You're kidding!" Warren said, appalled.

Colvin held up his hand. "I know what you're going to say."

"Yeah, and I'm going to say it, too. Why would we want to hire some kid who's never even graduated from college, especially at the price and on the terms she's demanding? That's crazy."

"We're trying to hire her so that we can exploit this metal she's invented. You have to see this statue to believe it, Paul. It's the most amazing thing I've ever laid eyes on."

"Why don't I just hop on a plane to New York, then, and go take a peek?" Warren asked.

"Why don't you just trust me, buddy?" Colvin said, putting an arm around the president's shoulders. "I know what I'm doing here. Believe me, if we don't snap her up now somebody else will. Look, we're going to put in an escape clause, right? So we can both walk away if it doesn't work out and nobody's a loser. Right?"

"If she walks she'll take that Intellimetal with her," the president warned.

"You've gotta trust our lawyers to write a better contract than that," Colvin said with a smile.

Clea was pleased. They'd accepted her without question. For the first time in ages she felt that she'd performed well. The only downside was that they hadn't risen to the bait she'd dangled in the way she'd expected. Could it be that they really weren't involved in the Skynet project any longer?

Cyberdyne had provided a limo and driver for her and the car was waiting out front when she exited the building. She didn't even acknowledge the driver when he opened the door for her, but stepped in and settled herself for the ride back to the hotel, lost in her own thoughts.

Clea woke up lying on a sofa, its firm cushions upholstered in blue-green tweed. The room she was in appeared to be a cheaply paneled conference room, with, unusually, a large mirror in the wall opposite the couch. *No. That is one-way glass. The room is institutional; government, not corporate.*

Her eyes searched the mirror for hints of movement from a possible hidden room as she sharpened her hearing and listened.

". . . took enough hypno to knock out an elephant! I thought she'd never go down," a male voice was saying.

"Maybe there's a flaw in the delivery system," another man answered, "because she just woke up. If she'd absorbed as much of the drug as you say you gave her, she'd sleep until tomorrow night."

Clea detected movement in the mirror, as though one of the speakers had leaned forward for a better look.

Well, well. I've been kidnapped! One of Cyberdyne's more aggressive competitors, perhaps? *Or Cyberdyne itself?* She considered the idea. It would be strange if it was them. For one thing, nothing in their dossier indicated that they played such games. For another, it seemed a criminal waste of their president and CEO's time if they had intended to negotiate by force all along.

Now who else might have an interest in my little inventions? And who else could or would employ such an extreme technique as drugging and kidnapping her? Organized crime came briefly to mind, but she dismissed the idea. They were hardly into research and development.

It's much more likely to be Tricker or one of his friends, she thought. *Excellent.*

She'd been wondering where the agent had got himself to; it looked like she might be about to find out.

Clea sat up, faking a wobbliness that she in no way felt, one hand to her brow as though her head ached. Which it should, but for the computer and nanites that had worked so hard to cleanse her blood. She blinked, and narrowed her eyes as though the fluorescent light bothered her.

"Hello?" she said, sounding shaky.

"That's my cue," said one of the men.

She heard a door open and close and there was a flash of light in the mirror. Then the door to the room she was in opened and she got up from the couch quickly. The I-950 immediately sat down again, resting her head against the back of the couch, her hand over her eyes as though dizzy.

"Take it easy, miss," the man said soothingly. "Are you okay?"

"Dizzy," she murmured.

She dropped her hand as though exhausted, keeping her eyes closed for effect. But her nose and ears told her where he was, even what he'd last eaten—hamburger with some sort of hot sauce. The glimpse she'd had of him when he walked in confirmed her suspicion. He worked for the government. His clothing and appearance were so artfully average that in a crowd he would be effectively invisible. It wasn't Tricker, but he might have been a close relative.

"That will pass," the man said gently.

She heard water pouring and then felt the touch of his hand. Opening her eyes, she saw that he was offering her a glass of water; when she took it he held out two aspirin.

"For the headache I'm sure you have," he said with a sympathetic smile.

Clea accepted the pills and took them with a sip of water, studying him over the rim of the glass. He was tall and slender, with muddy hazel eyes and a narrow face; his silvering blond hair was beginning to recede and there was an element of grayness about him somehow. But his voice was pleasant, as was his manner, both conveying trustworthiness.

Which was actually quite different from Tricker, who seemed to go out of his way to be abrasive. And yet this man reminded her of no one so much as of Serena's old nemesis.

He could be dangerous if he needed to be, she thought. *Or if he wanted to be.* There was the essential resemblance; like Tricker, this man was competently ruthless. *Not unlike myself,* she thought. *They probably work for the same agency.*

Clea swallowed. "Where am I?" she asked.

He didn't answer, but sat looking at her.

"And who are you?" She pulled herself up until she was sitting straight.

"Aren't you going to ask why you're here?" he prompted.

"Well, I assume you're going to tell me," she snapped. "Or are we just going to sit and stare at each other until we starve to death? But I've got to tell you, mister, if you're looking for a ransom you've got the wrong girl! My only relative is dead and all I've got in the world is a few thousand dollars in the bank. So what's going on here?"

"That's not entirely true, Ms. Bennet, now is it?" the gray man said. "You have the house and land in Montana, don't you?"

The I-950's eyes widened quite involuntarily as her mind flashed to that empty grave in the modest country cemetery. Should she have replaced the Terminator with a human corpse? Surely they wouldn't check her background *that* thoroughly?

"Oh yes," the man continued complacently, "we know everything there is to know about you. Certainly everything that is a matter of public record." He gave her a tight little smile. "And we've come to the conclusion that only we can offer you the resources to allow your inventiveness full scope."

"Who are you?" she almost shouted. All the time thinking, *Ah, so I was right. Tricker's gang.*

"My name is Pool," he said.

"Just Pool?" Clea demanded sarcastically, remembering Tricker's insistence on being called a simple, unadorned "Tricker."

"Yes," he agreed with a slightly deprecatory smile. "Just Pool."

Clea drew in a deep breath. "And who is *we*, Pool?"

The smile broadened. "*We* are your tax dollars at work, Ms. Bennet."

Setting her jaw, Clea tilted her head at a defiant angle. Actually she was delighted; the government had to have taken over the Skynet project when Cyberdyne's second facility was destroyed . . . by the Connors, again. But a human would object to this sort of treatment . . .

"And if I don't *want* to work for the government?" she asked.

Pool shrugged. "Then we would have to tell Vladimir Hill that the wonderful new material you've been letting him play with as though it was clay is one of the most carcinogenic materials ever devised." He paused as if to gauge her reaction.

Clea gave him one. "Nonsense!" she snapped, sitting forward. Then she looked queasy and leaned back again. "What are you talking about?"

"He'll probably be dead by next year," Pool said. "But that would allow him plenty of time to sue you. And, of course, there would probably be charges of criminal negligence. You'd probably do jail time." His eyes cooled. "In fact, you can count on that. And afterward, well, Cyberdyne wouldn't touch you or Intellimetal with a ten-foot pole, and neither would anyone else." He spread his hands. "Which would leave you with us. But not before we both lost a lot of time and effort and money. So why not just cooperate and we'll all be happy?"

Clea allowed herself to look shaken; her computer dropped her circulation slightly so that her face would go pale.

"Does Vladimir have . . . cancer?" Her eyes widened. "Do I?" she asked, her voice quavering.

"We don't know, actually, your tests aren't back. But the odds are good. As for Hill, in good conscience, of course, we can't let him remain at risk. We'll warn him quite soon, and if it's caught early enough there's always a chance that he might survive. You, too, of course. But we think you'd be better off if you suddenly became unavailable. Don't you?"

She nodded, looking shell-shocked, or so the mirror told her.

He smiled, an avuncular smile this time; Pool seemed to have quite a repertoire. "Very wise," he murmured. "You won't regret it, I'm sure. Our terms won't be quite as generous as Cyberdyne's, but our facilities are the best and our research budget is virtually unlimited." He stood, smiling down at her. "Why don't you lie back down and get some rest," he advised. "That drug can pack quite a punch. Later on someone will come and take you to your room, where you can have something to eat and relax. Then tomorrow we'll outfit you for your new job and by evening you'll be on your way."

"On my way where?" she asked, trying to sound crushed. Instead, her computer component was suppressing glee; this was turning out *exactly* as planned. And if it hadn't been *sixty-seven percent probability of terminating all units here and escaping without irreparable damage*, she calculated automatically.

His lips jerked into a mirthless smile, and he turned to the door. "I'd rather not say," he told her. Then he walked out the door.

She heard the click of a lock and then his receding footsteps. Clea covered her mouth as though feeling sick and leaned over, hanging her head. Then she lay down and, turning her back to the mirror, began to sob quietly for the benefit of whoever still lurked in the room behind the mirror.

It was too late now to do anything about her missing "uncle," she decided. Agents might still be loitering around asking questions, making it very risky to fill the empty hole.

I'll just have to take a chance on it, she thought. *But even if they do open the grave to find it empty, that proves nothing.* At least, nothing against her. Even so, it bothered her.

It was very hard, she reflected, to know when to stop refining a plan. *I should inform Alissa of the latest developments . . .*

CRAIG KIPFER'S OFFICE, SOUTHERN CALIFORNIA

ALTERNATE USES FOR INTELLIMETAL

- **Bullets: Intellimetal, once fired, will expand with the heat of the explosion, mushrooming into the most effective shape possible. On striking the target, it will break apart into smaller pieces, each piece seeking the primary electrical source in the body: the brain. Once there, each individual piece of Intellimetal will respond to the brain's electrical patterns by oscillating at a very fast rate as it seeks to rebond with other pieces of Intellimetal. This will effectively liquefy the brain.**

- **Mineworms: These antipersonnel devices will be planted like seeds in rows, while the "farmer" is protected by spe-**

cial gloves and boots, possibly special coveralls as well. When stepped on, the rods of Intellimetal will activate and burrow upward through boot, flesh, and bone, again in search of the body's primary electrical source. As an additional advantage, when anyone subsequently touches the body the activated mineworms will try to burrow into this subject as well.

Craig Kipfer sat back, his lips pursed as though to whistle but emitting no sound. There was some additional stuff in the girl's notes about possible security uses for her invention, but it was her ideas for weapons that both fascinated and chilled him.

He'd been around long enough to know that women could outdo men in viciousness; even so, he found it hard to associate these ideas with that young woman's lovely face. It proved once again the truth of an adage he'd been taught when he first started in this service. Beauty is a weapon. Feel free to use it, never let it use you.

From the moment he heard about that statue in New York, he'd been interested in Clea Bennet. And when she began throwing out ideas that paralleled the Skynet project during her meeting with Colvin and Warren, he knew that he wanted her to work for him, else he'd never have ordered her picked up. But this! *Talk about a bonus,* he thought.

Kipfer sat forward in his chair and pulled out his keyboard. He'd been of two minds about the woman; keep or kill. Pool was waiting for his orders.

Send her to Antarctica, he typed, then sent the message. After this, he'd hear about her in progress reports or not at all. Until, that is, such time as he had to review his decision to let her live.

RED SEAL BASE, ANTARCTICA

They arrived at night, delivered by an Osprey tilt rotor with no markings and no way to see out from the passenger compartment; Clea and two rather groggy-looking men—or perhaps they were just sullen. She decided to imitate their look and manner, adding a bit of frightened little girl to her demeanor.

They were hustled through the freezing darkness to a building like a shed. Clea had the impression of a vast reflective whiteness as they rushed through the dark, as though the surface of the moon were under their feet.

Once inside the shed, they were made to go down a flight of stairs into a small, unfurnished room. Two of the men from the plane were with them, silent, their eyes always moving among the three of them, as though they expected something to happen, both holding Ingram machine pistols.

The room began to move and Clea gasped. The men glanced at her apathetically, the guards sharply. She looked at them as though she wanted to say something, but then changed her mind.

Serena had definitely had the easier part to play, she decided. All she'd had to do was portray a ruthlessly efficient human. Whereas Clea was trying to convey inexperience, naïveté, brilliance, and humanity. She'd have to work at simplifying her portrayal as she went along. This was tedious.

She didn't know a great deal about Antarctica, but she rather thought that digging this deeply into it was something forbidden. She did know that according to international treaty, it was supposed to be free of military influence. This installation would seem to put the lie to that pretty notion.

It suddenly occurred to her that the more she interacted with humans, the more her thoughts became like Serena's. *Either my brain is overcoming any damage done by my accelerated growth, or I'm doomed to fail,* she thought sourly. *Or both.*

She wanted to contact Alissa but hadn't because her captors might be able to detect such communication. Better to wait until she knew more. But she resented the break in contact.

The elevator finally stopped and they were led out into a corridor lined with doors that had numbers and message pockets on them. The floor tiles and walls were beige and the ceiling had acoustic tiles and fluorescent lights. They could be anywhere on earth rather than literally at the end of the earth.

The three of them were marched down the corridor until they came to a door like all the others. One of the guards knocked, then opened the door, motioning them inside.

It looked like a small meeting room; a chalkboard and desk were placed at one end of the room with several rows of chairs in front of them. A middle-aged man in good physical shape sat on the edge of the desk; he raised his head to look them over.

Tricker! Clea thought, almost delighted to see him. It was like unexpectedly finding an old friend. Then, *He'll recognize me!* she thought. But he didn't seem to at the moment. He appeared bored, so much so that even though he was looking at them, he wasn't really seeing them. *I suppose I can keep out of his way.* Time would tell if he was going to be a problem. *I'll think of it as a challenge,* she decided.

Somehow he seemed to wear his tan chinos and plain gray flannel shirt as though they were a uniform. Casting a brief look at the guards, he nodded and the two men went out, closing the door behind them.

"Welcome to Red Seal Base," he said. "My name is Tricker. I'm the chief of security and I'll be your supervisor here. If you have any problems, or needs that we aren't meeting—and I mean anything—come and see me."

He looked them over as though trying to ascertain if they'd understood him, then he continued. "You're probably tired, so I won't keep you tonight. Tomorrow morning at 0800 hours I'll take you to the cafeteria and introduce you around. After breakfast, we'll take a brief tour of the base. It will be a brief tour, as you aren't allowed into most sectors. Then I'll show you to your own labs and you can get settled. After dinner, we'll have another meeting and you can tell me about anything that you need that we haven't yet supplied."

Tricker paused, assessing each of them with cool blue eyes. " 'It's important that you understand from the outset that you are not to discuss anyone's work with them, or to discuss your own work with anyone else."

Clea saw the two men glance at each other.

"Obviously," Tricker said, not even trying to hide his exasperation, "if you're working together, that doesn't apply as far as your own work goes. If you find this too confining come and speak to me and we'll see what we can set up. Do not"—he held up a warning finger—"simply decide to break this rule. You would regret that, I promise you." He looked at them; they looked at him. "Do you understand?"

"Yes," they mumbled.

"There are sandwiches and coffee in your rooms for tonight," Tricker told them, "but generally you'll eat in the cafeteria with everyone else. We'll do our best to make you comfortable here, folks. How comfortable is up to you."

Maybe he's asleep, the I-950 thought, surprised that he hadn't responded to her appearance. He certainly sounded it.

"The people outside will escort you to your rooms," Tricker said, rising. "You'll receive a wake-up call at 0700. Be ready for me to pick you up an hour later. Good night."

The two men and Clea looked at one another, then turned and toddled to the door, somewhat awkward in their heavy clothing. Outside two men and a woman were waiting for them, smiling for all they were worth.

"Welcome to Red Seal Base," they said cheerfully and more or less in unison.

"You must be Clea Bennet." The woman stepped forward offering her hand. "I'm Josephine Lowe, your buddy."

The I-950 just stared at her. This was almost unbelievably presumptuous, beyond anything she'd yet experienced from humans.

"You know, like in swimming class or fire drill," Josephine continued. "We're in a dangerous place, you know, and so they feel we should all have someone looking out for us; that way, if we have to evacuate in a hurry no one will get left behind. Unless"—she chuckled—"both buddies are together."

Lowe was plump, and crammed into a belted gray jumpsuit with sneakers on her feet. She was about forty-five with short blond hair brushed back from her rather ordinary face. She wore no makeup.

"I'm right next door to you," Josephine was saying.

Somehow Clea didn't find this reassuring in the least. She looked around and saw the two men going off with their buddies.

"You look exhausted, you poor thing," Clea's buddy said. She lifted her arm as though she was going to put it around the I-950's shoulders but didn't actually touch her. "Let me show you to your room. A little supper and a good night's sleep will do wonders for you."

Ah, Clea thought, *I look exhausted. That's why Tricker didn't recognize me.* Well, she'd have to see what she could do to continue looking mousy and uninteresting. Meanwhile she'd have to see what she could learn from this source. "Have you been here long?" she asked Josephine, smiling tentatively.

"Oh! Just ages, honey! At first I thought I'd go stir-crazy, but then I really got to like it here. We've got a pretty good mix of people. You'll see . . ." A hopeful note. "Do you like bridge?"

Clea followed her down the hallway listening to her nonstop chatter and wondering if, in fact, poor Josephine had gone stir-crazy and just didn't know it.

The cafeteria was the single largest room on the base, Tricker told them. With the exception of the warehouse, naturally.

Clea found it almost excessively institutional, with its rows of long, Formica-topped tables on either side of a wide central aisle. There were the same beige floor tiles and walls with the inevitable bulletin board for decoration. At the head of the room one picked up a tray and utensils and dragged it along to the place where food was dispensed. It was rather noisy, and smelled like a medium-priced chain restaurant; Applebee's, say.

The ceiling lights mimicked natural daylight, as did most of the lights on the base, so Tricker had told them. It didn't surprise her that the humans needed to be indulged this way. They were animals, after all, and six months of night or day was not a natural part of their cycle.

The people in the big room seemed to take a polite interest in the three new arrivals, watching them surreptitiously as they got their food and found seats. As Clea moved to join her fellow newcomers she found herself greeted with friendly smiles and nods. The I-950 found them rather . . . what was the word?

Ah. Creepy.

She joined the conversation already in progress at the table Tricker had chosen. He glanced at her as she set down her tray and continued to watch her as she pretended not to notice. When she looked up she smiled at him, then let her face drop as he continued to stare at her.

"What?" she asked defensively.

He spooned up some oatmeal before answering her. "You look familiar," he said.

Clea looked at him askance. "Is that a line?"

He swallowed the oatmeal and took a sip of coffee before he answered her, his gaze never wavering. "No. I've met you. I'm sure of it."

Shaking her head, Clea told him, "I don't think so, Mr. Tricker."

"Just Tricker," he said.

"Uh-huh. Well, *Tricker,*" she said, leaning forward, "have you ever been to Montana?"

He shook his head, spooning up more oatmeal.

"Well, except for one trip to New York and one trip to L.A., both in the last month, I've never been anywhere else. So I don't know how you could have met me. Do you?" She widened her eyes at him and took a sip of coffee.

The two men who'd arrived with her turned their heads back and forth between them. "Is this important?" one of them asked tentatively.

Clea thought that the fact he asked at all hinted at a habitual arrogance that circumstances had temporarily muted.

"No," Tricker answered. "Not at all." With a last, indecipherable look at Clea, he returned to his lecture about the base's rules.

"Ah, I see we have some new prisoners, Tricker."

The man's voice had a thick German accent and came from behind the I-950. *South German,* her computer half supplied helpfully. *Within fifty kilometers of Vienna, but not actually in Vienna. Originally middle-class.* She turned to look and found a tall, muscular blond man looking down at them.

Kurt Viemeister! she thought, and her heart leapt, like a human girl meeting her favorite musician.

Serena had decided that Viemeister was insane because of his extreme hatred for certain classes of human being and had stopped associating with him. But Clea had always felt her parent/sister was wrong.

If the scientist hated humans, well, so did Skynet, and so did the

Infiltrators, for that matter. Of course, they hated *all* humans, and wanted to exterminate them, but why was that reason to judge Dr. Viemeister for only hating some?

Though she was painfully aware that Serena entertained almost fond feelings for humans.

Subversive, misguided, and a failure, Clea thought dismissively. *She* intended to encourage Viemeister's efforts for Skynet. It didn't matter if he hated humans, but making Skynet sentient did.

Viemeister put his tray down beside Clea, giving her a pleasant smile. "Aren't you going to introduce us?"

Tricker took a sip of coffee and looked thoughtfully into the distance while the three newcomers watched him. Viemeister buttered his toast and salted his omelette as though he'd never said a word.

Clea rolled her eyes and gave a crisp "tsk!" Then she turned to Viemeister. "I'm Clea Bennet," she said, offering her hand. "From Montana."

"Charmed," he said, taking her hand gently and giving her a warm smile. He looked at the two men opposite them.

"Joel Gibson," a heavyset middle-aged man said.

"Maxwell Massey," his friend said. Maxwell had the dark looks of an East Indian.

"So what have they got on you folks?" Kurt said cheerfully.

Clea blinked as she realized his accent was much less thick than it had been. Serena had always suspected that he affected it. What he'd said was as interesting as how he'd said it, too. She glanced at the two men.

"See, now this is where you have to watch out," Tricker interrupted. "If any of you answer that question, you may find yourselves segueing into a conversation about your work. Now, what did I say about discussing your work?"

"But I already know something about Mr. Viemeister's specialty," Clea said eagerly. She turned to the scientist. "My uncle was a great admirer of yours and I've read all of your published work." Obviously gushing was the right tack to take with him; he fairly glowed in her infrared vision. "Your ideas on—"

"Hey!" Tricker interrupted. He pointed his spoon at her. "That's something you and I will have to discuss *in private.* Do you know why?" He drew out the last word.

Clea rolled her eyes again. "Because otherwise we'll be discussing Mr. Viemeister's work and we're not supposed to discuss one another's work." She raised her brows at him. "Did I get it right, teacher?"

"Yup," he said. Tricker scraped his bowl and ate the last spoonful.

"If you're granted permission to talk about your work to one another, you can yak about it all you want in private." He rotated his spoon, indicating the room around them. "Never in here. In here, none of us have jobs. *Comprende?*"

"Yeah," she said, letting a little insolence seep into her voice. Beside her Viemeister seemed amused.

"Great! If you folks are ready we should get started. I know you all have a lot to do today." Tricker rose and looked at them expectantly.

"I haven't finished my coffee," the I-950 hazarded.

"Well, too bad. Chop-chop, Ms. Bennet." He gave Viemeister an artificial smile. "Nice seeing you, Kurt." Then he turned on his heel and walked away.

Gibson and Massey scrambled to follow him, but Clea lingered, taking a last sip of her coffee. Then she gave Viemeister a conspiratorial smile, rose, folded her napkin, and slowly sauntered after the men.

Her walk gave the scientist something to watch if he was so inclined.

Kurt watched the young woman walk away. It looked as though the long dry spell was about to end. And to end very pleasantly indeed. As the girl followed Tricker and his chumps out the door, she glanced at him over her shoulder and gave him a delightful little smile. If only she were a blonde, she'd be a perfect Aryan.

Yes, definitely, things were looking up.

CHAPTER 19

Meg Horton, secretary to Roger Colvin, CEO of Cyberdyne, sighed as she looked at the tower of mail on her desk. It seemed the stack got bigger every day.

Taking her seat, she began sorting the mail into separate piles. Most of it was junk, and could be disposed of without opening. But one large envelope had a note written on the front.

Here's the material you requested.
Thank you for your interest.
Jesse Hooper

Inside was a stack of brochures from the Utah Tourist Bureau. Meg frowned, checking the address on the envelope. It was indeed addressed to Roger Colvin. The boss must be thinking of going skiing. Or turning Mormon. She added the material to the personal pile to go directly to his office and discarded the envelope.

Inside the envelope were several insectlike machines. As soon as the envelope hit the wastebasket they emerged and climbed out, dropping to the floor and scurrying to the nearest dark corner as they'd been programmed to do.

In Utah, the Terminator that had been assigned to monitor the bugs' progress took over their function, ordering one to remain below the secretary's desk while directing the others to various positions around the perimeter of the room to give the Terminator a broad view of the office.

It saw that the gap between the door to the CEO's office and the thick carpet inside was too small for the bug to slip through; the T-101 continued searching. In the ceiling there appeared to be a ventilator cover. That would be optimal placement. Once they were in the ventilation system, the bugs would have access to the whole building.

Soon it had one of the bugs stationed in Colvin's office and had sent the others off to explore and map the whole facility. Then it alerted the I-950 that the bugs were safely implanted. It arranged for their input to be recorded, then turned to other tasks.

Paul Warren looked up from the screen at his friend—the CEO of Cyberdyne—his face split by a delighted grin.

"I can't believe these numbers!" he said.

Roger Colvin grinned back at him. "Neither can I."

Their automated factories were a complete success, not one break-down in their pilot plant in over a year. Production clicked along 24/7 at a fraction of the cost of a human-run production line. Granted, it would take a while to amortize the capital costs, but with a guaranteed market like the Pentagon, that was a sucker bet. Best of all: No employ-ees equaled no unions and no support infrastructure for people, and all this minimized environmental impact—not that the environmental-ists appreciated that.

The intercom on Colvin's desk gave a warning chirp.

"Mr. Colvin," Roger's secretary said, "there's a Mr. Pool here to see you."

"Just Pool," a voice said.

"Sir!" they heard the secretary snap.

The office door opened and a tall, rather nondescript man of middle age entered. Behind him Colvin's secretary hovered, looking outraged.

"It's all right, Meg," Roger told her; he looked at Warren, then back at the intruder. "You must be the new guy," he said wearily.

"Pool," the man said, nodding in agreement.

"Just Pool?" Warren asked with more than a touch of sarcasm.

"Yes." Pool sat down without waiting for an invitation and opened his briefcase. "You might like to take a look at this," he said, handing Colvin a CD.

The CEO took it, his eyes never leaving Pool's. The government liai-son nodded once. "Sure," Colvin said, and replaced the one he'd been running. When he accessed the disc it showed a recording, obviously made with a high-end video camera, of what at first appeared to be one of their automated factories.

"Wait a minute," he said, leaning forward. He tapped a few keys and the picture froze. "Paul, take a look at this." He swung the monitor around.

"Hey!" the president said after a moment's study. "What's going on here? That isn't ours!"

"You guys building your own now?" Colvin asked coldly.

Pool looked back at him for a moment, then switched his glance to the president. "No," he said. "But unfortunately the situation is out of control. Factories like these are sprouting up all over, especially in the third world. Many of them," Pool continued with careful emphasis, "are making munitions."

"NATO. They're like . . . spy central. What are you doing about it?"

"Unfortunately there's very little we can do at this point." Pool closed his briefcase. "We know you're not involved," he continued, "because we've investigated. Thus far we haven't been able to pin it down, but you're right, unfortunately—it's more likely to be one of our 'friends' at NATO than anyone else."

"We're losing money here . . ." Warren began.

"You could always *try* suing," Pool suggested. "France is always a nice place to visit, though it would be a pity to spend your time there in a courtroom or locked up in a lawyer's office." He shrugged. "And I understand they're open to fiscal persuasion in the Balkan countries. But the problem is a little too universal for you to expect much success, I'm afraid."

Colvin sat back in his chair, genuinely shocked. They'd lost their exclusive contract. All their research and development, all their expansion plans, were just so much wasted time and money. They'd borne the start-up costs and someone else was walking off with the profit.

"How?" Warren demanded. "How did this happen? And how long has it been going on?"

"Almost from the beginning," Pool said. "That's why we assumed you two had something to do with it. Or at least someone in your organization. But we've found no corroborating evidence of that." He sounded regretful.

Colvin grunted like a man kicked in the stomach. The only thing they had going for them now was their contract with the government. He covered his eyes with one hand. "Where the hell is Sarah Connor?" he suddenly blurted. "This is certainly a Connor-sized disaster."

If he hadn't been looking directly at Pool he would have missed the moment when the agent froze.

"What?" the CEO snapped.

"Mr. Colvin?" Pool asked politely.

Colvin glanced at Warren, then back at Pool. He sat up straight, almost certain he could feel himself going pale. "Well?" he asked, his voice hoarse. "Where is she?"

Pool sat still for a moment, then he said, "We don't know, actually."

The announcement threw both executives into motion. Warren flung himself up and walked to the window, his back to the room. Colvin rose and, placing his hands on his desk, leaned forward slowly. "You what?" he asked quietly, one eyebrow raised.

Warren turned back to them. "Could she . . . ?" He waved a hand helplessly.

"Have leaked the information?" Pool asked. "No. Definitely not. We knew where she was when the problem began."

Colvin dropped back into his chair. "Could she have . . . associates?" he asked.

Pool shook his head. "Unlikely. Connor has always been a lone wolf. The degree and speed of this proliferation argue for some sort of organization. Frankly, gentlemen, we're completely out of ideas, which is why we decided to consult you."

"Oh, that's flattering." Colvin sneered. "The question is who benefits, and how?"

"Yeah," Warren said. He shrugged, then sat down himself. "If someone was blowing the factories up, I'd blame the Luddites. But I don't see how making this technology universally available fits in with their obsession."

"Well"—Pool rose—"keep thinking about it, gentlemen. If you have any ideas please feel free to contact me." He placed a plain business card on the CEO's desk. Like Tricker's, it bore only an E-mail address. Pool glanced from one man to the other, nodded once, and left without another word.

The two men were silent for forty-five seconds; then Warren spoke. "We are fucked," he said quietly.

UTAH

Alissa frowned. Some part of her had expected Tricker; had hoped for Tricker might be more accurate. Apparently this Pool was Tricker's replacement. He certainly seemed to be the same sort of human. It also seemed that the government's interest in Cyberdyne was limited to projects other than Skynet.

Both she and Clea had estimated a high probability that Intellimetal would prove a strong lure to Cyberdyne, which more or less ensured government interest. Her sister's casual mention of a Skynet-like entity was intended to prove irresistible to whoever had taken over the project, a doubly baited hook.

What they hadn't expected was that Clea would disappear so suddenly and so thoroughly. When she had vanished after her interview with Colvin and Warren, the little I-950 had naturally assumed that the government had intervened. But she had no idea of exactly where or from whom that intervention had come. The mysterious Tricker, she'd supposed. But he proved impossible to locate.

Now, with this Pool, Alissa hoped she finally had a lead.

She'd had some of her bugs hack into Cyberdyne's security system and through the company's cameras she watched the agent's progress through the building and out into the parking lot.

As he drove off she took note of the car's license-plate number and started a search. The address that came up wasn't very informative, a U.S. government motor pool, but it was a place to start.

She'd assign one of the T-101s. They were good at worming their way through bureaucratic baffle gab.

Swinging her legs and putting a finger to her chin, Alissa considered her sister's possible fate. It seemed unlikely she'd been murdered. Unless they'd completely destroyed her head, the computer part of her would have made contact. Unless they'd buried her in the equivalent of a Faraday cage, which was astronomically unlikely, it should have been possible to locate her.

No, a living Clea was somewhere shielded, or somewhere she feared that any attempt to communicate would reveal her true nature. This silence was more likely an act of will than a sign of misfortune.

In other words, things were probably going as planned. Except for the uncertainty and the Connors still being alive and on the loose. Alissa's lips thinned in displeasure. She needed to enter her next phase so that she'd be in a position to take care of them.

There would be no better time than the present.

RED SEAL BASE, ANTARCTICA

Clea was enjoying her new lab; it had all the equipment she could ever use, and any materials she wanted, however exotic, toxic, or illegal, were provided within forty-eight hours. She'd tested this and didn't even try to hide her glee when she was presented with some obscure and costly element.

Tricker had cautioned her that she couldn't continue to make such requests without producing tangible results. Clea had countered by giving him an extremely long and involved lecture on the advantages of pure science. He'd come as close to running away as she'd ever seen him.

The lab itself was small, but its efficient design made up for the lack of space. Its white walls and gleaming metal surfaces somehow gave it the illusion of size, though its dimensions were more those of a large walk-in closet. The overhead lights were the kind that mimicked natural light, making it more comfortable still. It suited her.

Meanwhile, her research into the T-1000 matrix was going very well and she was able to keep most of the work she was doing secret from the humans while seeming to produce a lot of new data. Their expectations, naturally, were based on what they thought a human could accomplish, so that, all in all, they were thrilled with her.

All of the scientists were watched all of the time. So the first thing she'd done was to spend long periods just sitting and thinking, or staring into a microscope. Once she knew they had a fair-sized archive of such activity, she became more active.

Her first real effort was to create some bugs, fiddling with the components so that no one thing seemed connected to another, then put them together as she walked from her lab to the cafeteria, or to her room; looking for all the world as though she was picking at her fingernails. When they were complete she set them loose in the ventilation system. One of her bugs was programmed to lurk in the tape banks and at her signal to run archival footage of her doing nothing at all.

They'd already collected some fascinating information for her, both about the other scientists and the base staff, as well as confirming her suspicions about being under observation. The entertainment value of spying on everyone else didn't make up for the lack of communication with the outside world, but she was working on that.

As part of her plan to keep the humans off balance regarding her real work . . .

She had a dozen projects going forward more or less simultaneously. She destroyed a great deal of what she accomplished without storing the information on their computers. She had her own, after all.

But she had to be careful. They sorted trash here with obsessive-compulsive thoroughness. Therefore they knew to the ounce what materials had been used and how. So she used only minute bits of things, working at speeds no human could duplicate on things the human eye could barely see. So far they suspected nothing.

One of her side projects was the creation of what she hoped would one day be a nano-machine. Right now it was huge, easily visible with the naked eye if you knew where to look. And, unfortunately, its range of functioning was extremely simple, requiring several to actually accomplish a task of any significance. About a dozen together were not much smaller than the bugs she and Alissa had created for surveillance. But they were much more complex and with time she was certain she'd find ways to diminish their size without losing utility.

Clea was gearing them toward affecting biological processes because she had a plan. But the one thing that was difficult to get here were animal test subjects. When she'd submitted that request Tricker showed up to suggest that she concentrate on Intellimetal.

Clea had carefully explained about how carcinogenic the stuff was and how, though she was trying hard to make it less dangerous, there was only so much a computer simulation could do. He'd stared at her for a long time, then said he'd see what he could do.

She could see why Serena had liked Tricker. The I-950 found it amusing to manipulate him, and moving him to sarcastic exasperation was actually pleasurable. In this she knew she was definitely becoming more like Serena; she found that reassuring *and* disquieting.

Checking a gauge, she made a note, solely to satisfy the watchers.

The I-950 had to admit that though she liked her lab she was feeling slightly claustrophobic. It wasn't being underground so much as it was the lack of information. The base was completely cut off from the rest of the world; no TV or radio, no telephone calls, and no Internet. This despite the very reasonable argument that cutting them off from observing the progress in their individual fields might slow their work, or even render it useless.

She'd been told that those who complained to Tricker had been given his *look* and told that they'd better hope not.

That Tricker, she thought with a secretive smile, *always trying to intimidate.*

Everyone treated the agent as though he was a power in the community, but the I-950 knew that the agent was in no way involved in decisions regarding the fate of the imprisoned scientists. *Well, perhaps as an end point,* she conceded. Though she had no evidence of that. But otherwise he had only a little more freedom than they did.

Kurt Viemeister had told her that Tricker was being punished for something and that was why he was here. The idea that the abrasive agent was subject to someone else's whim tickled her.

But she didn't actually know whether to be pleased or distressed that the agent was nearby. On the plus side, she knew where he was and what he was doing. On the negative, he was much too close to Skynet.

Clea glanced at her watch. It was almost time for her to meet Kurt for dinner. The I-950 was working covertly with Viemeister on his project and had put in a request to make it official. She had every expectation that it would be approved.

Hadn't she laid the groundwork for this long ago?

Her relationship with the human was surprisingly satisfying. He was a brilliant conversationalist and hearing his ideas about how he was planning to create the intelligence that would be Skynet was deliciously exciting. Her computer could barely restrain her emotional responses to him.

Instinctively the I-950 had been reluctant to try sex so far. Though she was mostly meat herself, the act itself had seemed a little *too* animal. However, Viemeister had taught Skynet to talk and to think, and so he was like the creator of her god, a hero to all her kind. In other words, more than merely human—an opinion which precisely corresponded with his own outlook. Moreover, something about him strongly appealed to her and she found herself slowly succumbing to his persuasion.

Of course he'd assumed her reluctance was due to her being a virgin. A quaint notion that she'd allowed him to keep. He'd asked her for the information and she'd provided it, finding it somewhat amusing that while it made him no less determined to have his way, it caused his manner to change entirely. Clea had decided it was probably best to let him think of her as young and naive.

It didn't hurt to have Tricker thinking of her that way, too. Especially since he continued to look at her suspiciously when he met her. He had told the I-950 that she resembled someone he'd known, but she sensed that he hadn't yet connected her to Serena.

But she'd been careful to keep her manner and her voice as different from her parent as she could. Still, she watched him carefully. After all, even Serena had been wary of his intelligence.

She hopped from her stool and headed toward the door. So far there was no need for her to do anything about him. When there was a need, she'd find a way. Clea snapped off the lights.

She found Kurt in the cafeteria. Seated alone, as usual. He'd once told her that he'd discouraged the other scientists from socializing with him.

When she'd asked him why, he said, "Because they're not very bright outside their own little field, and as people they're not interesting."

So she'd asked him, "Should I be flattered because you think I'm both intelligent and interesting? Or should I just assume you want to jump my bones?"

He'd laughed and assured her it was the former. She didn't believe him naturally, but took note that he could be diplomatic when he wanted to be.

Now she watched him watching her approach, and something in his eyes evoked a sensation of warmth below her waistband. The scrubbers stopped it, of course, but it had been very pleasant while it lasted. She gave him a smile, bold and shy at once, and kept walking, though with slightly more swing to her hips.

This was going to be an interesting evening. And . . . well, Viemeister was Skynet's creator, not Skynet . . . so it wouldn't be *quite* like incest.

■ ■ ■

Clea was feeling oddly pleased with herself as she went to confront Tricker. Every now and again a sense of well-being would sneak up on her. She knew that her processors were scrubbing endorphins by the bucket out of her system. If she'd known sex was so pleasant she'd have tried it much sooner. Though she suspected that the right partner was important.

The I-950 knocked on the agent's door and opened it without waiting for an invitation.

Tricker looked up, his blue eyes unwelcoming. "Yeah?" he snarled.

Clea gave him a dazzling smile and entered his office, leaving the door open behind her. "I was wondering if you'd heard anything about my request?" she chirped.

"Which request was that? You're pretty much a never-ending fountain of gimmees."

She pouted, then smiled at him. "My request to work with Kurt Viemeister," she said. "Has it been approved?"

"You really ought to stay away from that guy," Tricker said. "You're kinda young for him, for one thing."

"We've gotten very . . . close," Clea told him, and blushed, smiling at him.

Tricker held up a hand. "I don't want to know." He pulled forward a set of papers. "Your request has been approved. But you'll need to sign these waivers."

"Really?" she said, taking them and looking them over. "What's the point of that?"

"So that you'll know how serious what you're dealing with is." He stared at her, his gaze impossible to interpret.

Clea laughed. "What are you going to do to me if I tell someone about what I'm doing?" she asked. "Send me to Antarctica?"

"You never know." He sat forward in his chair, picking up a pen and offering it to her.

Clea rolled her eyes and took it. She signed the papers and handed them back to him. "I have another request to make."

"Surprise, surprise," he muttered.

"I'm finding it harder and harder to endure being indoors all the time," she said. "It's like the walls and ceiling are closing in on me."

"Hey, baby, it's cold outside," Tricker quipped.

Clea waved that aside. "I'm from Montana. Cold doesn't frighten me. But being closed up like this does. I *need* to get outside. I'd like to combine my time outdoors with a project I've thought up. I want to study some of the seals that live nearby."

Tricker sighed. He had a steady stream of scientists wanting to get away from the base. But not one of them had suggested simply going out for a nature walk. "There are plenty of scientists on this continent studying seals," he began.

"And it wouldn't hurt anything to have one more." She looked him in the eye. "Please," she said quietly. "I wouldn't have come to you about this except that it's really becoming a problem for me. I'm just not used to being indoors all the time like this. These other people have probably never been on a hike in their lives. I grew up in the mountains, and they don't call Montana the Big Sky Country for nothing." She let a few tears wet her eyelashes and swallowed hard. "I *need* to get outside," she whispered.

And she did. Not for the reasons she was alluding to, but to further her plans, to test her new micromachines on a living subject. And hopefully to send messages to her sister through a specially designed radio collar she intended to put on some lucky seal.

Tricker rolled his eyes. "So submit a request," he said. "I'll send it up the pipe."

"Thank you," she said, endeavoring to look more misty-eyed than ever.

"Hey, I'm not promising you anything."

"I know. But if you put your recommendation on it they'll take that into consideration, won't they?"

He just looked at her. She smiled slightly, and lifting her hand slightly, she turned and walked away.

Had she overplayed it? Time would tell. She thought she would get her way in this. If for no other reason than that he'd want to know what she was up to.

CHAPTER 20

Dieter entered the living room, where John half lay on the couch, reading a manual on source codes, a beam of bright sunlight spearing through one of the high clerestory windows to bring out the slight reddish hints in his dark hair. The Austrian dropped a package into the young man's lap.

John started as though he'd been asleep and looked from the package to von Rossbach. "What's this?" he asked.

"A package," Dieter said, with a slight edge of sarcasm.

John snorted. "Thanks!" he said, and rose. "I'll be in my room if you want me."

Sarah came in just as he was leaving and he leaned over on his way out to kiss her cheek. Her eyes widened and she turned to watch him go, then turned back to von Rossbach, her eyebrows raised in inquiry.

"Something came in the mail from that girl in Boston," he explained, sitting down in one of the leather chairs, the rest of the mail in his lap.

"Ahhhh," Sarah said thoughtfully. She moved slowly into the room. "What girl?"

This time Dieter's brows rose. "He didn't tell you about her?"

Trying to keep the hurt out of her expression, Sarah sat next to the big Austrian. "Uh, no." Her mouth twisted ruefully. "He *is* seventeen, and this *is* a girl and I *am* his mother . . ." She sighed. "I guess it's only natural he'd want to keep her to himself."

Dieter looked at her sympathetically. "But you're hurt anyway." As far as he could tell, they were unusually close. It was probable that until now they'd shared everything.

Sarah was quiet for a moment, then she wrinkled her nose at him. "A little. Maybe." Then she sighed. "It annoys me that I am, though, because, really, I'm pleased that he has someone. It would be nice if she were nearby . . ." She leaned toward him. "Tell me about her."

He shrugged his massive shoulders. "There's not much I can tell you," he said. "She's somebody he recruited on-line to keep an eye out for mysterious doings. Then, when we went to the U.S., he took her and her team the Terminator's CPU. She's a student at MIT," he added. "And clearly, something clicked between them."

"Hmmph," she said. "I guess I'll have to go to the source."

John closed the door to his room, tore open the box that Wendy had sent him, and pulled out her letter.

Hi, Sweetie, she'd written.

Well, that's flattering, he thought. One kiss . . . *On the other hand, we felt close right off.* Evidently three months' separation hadn't altered her feelings—and that was *extremely* reassuring. He read on:

> Some of us went to New York this week to attend the New Day show. That's the show that Ron Labane of the New Luddites hosts. It was wonderful! I can't begin to tell you how inspiring I find him. I wish you could have been with us. About a hundred of us from MIT went down in buses.

A hundred? John reread that, shocked. *A hundred MIT students went to the New Luddite show?* Those people must be more powerful than he'd thought.

The idea shook him. He'd assumed the group would be just another flash in the pan, a this-year's-cause sort of thing. Certainly not the kind of thing that would appeal to really intelligent people. *Like Wendy,* he thought, troubled. He straightened the folds of her letter and continued reading.

> I'm more convinced than ever that his brand of intelligent Luddism is the answer to so many of our problems: pollution, poverty, overpopulation. I have to confess to you right now that I took the pledge.

John looked up from her letter, frowning. She took "the pledge"? What the hell did that mean? He didn't think she drank.

> In case you're wondering just what I've pledged, I feel a little awkward about telling you. I know I should have discussed it with you, though that might be presumptuous of me. And maybe you'll say I was swept away by the enthusiasm of the crowd. But I did take it, and I mean to keep my word.

In case you haven't heard of the pledge, it's a promise to have no more than two children. If I divorce and remarry and my second husband hasn't any children, then I'm allowed to have one with him. Though ideally I would have had my tubes tied after I had my second child.

The hard truth is, the only way we're going to reduce our population is by making sacrifices like that. And reducing population is step one; everything follows from that.

Wincing, John lowered the letter and rubbed his brow with his free hand. *Oh, Wendy, if you only knew,* he thought sadly. Overpopulation was not likely to be a problem in a few years.

Anyway, I hope you won't be angry with me for going ahead on my own. But I know you're a sensible person and so I'm trusting you'll understand.

On a completely different subject, we also saw some of the sights while we were there and I got this for you at Lincoln Center. This is the most amazing sculpture; I'd love for you to see it for yourself. But the video is very good and has a "making of" section at the end that you'll probably find interesting.

Hope to hear from you soon. Love and kisses . . .

John pulled the video out of the mailing box and looked at it. On the cover was a photo of a weird-looking modern sculpture. He wasn't impressed, but then he wasn't a big fan of modern art. The back of the box was filled with not very informative blurbs from other artists and bits culled from critical reviews.

But, hey, if Wendy was impressed it must be really something.

He was trying, and he knew that he was trying, to suppress thoughts of Judgment Day. If there was a Judgment Day. Well, if there was, it would make Wendy's idealistic pledge seem rather foolish.

And yet, that she had made it moved him; still more, that she'd written to *him* about it. He felt toward her a tenderness more profound and respectful than he had yet experienced. He wanted to protect her, to shelter her from all harm. At the same time he admired her faith in the future. He smiled and shook his head.

Then he took the tape and inserted it into the VCR and sat back to watch.

There was a little explanation at first on how Lincoln Center had decided to erect a statue, and had commissioned the late Vladimir Hill to create it. Then there was a segment of film, greatly speeded up, that showed the thing actually moving. Its name was *Venus Dancing* and John's jaw dropped as he watched it doing just that.

The glittering column seemed to swoop and bend, stretching high and then stooping, the holes in its surface growing and shrinking as it moved. The whole thing seemed alive and its motion was graceful and very beautiful. Although, despite the pleasure of watching the lovely thing, something niggled.

Then the dancing segment ended and the "making of" section began. The sculptor, emaciated from his bout with cancer, described the process of creation. He told the interviewer that if he must die young, he had at least created the most unique sculpture in the world before he left.

Then there were scenes from the unveiling, where an almost unrecognizably healthy Vladimir was shown with a beautiful young woman who was the creator of Hill's new sculpting material, a substance she called Intellimetal.

It took a moment as he watched the smiling, blushing brunette, nervously adjusting her glasses. But it was that movement that attracted his attention to her eyes. The shock of recognition took his breath away.

"MO-OM!" he shouted, not moving from where he sat on the bed but only bellowing louder, "MOM! DIETER! COME HERE! NOW!"

Down in the living room the two adults looked at each other, then scrambled for the stairs, pulling weapons out of hiding places.

"What?" Sarah said, bursting into his room.

John pointed at his TV, unable to say anything. He didn't even make his usual crack about mothers who burst into their sons' rooms carrying guns.

Dieter and Sarah moved to where they could see what he was pointing at. Sarah sat down hard on the floor, pressing both hands against her mouth. Frozen on the screen was a face she wasn't likely to forget. *How?* she thought in horror. *She's dead! She's dead. She has to be dead!* No one could have survived that explosion, even if they hadn't blown away half her head first. She couldn't have escaped either; it was impossible.

And yet. This was Serena Burns. Jordan's former boss, the head of security for Cyberdyne. A new breed of Terminator—call it an Infiltrator—sent by Skynet.

"My God," she said. Then she took a deep breath and looked up at John.

"I'm not wrong?" he said, sounding shaky.

"I wish," she answered.

Dieter offered his hand and she took it. He pulled her to her feet easily. "So there was another one," he said grimly.

"Isn't there always?" John asked.

"So far," Sarah agreed. She brushed her hands over her hips. "Now we need to find out where she—*it*—is and what it's up to."

"I'll get in touch with Wendy," John said. "She might know something."

Wendy answered on the third ring.

"Bob's Brickyard, we lay anything," she said cheerfully. In the background there was raucous laughter.

"Wendy?" John said incredulously.

He was calling from his room, lying back on his bed propped up on some pillows; it was kind of late and he'd been afraid of waking her. *Guess I had that wrong,* he thought.

"Oops!" she said. Then he heard her talking to whoever was with her. "Hey, guys? I need a little privacy here."

There was a chorus of protest at that; it sounded like Snog and the gang. He smiled, remembering them. It took a few minutes, but she finally managed to get them to leave.

"I'm sorry it took so long," she said breathlessly when she came back.

"Good thing this isn't a pay phone," he said, letting her hear his smile.

They were silent for a while. John couldn't seem to wipe the smile from his face. Even though they didn't speak, he found intense joy just being in contact with her, listening to her breath—in a sense being with her for the first time in months.

"I've missed you," she said at last.

"I've missed you, too."

They fell silent again until Wendy said, "Why did you call? Did you get it?"

"Your package? Yeah. Actually that's what I'm calling about. Uh . . . there's something on it that might relate to Skynet," he said quickly, wincing slightly. This was a hell of a way to say thank you.

There was a pause, then she said, "Oh."

"Yeah. In the 'making of' part of the video they show this woman who invented the material the statue is made from. We need to find out about her. Where she is, for example."

There was silence again and John frowned; this time the silence had a very different quality. "Wendy?"

"Yeah. I just . . . I thought you might be calling about the pledge," she said, sounding disappointed.

John almost laughed. He'd forgotten about that. But he sensed that it was important to her, even if it was absurd to him. "I will always respect your decision on that. I know it's not something you did lightly. So if you thought I'd be mad or something, I'm not." He waited for her response.

"You just don't care," she said at last, sounding disappointed.

"That's not true," he assured her. "You care, and I care about what you . . . care about," he finished lamely. He hoped that would settle her down. They needed to get onto a more important subject.

She blew out a breath that whistled across the phone lines. "Okay," she said, her voice slightly flat. "What's up with this woman you want to know about?"

"Well," he said, "she should be dead."

"Uh-*huh*." She went silent, apparently waiting for more.

"We don't think she's entirely human," John ventured.

"Aaaaand what makes you think that?" Wendy asked.

"She almost killed my mother, but we killed her instead, and now she's attending parties. You can see why we're concerned."

"Yeah, that attending-parties thing, that's a real bitch." Her voice still had that flat quality, almost uninterested, and John didn't quite know what to make of it.

"You don't sound like you believe me," he ventured.

"Well. John. I've seen this woman's face and you're telling me you killed her. Which is freaky enough, by the way. Until you top it by telling me she's this inventor from the unveiling but she was dead *before* the unveiling. What am I supposed to think?"

"You're supposed to think this is more proof that Skynet is real," he snapped. *Now you doubt me?* he thought. *Now, after all these months?* "Are you guys still working on the CPU?" he asked, playing his ace.

She took a deep breath and let it out in a huff. "Yeah," she admitted. "We're making some progress, too. But this, John! This is like something out of a movie! And real life doesn't have a plot."

Oh yeah? Mine does. John held on to his temper; he needed her help and blowing his stack wasn't going to do him any good.

"Look," he said firmly, "I'd like your help on this. Can I count on you?"

Wendy was quiet for a while. "You really think this woman is from Skynet?" she asked, her voice sounding small.

"I'm convinced of it." John waited, holding his breath.

"I may know something," she said at last. "Give me a few minutes to get my notes together, then get on-line. I'll e-mail you what I have."

"Thank you," he said, his voice ardent with relief. He listened to the silence on her end and asked tentatively, "You're not mad, are you?"

"No. Just kind of creeped out. I'll see you on-line."

"Okay . . . Wendy?"

"Yeah?"

"I love you, you know." Somehow he sensed a smile, then he heard it in her voice.

"I love you, too," she said. Then, briskly, "Give me ten minutes."

"You got it."

They said affectionate good-byes and he hung up. For a few minutes he just lay back on his bed smiling. She loved him.

True, it wasn't 100 percent perfect; she also doubted his sanity. *But she's coming through for me anyway.* He kept on smiling. Love was really strange. But it was also the best feeling he'd ever had.

Okay, Wendy said, *I don't know how useful this will be, but to me it seems to tie in with what you want to know.*

Shoot, John told her.

You remember when I told you that Craig Kipfer guy said something that sounded like an order to kill someone?

Vaguely.

Well, I kept checking into this guy and finally broke through some kind of wall. About the same time he said "Send her to Antarctica," he was getting reports on someone from Montana. They were more detailed than you'd expect; there was a lot of material about her uncle, for instance. It looked for all the world like they were investigating her for a high-level, top-secret government job.

John took her at her word. He'd figured that since Wendy probably saw herself in a top-secret government job one day, she'd look into this sort of thing.

And this was about Clea Bennet? he asked.

No names were mentioned, Wendy wrote. *But Clea Bennet is from Montana, where she was raised by an eccentric uncle, recently deceased. All the particulars match, even if they didn't call her by name. So what do you think?*

I think I'd better look this stuff over. Thanks, Wendy.

No prob. I really do want to help, you know.

I know. Thanks. I'd better get to work on this.

Yeah, she said. *See you soon.*

I wish, John thought. *Love you.*

Love you, she wrote, then she was gone.

He began reading the reports she'd sent, finding them dry but very interesting. They did seem to match the few facts offered on the video.

Antarctica? he thought. *What are we supposed to do now?*

They'd gathered in Dieter's study to discuss Wendy's information. The comfortable room was lit by a single lamp and the light was dim, making the space feel more intimate. The French doors were open, letting in soft breezes laden with the scent of the garden.

Dieter was in the big chair behind his desk, feet propped up on a low filing cabinet. John and his mother were in the smaller, more formal chairs in front of him.

"You're kidding, right?" Sarah said. His mother wasn't so much frowning as looking puzzled. "I mean, it's not much to go on. Or I should say not much to go to Antarctica on."

John smiled at that. "No, but it's the best lead we've got." He tilted his head toward her. "So if you were looking for someone and you dug this up, what would you do?"

Sarah looked down, twisting her mouth wryly. After a beat she raised her hands in surrender. "I'd go to Antarctica."

Dieter hadn't said anything when John had presented Wendy's information. John looked over at him and found the Austrian apparently deep in thought.

"Hey," John said quietly. "Big guy."

Von Rossbach's narrowed gaze slid toward him.

"What do you think?" John asked.

"I think I remember hearing, just before I retired, the vaguest of hints about the possibility of someone creating a super-secret laboratory 'on ice.' At the time I thought it was a metaphor," Dieter said. "But maybe not." He took his feet off the cabinet. "Let me make a few calls, find out what I can about this."

"Meanwhile, John and I can do some research on what sort of equipment we'll need." Sarah turned to her son and smiled.

John glanced at Dieter, who looked away quickly.

"What?" Sarah asked, looking between them.

John hesitated. "Well . . ." He looked to Dieter for support, but the big man was looking out into the garden. John turned back to his mother and took her hand.

Raising her brows at the sentimental gesture, she looked at Dieter, too, frowned as he continued to stare out the door, and, her expression turning suspicious, turned back to John.

"You're still not a hundred percent, Mom." He took a deep breath. "Not enough to go hiking around Antarctica." He nodded once, looking deeply into her eyes.

Sarah frowned, then she let out an exasperated breath and looked away. To find herself confronting Dieter's concerned eyes. "Okay!" she said, throwing up her hands. "You're right. I'm not a hundred percent. But"—she pointed at John—"you're too valuable to risk. So where does that leave us?"

They both looked at Dieter.

He laughed and held up his hands. "Before we decide *who* is going, let's make sure of our destination."

"Sounds reasonable." Sarah rose and crooked her finger at John. "Let's leave our host to it, shall we?" With that, she walked from the room.

John followed her out, saying, "You're not mad, are you, Mom?"

"No, John, I'm not mad."

He was quiet a moment. "You sound mad."

"I'm not mad!"

Dieter smiled. She might not be mad, but she wasn't happy, either.

While they'd been thrashing out whether Sarah was to go or not, he'd been wondering if he dared call his old friend Jeff Goldberg, his former partner in the Sector.

I suppose I might as well, he thought. *Sully must have made a report by now, and even if he hadn't, they already knew about my association with the notorious Sarah Connor. Which means that Jeff knows, too.*

He went to the wall and took down a heavily framed painting, setting it to lean against the file cabinet. Then he worked the combination of the safe it had hidden. Removing the valuable papers and other odds and ends inside the surprisingly deep little safe, he opened a tiny secret compartment with a few deft touches. Inside was a cell phone.

In Vienna, Jeff had one just like it.

When Dieter had retired they'd decided to arrange a private means of communication in the event that either ever had need of the other's aid. At the time von Rossbach had been thinking that his partner, still active in a very dangerous profession, might need his help. It just went to show you; a backup plan was always a good idea.

He placed the phone on his desk and booted up his computer. Once on the Internet he sent off the coded message that would bounce through a few different addresses before it reached Jeff. Then he sat back to wait. It could be a while.

An hour and a half later the phone rang. Dieter snatched it up. "Yes?" he said.

"I don't even know why I'm talking to you."

"It's because in spite of everything you've heard, you know you can trust me," Dieter said.

"If I can trust you then why does it look like you've gone over to the other side?" Jeff's voice was stressed, not usual.

Dieter wondered if, in spite of their precautions, this call was being monitored—if Jeff was letting this call be monitored.

"You know me better than that," von Rossbach said dismissively. "What's the gossip about me?"

"*Gossip?* If it was gossip I could doubt it. I'm talking about official reports, Dieter."

"And what am I supposed to have done in these reports?"

"For starters, harboring a wanted fugitive!" Goldberg snapped.

"When was this?" *Careful,* Dieter thought. *You don't want to antagonize him any further.*

"You know goddamn well when. You were the one who sent me those sketches of her. Then you said the description didn't match. And of course I believed you because my good buddy wouldn't lie to me! Next thing I know, you're running around California recruiting for her army!"

Dieter was silent for a while as he gathered his thoughts. He'd thought he knew what he was going to say, thought he knew how to counter any arguments Jeff might throw at him. But now that the moment was here he found he couldn't use any of those glib explanations, because most of them were lies. He couldn't do that to a man who had been at his back through most of his dangerous career. He'd already done it too often.

Dieter took a deep breath and let it out slowly. "I owe you an apology," he said. "I did know it was probably her, but I was intrigued and wanted to investigate her by myself. Especially when you sent me that recording of a man with my face killing police by the dozen. I was bored here and feeling useless." He shrugged, though his former partner couldn't see it. "Then you sent Griego and I felt like I had to defend my turf. It wasn't sensible, and I know it wasn't professional, but I'd gotten to know her a little by then and I wanted to know more."

Goldberg was silent for a long time. "Go on," he said at last, his voice giving nothing away.

Dieter felt relieved. At least he was being given a chance to explain. "One night I went over to her house." He frowned at the memory. "I was bringing a dog for her son, more of a puppy, really." He took a deep breath and forced himself to continue. "Before I knew it we were under attack. By a heavily armed man with my face."

"Bullshit!" Goldberg snapped.

"I wish. God, do I wish you were right." Until this moment he hadn't realized how much he would give for all that had happened to have been a dream. "But you're not. The face was mine, but this man was no more human than that cell phone you're holding. I saw the body. It had no internal organs—just metal, wire, motherboards, stuff like that. There were sparks flying out of it and it took an incredible amount of ammunition to stop the damn thing."

"Do you think I'm an *idiot*!" Goldberg shouted. "What the hell is the matter with you?"

Dieter kept silent for a moment; he tightened his mouth and closed his eyes as if in pain. "Jeff," he said quietly, "I had a whole bunch of lies made up to tell you. I was going to be investigating this thing on my own, trying to find out how far Connor's influence extended. You know me. I'm good at being convincing when I need to be. You'd have believed me before I was finished with you. But you deserved the truth, so I took a chance and told it to you."

Jeff was breathing hard, his breath whistling though the phone. "Shit!" he muttered.

"Believe it or not, I know how you feel," Dieter commiserated. "Why would I tell you a story like this if it wasn't true? Don't you think I *know* how all this sounds? Why would I even try if it wasn't true?"

He stopped talking, waiting for his old partner to work it through.

"She could have talked you 'round," Jeff said at last. "Connor was a damned attractive woman." His voice was wary, but much less hostile.

"Yeah, and I'm really susceptible to wild stories and sexy women. That's why I was such a rotten agent." Von Rossbach sneered.

Jeff gave a short laugh. "Nooo, you were pretty good."

"I still am."

"Yeah, well. This is a pretty crazy story, buddy. You know that."

"Have you seen Sully's report?"

"Sully is, uh, undergoing psychiatric evaluation. You know he's one of ours?"

"Would I ask about his report if I didn't?"

"Good point."

"Jeff, Sarah Connor is crazy, her son is crazy, Sully's crazy. Now I'm crazy? Maybe instead they've been telling the truth all along?"

Goldberg gave a kind of hiss. "I can't go there, buddy. I just can't."

"Are you at least willing to think about it?"

After a rather painful silence Goldberg said, "Yeah. I could do that."

"Good. I need your help."

Jeff barked a laugh. "You cocky bastard! You sure you don't want to give me two more seconds to mull this over?"

"Yes."

"Well, what the hell. I figured you wanted something, otherwise we wouldn't be talking on these phones. Right?"

"You got it, buddy." Von Rossbach waited, wanting his friend to ask.

"So what do you want?" Jeff said.

"I'm trying to trace a possible kidnap victim."

"Whoa! If you're talking about Sarah Connor, she took off on her own. If you're talking about Dr. Silberman, how do you think we know that she took off on her own?"

Dieter winced. He wanted to tell the truth. *But I think I've tried Jeff's patience enough for one evening.* "What are you talking about?"

There was a pregnant pause from Vienna. Then Goldberg asked cautiously, "You don't know?"

"Sarah Connor is missing again?" Dieter asked. "Last I heard she was in an institution."

"If you don't know where she is and what she's doing, then why are you rounding up recruits for her cause?" Jeff challenged.

"Because I promised her I would before she disappeared from here. I don't know how much good I've done her. Being chased all over California by the Sector didn't help my efforts. But in any case, she's not the person I'm talking about."

"Oh." Jeff was silent a moment. "So, what? Are you a PI now or something?"

"No, just letting my curiosity get the better of me. This woman is named Clea Bennet, she's the inventor of something called Intellimetal. They made this sculpture in New York out of it."

"Yeah. *Venus Dancing,* it's called. It's all the rage, everyone's pretty excited about it. Nancy wants us to go see it for ourselves," Goldberg said.

"Clea Bennet has been missing for a little while now," Dieter explained. "I have some suspicion that it might have been the U.S. government that snatched her."

"You sure that suspicion isn't an effect of the people you've been hanging out with?"

Dieter let out an exasperated sigh. "This guy named Craig Kipfer's been getting reports on a woman from Montana. The reports read like Bennet's biography. Kipfer passed along an order, I quote, 'send her to Antarctica,' that jogged a memory for me. Just before I left the Sector there were hints of someone building an important and very secret research facility 'on the ice.' Do you know anything about that?"

Jeff was absolutely silent.

"Hello?" Dieter prompted.

"Kipfer isn't someone you should have heard about," Goldberg said at last. "He is like, ultra–black ops. As for the research facility . . ."

There was more contemplative silence, but Dieter waited it out this time.

"I can't believe I'm telling you this, but . . . yeah. It's there. We know where it's located, but aside from that we know very little. The only thing we can be sure of is that they're not doing nuclear testing. For once the Americans are playing their cards close to their chests. Though to be fair, it's not the kind of place that's easily infiltrated."

"So who have you got there?" Dieter said blandly.

Jeff laughed. "None of your business. Even if we did have somebody there you probably wouldn't know them."

"So where is this base?"

Dieter waited; would his friend come through for him? Jeff had no particular reason to cover for the U.S. government, but at the moment neither did he have a particular reason to help his old partner.

"You're not going to blow it up are you?" Jeff asked sourly.

Von Rossbach laughed in surprise. "No! That's not the plan anyway. I might try to rescue this young woman. Assuming she's there under duress, of course."

"Tsk!" Jeff said. "I thought you were out of the hero business."

"You going to tell me or not?" Dieter asked.

"Don't make me regret this," Goldberg warned.

"I won't. I swear," Dieter said, fingers crossed. After all, who knew?

"It's in west Antarctica." Jeff gave him the coordinates. "The base itself is slightly inland." He gave a brief physical description of the place. "You could hike there from the coast in three days."

"Thanks, Jeff."

"Dress warm."

"Yes, Dad. Give my best to Nancy."

"You bet." Goldberg paused. "God, Dieter, don't make me regret this, please."

"Don't worry."

"Just don't. Okay?"

"You'll get old and gray worrying like that," Dieter teased. "I'm just curious, is all. I like a good puzzle."

"If you hear from Connor—"

"I won't."

"Yeah, right. Don't blow anything up," Jeff warned.

"But that's the fun part!"

Jeff hissed in exasperation, then laughed. "Y'know, you're right."

Dieter laughed, too. "Bye, buddy. Thanks."

"I am so going to regret this," Jeff said, sounding more amused than worried.

"No comment. Bye." Dieter hung up.

This American base must be one of Jeff's projects, otherwise he wouldn't have the information at his fingertips like that. *A lucky break,* Dieter thought.

He'd check with Sarah and John to see how their research on supplies was going. Then he'd see about arranging transportation.

Sarah looked up as Dieter appeared in John's doorway. "It's amazing how many Web sites there are dealing with tourism in Antarctica," she said by way of greeting. "Apparently going there is really popular. Who knew?"

"Give me Paris any day," John muttered, typing rapidly.

"Ah, yes," said Dieter, "we'll always have Paris."

Sarah smiled. "I've always wanted to go there," she said. "My father said there was something special in the air of Paris. But, we could hardly expect them to put Skynet someplace so accessible."

"Or so pleasant," Dieter agreed.

"They could have at least put it someplace temperate," John complained.

"That's right," his mother said. "You've never lived anywhere cold, have you, hon? We'll have to put some antifreeze in your blood."

John gave her a look. "Thanks, Mom. I knew I could rely on you."

"What are mothers for?" she asked brightly.

"To justify Mother's Day?" John asked. He tapped a final key and the printer began to hum.

Sarah punched his arm lightly and turned to von Rossbach. "Did you find out anything?"

"There *is* a top-secret American scientific installation in west Antarctica," he said. "About three days in from the coast. It's a mostly underground facility with some sham huts on top."

■ ■ ■

John took some papers from the printer and handed them to Dieter. Who took them and looked them over.

"A lot of stuff," he said.

"I pared it down to the essentials," John said. "We're not there for the scenery, after all. It's the food that concerns me. We'll need a ton of it. I get the impression you're supposed to eat a pound of butter a day."

"Cold burns calories," von Rossbach said. He became quiet for a moment.

"What?" Sarah asked, coming into the room and sitting on John's bed. Dieter looked up, his eyes meeting hers. John turned to look at him and von Rossbach glanced his way.

"Why are we doing this?" he asked. "We don't know for sure that this woman is there, or that Skynet is there. We could be running off half-cocked here. And to do what, exactly?"

Sarah and John stared at him as if he'd suddenly broken out into a Broadway show tune, then glanced at each other and away. After a moment of chewing her lips Sarah looked at von Rossbach.

"If that thing is there, and we have good reason to think it is, then it's there for Skynet. That's what all of these things are for—the Terminators, whatever Serena Burns was, whatever this thing is. They exist to protect Skynet, and/or to kill us. It's just a question of who strikes first."

"What about the rest of the facility?" Dieter asked.

"Our one goal is to destroy this thing and Skynet," she answered. "Nothing else."

"So you're talking surgical strike?" Dieter said.

"By preference," Sarah said. "But what I'm talking is whatever we have to do."

"Same as ever, big guy," John said. "The goal is always the same, however many times it takes." He sighed and lifted his arms, then dropped them in a full body shrug. "Hey, at least we get to travel."

Dieter was silent a long time. Abruptly he rose.

"All right," he said. "I'll arrange travel." As he walked toward his study he thought, *Jeff's going to kill me.*

"Yes?" The woman's voice was sultry and inviting, a voice designed to tickle and suggest.

"I would love to take you out to dinner."

"Dieter!" Vera Philmore exclaimed in delight. "How marvelous to hear from you! Where are you, darling?"

"I'd rather not say," he answered carefully. "But as I said, I'd love to take you to dinner."

"When and where?" she purred.

"Tierra del Fuego."

Vera laughed out loud. "Do they even *have* restaurants there?"

"Some very good ones." He picked up a pen and tapped it on the desk. "But I must confess, I need a favor."

"Oooh. I knew there'd be a catch," she said, putting a mock pout in her voice. "Maybe I should put in a catch of my own."

"Careful, you'll frighten me away."

Vera gave a throaty laugh. "What do you want, sweetheart? Not more money, I hope."

"No," he assured her. "I'd prefer to explain to you face-to-face."

Suddenly the banter was gone from her voice. "So this is a serious thing?"

"Yes," he agreed. "But—always excepting the seas and the weather down there—what I'm asking shouldn't put you, or your crew, in any personal danger."

"I see."

Dieter waited, letting her think it over. "Have you ever been to Tierra del Fuego?"

"Of course not, darling!" she said, and laughed. "It's not exactly a spa, is it?"

"There's nowhere else on earth quite like it," von Rossbach assured her.

"Sweetie, there's a whole lot of pissholes on this planet that could make the same claim. That doesn't mean I want to visit them." She gave a deep sigh. "All right. Where and when?"

"Ushuaia," he said, "it's the capital. Two weeks from today?"

"I'll be there," she said. "This had better be one very good dinner, baby."

"I'll make sure of it," he promised. "Will you be staying at a hotel, or . . . ?"

"I'll be on the yacht, of course, dear. That's what it's for, to protect me from bad hotels. See you then." She made the smacking sound of a big kiss and hung up.

Dieter depressed the receiver button and began dialing the restaurant that the travel agency had recommended. *I hope this place lives up to its reputation,* he thought. He didn't want to have to make up for bad food.

CHAPTER 21

HARTFORD, CONNECTICUT

Ron Labane entered Hartford feeling *good*. Not even the general atmosphere of industrial decay—the abandoned mills, some converted to glitzy malls, and the tract housing from the vanished heyday of the textile factories—could depress him. He'd turned the radio to a classic-rock station, and tapped out the rhythm of "Dreamboat Annie" as he drove.

Things were moving along better and faster than he'd ever anticipated. There were now two Eco Party U.S. senators and eight congressmen in Washington and a lot more who were state representatives, five Eco Party governors: two on the West Coast, three on the East.

Ten years ago they were nothing.

It was a thrill to realize that the United States at last had a three-party system and that, in large part, it was due to *his* influence. The *New Day* show, the books, the clubs, the new magazine, all of these had changed the attitudes of millions of Americans. All because of his grand vision.

Ron grinned. He felt better than good; he felt invincible. Just before heading out for his speaking engagement at U. Mass. he'd gotten a surprise visit from Eco Party chairman Sebastion MacMillan and his closest associates. He felt a surge of pure pleasure as he remembered the meeting.

NEW YORK

"Mr. Labane," MacMillan said, "I realize that this is short notice, but I hope you can spare us a few moments of your time."

Ron looked at the professorial gentleman at his door in surprise, and at his three associates. Then he smiled.

"Come in," he said, stepping aside and gesturing into his austere yet elegant apartment with its handcrafted third-world textiles and slight odor of organic sachet. "Can I take your coats?"

"No, no, we won't be staying that long." The chairman took note of Ron's small suitcase. "And you're going somewhere, I see."

"Yes, Amherst, up in Massachusetts. I'm speaking at the university there." He chuckled deprecatingly. "I don't want to get the reputation of only speaking to the Ivy League."

The three men and one woman looked at him as though he'd said something profound. "Your egalitarianism is one of the reasons we want to speak to you," MacMillan said.

"Sit down, please," Ron invited, and led them into the living room.

He looked them over as they took their seats. The rumor was that the chairman had sent around copies of *Dress for Success* as soon as he'd taken over and had demanded that everyone in any position of authority make it their bible. Undoubtedly it had helped. These people had always looked intelligent; now they also looked professional and therefore trustworthy. Ron looked over and met MacMillan's eye.

This is someone I could work with, he thought. He made a mental note to invite him onto the show.

"I'll get right to the point," the chairman said. "In ten months one of New York's senators will be leaving Washington for good. We'd like you to be our candidate for that office."

Ron was genuinely stunned. He'd assumed that they wanted him to do something for them. It seemed it was the other way around.

MacMillan smiled warmly at him. "I've studied your career, Mr. Labane. It seems to me that the logical next step for you is public office. Your genuine dedication to ecological causes is both unselfish and unquestionable. To the general public you're a hero; to those of us involved with the cause you're a leader. We'd like to take that a step further and make you a leader with power."

The chairman pulled his briefcase onto his lap and extracted a slim file. "The party ran a straw poll to see how the idea of you as our candidate struck people."

He held out the file and Labane took it. Ron glanced at the other party members, who all nodded, smiling; then he opened the file. After a moment he looked up at the chairman, astounded.

MacMillan smiled comfortably. "We've never had a result like that when we've floated a name." He shook his head. "As you can see we didn't restrict the poll to party members either. If you ran on our ticket today you'd be elected. In a landslide."

Ron smiled and shook his head, then he blew his breath out in a whistle. He laughed, he couldn't help it. "This is *ve-ry* flattering."

"Don't answer tonight." The chairman held up his hand. "We know you'll want to think about it. After all, this would be a big step."

He rose and the others followed suit. Taking a step forward, MacMillan held out his hand. Belatedly Ron rose to take it.

"All we ask is that you consider it seriously. I honestly think that now is the time."

Ron shook the chairman's hand. "I'll certainly give it some thought," he said. "I'm caught completely flat-footed here, I"—He shook his head helplessly—"honestly don't know what to say."

"I'm hoping you'll say yes," MacMillan said, smiling. He started slowly for the door. "In a few years I think this country will be ready for a presidential candidate from our party." He put his hand on Labane's shoulder. "We need to do everything that we can to make that day a reality."

He stopped and smiled at Ron.

"That would certainly be a wonderful day for this country," Ron said, his head whirling. *I'm already sounding like a politician,* he thought.

The chairman grinned as though he shared the thought. "Our contact information is in the file." MacMillan held out his hand again and Ron shook it. "Good night."

"Good night," Ron said.

The other three party members filed out behind the chairman, each offering his or her hand for a firm handshake, making eye contact and saying a polite good-bye that implied great pleasure in their brief acquaintance.

After closing the door behind them, Ron simply sat down on the chair in the foyer and stared at nothing.

No, not at nothing: into the future.

HARTFORD

A very pleasant memory. Even sitting down driving, Ron felt ten feet tall. The numbers had indicated that he would be the near-unanimous choice of New York voters.

"Unanimous!" he said aloud, and laughed. New Mexico probably hadn't hurt . . .

This was heady stuff. *Should I expect to hear from the Democrats next?* he wondered. Not that he would accept an offer from them. He didn't think his support would be unanimous with the Democrats.

His support! He was definitely thinking like a politico already. *Must mean this was meant to be.*

As Ron pulled off the highway and into the parking lot of the cheap motel, he frowned. *I'll have to be more careful,* he thought. A lot more careful. *Maybe this should be the last one.*

The last of hundreds of clandestine meetings that he'd held over the last few years. Meetings designed to give the last little nudge to people who didn't need very much in the way of a push in the first place.

But his presence had helped. Had helped to keep even the most aggressive and angry extremists from becoming too violent. While at the same time offering direction and ideas, ideas that had been making headlines for a long time now. Some people called it a "terrorist network," but that wasn't how things worked. It was more in the nature of an umbrella.

He sat in his car looking at the cabin where the meeting was being held. Maybe he should just not show up at all. The truth was, of all the crazies he'd had contact with over the years, these people were the only ones who truly scared him.

At least they haven't killed anybody. Yet.

No one that he knew about anyway. But when he looked in their eyes he could see that in their hearts they'd murdered thousands.

Hell, they were so misanthropic that the only reason they could tolerate one another was because of their dedication to their cause.

A cause which Ron had gradually come to see was not quite the same as his own.

His fingers tapped the steering wheel and he felt his reluctance grow the longer he sat. Ron frowned. He was cagey enough to know that he wasn't worried about what effect being seen with these people might have on his potential political career. He could always say he was trying to rein them in, and he thought he'd be believed.

The problem was that he didn't trust them. They looked at him like they hated him; even as they hung on his words and did as he directed, he could feel their loathing, like an oily heat against his skin.

He pictured them in his mind's eye as he'd seen them last. They were all young, all white, seven of them, three women and four men. He didn't know their real names; they certainly weren't born with names like Sauron, Balewitch, Maleficent, Dog Soldier, Death, Hate, and Orc. They were pale, and underfed, with stringy hair and a slightly swampy smell about them, as though they lived underground.

Ron smiled at the thought. They most certainly did.

And they were angry. Their bodies were stiff with rage, even though their faces were usually blank, until you looked at their eyes. There was emotion enough in those eyes all right, none of it wholesome.

They didn't talk about their families or their pasts, so he had no idea what forces had molded them into the dangerous people they'd become. But they spoke freely of their education. Each of them was brilliant, each had received scholarships and had attended prestigious universities.

And each one thinks he or she is the smartest one in the group and should be in control, Ron thought.

They thought they were smarter than he was, too. It didn't take a genius to guess that they were jealous of him and resented his influence—on them and on other people. Influence they wanted for themselves.

He gave a shudder and pulled the keys from the ignition with a jangle of metal. This wasn't going to get any better with waiting.

He strode to the door of the cabin and gave the prescribed knock. Two knocks, pause, one knock, pause, five knocks, pause, one knock.

"Who is it?" a surly male voice demanded.

"English muffin," Ron said wearily. There was a peephole in the door for crissake!

The door swung open on a darkened room and Labane entered with an audible sigh. He closed the door behind him. "May we have some light?" he asked with exaggerated patience.

Maleficent turned on the lamp beside her chair and glared at him with what appeared to be heartfelt contempt. "You're late," she said coldly.

"Yes," he agreed. "I was delayed starting out."

Ron went over and sat on the bed, almost landing on Sauron's legs, since that worthy disdained to move them. "It's been a while," Ron said.

"Meaning?" Balewitch snapped in her foghorn voice, ice-pale eyes blazing. She, more than the rest, was inclined to take every remark personally.

"Just an observation," Ron said, his voice carefully unapologetic.

He decided to say nothing more. They'd asked for this meeting; therefore, let *them* talk. The old Buddhist stuff about the power of silence had something to it; if you made the other guy speak first, you had him off balance. He waited, and waited, feeling like a mailman surrounded by Dobermans on speed. After what felt like an hour of charged silence— in reality about five minutes—Ron got to his feet and moved toward the door.

"Thanks for inviting me to your meditation session," he said sarcastically. "But I've still got a couple of hours of driving to do and a great deal of meeting and greeting at the end of it. So if there's nothing else you wanted—"

"Sit down," Hate said, his uninflected voice weighty with threat.

"No, I don't think I will," Ron said, clasping his hands before him. "I will give you a few more minutes. What do you want?"

"Now you're meeting with political mavens you think you're too good to spend time with us?" Sauron asked.

Ron's head snapped around to glare at him, hiding the curdling horror he felt inside. For the first time he realized that Orc was missing. *How long have they been watching me?* he wondered, feeling the back of his neck clench with a sudden chill.

Sauron sneered at him. Sauron was the smooth one; he was able to hide his feelings most of the time. He wasn't bothering now. "MacMillan and his school of sycophants," he drawled. "But they didn't linger."

"No," Labane agreed. "They said what they came to say and they left." He looked at each of them. "Their arrival was as much a surprise to me as it was to Orc."

"We weren't surprised," Balewitch said. Her graying bristle-cut clean for a change, she stared at him as if he was a spot on a white wall.

"Is that why you asked me here? To discuss their proposal?" Ron asked, trying not to let them see how disturbed he was.

"Have you sold your soul yet?" Death asked, looking at him sidelong through a dark curtain of her lank hair.

Ron snorted. "They offered to sponsor me as a candidate for the Senate from New York," he told them. Even though they probably already knew that.

"And?" Dog Soldier asked, his voice disinterested.

"And, I'm considering it."

Maleficent actually hissed. Ron looked at her, one brow raised. "That's where the evil is," she said.

"That's where the *money* is," Dog Soldier corrected.

Maleficent shot him a glare that should have singed his hair.

"That's where the power is," Ron interrupted.

"The power to change things?" Dog Soldier asked, a smirk playing on his lips. "The power to right all the wrongs, cross all the *t*s, dot all the *i*s."

"Yes," Ron said. "Why shouldn't I want that kind of power? Think of the good I could do for the cause with that kind of influence."

There was the strangest feeling then, as though, without moving, they'd all drawn back from him in disgust.

"That's the sort of thing someone who'd already made up his mind might say to excuse being greedy," Sauron observed. "You already have a lot of influence with your little television show."

"Influence with power behind it will go a lot further," Labane insisted. "And there's no telling how high this road could climb. This is a golden opportunity for our cause."

The six of them exchanged glances around him.

"I suspect that we have different goals," Death told him.

"We all want to save the planet!" Labane said in exasperation.

Once again their eyes met, excluding Ron.

"Fine," he snarled. "Just forget it. I'm outta here."

"Ron." Sauron stopped Labane with his hand on the doorknob. "Just in case the thought has crossed your mind, I'd like to discourage you from any ideas you might have of turning us in." He shook his head. "That would be a *very* bad idea."

"I *do* know something about loyalty," Ron said.

"If you're going to be a politician that'll be the first thing to go," Dog Soldier told him, snickering.

"You do us the dirty and you'd better watch your back, Labane," Death warned, her dark eyes narrowed to slits.

"You know what?" Ron said. "Don't call me, I'll call you."

"Thanks for dropping by, Ron," Sauron called just before the door slammed.

They were quiet for a while. Then Maleficent observed, "He's gone over to the other side. He just doesn't know it yet."

"And he never will," Dog Soldier said. "That kind of insight takes time."

"Death to traitors," Balewitch growled.

They crossed glances again. This time they smiled.

ROUTE 91, MASSACHUSETTS

Ron felt better once he'd left Connecticut behind him. Being with that crowd was always a trial, but tonight! Tonight had been different. The idea that they had been watching him made his stomach clench like an angry fist. How dare those sick little bastards spy on him? *How long has this been going on?*

And how far had it gone?

The thought frightened him and the fear broke the fever of his outrage with a cold sweat. Had they been in his apartment?

No, he assured himself, *they couldn't have; I'd have smelled them.* The contempt felt good.

Besides, he paid a premium to live in a building with first-class security. It was one thing to watch MacMillan enter his building and to guess where he was going. It was quite another to actually break in.

His eyes flicked to the mirror to watch a car coming up behind. A little frisson of fear shivered through his belly. Was it them? Were they up to something?

As the vehicle passed him he saw that it was one of those pickups with a complete backseat and what seemed to be an eighteen-foot bed—known in some circles as an "adultery wagon." Ron relaxed, feeling himself loosen, almost deflating behind the wheel. Even in deep disguise, that crowd wouldn't go near one of those things. *Unless they planned to bomb it.*

He forced himself to be calm. They had no reason to be after him. He'd never betrayed them. *And I don't need to betray them now.* Without him to keep them on an even keel, they'd be in police custody in a month. Most likely they'd betray one another.

Geniuses! He gave his head a little shake. A lot of the time they had no practical sense at all. They wouldn't last long enough to create problems for him.

And if they did . . . well, he knew some other people, too.

THE VICTORIAN INN, AMHERST, MASSACHUSETTS

Labane entered the pleasant guest room—plenty of froufrou and color, to match the theme—and flung his jacket onto the tiny sofa; then he pulled off his tie and threw that down, too. Unbuttoning his cuffs, he entered the bathroom, unbuttoned his collar, and turned on the tap. He splashed cold water on his face, dried off with one of the inn's luxurious towels, and stared at himself in the mirror.

He looked almost as exhausted as he felt.

Last night had run later than he'd planned, but the company had been good. Besides, he suspected that he'd been too keyed up for an early night. Then today there was the traditional campus tour, followed by the obligatory meeting with the campus's ecology clubs, an interview with the local press, a formal dinner with the president of the college and all of the faculty and guests from the surrounding colleges—of which the area held a multitude—and *then* his address to the college. After which there was a mill-and-swill where some people introduced themselves and spoke with him, and more people stared at him from a distance as though he were on exhibit.

God, it was good to be alone again. He went back into the room and sat in one of the comfortable club chairs; he wondered idly if they were Victorian. Didn't seem likely. The chair didn't try to make him sit ramrod straight and the cushions accepted the shape of his posterior without the apparent resentment of true Victorian furniture.

He'd ordered coffee, and though he knew that the average guest would have been denied, his celebrity status got him what he wanted.

Ron smiled; life was good. He was tired, but it was worth it. Seeing all those eager young faces, knowing they were hanging on his every word, shaping their lives to fit his philosophy. He closed his eyes, hands folded across his stomach, and sighed contentedly. It just didn't get any better than this.

There was a discreet knock at the door.

"Room service."

"C'mon in, it's open," Ron called out from his chair. "You can just put it there on the coffee table."

Then he realized that there was more than one person entering the room. He opened his eyes, annoyed, but smiling through it. Sometimes being a celebrity got you what you wanted, but sometimes the fans wanted something back in return; like the opportunity to show you off to their friends.

Then he realized he was looking at Hate and Dog Soldier. The artificial smile froze on his face, then slipped away. "What's up, fellas?" he asked.

Hate handed Dog Soldier a pillow from off the bed. Dog soldier pulled out a huge gun and wrapped the pillow around it.

"Wait a minute!" Ron said, holding up his hand.

"Not even," Dog Soldier said cheerfully, and shot him between the eyes.

At least that was where he'd been aiming. With large-caliber ammunition it was sometimes hard to tell exactly where the bullet struck.

Hate picked up the phone and dialed room service. "I'm so sorry," he said in a nearly perfect imitation of Labane's voice. "I have to cancel that request for coffee. I'm suddenly so tired I couldn't even take a sip. I apologize for the inconvenience."

Dog Soldier watched him as he put the gun down on the coffee table.

"Oh, thank you," Hate said into the phone pleasantly.

Dog raised a brow as he flung the pillow back onto the bed and took out a small box.

"Well, that's always nice to hear," Hate said.

Dog got to work on the gun, unscrewing the handgrip and carefully replacing the grip plates with those that had been handled by their mark.

"Really," Hate said, rolling his eyes and gritting his teeth even as he kept his voice friendly and cheerful. "All that way? Just for me?"

Dog Soldier grinned and shook his head.

"Well, thank you, but I really must go. Yes. Yes, everything is wonderful. Yes. Thank you. You're very sweet. I must go. Yes. Good night." Hate put down the receiver carefully. "I was ready to go down there and blow them all away," he snarled. *"Cattle!"*

Dog chuckled. "I don't blame you, man. People get to me the same way. Save the planet—kill all the people!"

Wendy walked along the dark street feeling totally jazzed. She'd been invited to a private meeting with Ron Labane! She gave a little skip and hugged herself.

When she'd heard Labane was going to be speaking here tonight, she'd made arrangements to stay with her friend Diana, skipped her classes, and took a bus to Amherst. His speech had been wonderful, and even Di, who really wasn't that interested in ecology, had agreed about that. She'd been invited to go along to this meeting, too, but hadn't wanted to.

Wendy sighed. Di was a good friend, but she was more into dancing and dating than saving the world. Wendy would have loved her company tonight. It would have been so good to share this opportunity.

It was just pure luck that they'd found themselves behind two guys who worked on Labane's show in Oklahoma City. One of them, Rich, was kind of creepy, but the other, Joe, was friendly enough. He'd reminded her a little of Snog, a good sense of humor and obviously very smart.

They got to talking and Joe invited them to this private meeting. He explained that Mr. Labane was especially interested in talking to students in the high-tech area.

"Well, that lets me out," Diana had said, grinning. "I'm an art major."

"Hey, you can come," Joe said.

"Got a date," Diana told him.

Di had told Wendy later that she thought he was hitting on her. "When I want a guy to hit on me," she said, "I'll let him know it."

Joe didn't act like he'd been rejected, though. He kept talking with them and joking. He was wearing latex gloves. When Wendy had asked him about it he told her that he'd been burned when a battery exploded and the gloves protected him while making it possible to handle things.

He claimed that they had a special pass, but he couldn't find it. He kept handing her things from his pockets as he searched for his pass. The weirdest collection of stuff—metal and plastic and wire and string—but no pass. In the end they'd bought tickets like everybody else, which Joe's friend was clearly annoyed about.

"Did you believe him?" Di had asked later.

"Sure," Wendy said.

"I hope you're not letting yourself in for a nasty experience going to meet these guys," Diana warned. "There was something fishy about those two."

"It's at the Victorian, Di," Wendy had said in exasperation. "That's where Mr. Labane is staying."

It kind of annoyed her, Diana coming on so superior like that. As if U. Mass. Amherst was a hotbed of sophistication next to Cambridge and MIT.

I bet she's sleeping around, Wendy thought cattily. She'd known other girls who suddenly felt all worldly because they were suddenly "doing it" regularly.

Wendy entered the lobby and looked around; the man behind the desk had his back turned as he filed something. There was a lot of ornate furniture with red plush upholstery and matching drapes. The wallpaper was a sepia-toned print of acanthus leaves; the carpet had plate-sized pink roses all over it. She wrinkled her nose; it was very nice, she supposed, just not her style.

She went to the ornate staircase and climbed to the second floor. Mr. Labane's room was 207, at the far end of the hall. The hall was quiet and the ambience here was restful. She wished she could stay in a place like this; Diana's dorm was as noisy as the inside of a drum at a rock concert.

She found the door to 207 slightly open, but the room was quiet. Biting her lower lip, Wendy hesitated. She really didn't want to be the first to arrive. How would she explain her presence if Rich and Joe weren't here? By the same token, she'd look stupid hanging out in the hall like this. And if she was first she'd actually get some private time with Mr. Labane. Taking a deep breath, she knocked twice.

"Come in." It was Ron Labane's voice.

She clasped her hands as her excitement surged, then nervously pushed the door open. Just inside the door on the left was the bathroom; Joe was coming out as she entered.

"Hi," she said happily.

Smiling broadly, he lifted his hand as if to blow her a kiss and blew a fine powder right into her face.

Wendy started to suck in her breath in surprise, gagged, and fell to the floor unconscious.

"Gets 'em every time," Dog Soldier said, brushing off his hands.

"Get her out of there and close the door for crissake," Hate snarled. "Couldn't you have waited until she was further in?"

"Picky, picky, picky." Dog grinned. He grabbed Wendy under the armpits and dragged her a few feet, dropped her like a sack of potatoes, and stepped over her to close the door. "That was easy," he said, watching Hate position the girl on the floor beside Labane.

"Yes," Hate agreed. He spread the girl's right hand and touched the gun to her fingers in a number of different directions. "Why did we have to replace parts if we could do this?"

"Extra measure of safety," Dog said. "Dude I knew got caught because of a fingerprint on the inside of a mother-of-pearl handgrip plate. Besides, we didn't know if we'd have the leisure. She might have brought a friend."

Hate nodded, not looking up. Then he placed the gun in the girl's hand. Lifting Wendy up, he brought her close to Labane, the gun pressed against what was left of Ron's head, Hate's hand over hers on the gun. Dog wrapped the pillow around her hand and Hate pulled the trigger.

Wendy got most of what splashed, though Hate caught some blood and matter on his face and hair.

"Shit!" He dropped her and headed for the bathroom. He took a handful of toilet paper and cleaned off the worst of it, then pocketed the mess. "Let's get out of here," he growled.

"Sure," Dog said. "Bye, Wendy."

They pulled the door quietly to behind them and went down the back stairs, exiting through the inn's rear door, where Hate had unscrewed a bulb earlier, leaving the back path in darkness.

"You wanna make the call, or shall I do the honors?" Dog asked.

"You," Hate said. Why should he take the risk of having his voice recorded?

"Oh! Y'know what?" Dog Soldier said. "You could imitate Ron! You could call up and say this coed stalker was threatening you and you'd seen her in the hotel and the cops should come and take her away, or something." He grinned excitedly. "It would be so cool!"

Hate stopped walking and looked at him. Actually, it *would* be cool.

Perhaps, thanks to a superior gag reflex, Wendy hadn't inhaled as much of the drug as Dog Soldier had assumed, or perhaps she had a resistance to it—for whatever reason, she returned, more or less, to consciousness before Labane's killers hit the back door.

Slowly she realized she was lying on the floor, and she wondered how and why this was so. Then, for what seemed like a long time, she stared at what looked like a very messy piece of raw meat. All at once she realized what it was she was looking at and her stomach rebelled.

Wendy tried to rise but couldn't. She threw up on the carpet and partly on the corpse. When she was through retching she pushed herself away from the body, weeping, her head turned away. She took shallow breaths, afraid the smell would make her vomit again, and struggled to her feet, sobbing.

Staggering to the bed and grabbing one of its posts, she looked around the room. A very nice room. Wendy swayed, blinking, feeling the sweat dry off her face as she tried to make sense of what was happening. A quick glance at the floor told her the body was still there.

Hadn't there been something in her hand? She looked at her hand clasped on the carved wood. Nothing there. But there had been something. Wendy looked down at the floor, but not at the body. There was a gun. It was lying in a pool of blood going tacky. The gun had been in her hand. She looked at her hand; there was blood on her fingers. And the smell . . .

Wendy's knees gave way and she dropped, holding on to the bedpost for dear life. No! No matter what, she knew that she wouldn't kill anybody. Wait, she didn't even *have* a gun. She loved Ron Labane and everything he stood for; nothing could make her hurt him.

Wendy forced herself to take deep breaths, fighting the dizziness and the panic.

Her legs steadied and she leaned her forehead against the bedpost, trying desperately to remember what had happened. Something came to her—Joe coming out of the bathroom, lifting his hand . . .

I have to get out of here, she thought. *I have to find Diana.*

She got to the door, having trouble keeping her feet, weaving left and right as though she was drunk. Her stomach wanted to heave again, this time because her head was whirling, but she forced herself to move.

Back stairs, she thought muzzily. *Too many people out front.* Wait, shouldn't she tell them? Someone had been murdered after all. She stood in the hallway, feeling as though gravity wanted to pull her flat to the carpet, trying to make up her mind.

Deep inside, some instinct warned her to go, to sneak out. *Good idea,* she thought. She wasn't sure what was going on. She could always go to the police later, when she figured out what had happened.

Once outside, she headed in the opposite direction from Hate and Dog. She thought she'd take a shower as soon as she got back to the dorm. She always felt dirty after she threw up and . . . she thought she smelled blood. Wendy caught her breath in a sob. Had that really been Ron Labane? What had Joe done to her and why?

He seemed so nice, she thought plaintively.

"Hey, sleepyhead!" Diana nudged Wendy a little harder, not entirely pleased with her friend right now. "Wake up!"

With a wrenching effort Wendy managed to say, "Unh." If Diana hadn't started gently slapping her face, she'd probably have dropped off again. "Nnnno," she murmured, raising her hands. "Stop."

"Listen, Sleeping Beauty, we've got an hour and a half to get you dressed and fed and onto your bus. C'mon"—she tugged on Wendy's nightgown—"sit up. That's a good girl."

Wendy pressed her hand to her aching brow and felt her stomach clench. *Oh God,* she prayed, *not again.* She'd thrown up three times last night. "Oh God," she said out loud, her voice sounding rusty.

"What the hell happened to you last night?" Diana asked. "I come back, you're passed out on *my* bed, thank you very much, your clothes are in a soaking-wet heap on the floor." She raised her hands and did a little hootchie dance move. "Whoo-hoo! Those intellectual dis-*cussion* groups. Wild times, I'm tellin' ya! Wild times!"

Wincing, Wendy looked at her friend through narrowed eyes. "I have a headache," she said pitifully.

"Thought you might." Diana collected two tablets and a glass of water from her night table. "I put your clothes, including your shoes"— she raised a brow—"in the dryer. What happened?"

Wendy looked at her, her mind blank for a moment, then an all-too-vivid memory crowded in. She made an involuntary sound of disgust that sent Di arching back.

"You're not going to be sick again, are you?"

Wendy shook her head, then wished she hadn't. She put one hand to her aching brow and took another sip of water. "You were right," she said. The story took shape as she spoke, almost as if she were channeling it. "Those guys didn't know Ron Labane at all. They met me outside the inn and said I was too early." She let out a soul-deep sigh. "Let's go for a walk, they said. When we were a ways from the inn they admitted that they'd tricked me. Then they asked me if I wanted to do a threesome with them."

"Bastards!" Di snapped. She put an understanding hand on Wendy's shoulder.

Wendy smiled sadly at her and covered her friend's hand with her own, then she went on with her lie. "I told them they were assholes and to get lost." Her throat grew tight and tears threatened; she fought them back, but when she continued her voice sounded strangled. "The next thing I knew I was sitting on a park bench and I'd thrown up all over myself." She covered her eyes, for a moment, then looked at Diana.

Her friend sat with her mouth open, an uncertain look on her face. "Are you all right?" Di asked carefully.

Wendy nodded, looking down at her lap. "Yeah," she choked out. She shook her head. "I don't think they even tried to touch me. You can tell. You know?" She looked at Di.

Diana nodded. "Yeah. I know." She bit her lips and said solemnly, "Do you want to go to the police?"

Wendy gave her a deer-caught-in-the-headlights stare, then shook her head vehemently. "Oohhh," she groaned, clutching her temples with both hands and wincing. "No. No time, for one thing. I've got a bus to catch. And while it was a dirty trick and they're a pair of assholes, they didn't actually hurt me. They didn't even take my wallet. I checked." Wendy sighed, then wrinkled her nose. "I guess I'll have to chalk it up to experience."

Turning down the corners of her mouth, Di nodded. "Get dressed," she said suddenly, rising from the bed. "We'll catch a burger at the bus station. We've only got about an hour and ten minutes."

They were walking to the bus station, a good half-hour walk, at Wendy's request. She'd explained that she thought the exercise might clear her head. It did seem to be helping, though her mind was still a confused knot.

"Fuck me!" Diana suddenly exclaimed.

Wendy frowned at her. "You're one of my best friends, Di, but frankly, you're not my type."

Diana tossed her a disgusted look and pointed to a newspaper box standing at the corner of the building beside them. Wendy stepped closer to look at it and her breath froze in her chest.

ECOLOGY SPOKESMAN SLAIN IN LOCAL INN

"Oh, my God," she said. Somehow it felt like she was just finding this out.

"Are you okay?" Di asked. "You just got really pale."

"I'm fine," Wendy said in a faint voice. She dug in her jeans for quarters and bought the paper. "I just can't believe it."

She didn't want to believe it. The memory of Ron Labane's shattered head and the smell of his blood hit her and she staggered. Di took her by the shoulders and guided her to the curb, where she made her sit down.

"If you're feeling faint you should duck your head between your legs," Di said gently.

"I—I'm okay." Wendy looked at her friend and smiled faintly. "It's just . . . such a shock." She took a deep breath. "And I was there. I was right th—"

"Stop right there," Di said firmly. "You were not right there. You were in the neighborhood; that's not the same thing at all. What you're saying is like saying everybody in Amherst was right there, and we weren't. So if you think you could have saved him just by standing next to the inn or have known what was going to happen, you're wrong. Don't you take that on yourself."

Wendy smiled at her; she couldn't help it. A wave of affection caused her to hug her friend in gratitude. "Thank you," she said. "I needed to hear that."

She knew in her heart that if she confessed to waking up beside his body with a gun in her hand, Diana would still have believed in her innocence. She was that kind of friend.

"C'mon," Di said, standing and snatching the paper out of her friend's hands. "You can read this on the bus."

There were a couple of policemen talking to a young, dark-haired woman as they entered the bus station. One of them glanced at Wendy and Di as they walked by. When they entered the Burger King he looked away.

"You've only got twenty-five minutes," Di said, checking the clock.

"Then I guess I'd better skip the Whopper." Wendy sighed. "I'm not really all that hungry."

"Get some fries, then," Di suggested. "And some orange juice."

"*There's* a combination," Wendy muttered. But she did as her friend suggested. It was easier, and she was too tired.

Glancing out the window, Di pointed. Wendy looked out and saw the cops talking to yet another dark-haired girl.

"Whaddaya think is going on?" Di asked.

Wendy shook her head. "Maybe somebody ran away," she suggested.

"Huh." Di shrugged. "Maybe they're trolling for dates."

They looked at each other and grinned. Then they passed the next few minutes in eating and idle chatter.

As they walked to the bus bay for Boston, Di said, "Y'know, you might want to think about reporting those guys. I'll back you about their invitation. I mean, you got away okay, but somebody else might not be so lucky."

Wendy nodded. "I know," she said. "I just can't right now. I still feel kind of sick and I just want to get to my own room. Y'know?" She looked up into her friend's sympathetic face and reached out for a good-bye hug.

"Excuse me, girls."

They looked up to find themselves confronted by the police they'd noticed earlier.

"Could we ask you a few questions, please?"

"Sure," Di said.

Wendy nodded, then she pointed vaguely toward the bus bay. "My bus is boarding, though."

Both looked at her as though expecting her to continue.

Wendy cleared her throat. "Sure, what do you want to know?"

They wanted to know if Wendy and Diana knew who Ron Labane was, did they go to his speech, how did they feel about him, and most important, where had they been last night.

"Well, I went out clubbing," Di said happily. "But my buddy here got food poisoning and spent the night at the dorm yawning in Technicolor."

For some reason the phrase sent a spasm though Wendy's stomach and she put her hand over her mouth, just in case.

"Sorry," Di said, wincing.

"So you were by yourself last night?" one of the cops said. They both moved slightly closer to her.

"Well," Di said, wincing again, "I just couldn't . . . I mean, she was soooo sick. She said it was okay if I went out. But I kept coming back to check on her, so it isn't like I deserted her." She gave the cops a kind of an accusing look.

"How many times did you look in on her, miss?" the cop asked.

"Oh, I dunno. Four?" She'd changed clubs four times, so that seemed right. Di looked at Wendy.

"I think so," Wendy said. "I was kind of out of it."

The cops looked at her. "You do look a little pale," one of them said.

"There's a flu going around Boston," Wendy said, quite truthfully.

The cops moved back slightly. Just then the station announced the last call for her bus and Wendy pointed outside. "I have to go," she said.

The two policemen looked at each other. "Okay, thanks for your cooperation. We'll get your address from your friend here, in case we need to speak to you again."

"Okay." Wendy hugged Di. "Thanks," she said, meaning it. "I'll call you later."

"Yeah. I want to be sure you got home okay."

As the bus pulled out Di was still talking to the police, but they were laughing at some joke she'd made. Except for the uniforms, they could have been any pair of young guys flirting.

Wendy read the paper as the roadside ribbons of urban sprawl, interrupted by occasional patches of woods, rolled by outside the grimy window of the bus. Labane had made a call to the police to report that a young woman with long red hair had been stalking him, threatening him. He'd asked the police to investigate, but by the time they arrived at the inn he was already dead. Three high-caliber gun shots to the head from close range, the coroner reported.

They're looking for me, Wendy thought. *They just don't know it yet.* But they'd find her name on the list of *New Day* show attendees, they'd find her name on the pledge list, she'd subscribed to the magazine, her name was all over his lists. Just the way a stalker's would be.

She'd been well and truly set up by those guys.

Somewhere along the way she drifted off to sleep again. She came to with the bus driver giving her a gentle shake. "Miss," he said quietly. "Miss."

She looked into his fatherly face for a moment, confused. Then she asked, "Are we there yet?"

He grinned. "Yep. I came back to get something and I noticed you. You almost got a trip back to Amherst." He raised his brows. "Good weekend?"

She shook her head tiredly, then smiled. "Memorable anyway."

"Good for you," he said. "Make as many memories as you can." He tapped his head. "Supposed to be good for your brain."

"I'll keep that in mind." Wendy smiled as she slipped out of the seat.

"You got any luggage down below?" the driver asked.

She shook her head and pulled her duffel from the overhead rack. "Just this. Thanks."

They made their way down the aisle and he waited for her to get off before he closed the door, then they said good-bye and went their separate ways. Wendy moved slowly through the crowd of travelers, still feeling groggy. She wandered out the front doors and stopped to look around.

John, she thought. The name brought her head up. Yes, John. He'd been running from the cops since he was, like . . . born! *I need to talk to him.*

Gripping the strap of her duffel, she turned on her heel to go back into the bus station to the bank of phones and ran smack into Yam's narrow chest.

"Hey!" she said, and gave him a one armed hug. "Am I glad to see you!"

"Me, too," he said. "Keep walking, we've got to get out of here; the cops are looking for you."

"Oh God," she said. "Already?"

"Yep, we're supposed to meet Snog at the Coop."

Yam explained that they'd pooled their resources and come up with fifteen hundred in cash for her.

"Snog got to your computer; there wasn't anything there that needed to be erased, but we had to check. Did you leave any disks or anything around?"

"No. All my stuff is at the central drop." She shook her head. "I don't do written notes. At least not about that." She was referring to the CPU John had given them.

"Good." He gave her a brief, nervous smile. "C'mon."

Upstairs at the Coop they found Snog and Carl waiting for them at a corner table near the big windows that looked out on the alley and the brick wall opposite. Snog rose and enveloped her in a hug. Then he stepped back, his hands on her shoulders.

"Thweetie," he lisped, "you *tho* need a makeover."

Wendy blinked at him in astonishment. "Hey, thanks, Snog! "That just caps my day!"

"No, no, no. You don't understand," he said, grinning. "Here, sit down before you fall down."

That didn't make her feel much better, but she let herself be persuaded.

"Cuppa joe?" Carl asked.

"Please," Wendy said with heartfelt gratitude.

"Decaf," Yam said, sitting down beside her. They all looked at him. "I've got some schematics to draw later," he explained.

"Ah," they all said at once.

"Here's your passport." Snog slid a blue booklet over to her.

"I don't have a passport," Wendy said, confused.

She opened the cover and stared at the photo inside. The girl was a goth-rock vision with multiple piercings on lip, nose, eyebrow, and ears. Her short hair was purple; in fact, in her physical description the color was listed as brown/purple. The girl stared out of the picture with an unnerving intensity, as though, somehow, she could actually see Wendy looking at her. Wendy snapped the cover shut.

"Who is this psycho?"

Snog laughed. "That's my sister, Carolyn. I'll have to tell her you said that; she'll laugh. She belongs to a band in Canada and one time when they pulled her license she decided she needed another ID to get across the border. It's okay, she never uses it anymore since she got her license back."

"Snog, I don't look anything like your sister!"

"You will once my girlfriend gets through with you."

"You have a girlfriend?" Yam said.

Carl, who had returned with their coffees, looked askance at Snog.

"Well," Snog said, pulling his head back and looking down into his cup, "she's a friend, and she's a girl . . ." He glanced up at them. "Okay, she's more a friend of my sister's, but she kinda likes me."

They all stirred their coffee and he looked around the table at them.

"Hey, she likes me enough that she agreed to make Wendy look like Carolyn."

"I really appreciate this, Snog," Wendy said, looking up at him. "But I just can't get my face pierced." Wasn't she in enough trouble without adding physical pain, too?

"No, no, no. This is the cool part." He held up his hands. "She's a makeup artist. She can fix you up with fake piercings. And the great thing is, even if you aren't a perfect match, nobody over twenty-five can look someone with eyebrow piercings in the face."

"You have a point," Yam said after a thoughtful sip of his coffee.

"Am I going somewhere?" Wendy asked. "And if so, where?"

"Yeah, you're going somewhere," Snog said.

"You can't stay here." Carl shook his head sadly. "Brad says the cops are all over your dorm."

"Is that where he is?" Wendy asked, relieved. She'd been afraid he thought she was guilty.

Snog slid two phrase books over to her, one Portuguese and one Spanish.

She looked around the table at their serious faces.

"John," Yam said, and shrugged. The others nodded.

"Who else that we know can tell you what to do?" Snog asked.

Wendy looked down, biting her lips, fighting the tears that wanted to come. "I didn't do it, you know."

"We know that." Carl placed one of his big hands over hers. "But Brad says the cops are acting like they've got something pretty solid on you."

"Do you know what that would be?" Yam asked.

Wendy nodded, then waved a hand in a negative swipe. "I'm not going to tell you anything. The less you know the better."

Snog slid a packet across the table. Wendy opened it to find a ticket to New York and one to São Paulo, Brazil. She looked at him, her eyes wide with unasked questions.

Shrugging, Snog explained, "He once said that if I needed to meet him face-to-face, I should send him a message, go there and wait." He glanced up at her. "I assumed he told you the same thing."

She nodded. Actually, John had trusted her further than that, but saying so might hurt her friend's feelings, so she kept it to herself.

"We should get going," Snog said, rising. "You'll need some new clothes of the right type and then we get you made up. Your flight leaves at seven and they like you to be at the airport at least two hours before that."

"I can't thank you guys enough." Wendy reached out and touched Carl and Yam, looking up at Snog with tears in her eyes. "I am innocent, but I can't prove it."

Snog grinned and spread his arms. "Hey, that's why we're helping you. C'mon, let's get cracking."

SÃO PAULO, BRAZIL

The customs agent stared at her in fascination and Wendy couldn't blame him. She felt like a complete clown. Not only was her hair rinsed purple, and her makeup taken to the extreme, her face covered with various types of faux piercings, but both arms writhed with intricate tattoos.

The vintage black velvet dress was hot even inside the air-conditioned building; she didn't want to think what it was going to be like when she got out into the smog-sizzling tropical atmosphere of Brazil's biggest city. It hung on her like a bag, and the brand-new army boots were killing her. *Once I get them off I'll probably have to go barefoot for a week,* she thought. Her feet and ankles were undoubtedly destined to swell to twice their size. She'd been moving from one form of transport to another for the last fourteen hours.

The customs agent went through his list of rote questions, then hesitated.

"I must warn you, senhorita, that having anything to do with drugs in this country is a very serious crime."

Wendy smiled sweetly. "Oh," she said, shaking her head carefully lest she shake something loose, "thank you, but I'm not into that. I'm into Christian goth rock. We sing about the sufferings of our Lord, not sex and drugs. See." She held out her empurpled arms. "I'm totally clean. Do you believe that Jesus is your personal savior?"

"Yes," he said, quickly stamping her passport. "And I have a very active patron saint. Welcome to Brazil, have a nice day. Next!"

Was that a note of desperation I heard in your voice? she wondered as she moved toward the Hertz counter. Wendy put on a pair of huge, black-rimmed sunglasses she'd bought in New York. She slipped them down to rest on the tip of her nose as she got to the counter and, taking out her Portuguese phrase book, prepared to do battle.

At the sight of the book a look of subdued horror crossed the clerk's face. "I speak English," he said quickly. "American?"

"Yes," she said, relieved. "How did you know?"

"The last plane in was from New York. You will pardon my observing that you look like New York. Yes?"

Wendy laughed. "I suppose I do," she said, trying to sound as though she enjoyed the way she looked. "I'd like to rent an economy car." She plunked Carolyn's Visa card on the counter.

("Don't worry," Snog had insisted. "She won't even notice it's missing.")

Actually Wendy was willing to bet that she would. At the very least she'd notice when charges from Brazil started showing up on her statements.

"May I see your driver's license, please," the young man said pleasantly.

She handed over her own Massachusetts license.

"This is a different name from the card," he said. "I'm afraid I can't accept this."

"But it's obviously me," Wendy objected. "Carolyn Brandt is my stage name, the one I travel under." She handed him the passport. "See, that's me, too." She offered him a brilliant smile. "I explained all that to the Massachusetts DMV and they said no. They said I had to take off my makeup and rinse the dye out of my hair and use my birth name. The federal government," Wendy said loudly, "was willing to accept me as I am, but not Massachusetts. But really, a federal document supersedes a state document," she said confidently.

He looked up at her, comparing the pictures from the license and the passport with what he saw. "It does seem to be you," he said.

Wendy smiled and nodded. He began comparing signatures. Fortunately Carolyn's handwriting and her own were very similar, hers being slightly neater.

"This handwriting is a little different," the clerk said, pointing to the license.

Wendy nodded. "They made me write it three times. It has to be legible, they said." She scrunched up her face and felt one of the brow rings loosen. "So are we all right, or what?" she asked, suddenly impatient.

The young man hesitated, still. "How long did you want to rent the car for?"

"Ten days," Wendy said without hesitation.

That way, if John didn't want to help her, she could get it back here easily enough. She supposed that she could lose herself in a city this size. *Hell,* she thought, *maybe I can start up a Christian goth-rock band.*

The young man made his decision and processed her request, sold her insurance. "Very wise, miss." And had her sign the rental agreement.

Wendy had bought a wrist brace when out shopping with Snog and it supplied the requisite messiness to make her handwriting an almost perfect copy of Carolyn's. Certainly it brought a look of relief to the clerk's face.

She stopped at the bank window to change her U.S. money into Brazilian currency, and remembered to buy some guaranies for when she entered Paraguay. Within ten minutes, a map on the seat beside her, she was on her way.

I hope John won't be mad, she thought.

CHAPTER 22

Kurt Viemeister swaggered through the bland corridors of the base's living quarters to find Clea Bennet's door open. Putting his hands on either side of the doorway, he leaned in and looked around, pleasantly conscious of the way his broad sculpted shoulders and thick-muscled arms rippled beneath the thin T-shirt.

The room was just like a generous ten-by-fourteen cubicle, painted off-white, with a full bed, bookcase, cheap desk with an uncomfortable chair, bedside table, bureau, and a first-rate computer. Space was at a surprising premium in the base; armoring against the Antarctic was almost as much trouble as guarding against the environment of the moon.

Clea was packing.

"Going somewhere?" he asked, half humorously. *As if there was anywhere to go.*

"Yes," she said, coming out of the tiny bathroom. "Kushner, Locke, and I are going seal hunting." Clea gave him a sidelong smile. "In a manner of speaking."

"What about our work?" Kurt snapped, straightening.

The I-950 turned a cool look on the self-styled superman.

"Hey, Kurt, why don't you say that a little louder, I don't think Tricker heard you. Or, you could wear a T-shirt that says 'I break the rules, please punish me.' " Clea raised one sardonic brow at him as she crossed the room to take something from her bureau drawer. "If you want me to work with you it wouldn't hurt you to *ask* for my assistance. *Officially.*" She gave him a very false smile. "I suspect Tricker thinks I want to be your groupie."

Viemeister frowned. "I will speak to him now, this hour. I don't want you wasting your time fooling around with dumb animals."

Serena had been right; Viemeister was ridiculously lacking in social skills, and laughably unaware of it. The man was convinced that it was his choice entirely that people left him alone. He was equally convinced that if he wanted someone's company he could charm them into liking him.

Fat chance! Clea thought. Viemeister had brains and good looks—but then, so did a very bright Doberman. *Apparently he's never tested that I-am-charming-when-I-want-to-be theory.*

She turned to him with a slight smile. "Kurt, I'm going stir-crazy down here. I want to see some sky." She tilted her head toward him. "Okay?"

"I didn't even know you were interested in pinnipeds," he said sullenly.

The I-950 laughed. "I'm interested in everything. Especially wringing concessions from Tricker. It amuses me."

Frowning, Viemeister took a deep breath and crossed his massive arms over his swollen chest.

Is that for my benefit? she wondered.

"I don't like Tricker," he announced.

"Big surprise there," Clea said. "I doubt he'd win a popularity contest hereabouts. If you don't like him it should please you that I enjoy torturing him."

Kurt snorted. "I suppose it should. But it concerns me that you claim to be going stir-crazy. It is a weakness, and you should fight any weakness in your character."

"It's a state of mind, and I'll do what I like."

The I-950 gave him a hard look and watched him lift his head, like a bull scenting a challenger. She smiled and looked away, a dimple in her cheek. "I'll be back in a week," she said. "You're just jealous because I'm getting to do something different."

His stance and expression softened slightly. "Perhaps I'm jealous that you're going to be out on the ice with two other men."

Clea laughed and went to embrace him, chuckling as his arms wrapped around her. She leaned back and looked up at him, her eyes sparkling. Yes, she was definitely developing a sense of humor.

"You *have* to have seen these guys," she said. "Kushner is a potato with legs and Locke looks like the mummy of Ramses the Second walking." She poked him in the chest, perhaps a little too hard, but he was *such* a jerk. "I've made my choice, and that ought to tell you something about my taste in men."

This time he laughed, and something in the way of it was intended to remind her she'd been a virgin until she met him.

"Exactly," she purred.

Clea pushed herself off from his chest, forcing him to let her go, though he obviously didn't want to. Arching a brow, she asked, "Weren't you going to go ask Tricker to allow you my services?" She smiled wickedly.

"I can't dissuade you?"

"Uh-uh."

"Then I may as well go." He turned on his heel and walked out without another word.

Clea snorted, knowing he heard her because she knew exactly how to direct sound to her intended hearer. She knew he'd been deliberately ambiguous, assuming that she'd wonder if he'd even bother to ask Tricker for her assistance in his work.

As if he'd risk alienating her. Poor Kurt was a very lonely boy and she'd made a point of filling his off-hours with lots of rigorous exercise and stimulating conversation. What *he* considered stimulating conversation anyway, which alternated between talking about how wonderful he was, his absurd politics, and his project. Clea actually enjoyed talking about that last subject though.

So, no, he wouldn't risk antagonizing her. By the time she got back, everything should be settled and then she could begin work on the most important thing in the world. A thrill of anticipation shot through her.

Skynet!

Clea approached the downed leopard seal at a jog, moving effortlessly over the irregular, slippery surface of the ice. Had the humans been watching, she would have crept up on it, as if it was going to jump up and savage *her*. But she could plainly see that it was unconscious, and hear the rhythm of its heartbeat and breathing.

The I-950 quickly plucked the orange-tipped dart from its side and stowed it away in her pouch. Then she pulled out a radio harness, tested it, and fitted it around the seal's body. Pulling out a punch, she attached a tag to its flipper.

All of this was done at speeds far exceeding the human norm. It kept her warmer and she saw no reason to suffer when there wasn't anyone to witness her relative comfort. She couldn't push her metabolism too hard, unfortunately, as the supply of food was both limited and carefully calculated. So, like the humans accompanying her, her socks froze to the soles of her feet and she actually needed the multiple layers of clothing she wore.

Pulling a syringe out of her jacket, where it had been kept warm until this moment so the saline medium didn't freeze, she carefully flushed the needle to eliminate air bubbles. Inside, just barely visible to the most refined sight her augmented eyes could manage, were the microscopic machines that would allow her control over this animal.

She regretted the size of the things, but it was the best she could do with the materials at hand, the constant surveillance, and supplies so carefully monitored. The I-950 had only gotten away with the limited number she'd managed to cobble together because she was using minute pieces of parts she then destroyed in "experiments."

Each machine had a tail, like a sperm, that would allow it to swim through the fluid surrounding the seal's brain to the area it was programmed to affect. There it would gently drop onto the surface of the brain and adhere itself by releasing a microscopic drop of surgical glue. Then tiny filaments would spin out, attaching themselves to crucial parts of the mammal's brain—essentially a more limited form of the machine-neuron symbiosis that made up her brain, and derived from the same technology.

Not for the first time, she wondered how much of what Skynet would know in the future would come from research, and how much through a closed timelike loop from *her*. With an effort, she pushed these musings aside; the question was simply unanswerable, as was the question of where the information came from in the "first place." That was meaningless, when time travel was factored into the equation.

The machines would respond to signals sent through a special transmitter she'd added to the one on the radio harness. This should allow her to see and hear through the animal's eyes and ears. How well that would work, exactly, she had yet to find out. The transmitter would also allow her to excite certain portions of the seal's brain to elicit a desired response. Relentless, violent rage, for example. In a world without Terminators she had to improvise.

Clea plunged the needle into the seal's neck at the base of the skull and inserted the machines.

"Clea! What did you just do?" Hiram Locke trundled gingerly over to her across the ice. "Did I just see you inject air into that seal?"

She couldn't see his face at all, as it was covered by a fleece balaclava and mirrored goggles, but she could tell from his voice that his expression as disapproving. "Hiram!" she snapped back. "Wouldn't that kill the animal?"

He hesitated. "Yes," he said.

"As we both already know that, what possible reason would I have to do something so stupid?"

Locke looked around, as though hoping for backup. "What were you doing?" he asked uncertainly.

"I was trying to get a blood sample. But my fingers are numb and I missed the vein. Would you like to give it a try?" She stood and held out the syringe.

"No, no," he said, backing a step, holding up his mittened hands.

She took a step closer to him. "I had the impression you didn't think I knew how to use one of these." Her voice was hard, leaving no doubt as to how she felt about his interference. "Wouldn't you like to demonstrate?"

"Sorry," Locke said, continuing to back away. "I spoke out of turn."

"What do you want?" Clea asked.

She wasn't happy that he'd come looking for her. He was supposed to be a couple of miles away with his partner. She'd been taking chances and he might have seen something. But the risks had been unavoidable. Her time alone was severely limited; safety regulations demanded that no one go out on the ice alone. She'd only managed to acquire this time by making herself completely unendurable to the two humans.

Still, I shouldn't have been taken unaware like that.

With her whole head muffled by a balaclava, goggles, and a fur-trimmed hood, even her computer-enhanced senses were severely hobbled. She judged that she was currently human normal in the realm of her senses. Which put her way ahead of her companions.

Still, she should be more alert than a human. Especially because of the reduction in her abilities. Clea wondered if at some level she was trying to get caught. *Or perhaps I'm looking for an excuse to kill a human.* Perhaps it was frustration over how long it was taking to get Skynet on-line.

The computer that would one day be Skynet was exceptional, but it was just a machine, completely empty of consciousness. Being in the presence of such a truncated version of her creator was acutely painful in the emotional sense. It certainly kept her own computer busy balancing her brain chemistry. Perhaps too busy.

"We were concerned," Locke said. "You're not supposed to be alone out here. If anything happened to you . . ."

She laughed at him. "If anything happens to me it will be my own fault and there'd be nothing you could do about it."

"Well, I don't want to be the one to tell Tricker that you were left alone out here like this." His voice was sullen.

"Then don't tell him." Clea shrugged one shoulder. "What he doesn't know won't bother him. Do you think I'm going to complain to him about it when we get back?" She leaned toward him. "Look, I have my work and you have yours. And guess what? My work is more important to me than yours is. I don't want to help you, or hang out with you, when I could be accomplishing things on my own."

They'd discussed all of this, ad nauseam, before they all set out to work this morning. Possibly the human was nervous and wanted to cover his butt in case Tricker somehow found out about her working independently.

"By the way, if we're not supposed to be alone out here, where the hell is Kushner?"

Locke shuffled his heavily booted feet. "He'll be all right."

"Well, so will I!" Clea snapped in frustration.

The scientist drew himself up. "But *you're* a woman."

Does he honestly think I'm unaware of my gender? she wondered, momentarily confused. Her computer gave her a prompt. *Human females have historically been considered the weaker sex.* She almost laughed aloud.

"Yes," she agreed quietly, "I'm a woman." *Sort of.* "But I'm also a *lot* younger than both of you and in much better shape. I suggest that you two watch out for each other and leave me to my no-doubt-deserved fate."

"There's no need for you to get snippy," Locke said huffily. "I'm only trying to help."

"There's no need to get patronizing. Go away, I'm busy."

They stared at each other. *It's a good thing he can't really see my face,* the I-950 thought. *He'd probably have a heart attack.* Of course, then at least half of her problem would be solved.

Killing them both was so tempting. She could toss the bodies down a crevasse today, and by the time searchers found them, the two would be so frozen no one would be able to tell exactly when they'd died, and even if she beat them to a pulp they'd most likely attribute the wounds to the fall. Then she'd be free to work in peace. A perfect solution.

Except . . . it would also redouble Tricker's surveillance. She sighed, looking around at the white, white landscape with its drifting wisps of ice crystal under the deep-purple-blue sky. In the long run she supposed the best thing to do was to simply put up with them. *But it is so tempting. Without them, I could imagine there were no humans in the world at all. This place is . . . clean.*

"Look," the I-950 said, trying to sound conciliatory, "I'll call in every half hour, and if anything, anything at all seems to be going wrong, I'll call you and immediately head back to camp." Clea shrugged. "What more can I do? If I don't do this now it will be time to go back and I'll have accomplished nothing."

Locke folded his arms across his chest and seemed about to speak.

"Unless you'd both like to give up some of your time out here to stay with me while I work?" she suggested.

He barked a laugh. "The thing is, Tricker . . ."

Here we go again, she thought. "Who's going to tell him?" Clea demanded. "I'm not." She shrugged. "Look, it's cold out here and we're losing working time. Why don't we discuss this later, back at camp?" Just like they had every day so far.

After a moment's hesitation he nodded. "All right," he said. Then, almost reluctantly, he turned and tottered off.

Clea watched him go. Suddenly an image of him squirming on the ice with blood pouring from his mouth came to her. *If only,* she thought, and regretted the virtue of necessity.

She looked down at the seal. Its heartbeat was normal and it seemed to be sleeping naturally. The circuit that activated the machines she'd implanted was controlled by another one in her complex and somewhat bulky wristwatch. Clea activated them, testing each one in turn and getting a positive signal. Now all that remained was to give them an actual field test.

Something to look forward to, she thought.

She looked behind her and saw Locke disappearing around a wind-sculpted ridge of snow touched with exquisite shades of pale blue. Clea watched for a full minute and saw no sign of him, not even in the ultraviolet stage. Her ears hadn't picked anything up that sounded human either.

Picking up her backpack and sliding it on, she jogged off, looking for another leopard seal. Time wasted delayed Skynet's advent.

Kurt was there to greet her, in the chamber that resembled an air lock when they came in off the ice. Clea grinned and ran into his arms, wrapping her legs around his waist and kissing him passionately.

"We have permission to work together," Kurt murmured in her ear when they came up for air; then he licked her neck.

The I-950 giggled and snuggled her head into his shoulder. "Good," she whispered.

"I hate to break this up, kids," Tricker said, "but we have some things to discuss."

Clea continued to cling to Viemeister like a monkey as she glanced over her shoulder at Tricker. She offered him a lazy smile. "Oh? Then let's make an appointment," she suggested.

"Hey, I'm free now," he said, appearing totally unimpressed by their display of heated sensuality.

The I-950 looked adoringly at Kurt. "But I'm busy," she said. Then she looked over her shoulder again at Tricker. "Perhaps in a couple of hours?"

"Perhaps now?" Tricker didn't try to hide his dislike for either of them most times; now he seemed to be doing his best to project it. He had an extremely effective way of suggesting what he was seeing when he looked at a person—something reminiscent of a small, yapping, incontinent dog that *might* be too valuable to be put down.

Viemeister moved his hands from Clea's waist to cup her buttocks; he hoisted her up and she laughed. "Two hours," he said, and started to walk off.

"Kurt," Tricker said, pointedly not looking at the muscular scientist and his comely burden, "you make me wait, I make you wait."

Kurt and Clea looked at each other and sighed as one, then smiled wickedly. He let her down slowly, and she came over to the security chief.

"What exactly is there to discuss? You've received permission for me to work with my friend. So . . . ?" She shrugged, her eyes wide.

"I need to know what you're going to do about *your* work," he said through clenched teeth.

"I think this is more important," Clea told him. *If you only knew how much more important, human.* "Once my attention is engaged like this, it's very difficult for me to concentrate on anything else."

"So you're just going to abandon the work you were brought here to do?"

"Well, actually . . ." She produced a disk and handed it to him with a sweet smile. "It's largely finished. I think you'll find several people here—" she named them—"can handle the remaining details. That's okay with you, isn't it?"

Tricker bit the inside of his cheek. "Sure," he said after a moment. He gave her an insincere smile. "Run along, kids. Get some work done." The sarcasm was as thick as butter.

"All in good time." Clea blew him a kiss, then engulfed Viemeister's muscular arm in a hug and looked up at him. "All in good time."

She walked off with Kurt, feeling as happy as it was possible for her to feel without Skynet whispering in her mind. She looked forward to the sex she would soon be having with Kurt. And it was good that she now had official permission to work with him on Skynet. No one on earth, with the exception of Alissa, could offer more help in developing its intelligence. As a bonus, she'd annoyed Tricker again.

Serena had regarded him as an exceptional human being. But Clea wasn't finding him to be that formidable; he hadn't even pursued her resemblance to her parent, which, frankly was a relief.

It was also a relief to know that she'd finally convinced her computer to allow her natural reactions to sex to prevail. She'd successfully argued that as she was less experienced than her predecessor, she was less able to fake her reactions. Therefore, it was reasonable to assume that someone as intelligent as Viemeister would almost certainly detect her lack of enthusiasm.

Her stomach fluttered pleasantly in anticipation. Life was good.

ROUTE 9, PARAGUAY

Wendy had somehow thought of Paraguay as a small country. She supposed that was because it looked like a peanut nestled between Brazil and Argentina. But the place was as big as most American states and its character had changed completely since she'd passed the Brazilian border. Lush semitropical forest full of smoking clearings had given way to flat, dry grasslands where scattered cattle grazed between occasional clumps of palms. It smelled strange, too: hot in a way that had nothing to do with the temperature; dusty, like spices and acrid musk. Even the smells of cattle were alien. She'd been a city girl all her life.

According to what John had told her, he was living on a farm or something just outside Villa Hayes. Sometimes it sounded like he was talking about Dogpatch, and sometimes like the Ponderosa.

She was tired, and she was hungry, and she was fighting the feeling that she was hopelessly lost. It was hot and everything that she'd brought with her was made of black velvet at Snog's insistence. She'd kill for a T-shirt and shorts right now.

Money was rapidly running out, making her want to continue to drive, not stopping for bed or food, but she could barely keep her eyes open. Besides fighting sleep, she was fighting the sneaking suspicion that John wouldn't be too happy to see her.

Should she call him, warn him that she was coming? What if he said no, he wouldn't help her? Wendy's heart beat faster at the thought, exhaustion allowing panic a foothold.

Her ordinary sunny self-confidence was gradually eroding in the face of the sheer foreignness of her surroundings, not to mention her circumstances. She was homesick and scared and very lonely. Wendy found it disconcerting to realize just how protected she had always been until now. She'd always considered herself an independent, self-sufficient type of woman.

But I'm really just a clueless college girl on the lam.

Wendy licked dry lips and decided to press on, deciding she wouldn't give John a chance to say no. After everything else she'd been through over the last few days, she was learning to take things as they came.

VON ROSSBACH ESTANCIA, PARAGUAY

Epifanio Ayala, von Rossbach's overseer, watched the plume of dust approach the main house of the *estancia* and assumed it was yet another delivery. They had received many such in the last few days: although little remained, for Don von Rossbach and young John had taken the accumulation away to Asunción in the *estancia*'s truck today. Epifanio's wife, Marietta, from whom almost no secret could be kept for long, had informed him that these things were mostly very warm winter clothing and expensive camping gear.

"Maybe they are going mountain climbing," he'd suggested.

Marietta had only shrugged and rolled her eyes expressively. But he'd known what she meant. Ever since he'd met Señora Krieger, Señor von Rossbach had been going away without warning to do who knew what.

Epifanio shook his head as he watched the dust plume grow closer. The señor was a nice man, and Señora Krieger and her son, they were nice, too. But since they'd come home, Epifanio himself was the only one involved in running the *estancia*. True, he was the overseer, it was his job. But not so very long ago Señor von Rossbach had taken an interest in every aspect of the ranch, riding out to check the cattle, making plans to improve the stock and the land. It was worrying to see such a change in him.

Marietta thought it was for the best. "He is much more alive," she'd insisted. And she favored the señora's presence. But that was a woman for you, always hoping for romance. To him it seemed there was never a woman more cold and businesslike than Susan Krieger. Although she, too, was neglecting her business, staying mostly at the *estancia* fiddling with the computer. And that bandage on her hip . . . He was a peaceful man, but he knew a gunshot wound when he saw it.

The dust wasn't coming from a delivery truck, it seemed, but from a small sedan, so covered with dirt that its original color was completely hidden. His brows rose. Those were Brazilian plates—common enough in Asunción, but not in the country.

Epifanio rose from his seat on the *portal* and went down the steps to stand before the great house, patiently waiting for the car to arrive. No doubt it was some lost traveler, for the vehicle certainly didn't belong to anyone Ayala knew and the señor and his guests never received visitors.

He could dimly see the figure of a woman through the dirty glass of the side window as she pulled up beside him. Epifanio waved some of the swirling dust that accompanied her aside with his hat and took in details to relate to Marietta later on.

The car was new and designed for city driving; its low-slung chassis must have had a hard time on the rough roads surrounding the *estancia*. A very impractical vehicle, with no storage capacity to speak of and much too small for a family of any size. It seemed to be a pale blue under the dust.

The woman inside slumped behind the wheel, unmoving, and after a moment Epifanio tapped lightly on the window to get her attention. She lifted her head with a start, as though she'd fallen asleep, then she rolled down the window.

He saw that she hadn't been sleeping, but reading. It was a girl, perhaps nineteen years old and very tired looking, dressed in black velvet and sweating because of it. She glanced from him to her book and brushed a hank of sweat-soaked dark hair back from her face with one hand.

Then she told him, in terrible Spanish, that she was looking for John Krieger. Really, it was only the name that gave him a clue as to what she wanted. *What a terrible accent,* he thought. She probably didn't speak Spanish at all, but was parroting phrases from the book.

"Señor Krieger is not here right now," he said politely. "He will not be back for several hours, I think."

Epifanio had taken care to speak slowly so that she would understand, but the girl looked back at him with big eyes that held no more understanding than a cow's. *Sí. No Spanish at all.* And not likely to speak Guarni, which was his only other language beyond a few words of German. She looked so tired, and so lost, that he couldn't help but take pity on her.

"Señora Krieger? Perhaps she could help you?" he offered.

Alarm flashed briefly in her eyes, then her mouth firmed and she nodded once. Opening the door, she stood, as stiff as an old lady. Then she said, "*Sí.* Señora Krieger, *por favor.*"

Epifanio smiled at her, pleased at their progress, and gestured toward the *portal* with his hat, holding out his other arm as though to herd her into the house. To his surprise she put her hand on his arm to steady herself and he instantly took her elbow to support and guide her.

Marietta was going to love this.

Sarah looked up from her work, frowning, at Epifanio's knock. Beside him was a young woman in a long-sleeved, ankle-length, and ill-fitting black dress. If her hair hadn't been purple Sarah would have thought she was a very young nun. Suddenly something about the girl clicked and Sarah said to herself, *American.*

"Yes?" she said aloud.

"Pardon my intrusion, señora. But the young lady"—he gestured at the girl with his hat—"is looking for your son, I think."

Sarah's eyes flicked to the girl, and if looks were bullets Wendy would have been dead before she hit the floor. Only part of it was due to the continuing dull pain in Sarah's hip. "Thank you, Epifanio," she said, rising from the desk. "I'll take care of it." Switching to English, she said to the girl, "Won't you come in?"

The girl swallowed visibly and, with a nervous glance at the overseer, tottered stiffly into the room.

Sarah frowned. "Are you ill?" she asked.

"No, ma'am. I've just been driving for a very long time." The girl gave her a nervous smile. She dropped into the chair that Sarah had indicated like a sack of potatoes.

What a wuss. "Hungry?" Sarah asked crisply.

"Yes, ma'am."

She asked Epifanio to tell his wife to bring sandwiches and fruit juice and watched him go before she sat down again. Then she looked across the desk at her—no, at John's visitor.

"You're from MIT," she stated. John's recruits had been sending reports every other day, but there had been no word in over a week. Obviously something had gone seriously wrong. Perhaps wrong enough to send a messenger. "What happened?"

It was hard, but she kept the anger out of her voice as much as she could. This child was so spooked she'd probably faint if she had any idea how close to killing mad Sarah was. She should reserve her anger for John, who had obviously given out just a little more information than he should have. Forcing herself to seem calm, Sarah leaned back and waited for the girl's explanation.

God, what a bitch, Wendy thought. It had never occurred to her that John wouldn't be home when she arrived, and she longed for him now more than she longed for sleep. If she'd thought about his mother at all it was as a distant presence to whom she would be brought after she'd explained everything to him and at least had a shower.

She hadn't felt this much like an importunate intruder since her first interview at MIT.

Well that was nothing, Wendy told herself, squaring her shoulders, *and I'll get through this.* After waking up to find one of her heroes blown to pieces in front of her and the police after her for the murder, one overbearing woman shouldn't be too hard to take. But, oh, how she longed for John.

She took a deep breath and rapidly gave John's mother a succinct report. By the time she finished she was slurring her words in exhaustion. Just then a motherly-looking woman came in with a tray of food.

John's mother cleared a section of the desk and said something in
Spanish. The woman gave Wendy a thorough looking over and a slight
smile.

Wendy could feel her color rise. She'd never felt—she'd never *been*
so grubby in her life. She actually smelled! Tired as she was, the embarrassment she felt was almost too much. Tears welled up in her eyes
and she looked down, hoping to hide this final humiliation from John's
hard-assed mother.

I will not cry! she thought fiercely. *I will not.*

Sarah poured juice into the glasses, glancing at Wendy from under her
lashes. The kid looked like she was going to break down and bawl at any
moment. *My God, what a wuss!* What did John see in her?

She handed Wendy a glass of juice and the girl took it with an almost
inaudible "thank you."

Sarah sat down and took a sip from her own glass, watching Wendy
take careful sips of the juice. "Not thirsty?" she asked. "You don't have
to drink it."

The girl glanced up, then looked down again. Yes, her eyes were red
and her eyelashes moist, a real crybaby.

"I haven't eaten or drunk anything for a while," Wendy said at last,
her voice sounding surprisingly strong. "And I'm nervous, so I'm just
being careful." One corner of her mouth lifted and she raised her eyes to
meet Sarah's. "I wouldn't want to be sick all over your parquet floor."

"Thank you," Sarah said, her chin resting on her fist. "It's not my
floor, but I appreciate the thought." She straightened up and crossed her
legs, taking a sip of her juice. "What I don't appreciate is that you're here,
and why."

Wendy dropped her gaze to her drink and went absolutely still as
once again, color flooded her cheeks. She tipped her head to one side.
"I guess"—her eyes met Sarah's—"that we thought you might be able
to tell me what to do."

"Because of being unjustly accused and all?" Sarah asked with a
wave of her hand.

Wendy nodded, her gaze unwavering; something in her eyes told
Sarah that she had caught the sarcasm and didn't like it.

"To be honest," Sarah said, picking a speck of lint from her skirt and
smoothing down the fabric, "I don't think I've ever been unjustly
accused."

She grinned at Wendy's undisguised astonishment. "I've done it all," she said breezily. "I've bombed, I've run guns, I've smuggled drugs. Extortion, bribery, destruction of property, assault and battery." She ticked her crimes off on her fingers. "I'm guilty, guilty, guilty. I've never killed anybody—anybody human—and I've never been involved in a kidnapping—not that I didn't have opportunities—and I've never sold myself. But other than that . . ." She shrugged, watching for the girl's reaction.

"Even better," Wendy said after a moment's pause. "If you're guilty of all that and you're still not in jail, you could probably write a book on the subject."

Sarah was taken by surprise. *So, maybe the kid does have a spine,* she thought. She hoped so if John was in any way involved with her. Still, she'd come here in trouble and possibly dragging trouble behind her. "One of the ways we've stayed out of jail is by not allowing people being chased by the police to come directly to our door," she said pointedly.

"Nobody knows where I am," Wendy said. "The closest anyone could trace me is São Paulo."

"That's closer than I like," Sarah snapped.

"Look," Wendy said carefully, "I didn't stop driving once I left São Paulo. I bought a bunch of food, which ran out the day before yesterday, and juice, which ran out last night. I haven't stopped or spoken to anybody since I left the border except three times to buy gas. And since I got lost twice on lonely roads with no human beings around for as far as the eye could see, and since from here that's pretty far, I seriously doubt I was followed. Okay?"

Sarah felt herself relax marginally. She chose a sandwich and started to nibble. To her amusement the girl seemed to take it as a signal that she, too, could begin eating and chose one for herself. *Well, I suppose she's right. I don't approve of her being here after all.*

"Nonstop?" Sarah said, raising her brows. "All the way from Brazil?"

"Yes."

"Quite a drive," Sarah commented.

"Especially if you get lost," Wendy agreed, nibbling delicately at the home-baked bread.

"Did you have to ask for directions?" Sarah asked casually.

Wendy looked up at her, impatience briefly plain on her face. "No," she said carefully. "I worked it out by myself." She put the sandwich down and then looked Sarah full in the face. "I would never do anything that might cause John the slightest risk."

The two women locked gazes and Sarah felt a sinking feeling in her middle. *No doubt this is how every mother feels when her son gets his first serious girlfriend.* And, if anything, Wendy, here, appeared deadly serious. *I wonder how John feels about her?* Was he going to be thrilled to see her, or was he going to react as though she was a stalker?

That thought sent another spasm of uncertainty through her gut. After all, she had only Wendy's word that she'd been framed. *And do I know anything about her? Nooo.* John had barely mentioned her name. She waggled her foot thoughtfully. He could be shy about confiding in his mother about it, or he might be as surprised and dismayed as she was to find out that he had a girlfriend. *And . . . there was a time when I was a student with a part-time job, too. And then my world fell apart.*

Well, she'd find out when he got home. In the meantime . . .

"You look exhausted," she said. Wendy looked up at her. "Why don't we take this"—she stood, wincing slightly at the pull of the healing wound, and picked up the tray—"upstairs. I'll show you your room for tonight. There's a bathroom en suite, so you can have some privacy. Just leave the tray outside the door when you're finished."

Wendy stood, still a little wobbly. "Thank you."

Sarah glanced at her. The kid was dead on her feet. *I know what that feels like.* She'd felt that way often at the end of a hard trip. *We'll see,* she thought, and turned to lead the way upstairs.

CHAPTER 23

Wendy couldn't sleep. She had, perhaps, dozed a bit, but for the most part she had simply lain still, too tired to move, too wide-awake to truly rest. Her cramped body felt as though she was still in motion. Very distracting.

She had heard people moving about downstairs for some time, and an occasional voice speaking Spanish. But things had quieted down now that darkness had fallen.

I wonder what time it is. Not late, she thought, perhaps nine o'clock. But for farm people that must be the same as midnight. They had to be up with the sun, didn't they? She listened carefully and heard no human voice, though the night was alive with the sound of insects. Different insects from the ones she was familiar with. The air smelled different, too, dusty and spicy, kind of like a kiln did when baking pots.

She heard a car in the distance and smiled to herself; she hadn't realized that she'd missed the sound of traffic. She tracked its progress by ear and her heart began to beat faster as it approached. *It must be John!*

Wendy wanted to spring to her feet and dance down the stairs to meet him at the door. Indeed, that was her intention, but she couldn't seem to gather the energy to do so and lay on the bed urging herself up, too paralyzed by exhaustion or uncertainty to get her muscles in gear.

The car drove by the house and her heart sank. She'd been mistaken after all; it was somebody else coming home. Wendy sighed, feeling discouraged and out of place. *I shouldn't have come,* she thought. She was suddenly amazed that she'd had the nerve to do so. John had no obligation to her. How dare she throw herself at him like this? What in God's name had she been thinking?

She covered her face with her hands and groaned aloud. *I'll leave in the morning,* she thought. Before or after she'd seen John? One part of her longed to see him, to hear his voice and to hold him in her arms. Another cringed with embarrassment and dreaded seeing him, fearing rejection. Wendy sighed and dropped her arms to her sides.

What's done is done. Face the music and move on. Certainly Sarah Connor would like her to move on; there'd been no mistaking that.

Her head lifted slightly and she strained her ears. Had that been the sound of a distant door closing? It might be John's mother finally coming upstairs. Assuming she had a room upstairs.

Maybe she's coming up to smother me with a pillow to round out her list of crimes. In a way, Wendy supposed that would simplify things. And Sarah had certainly looked like she wanted to kill her for a split second there. *Not that I intend to let her.*

Wendy sat up and swung her legs over the side of the bed, surprised at how much better she felt. The dizziness was gone completely, though her limbs still felt heavy. She stood up, the old nightgown that Elsa, the housekeeper's niece, had loaned her falling softly to midcalf. Tiptoeing to the door, she released the latch carefully, letting it swing open slightly.

She heard a man's deep voice and the sound of booted footsteps downstairs. Then her heart leaped; that was John's voice, followed by his laugh. Sarah rushed out of the office and shushed them. That was followed by a tense silence. After a moment Wendy heard stealthy footsteps on the stairs and she closed the door and hurried back to bed, lying down and forcing her breath to a steady, slow, and audible rhythm.

She caught herself falling asleep despite her excitement and thought, *I should have tried that before.* Wendy counted slowly to a hundred before she dared to open her eyes to slits and tried to see if anyone was at the door. Unfortunately she was facing away from it. *Note to self: Next time think about position.* After a few more tense moments she decided to risk turning her head.

No one was there. Her heartbeat decelerated but by no means returned to normal. Wendy sat up slowly and once again tiptoed across the room. She opened the door, holding her breath, half expecting to find herself staring into Sarah's disapproving eyes. Still, no one was there. Wendy let her breath out slowly in relief.

Slipping through the door, she slunk to the top of the stairs. From there she could hear voices. They seemed to be coming from the office where she'd met Sarah, but they were muffled by the room's heavy door. Wendy crept down the stairs and made her way to the office. The hall was dark and she had to steer her way past dimly seen obstacles, not always successfully. Despite the pain, she thanked God that stubbed toes made no sound when they contacted mahogany furniture.

Once she reached her goal she found herself stymied by the thickness of the elaborate door. She couldn't make out a word, but the tone of John's voice was not happy. Wendy stood straight, biting her lower lip, then she took a deep breath and moved down the hallway to the room next to the office. The door to this room was open and it, too, had French doors opening onto a walled garden. She tried the knob and found them locked, but she located the key by feel. Screwing her eyes shut and clenching her teeth, she turned the key with the greatest care, slowly, slowly easing the latch back. At last, without a click, the door stood unlocked. Wendy shook her hands out and just stood for a moment, letting her galloping heartbeat slow.

The way my luck is going, she thought, *the hinges will scream like a banshee.* She turned the knob and opened the door; it moved silently and cool night air washed over her, prickling the skin of her bare arms. Peeking out, she saw that the doors to the office were still open and at last she could hear what was being said.

"She's *not* a stalker, Mom." John's voice sounded weary, as though he'd already said it again and again.

"How do you know that?" Sarah challenged. "And how did she know how to find you?"

Dieter was sitting behind his desk, looking grim as he watched mother and son argue. John was seated in one of the guest chairs while Sarah paced the floor like a caged tiger.

"She found out where I was a few minutes after I first contacted her," John admitted. Then he ducked his head, looking up at his mother from under his eyebrows as he waited for the explosion.

There wasn't one. Sarah stood absolutely motionless and looked at him. "Do the rest of your little friends in Massachusetts know where we are?" she asked quietly.

"No, Mom. Just Wendy, and I asked her not to tell, so I know she didn't."

"You know she's not a stalker and you know she'd never tell anyone where we are. How did they know to send her to Brazil?"

"I told Snog that if he ever had an emergency and needed to get to me, to meet me in São Paulo." He looked his mother in the eye, though the steadiness of her stare made him want to flinch. "It's one of the biggest cities in South America," he explained, "and it's far away from here. Which makes it perfect for a meeting like that."

"Except that your little playmate didn't wait for you in São Paulo, she came directly here!" Sarah folded her arms across her bosom and took a deep breath. "And it's not like she's accused of murdering some nobody. Ron Labane was a celebrity."

"She didn't kill him, Ma."

"How can you be sure of that?" Sarah asked as she resumed her pacing. "How well do you actually know her?"

"Well enough," John said, standing in her path. "She's not a killer." He lowered his head to look directly into her eyes. "Do you think I don't know one when I see one?"

"It's not an exact science," Sarah snapped. "You can't point at someone and say, 'There's a killer,' or at someone else and say, 'There's someone who wouldn't kill to save their own life.' If you think you can you're kidding yourself." They stood eye to eye for a long moment. "Why do you think she couldn't have killed him?"

"First, because she thought the sun rose and set out of his ass. Second, because she had no reason to. Third, because there's nothing in her experience that would make her a killer."

"You don't know that she didn't have a reason," Sarah argued. "You haven't even spoken to her."

"Well, if she did have a reason then it was self-defense," John shouted. He struck his chest. "I *know* her! I trust her; and that should be enough for you."

They both stood there, glaring at each other and breathing hard.

"What really matters," Dieter said calmly, "is whether or not she was followed."

"There's been no sign of anyone." Sarah looked away from her son and moved toward the desk. "She says she drove straight from São Paulo and only stopped three times for gas. She says she didn't ask for directions and that she kept checking to see if anyone was behind her. Which I believe because she was obviously scared as a rabbit."

"Of course she is!" John snapped in exasperation. "Weren't you?"

Sarah spun on her heel to face him, her mouth open for a retort.

"No," Dieter said.

They both looked at him, their mouths open.

"There's no point to continuing this argument. You've both totally lost your focus." He tipped his chair back and took a whisky decanter and a cut-crystal glass off the low filing cabinet. "The truth is, we won't know anything until we've spoken to the girl."

"I spoke to her," Sarah snapped, pointing to herself.

Dieter poured himself a measure of the single malt and replaced the decanter. He swirled the rich liquor around the glass and then took a sip, closing his eyes with pleasure. "I've been looking forward to that all day," he said. Then he put the glass on the desk and pulled his chair forward. "If you met her with that fire in your eye, Sarah, I doubt that you got much information out of her."

"Thanks a lot," she said, clearly wounded by his remark. "But I got enough out of her to know she's a liability. We've got to get rid of her."

"What?" John's face was a mask of disbelief. He took a step toward his mother. "I can't believe you said that."

With a puzzled expression on her face Sarah looked from John to Dieter and back again. "For heaven's sake, you guys! All I meant was that I'm not willing to baby-sit someone with the law hot on her trail while you're gone!"

"You're pretty picky all of a sudden," John said hotly. "Wasn't so long ago you—"

The flat of von Rossbach's big hand hit the desk with a resounding slap that made them both jump. He glared at them until they both looked sheepish. "As I said before"—his voice was deadly quiet—"we need to speak to the young lady. Would you care to join us, miss?" Dieter looked to the French doors.

John followed his gaze. "Wendy?" he said.

Wendy peeked around the bush that had concealed her, eyes wide.

"Wendy!" John repeated joyously, and stepped toward her.

She flew into his arms and he held her tightly, burying his face in her hair. They held on to each other tightly for what seemed like a long time, and yet too short a time; his hands stroked her back through the thin nightdress, leaving a trail of warmth on her chilled skin. She opened her eyes to catch Dieter's half smile.

"Hello," he said.

She smiled back at him.

"Those who eavesdrop seldom hear good of themselves," Sarah said self-righteously.

Wendy wrinkled her nose. "Tell me about it," she growled.

Dieter laughed out loud. "From Sarah's description I thought you were some kind of shrinking violet." He grinned at Sarah's offended look. "Please sit down," he invited, indicating the chair before his desk.

John took her hand and led her to the chair, taking the seat beside her without releasing her hand. They smiled at each other as though they were alone and completely at peace. Sarah stood behind them with her arms crossed, frowning—looking, and no doubt feeling, very much left out. Dieter sighed, not certain if it was at this example of young love or at Sarah's apparent jealousy. He knew that she wanted her son to have someone, just not right now.

Ah, but Sarah, he thought sadly, *better now than never at all.*

"What happened to your hair?" John asked.

Wendy touched it with her free hand. "We cut it so I'd look more like Snog's sister. I'm using her passport." She looked at Dieter. "That car I drove here in was rented using one of her credit cards."

"When is the car due back?" he asked.

Wendy shrugged. "I took it for ten days; I've got seven left. I didn't know how long it would take to get here, or what would happen when I arrived, so I went for a fairly long time."

Dieter nodded, considering. "We'll take it back for you," he said. "I'll pay the bill in cash so there'll be no paper trail."

"Thank you," she said, looking awkward. "But I'm already imposing so much—"

"Don't worry," von Rossbach said with a magnanimous wave of his hand.

"Especially at this late date," Sarah muttered. Then she rolled her eyes at Dieter's disapproving expression. Throwing up her hands, she went to sit in the far corner, in the office's only other chair.

"Tell us what happened," von Rossbach invited.

Wendy glanced at John, who nodded. She licked her lips and began.

When she was finished Sarah said, "That was a lot more coherent than your first recital."

Wendy looked at John and smiled at him before answering. "I'm much more rested." She glanced over her shoulder at Sarah. "And John makes me feel more secure."

"The only significant connection between you and the murder would be your fingerprints on the weapon," Sarah observed. "Why didn't you take it with you?"

"Gimme a break!" Wendy snapped. "I was drugged and in shock. For a moment there I was going to run down and report the murder to the desk clerk. All things considered, I think I did pretty well. This might be everyday stuff to you, but it's all new to me. So just back off, okay?"

Sarah blinked and John tried not to smile. Dieter maintained a neutral expression—with difficulty. "Given what you've told us," he said, "I doubt you were followed." He looked over at Sarah. "I also doubt you can be traced. That is"—he turned back to Wendy—"unless your friends . . ."

She shook her head. "No. They wouldn't turn me in. Nor do they know where I am. I've never told them this is where John lives and there's nothing on my computer or in my notes about anything." Wendy shrugged. "So things are as safe as they can be under the circumstances."

Von Rossbach nodded. "You look tired," he said gently. "Why don't you go back to bed? We can talk some more in the morning."

Wendy glanced uncertainly at John, who squeezed her hand. "I'll go up with you," he said. "I'm tired, too." But the look he gave her promised at least a few minutes together. Hand in hand they left the room without looking back.

After they'd gone Dieter and Sarah sat quietly for a few moments. Then Sarah got up from her chair and approached the desk.

"I've never seen you like this," Dieter observed.

Sarah snorted and half smiled. "I've never felt like this," she admitted. As she took Wendy's seat she raised and dropped her hands to slap her thighs. "It's just that I don't know anything about her."

The big Austrian laughed and quickly said when she frowned, "My mother said exactly that when I got my first serious girlfriend."

Sarah grimaced. "Yes, well . . ." She gave him an assessing look. "How did you know she was out there? I didn't have a clue."

"The shampoo in the guest bathrooms has a very strong scent," he admitted.

She tilted her head, looking at him in amused surprise. "I'd noticed that, but I never realized there was a reason for it." She shook her head and laughed. "But even so, I didn't smell her."

"I thought that was why you stopped using it," he said. "So I wouldn't know where you were."

"Not likely," she said. "I stopped using it because the smell made me gag." They grinned at each other until she lowered her eyes.

"It's obvious that she adores him," Dieter said, his expression sympathetic.

Sarah instantly went on the offensive. "She also allegedly adored Ron Labane, and look at what happened to him!"

"Oh, come on, Sarah! She's a victim of circumstance. John backs her up."

"And the neighbors always say, 'He was such a quiet man,' " Sarah snapped back.

"It's pure coincidence that she got involved with the murder. The killers were clever, but they couldn't know how resourceful she would be."

"I don't believe in coincidence, or accident, or happenstance when it affects John," Sarah said firmly. "I can't afford to." She looked in his eyes. "*We* can't afford to. Especially not now."

He lowered his head and looked at her from under his eyebrows. "Do you think she's a Terminator?"

Sarah threw up her hands again and looked away. "Before Serena Burns I would have sworn it wasn't possible. Now?" She shook her head. "Who the hell knows."

In Wendy's room, on Wendy's bed, the two young lovers lay entwined. John was still completely dressed, Wendy was far less so and not minding that a bit. She tugged at John's shirt as she kissed him, inhaling his scent, her eyes closed in sheer pleasure.

John stayed her hand, captured it, and brought it to his lips. He kissed it and smiled at her, his eyes begging her to understand. "Mom's still awake," he said softly.

Wendy groaned, then buried her face in his neck. "I love you," she said passionately. After a moment she said timidly, "But I don't think your mother likes me at all." She looked up at him. "She's not what I expected."

John laughed lightly. "Right now she's not what I expected. But then, you're my first girlfriend and a total surprise to her. Mom doesn't like surprises. One time I baked a cake for her birthday, lit the candles, and hid behind the door. When she came in I jumped out and yelled, 'Surprise!' and she pulled a gun on me." He chuckled. "It's a wonder I wasn't shot."

Wendy stared at him, wide-eyed, as he recounted what he apparently thought of as a fond memory.

Noticing her mood, he gave her a squeeze and kissed her forehead. "Once she gets to know you, she'll like you," he assured her. "I know she will."

"I hope so," she said with a sigh, and kissed him again.

After a few heated moments they came up for air. John held her more tightly and groaned. "I wish we had more time!" he said fervently.

Wendy's head went back and she studied his face in the dim light of the bedside lamp. "Before your mother comes up to bed?" she teased.

He sighed and shook his head.

"Then what *do* you mean?"

"Dieter and I have to go somewhere," he said. "We'll be gone for a few weeks at least." *Or forever,* he thought, *depending on how things go.*

"Where are you going?" she demanded, frowning.

"Shhh." He laid his finger on her lips. "Don't worry, you can stay here with Mom."

Wendy sat up and looked down on him. "I'd rather go to hell," she said frankly. Then she drew close to him again, snuggling into his arms. "Or with you."

He shook his head.

"Please," she begged.

"Wendy," he said, tracing the curve of her cheek with his finger, "I can't. I'm sorry to say no to you. But I just can't."

She closed her eyes and let out a shaky breath. After a moment she nodded. "Fine," she said. "I understand."

John looked at her in concern; he thought that her eyelashes had grown moist. Before he could speak Wendy said, "I'm really tired. I should go to sleep now."

She still hadn't opened her eyes and John felt a sinking feeling as she drew herself from his arms and turned her back on him. He reached out for her.

"Good night," she said.

John drew back his hand, confused. He knew he'd somehow mishandled this situation, but genuinely didn't see any alternative. In his heart he understood that Wendy felt rejected, but he could hardly take her to Antarctica for a raid on a military facility.

He'd missed her so much, had wanted to see her and hold her for so long. *But not now!* There was just no time. No time to be with her and maybe not even time to heal this breach. He let out his breath in an almost inaudible sigh and reached out to touch her bare shoulder.

"We'll talk tomorrow," he said. Leaning over, he kissed her neck. "Sleep well, sweetheart. Good night."

Getting up from the bed, he left the room, closing the door softly behind him. On the way to his room he reflected on how he'd often wondered as a kid how adults could say things like *sweetheart* and *darling* to one another with a straight face. He thought of the girl on the bed and smiled. *And now I know.*

Wendy heard the click of the latch as he left the room and raised her head from the pillow. She gave one self-pitying little sniff, then steeled herself. She was going with him. He just didn't know it yet.

John's mother made no comment when he announced at breakfast that he intended to ramble around the *estancia* with Wendy that day. The very lack of reaction raised Wendy's hackles even more than John's blithe assumption that she'd go with him.

"Do you ride?" John asked her, smiling.

" 'Fraid not," she said. "I wanted a horse when I was little, until my dad explained about mucking out. Then I changed my mind and made do with Bryer's figures and glossy calendars." She grinned. "Truth to tell, we had a hard time affording my cat."

"I can teach you," John offered.

She smiled at his eager expression, her heart giving a little extra thump, and decided to forgive him. "I'd like that. But first I'd like to enjoy your company with no distractions. I"—she was about to say, *I've missed you,* but suddenly remembered that they weren't alone and became shy—"can't wait to hear about what you've been doing," she finished lamely.

"Likewise," John said. "Are you finished?"

Wendy instantly laid down her napkin, saying "yes" despite the food remaining on her plate.

"May we be excused?" John asked his mother. Sarah was examining a printout that Dieter had given her and didn't hear him. "Mom?" he said again, somewhat louder.

She looked up at him. "What?"

"May we be excused?"

Sarah glanced at their barely touched plates and shrugged, slightly bemused that he would even ask. "Of course," she said. When the two young people left in a clatter she turned to Dieter. "Suddenly he's exquisitely polite."

"She's the older woman," Dieter observed. "Maybe he's trying to appear sophisticated."

Sarah gave a little laugh and shook her head. "This thing between them—it's for real, isn't it?"

Dieter nodded, suddenly solemn. *This thing between us,* he thought, *is that real?* Aloud he said, "I'm glad of it. It will give him something special to come home to."

"Hunh!" Sarah said. "That puts me in my place."

"You know what I mean." He laid his hand on hers for a fleeting moment. "He's young and she's a pretty girl; the thought of her will keep him going."

Sarah leaned her chin on her fist and raised her brows. "So did you have some Dulcinea in your life when you went into the field?"

He gave her a look that seemed to liquefy her bones. "Maybe," he said laconically. He gestured toward the printout. "What do you think?"

Sarah straightened and, lowering her eyes, picked up the papers beside her plate, feeling desired and rejected at the same time. "O-kay," she said, all business again. "This looks excellent. I'd be happier if we had a few more storage depots in central Mexico, because I think the U.S. and Canada will be hit harder. And I'd love to get my hands on something bigger than 120mm mortar." She looked up at him. "Don't worry, I know that's impossible. But this is impressive. We'll be in much better shape than I ever could have hoped for." One corner of her full mouth lifted in sardonic amusement. "Clearly your contacts are more reliable than mine."

Dieter snorted. "More money buys better contacts."

■ ■ ■

John cut an apple with his pocketknife and gave the piece to Wendy, who offered it on her open palm to an enthusiastic Linda, Sarah's mare. She smiled at the feel of the horse's soft muzzle and warm breath.

"You breathe into their nostrils to introduce yourself," he told her.

Wendy leaned forward and blew gently, but it seemed to her that Linda wasn't very interested, or else she was doing it wrong, or maybe the mare just wanted more apple. "Gimme," she said, taking the fruit from John's hand. She offered it to the horse and got a very positive reaction. "I think she just smiled."

Watching and listening to the horse crunch up the apple, John was inclined to agree. He put his hand between Wendy's shoulder blades and scratched gently. She turned to him, her eyes twinkling, a dimple in her cheek.

"Are you getting us mixed up?" she asked, tilting her head at Linda.

"Sorry," he said, blushing. "No, not at all."

"You're distracted, though." She leaned an elbow on the corral fence. Linda nudged Wendy hopefully, knocking her off balance. John caught her, steadying her while he looked into her eyes.

"I love you," he said.

She smiled. Leaning forward, she brushed a kiss across his lips. "I love you, too. But"—she held up a finger to forestall his kiss—"*I* am not so easily distracted. Tell me what's on your mind, John. It isn't me, or at least not all me."

He looked at her, his face grim, his eyes concerned. Then, looking up, he pointed to a tree. "Let's go sit over there."

As they approached the shade Wendy saw that a blanket and a picnic basket had been left there and she turned to John with a smile. "No wonder you were willing to walk out on breakfast. When did you bring this out?"

"I didn't," he answered, collapsing bonelessly onto the blanket. "But I have friends in the right places." He opened the basket and offered her something wrapped in a napkin. Wendy accepted it, going to her knees beside him. It turned out to be an extremely moist sort of savory pastry.

"It's good!" she said around a mouthful of oniony, cheesy, corn-muffin-y stuff.

"It's called *sopa paraguaya,* a traditional breakfast food. Marietta, the housekeeper, makes the best." He opened the thermos and poured them each a cup of coffee with the milk and sugar already added.

"This I'm not so crazy about," she said, making a face.

"Hey, it's got caffeine." John took a long swallow. "I didn't sleep much last night."

"Me either," Wendy said.

They were quiet for a while, filling the silence with eating and drinking. Marietta had packed fruit juice and Wendy eagerly drank that, leaving the too-sweet coffee to John.

"Tell me," she finally said.

He looked at her questioningly.

"Don't give me that look," she said, giving his shoulder a shove. "It's so on your mind I can practically see digital letters running across your forehead. But if you insist I'll make it easy for you. When are you leaving, and where are you going, and what are you going to do when you get there?"

He bit his lips and looked into his coffee as though trying to divine the future from it.

Wendy gave him another shove. "What's the point of holding out on me? Given where I am and what I already know."

"Good point," he admitted at last, sitting up. He shook his head. "Mom will kill me for this."

Wendy laughed. "I seriously doubt that. Me, maybe. But from her at least, you're safe."

John grinned and, putting his hand behind her head, pulled her toward him for a kiss, then let her go. "We're going to Antarctica."

"Cool," she said, then laughing, held up her hands. "No pun intended, honest."

He smiled, then frowned. "They've started up the Skynet project again at a secret base they've got down there. We're going to take it out."

"Blow it up, you mean," Wendy said.

Her face grew thoughtful and John kept silent, putting off what he saw as an inevitable argument. She would give him reasons why she should come and he would refuse. Then she'd be hurt and would in turn hurt him, by withdrawing, or even, perhaps, by saying something in anger. He lay down on his back and looked up at the tree and the blue sky just visible through its canopy of leaves.

"I think you might be making a mistake here," she said slowly, still obviously thinking hard. "You blow this thing up and they just rebuild it somewhere else."

John looked over at her, but said nothing. Wendy turned to him eagerly.

"What you need to do is get something into the programming that will also become a part of their stored data. Something that will prevent the thing from becoming sentient!"

John blinked. "Can that be done?" he asked, sitting up to face her.

"Yes. And it will probably be a lot easier than trying to make a machine sentient in the first place. And you know what?" She leaned close as though to kiss him. "I've already done a lot of the work. So you do need me to come with you." Then she did kiss him.

John pulled his head back after a moment to give her a speculative look. "I'm not all that easily distracted myself, sweetheart. If you can write a program that will do this, why can't *we* install it? Dieter and I are both computer literate."

Wendy gave an exaggerated sigh. "Well, I have most of the ideas down," she admitted. "But I was coming at the problem of AI from a different direction—namely, creating self-awareness, not stifling it. So I'd have to rewrite the program." She shrugged. "And that will take a little time."

"We don't have years," he said, disappointed.

"It won't take years. I've already identified a number of factors that indicate sentience. Well," she admitted with a deprecatory shrug, "I've gotten a huge boost from Kurt Viemeister's articles. But those were just a springboard. I've gone much further. I can do this!" she insisted. "By the time we get there I could have it ready to go." Wendy tried to keep her expression neutral and to hide any trace of the mantra *take me!, take me!, take me!* that yammered in the back of her head.

John looked at her in astonishment. "What you're saying is we wouldn't have to blow it up."

"Not at all," she agreed, nodding enthusiastically. "It will be better if you don't because this way you'll corrupt all of their updated information. Just make it look like blowing it up was your goal, but you were prevented from following through and the program should pass unnoticed." She bit her lip. *Don't say too much,* she cautioned herself. *Let him work it through.*

John looked up from his reverie. "Let's go talk to Dieter."

"*Should* pass unnoticed?" Dieter said. He folded his arms before him on his desk. "My dear Wendy, we can't afford *should*. We need to kill this monster."

"Which John tells me you've already done twice!" Wendy challenged from her chair in front of him. "So killing it isn't working. You need to prevent this thing from *becoming* a monster. Maybe something less obvious and less destructive is the answer. Let them have their Skynet!" She waved her hands in an expansive gesture. "Just don't let that Skynet reach its full potential. All they're looking for is a tool, not something that's going to try and take over the world. Let them have what they want while making sure you get what you want. They'll never even suspect anything's wrong—because from their point of view, nothing *will* be wrong!"

She stopped talking, looking at him as though willing him to give her a go-ahead. Von Rossbach pushed out his lower lip as he thought and John stood behind Wendy's chair, tapping his foot nervously.

"How likely are they to find this program you're proposing?" Dieter asked.

"Not very," Wendy assured him. "A program like the one that makes up Skynet is extremely complex; there are millions of lines of text involved. I could never have done it without that data that John gave us, from the thing's . . . head. What I'm intending isn't going to interrupt Skynet's function, so it won't cause problems for the designers. All I want to do is prevent unintended consequences, and I can do that by spreading my program out quite a bit so that it won't stand out as something alien." When von Rossbach still looked dubious she hastened to explain further. "They'll certainly check the program after your visit," she admitted. "I know I would. But they'll be looking for key words that will involve self-destruction. While our goal isn't to destroy but to get the computer to ignore certain data. Something like that won't stand out. And unless someone is so anal that they insist on going over every single line of text, it will not be noticed."

"Where's your mother?" Dieter asked John, who shrugged. "Let's go find her."

Sarah was in John's room working on his computer. She glanced up with a distracted frown as they came in, then looked a question at them.

"Wendy has a new idea that we'd like to run by you," Dieter said.

Sarah turned to the girl and gave her all her attention. After Wendy had finished explaining she sat quietly rocking the desk chair as she thought. "It could work," she said at last. "Maybe destroying Skynet *is* impossible; it certainly feels that way. But sabotaging it . . . ." Sarah chewed her lower lip, then nodded once, firmly. "Yes. Let's try it. It isn't like bombing the place isn't taking a risk, too. And this way they won't feel the need to start all over again. And"—she glanced at her son—"John can stay here."

John simply stared at her in shock and Wendy caught her breath in a gasp. "You've got to be kidding," he said.

Sarah shook her head. "Completely serious. The mission doesn't need you and I don't think that with this new plan there's any excuse for putting you at risk like that."

"Mom, you're asking me to send my *girlfriend* in my place! Do you think I'm going to just stand by and let you do that?"

"I expect you to weigh the risks against the benefits and to come up with the same results that I have." Sarah met his eyes with a hard look.

"I can't believe this," John said, turning his back on her. Then he swung around again. "Wendy hasn't had the training to take on something like this."

"You haven't been around snow since you were four, kiddo," Sarah reminded him. "And Dieter can take very good care of her. I was trusting him to take care of you, so now he can do the same thing for her." Slowly she realized that he was more angry than she'd ever seen him; the skin around his nostrils was actually white. "Besides, you don't have enough supplies for three people."

"Those could be acquired." Dieter shrugged in the face of her glare, his face unreadable.

"I'm going, Mom." John was breathing hard, but his voice was calm and his eyes were cool. "That's the end of it." Then he turned and started to walk out of the room.

Sarah sprang to her feet, hiding a wince. "John! It's an unacceptable risk!"

"Mom, I ask you, what good will I ever be if I stay here safe and warm while sending someone I love out to maybe get killed. How would I ever be able to call myself a man?" He glared at her from the doorway.

Wendy had been watching them wide-eyed; now she spoke up, her voice shaking. "I won't go without him."

Sarah's eyes widened and her head snapped around to face the girl. She could feel the blood draining from her face. Then she looked at Dieter. The big Austrian stood like an oak, his arms folded, his eyes downcast.

"Sarah, you have not healed completely. You would be a liability. You know it, we all know it. Why not admit it?"

"If you'd all already decided this was what you were going to do, then why in hell did you interrupt my work?" she demanded fiercely. "Get lost, I've got things to do." She sat down and began typing.

John looked at von Rossbach, who tossed his head in the direction of the door. Wendy scuttled out first, followed by John. Dieter gave Sarah's back a long, last look.

"You're right," she said, in an almost whisper.

"What was that?" he replied politely.

"I said, you're right. I'm not fit to go into the field right now. I'll be more useful here." A pause. "Harder to wait than to do."

Dieter smiled and pulled the door gently to.

CHAPTER 24

John stood alone on the deck, so deep in his own thoughts he barely noticed the driving rain that competed with the seawater blasting under his oilskins. The sky above was steel gray, the same color as the rough-sided mountains of moving water before and behind, topped with frothing white where the keening wind slashed their tops into foam. It was a storm fifty million years old, here where wind and water circled eternally from east to west about the Antarctic coasts. The young man ignored it, save for the tight grip on the railing and eyes slitted against the spray.

He had been brooding ever since the stiff leave-taking with his mother. He'd been busy breaking down the moments before good-bye into smaller and smaller pieces.

From the time when she'd first sent him to the academy, his mother had insisted on carrying his bag out to the car for him, no matter how heavy it got. As he grew and realized that despite his mental image of her, Sarah Connor was not a towering Amazon, he'd tried to take over that task; but she wouldn't allow it. It became a kind of good-natured contest between them. A contest he'd never won until that morning.

He'd dragged his duffel downstairs to find her already on the *portal,* looking out into the yard, unsmiling, arms crossed, her back military straight, the fingers of her hands digging into her arms. The bag was a little thing—really an unimportant thing—but it signaled her displeasure to him vividly and he regretted the rift between them.

"Did you forget anything?" she'd asked, obviously unable to break old habits completely.

"Nope," he'd said, just as he always did. "Got my toothbrush, my comb, and an extra pair of shoelaces."

That had earned him only a slight, distant smile.

Wendy, in her eagerness to avoid contact with his mother, was already in the car, in the backseat—crowding the far door in an effort to escape Sarah's gimlet eye. Knowing Wendy might be watching them made him feel even more awkward. John was disappointed that the women in his life hadn't taken to each other, but under the circumstances he had decided to just let it ride.

Sometimes you *could* put off trouble.

■ ■ ■

Through the windows of the lounge Dieter watched the young man automatically adjust his stance to the rolling of the big yacht, ignoring the V-plumes of spray that erupted skyward every time it dug its bows into the cold gray water.

"It's freezing out there," Vera observed. She shivered dramatically, causing the ice cubes in her Scotch to clink. "But it is fantastic." Her eyes glowed as she watched the steel-colored sea heave itself into mountains of water. "I love the sheer power of it! I'm so glad you convinced me to come down here, darling." She wrapped her arms around one of his and grinned up at him mischievously.

Dieter knew she was well aware that he got nervous when she did that and he smiled down at her in a carefully pleasant but not encouraging way.

She indicated the direction of Wendy's cabin with a tip of her well-coiffed head. "That nice little girl has been pretty broody, too."

"No"—Dieter patted Vera's hand—"not brooding. She's working on something. It has to be done by the time we reach our landing point, so she's just concentrating."

With a very unladylike snort, Vera said, "Yeah, right. And Johnny?"

Dieter shook his head. "He's eighteen."

"Ah," Vera said wisely. "That explains a lot."

John blinked and studied the waves as they roared toward the yacht, broke at the bows, and cataracted down the sides, doing his best to empty his mind and simply feel. He was out here to acclimate himself to the cold, and the mealy scent of the everlasting ice was strong. He kept telling himself that this was a useful exercise that would test his endurance. *I'll build confidence knowing I can keep going through the discomfort. Jungles I'm used to, and mountains, but not ice.*

Unfortunately he suspected that in reality he was enduring the discomfort because he felt guilty about leaving his mom behind and didn't want to discuss his feelings with Dieter and Wendy.

Not that Wendy seemed to be on the same planet with the rest of them at the moment. Sometimes she looked right through him, her head moving in little jerks as her eyes roved the room and her fingers tapped in a keyboard rhythm on the tablecloth. What she was like the rest of the time he didn't know since he only saw her at meals.

My girlfriend, the zombie, he thought bitterly, knowing he was being unfair. He paused in his thinking. *I'm whining! I'm actually whining—*

and to myself! Did other people do that? *It seems I do.* So what was he supposed to make of that?

His feet and fingers hurt from the cold and the hairs in his nose felt like they were snapping off with every breath. Maybe his body was whining, quite justifiably, and this was the way his mind was interpreting its complaints. He sighed and could have sworn that he saw ice crystals fall from the plume of his breath. Impossible, with the air this saturated with moisture, but they *should* have . . .

The whining might not be justified, but the guilt was. Or at least it was understandable. By insisting on coming, he'd broken with a near-lifelong habit of assuming that his mother understood the situation better than he did. At least as far as Skynet went.

But he'd been right. *I'm supposed to be a great leader. Nobody is going to follow someone who makes preserving his own precious pink personal buttocks the maximum priority.*

His mother's still face came before his mind's eye. He had sensed her deep unhappiness and ignored it, choosing instead to crack jokes and to lift her off her feet with his good-bye hug. It was as if he was saying, *See, Mom. I'm all grown up. I'm bigger than you are!* Suddenly he felt very gauche.

He wondered if he shouldn't have confronted the situation, let her tell him what was on her mind. *Like I didn't know,* he thought grimly. Wendy was coming with them and Sarah couldn't. Wendy was an unknown quantity, an untested weapon, and Sarah wasn't going to be on hand if that weapon failed.

He had to give it to her; his mother knew how to cover his back, even if some part of him resented her presence there more and more as he grew older. At the same time he appreciated her devotion, even if he didn't want to examine it too closely. *How hinky is that?* he wondered, and decided not to examine that question too closely either.

Maybe he was just tired. The cold really burned energy and the heavy clothing he was wearing was . . . *heavy.* Still, he didn't move to go into the warmth of the lounge. Maybe he was punishing himself in some daft effort to make it up to his mother because he felt guilty. Guilt again. Though considering his insensitive behavior at their parting, he had good reason for feeling it.

Aside from that, whatever his mother felt, to him Wendy wasn't a weapon of any kind. What she was, quite simply, was the most important person in his life. *Uh-oh. Did I really think that?*

He'd been aware that he had very strong feelings for her, but he hadn't realized until this moment the depth of those feelings.

But Mom knew. She was as sensitive as a cat when it came to gauging people's feelings. Which might explain her distrust and resentment of the younger woman. Replaced and abandoned. The thought made him want to squirm.

But, hey, wait a minute. Look at it from another angle and this just clears the way for her to get together with Dieter. If everything goes according to plan this could all work out as neatly as a Gilbert and Sullivan operetta.

It unnerved him that he honestly didn't know if he was being sarcastic or not.

A wave heaved itself over the railing and drenched him from head to foot. *And on that note . . .* Grasping the safety line, he made his way to a door, grateful that he could choose to go in. One or two of the crew had to stay outside at all times, and every one of them came from the tropics. At least he'd *seen* snow.

Wendy saw John move past her porthole and flew to the door; throwing it open, she rushed down the corridor, opened the hatch to the deck, and flung her arms around his neck.

"I'm done! I'm done! I'm done!" she sang, hopping up and down. Her eyes grew round. "I'm cold! I'm cold! I'm cold!" She turned and fled back through the hatch.

He followed her in, grinning at the sight of her shivering, her teeth chattering as she hugged herself. As soon as the door was closed she rushed him again, then pulled back.

"You're wet!" she said in dismay. Then she looked down at her shirt. "I'm wet!"

He could see that. He could also see through the thin wet fabric that she wasn't wearing a bra. *Now* that's *a sight for sore eyes!*

"Never mind," Wendy said. Suddenly all business, she took his hand and towed him toward her cabin. She opened the door and turned to him, her eyes glowing. "Come in," she invited, tugging him forward.

"I'll come back," he promised. "I'm drenched."

Wendy laughed. "Use my shower," she suggested. Her voice dropped and went slightly husky. "I'll scrub your back." Then, taking him by surprise, in one smooth movement she pulled him in, closed the door, and leaned against it.

John blinked. *Scrub your back* was pretty unequivocal. He could feel himself blushing, but he was pretty sure that it was more about desire than embarrassment. He glanced at the porthole and Wendy moved to the wall and drew the short curtain over it. Turning, she raised a brow at him, then without a word went to the door and locked it.

"That should ensure privacy," she said. Wendy moved closer and looked up at him. "And your mother isn't here now, so there's no need to be shy."

He backed up a step and said uncertainly, "I just don't want to take advantage of you."

"Pleeease!" she begged him, crossing her eyes and shaking her folded hands in the classic pleading posture. "Take advantage of me! I've just done the impossible and I want to celebrate, *and* I want *you*! Moments like this only come along once in a while, John," she said as she began untying the ribbons on his life jacket. "You have to grab them while you can."

Beer commercial, he thought irreverently. Then, somehow, the life jacket was on the floor and she was reaching for something else. John grabbed her hands.

"We've only known one another for a little while," he protested. "I don't want you to feel that you have to rush into anything you may regret."

She stared at him as though he'd been speaking Swahili, then she blinked and looked determined. "I've known you long enough to know that I won't regret this, John. But here's the deal. Once we land, we're not going to be alone for however long it takes us to do this thing. And we'll be in a place so cold your breath sticks to your lips. *And* we could all be killed. Okay? Do you get what I'm telling you?"

"Now or never?" A smile tugged at the corners of his lips.

"That's one of the things I love about you, sweetie," Wendy said, attacking the half-frozen zipper on his jacket. "You're quick on the uptake."

By the time they were finished undressing him, they were both on the floor, panting and laughing. He flung the last sock onto the formidable pile of garments and fell onto his back. Wendy leaned over him, smiling. Then she straddled him, putting her hands on either side of his head and her knees on either side of his hips; she held herself above him grinning at the way he lay blinking up at her. She leaned forward and planted tiny, nibbling kisses on his lips.

"You're not going to tell me that you're too tired to move, are you?" she asked.

Putting his arms around her waist, he gently tried to pull her closer. "C'mon down here," he growled, "and I'll show you how tired I am."

Wendy grinned, but resisted. "Ah, but you're so far ahead of me," she complained.

He sat up and Wendy retreated until she was sitting on his thighs. John reached out and undid the top button of her shirt and Wendy drew in a shuddering breath, causing him to look up at her. "Don't you dare stop now," she warned.

Grasping his head, she pulled him to her for a passionate kiss. He matched her ardor, running his fingers through her hair, then down the curve of her neck and back, drawing her closer, deepening their kiss.

Wendy pulled back, panting. "I love you," she said. Then she gave him a gentle push. "But we still have this clothes problem." She got to her feet and began to unbutton her cuffs.

"No," John said, standing. "Allow me."

Grinning, she held her arms out. "I am entirely at your disposal."

"Not like loading stuff at a dock," John said.

"No," Dieter said. "More creative."

More of a pain in the ass, John thought, looking shoreward.

The yacht was anchored in the lee of a headland. The shore was shale and rock, rising to high rocky hills whose black expanse was split by fingers of white—the outliers of the great interior ice sheets of Antarctica. Nobody had bothered giving the bay a name; *Desolation* would be about right. The rocky upthrust to the east sheltered the *Love's Thrust* from the westerlies, but there was still a definite chop, with white-caps on the short steep waves. That made the big pleasure craft pitch at its anchor, a sharp rocking motion more unpleasant than the long surges of the huge deep-ocean waves. Several of the crew were looking green as a result, which wasn't helping with unloading.

Getting the big inflatable raft over the side had been a nightmare. Getting heavy parcels into it was worse. Right now the boxed snowmobile was swinging up on the pivoting boom.

"Slowly . . . slowly . . ." Dieter said, leaning over the side and making hand signals to the man operating the power winch. "Slowly . . . *I said slowly, dummkopf!*"

John hopped nimbly over the side and slid down the rope ladder, landing easily on his feet and helping the two crewmen guide the big Sno-Cat down. The raft was a military model, with aluminum stringers to stiffen the bottom; it had been designed to take a dozen troops and their gear into a beachhead or on a commando raid. With three men gripping the front and two corners of the crate, and Dieter blasphemously directing the winch operator, they managed to get it down despite the continual seesaw of differential movement between the two crafts. Which was fortunate, because if the crate had come down really hard, it would have gone straight through the bottom.

The crewmen threw John looks of surprised respect as he helped guide the crate down and lash it firmly in place. He gave them a grin and a thumbs-up—*Hey, I'm a lad of many skills, thanks to Mom*—and swarmed back up the ladder to the deck.

"That's the last of it," he panted.

Dieter and Wendy were there, their hiking clothes covered with a final layer of orange water-resistant coat and pants, to find Vera waiting for them, a vision in pink. Her fine skin looked greasy from the sunblock she wore, and the big pink sunglasses that shielded her eyes from Antarctica's fierce ultraviolet rays made her look like an owl with bloodshot eyes.

God knows where she found a pink anorak, John thought. But he wasn't really surprised. By now he knew that whatever Vera wanted, Vera got. *Well, with the exception of Dieter. So far.*

"Sweetie," she said, rushing forward to give John a farewell embrace. "You take care of that nice girl, now. Y'hear? And take care of yourself, too."

She planted a kiss on his cheek, then pushed him away and gave him a swat on his bottom. Then she turned to Wendy, leaving John to wonder if that was a grandmotherly slap on the tush or a lecherous one.

Too fast to be lecherous, he decided. *Besides, there's Dieter right in front of her.*

Vera kissed Wendy on both cheeks, then tugged her sunglasses down to give the girl a conspiratorial look. Wendy giggled and blushed, then enfolded the older woman in a fond hug. "We'll see you soon," she promised.

Vera tapped Wendy's nose with a pink-gloved finger. "You'd better," she warned. Then she pushed her sunglasses back up and turned to Dieter, one hand on her hip. "Well, big boy," she said, somehow managing to slink toward him in her parka and heavy boots, "looks like this is it."

"I sincerely hope not." Dieter smiled. "Or you might not come back for us." Then he took her in his arms and gave her a kiss that made her moan for more. When he finally let her go she staggered slightly and he gently held her shoulders until she seemed steady on her feet.

"Wow!" she said, grinning. "I'll come back for sure if you'll promise me another just like that one next time I see you."

He chucked her under the chin. "I'll look forward to it," he promised.

Vera waggled her brows. "So will I, honey. So will I."

With that, John handed down the last duffel and swung out onto the ladder that led down to the Zodiac. Wendy followed, and when she was far enough down he took her by the waist to steady her as she stepped down from the ladder. Dieter handed down Wendy's equipment and then his own duffel, following it down with economic efficiency.

The crewman fended the huge inflatable boat off the side of the yacht and started the motor. The three travelers looked up from their seats to wave at Vera and her merry crew, who continued to wave at them all the way to the shore.

Giovanni, Vera's handsome crewman, efficiently beached the Zodiac onto a smooth spot on the shale so that they didn't have to wet their feet to step ashore; it was less than a dozen paces to the beginning of the snow. All four of the men joined in pushing the crate containing the Sno-Cat up a collapsible metal ramp, over the side of the Zodiac, and then down to the beach. Then the Italian tossed them their bags. Returning to the motor, he pulled the boat off and turned it in a sway and flurry of foam.

As he headed back to the yacht he waved and shouted, "Good luck!"

Wendy waved back while John and Dieter strapped the duffels to the pile of supplies on the sledge. Two of them would ride the Sno-Cat while an unlucky third took a more precarious ride atop the supplies. They'd fashioned a sort of seat out of the softer goods they carried, but it was still going to be tricky.

"There's sure a lot of wildlife around here," Wendy commented.

John had to agree. He'd known the animals were there but somehow it hadn't registered. Off to the right, far enough away to mute both their sound and smell was a huge . . . *herd,* he supposed . . . of penguins. To the left a small pod of seals lounged.

Dieter looked back and forth between them. "It's unusual for that many leopard seals to get together," he said quietly. "They're usually solitary creatures. I don't see any pups, so that can't be it . . ."

"I think the penguins are watching them," Wendy commented.

"Leopard seals eat penguins," Dieter said. He looked at them for a few moments, unable to shake the feeling that while the penguins were watching the seals, the seals were watching the humans. He shook off the feeling and went back to work.

"Would you hold on to this for me, hon?" John called out.

Wendy turned away from the penguins and headed toward the sledge. Suddenly something hit her in the head with enough violence to knock her down.

"Wendy!" John shouted, and rushed over to her. "Are you okay?"

She rolled over, one hand holding the back of her head, tears in her eyes. "Yeah," she said. "I guess so. What the hell hit me?"

John looked up in astonishment at the bird that had struck her. It looked like a huge brown pigeon wearing an unpleasant expression on its avian face. He pointed and she looked up.

"That was a *bird*? It felt like a rock. A *big* rock. Was I near its nest or something?" she asked, looking around.

"That's a skua gull," Dieter said. "They do that. No one knows why."

"Bastard," Wendy muttered, getting to her feet. She kept a weather eye on the sky, though the bird only dive-bombed them one more time.

Finally everything was secure. "So," Dieter said, "do we draw straws or what?"

Suddenly Wendy rushed past him, climbing up the pile of supplies as agilely as a monkey to plop down among the duffels, her legs stretched out before her. "C'mon, guys," she said cheerfully, "let's go! Maybe the damn birds won't follow us inland."

"Good enough for me," John muttered.

Dieter grinned and took his place on the seat of the snow mobile. "Then by all means," he said, starting it up, "let's go."

CHAPTER 25

Useless!" Clea shouted, and swept the desk clear of print-outs pens and calculators. "Useless!" She kicked her chair and sent it rolling into the wall hard enough to dent the plaster. The action wasn't even satisfying; the huge weight of rock and ice above her seemed to swallow her anger, and the antiseptic air of the base to muffle even the sound of a scream.

Inside her brain her computer governors worked to calm her. But Clea resisted, unleashing a seemingly bottomless well of fight-or-flight chemicals into her bloodstream.

Useless, stupid machine! she thought at her own computer. Why didn't it have the information that she needed? Where was the program that would turn Skynet from a sophisticated toy into a sentient being? Why hadn't it been included? She had useless information to burn, but the one tiny clue she so desperately needed was missing. A murmur of quantum formula ran through the mechanical part of her brain, and she dismissed it with fury.

We're so close! she thought, feeling herself calm as her computer succeeded in getting her brain chemistry under control . . . But diminishing the strength of her frustration didn't erase it. She stood with her hands on her hips glaring at the computer screen and its offending lines of text. Then she began to pace like a caged tigress.

"Your lack of self-control does you no credit," Kurt Viemeister said coldly. He hadn't looked up when she'd swept her desktop clear and he didn't look up as he spoke, but his posture and his fixed expression revealed his disapproval as loudly as any words.

You idiot human, Clea thought bitterly, turning her glare on him. *I thought you were the one that made Skynet live.* Unfortunately the work he'd been producing proved that he wasn't, and even more unfortunately neither was she. She shook her head in disgust and turned away.

"Where the hell are you going?" Viemeister shouted at her back.

She turned at the door of the lab to snap, "Your lack of self-control does you no credit, Kurt." Then, with a look of profound contempt, she turned away. Petty, perhaps, but satisfying—unlike anything else in her life right now.

Clea went directly to her room; she needed desperately to get away from humans or she might just have to kill one. *I should not terminate any humans at this point. It would be non-mission-optimal. But what if I simply* must *kill someone?*

She slammed the door behind her, then paced the small space for half an hour, burning off the rest of the bad chemistry—the hormones had sunk into muscle tissue as well as her brain.

Finally she threw herself down on the bed, covering her eyes with her forearm. It was time to calm down and start thinking. She decided to take a few moments to check on her seals.

Seal vision was not the best and she regretted that she hadn't made some provision to enhance what they saw. But if they saw anything really interesting her internal computer could sharpen the images for her. What she saw through their eyes might be almost as boring as the base, but it was a change of scenery. Which, after far too many weeks in this lockbox, she needed now and again.

While she watched, courtesy of her implants, the vague shapes of penguins toddling about in the distance, Clea idly wished that she could talk to Alissa. But the Terminator she had managed to contact while out on the ice had informed her that her sibling was undergoing the growth process and was unavailable. Alissa would probably remain unavailable for at least another week, depending on how hard she was pushing herself.

The I-950 sighed and changed her input to another seal for more blurred views of rock, ice, water, and penguins . . . then sat bolt upright in surprise. What she was looking at was a small group of humans loading up a sledge. Making the seal look around she caught sight of a Zodiac plying its way to a dimly perceived ship of some kind in the distance.

Well, well, she thought. *Who is this?* New arrivals for the base? Why not helicopter them in the way they did everything else from supplies to scientists? *Maybe they're not coming to the base.* But what else was out there?

A skua, going by the general size and shape, knocked the smallest human down and Clea laughed aloud. She'd had that happen to her once; thereafter she'd amused herself by knocking the skuas out of the air. It was a pity she hadn't been able to catch one to implant with her little chips, but they'd all been dead when she retrieved them. Besides, the chips were designed for mammalian nervous systems, and an avian one might not be able to support the machinery—avians were *literally* birdbrains. Still, she longed for the kind of clear vision a flying predator might provide.

The humans finished their packing and headed inland. Clea watched them go, chewing her lower lip indecisively. Then on impulse she sent four of her seven seals after them; at the very least they'd be something different to watch.

Besides, she suspected that at this moment she knew more about the situation than Tricker did, for there had been no incoming communiqué warning of new arrivals. *Perhaps it's a surprise inspection,* she thought. In which case she could arrange to be on hand to witness Tricker's discomfiture. The idea gave her a nice feeling of power.

It was a fairly nice summer's day in Antarctica. *The temperature must be around thirty-five or so,* Wendy thought. There was only a gentle breeze stirring the air and the sky was a light blue gray, indicating a high overcast. She was merely miserably, uncomfortably cold instead of freezing as she'd expected.

The scenery around them was ice and hard-packed snow, windsculpted into weird and graceful shapes like a Salvador Dalí painting in monochrome. Sometimes a mound of snow would heave up like a wave frozen as it crested, frilled with a lacy edging of clear ice sparking on its underside; in the distance cliffs of ice seemed to bear tiny ruffles of white and blue and pale emerald green. More than once the beauty of the place took her breath away.

The three of them were dressed all in white, the sledge wore a white tarpaulin, and the snowmobile was painted pure white as well. *It's Ghost Troop!* she thought. It seemed to her that very little here was really pure white; to Wendy's eye they actually stood out against shades of cream, blue white, palest beige. Although the light was so flat it made things look strange, so that if anyone was watching maybe they couldn't tell where they were going, or how far away they were. *Or even that we're here?* Well, maybe that was too much to hope for.

On the other hand, it's too cold out here to have people posted with nothing but a parka and a pair of binoculars for any length of time. Cameras would freeze, I suppose. Someone had told her that on the yacht; Antarctica was actually a worse environment for machinery than the moon. So the odds were good that they were unobserved. She looked up again. *And that overcast, slight as it is, would obscure satellite observation, if there is any. So I guess we're safe.* The sledge went over a bump and her teeth clopped together. *Not comfortable, but safe.*

The plan was to travel at an easy pace for the next two days. They'd actually unpacked a stove to cook up some stew for lunch, which they'd eaten in the lee of the supply sledge, along with a whole loaf of bread.

Wendy had tried to refuse the bread, but Dieter had buttered a huge slice thickly and put it into her hand.

"Eat it," he'd insisted. "You're not going to get fat at the rate you're burning calories."

So, reluctantly, she'd done so. And she did feel better for it. After lunch John had slipped her a couple of chocolate bars and she'd gobbled them up.

Guilt-free chocolate, she thought happily. *What a concept.* She was already looking forward to supper.

By the morning of their third day on the ice, as Wendy lay on her stomach staring at the hidden base's wind farm, all she was looking forward to was getting somewhere warm. Even if it was only for a little while. The sky had become completely overcast by late the first afternoon and the temperature had plummeted accordingly, giving even the most expensive of their travel gear a harsh, and as far as she was concerned, not altogether successful test.

Wendy had thought that as a New England girl she'd be better able to endure the cold than John. She glanced at him. He seemed completely unfazed by the temperature, the hard travel, the cramped sleeping quarters, or what they were about to do. On the one hand, she admired him; on the other, she was convinced they'd all gone barking mad.

John turned to Wendy and gave her a thumbs-up, smiling encouragingly as he did so, even though she couldn't see his grin. He couldn't see her expression either since they both wore balaclavas and huge dark goggles, not to mention skin-protecting ointment that smelled bad and made them look like ghouls three days dead. But he could tell by the position of her head that she was giving him a blank and puzzled look.

She's so slender, an easy candidate for hypothermia. She seemed to be growing weaker, too, despite all the chocolate and PowerBars and buttered bread they could force on her. He was looking forward to their day of rest when she could languish in her sleeping bag inside the tent for as long as she wished. Not that it would be a visit to the tropics, by any means, but it was a damn sight better than what she was experiencing now. Not that she'd uttered one word of complaint.

Moved by her pluck, he gripped her shoulder and she bent her head to touch her swaddled cheek to his gloved hand. Dieter recalled his attention by slapping his shoulder. The big Austrian signaled that there was no one around and the little gizmo in his hand detected no listening devices. *So why,* John wondered, *aren't we talking?*

Then he decided it wasn't worth asking. It seemed the cold was getting to him, too.

The two men rose and trundled over the gentle rise toward the windmills. The few supplies necessary for the sabotage were in insulated packs that they had stuffed inside their parkas to keep them from freezing. Time to take out the target.

The windmills stood on a slight rise, where the basalt rock beneath crested up beneath the ice. The inhuman whine of their giant blades came whickering down through the frigid air, like a mechanical snarl beneath its chill.

"Why do operatives say things like like 'terminate' and 'take out' instead of 'kill' and 'blow up'?" John asked.

"The business is hard enough as it is," Dieter answered.

John unscrewed the panel that led to his first windmill's inner workings. Awkwardly, he attempted to unscrew the cap on the bottle he'd carried inside his jacket and found it impossible. Stripping off the heavy outer gloves, he allowed them to dangle from cords attached to his sleeves, leaving only his polypropylene glove liners to protect him from the cold—which, since that wasn't what they were designed for, they didn't. Almost immediately his fingers began to go numb. But at least he could handle the small bottle. Removing the "eyedropper" top, he sprinkled a liquid onto the plastic seal at the top of the unit's hydraulic pump. The liquid was supposed to break up polymer chains, causing the seals to disintegrate.

Putting the liquid back into an inside pocket, he brought out a calculator-sized instrument that he would use to reprogram the windmills' computerized governor. He pulled out the motherboard and attached clips, then set to work. By the time he reinstalled it in its slot, the windmill was already pumping faster, spreading the damaging liquid and on its way to dashing itself to pieces.

Putting his gloves back on, John screwed the protective panel back on and moved to the next one. There were twelve in all, modular units about fifteen feet high and built sturdy to survive the frequent high winds and the bitter cold. But no attempt had been made to protect them from sabotage. Why would there be? Who would be out here looking to commit acts of vandalism in Antarctica?

Li'l ol' me, John thought. *Just li'l ol' me.* Well, and Dieter. *Oops, looks like the big guy spilled some.* Von Rossbach's glove liners were in shreds where the liquid had touched them. John watched him peel them off, wincing at the heat caused by their destruction.

"It felt good at first," Dieter said when he noticed John watching him, "but now it's burning. He shoved the ruined gloves into his breast pocket, then worked his reddened hands. "Could just be the cold," he muttered, slipping his outer gloves back on.

John looked around. Dieter was finished and he was halfway through with his last one. Checking the watch attached to the outside of his sleeve, he raised his brows. *Good job!* he thought. They'd obviously allowed more time for this than necessary.

In less than five minutes he was tramping up the low rise to rejoin Wendy. Behind him the windmills had begun to run crazy, spinning like tops in the wind. Soon the governors would burn out and without the seals so would the hydraulic pump, while the blades broke up under the stress.

Which meant that the hidden base would be completely out of power in less than a day, turning the place into a deep freeze. But just in case the base had some other means of generating electricity, their next stop would be a visit to their water-pumping station. Behind him the level whine was grating higher, turning into a protesting squeal as the ultra-tough composites began to stress beyond their design parameters.

CRACK! Dieter and John both spun and began to drop, an automatic response to what their trained reflexes interpreted as an exposion. They completed the movement; one of the windmills had disintegrated, and lethal splinters might well reach across the three hundred yards to the two men.

"Didn't think it would happen that fast," John said.

Dieter looked up, brushing himself free of snow. "The wind is picking up," he said. "Must be nearly fifty by now."

Wendy was already seated on the snowmobile, and when she saw them come over the rise she started it up. The movement of her head looked a little wobbly to him, and her hand as it reached for the starter had seemed clumsy and slow.

Suddenly he noticed something he'd missed while working below. His haste had kept him relatively warm, but the temperature had dropped. *And Dieter was right. It* is *getting to be storm level.* John looked up at the sky and realized that the hurrying clouds were also thicker and more threatening.

He glanced at Dieter.

"We'd better hurry if we're going to make it before this storm breaks." The Austrian looked from John to Wendy. "I'll ride in front of Wendy to shield her from the wind," he offered. "Also, I'll probably throw off more heat than you would."

John nodded and headed for the sledge. As they rode away he saw one of the blades on the second windmill fly off and strike the one behind it, breaking two of its blades and starting a chain reaction of destruction that brought a smile to his weary face. *A job well done,* he thought with satisfaction.

After her blowup in the Skynet lab Clea had gone to her own lab to work on her abandoned projects. For one thing, it gave her more freedom to watch the three mystery travelers. For another, it gave her some relief from Viemeister's irritating possessiveness.

He'd been avoiding her conspicuously in the cafeteria, which had given her an opportunity to meet some of the other scientists. To Kurt's great annoyance, which of course she enjoyed. His self-imposed distance meant he was less likely to burst in on her while she was spying on the travelers. A small bonus that did little to make up for the disappointment the human had caused her.

One of the seals, the smallest, had dropped dead of exhaustion after nearly thirty-six hours of humping its way across the ice—the animals weren't designed for overland travel. It had made a useful snack for the others, though. Fortunately the humans allowed themselves rest and meal breaks, and so the other three seals were able to keep up, though they were hardly thriving.

The I-950 had begun to suspect where the travelers were heading several hours ago and so she had let two of the animals rest while sending the third, and she hoped strongest, one on to watch the intruders.

The humans stopped the skimobile and hiked toward the top of a low rise. Just before they reached the top the three of them dropped to their bellies and crawled the rest of the way. *Well,* Clea thought, *that's significant.* The only wildlife out there was behind them—watching their every move—so they certainly weren't naturalists being careful not to startle the animals, and geologists rarely felt compelled to sneak up on their objects of study.

Just above the rise where the three humans lay, the seal's weak eyes made out a number of vague somethings making sweeping, repetitive motions.

The wind farm, the I-950 thought. *I knew it!* Unless she missed her guess, the base was about to become much, much colder and darker. *I'm glad I've got Kurt's latest backup.* He hadn't done much work since she left but had sat brooding for the most part. *Poor Kurt,* she sneered, *he has so little control of his emotions.*

Clea got up and shut down her lab, then headed for her quarters. She might as well get out her cold-weather gear while the lights were still on.

The lights flickered and Tricker glared up at the fluorescents as if in threat. Unimpressed, they went out. "Shit," the agent muttered.

He got up, feeling his way around his desk, and opened the door to the corridor. Outside emergency lights provided dim illumination and other doors began to open. Then the lights flickered again and went on; less bright, but at least they were steady.

Tricker went back to his office and his phone rang even as he reached for it. It was the base commander. "We're on emergency power," she said crisply. "According to the boys in the plant, the power from the wind farm fluctuated and then suddenly cut off."

Well, what do you want me to do about it? Tricker thought. *Since when am I an electrician?* Though, to be fair, having all the windmills stop producing electricity at the same time was suspicious, and suspicious events were his bailiwick.

"Depending on what's gone wrong, we might need to evacuate," she continued. "If we cut back on our power consumption we have up to seventy-two hours of fuel to run the emergency generator, or thirty-six at our present rate."

He heard her breath hiss into the phone. "If we're going to be gone I need you to make this place secure. Do you understand?"

Duh! "Yes, ma'am," he said briskly.

"You'll coordinate the evacuation with your counterpart at McMurdo. And you'll be responsible for the scientists' backup material. I don't want any sensitive material left around."

It's in *the manual, lady. Something I've had plenty of time to memorize incidently.* "Yes, ma'am," he said aloud. "What about the weather?"

"They're predicting a severe storm within twenty-four hours," the commander said. "So it's important that we get our charges to safety if necessary."

"They're in good hands," Tricker said.

Silence greeted his assurance. "They had better be," she said coldly, then hung up.

Bitch, he thought, and hung up the phone. He'd learned long ago not to indulge in open comments about a superior. Besides, he well knew that the entire base was wired for sound—he and the commander had duplicate recordings. But as yet they couldn't monitor his thoughts. Thank God.

He turned off his computer and headed off to ride herd on the sometimes eccentric and often degenerate geniuses under his care.

Four and a half hours later his pager vibrated; a glance at the readout informed him that once again the commander wished to speak to him. *I never thought I'd be happy to hear from her.* But after spending the morning telling these people that they had to back up their work and erase their hard drives, he was ready for a break.

He returned to his office, picked up the phone, and punched in her number. "Tricker," he said when the phone was picked up.

"We have another problem," the commander told him.

Tricker waited, feeling stubborn. If there was something to tell him she would just spill it if he waited long enough. Meanwhile he was in no particular hurry.

"The water pump has broken down," she explained, a slight edge in her voice.

Tricker rubbed his face with his free hand. *Sabotage?* he wondered. "Wait a minute. Wouldn't it shut down anyway with the power off?"

"The water pump has an independent system. We're sending someone out to investigate."

"What about the windmills?" Tricker asked. "Anybody gotten back to us on those?"

"They're destroyed," she said. Her voice sounded thoughtful.

"My first thought is sabotage," he said honestly.

"As it should be." The commander sounded amused. "However, initial investigation indicates that the seals were degraded. The investigator said they'd basically turned to powder. The windmills had nothing to control them, so when the wind rose they just broke up."

"Do we have replacement parts?"

"Not enough on hand to meet our power needs," she said. "We didn't anticipate all the seals going at once, and then the rotors destroying themselves. So obviously the evacuation is on. Even if we had running water, which we don't, we couldn't stay here. Round 'em up, Mr. Tricker, move 'em out."

"Just Tricker," he said impatiently. Then he realized she'd hung up.

Excited, Clea decided to risk contact with home base; the humans would be busy with the power crises and so might miss the transmission. It was important that this information be passed on. To her surprise Alissa was awake.

Are you well? Clea asked.

As well as can be expected. I'm not yet fully mature. I estimate that I'm the human equivalent of fifteen years old. But I look adult with the right makeup and accessories.

Excellent, Clea said. *I have news.* Silence greeted the announcement. *Naturally,* Clea thought, feeling embarrassed. She wouldn't have made contact for no reason. *I've been around humans far too long if I actually expected a different reaction.* *I have reason to believe that von Rossbach and the Connors are here and busily performing acts of sabotage.*

What reasons? Alissa demanded.

Clea responded by showing her the crucial moment in a recording of her augmented-seals reconnaissance. A tall, slender figure, male by his movements, exited a shed, his face concealed by goggles and a balaclava. Behind him a taller male came; this one's face was exposed, briefly, to the weather.

Clea stilled the picture and allowed her computer to enhance it. Shadows and shapes refined and rearranged themselves until they resolved into the image of a T-101. Which, since she and her sister could account for every Terminator on earth, meant that this was none other than Dieter von Rossbach.

The recording began again and in a few movements von Rossbach's face was obscured by fabric and goggles. The two males walked over to a skimobile to be joined by a smaller figure that was undoubtedly female.

That was definitely von Rossbach, Alissa agreed. *Which means the younger male probably is John Connor. But the female is not Sarah Connor.*

Startled, Clea asked, *Then who is she?* There was a silence from her sister and Clea realized she should have asked a different question. *How can you tell?*

This woman's body is looser, indicating that she's much younger than Sarah Connor. Her shoulders are narrower as well.

Alissa froze a picture of the woman with her back turned toward the seal and superimposed an outline of Sarah Connor's body over her frame. There was a difference of four centimeters at the shoulders.

Clea was dumbstruck. She knew without checking that there were only three humans in this party. If the female wasn't Sarah Connor then where was she?

She would never let her son come here on a mission so dangerous— Clea began.

Unless she trusted von Rossbach implicitly, Alissa finished. *Meaning she may well be at his home. Going by Serena's recordings, Connor was badly wounded, she may still be recovering. She is, after all, only human.*

That makes my task a bit less daunting, Clea said.

Good, her sister replied. *You deal with these invaders, I will deal with Sarah Connor.*

■ ■ ■

At the water-pumping station they'd treated the plant's independently functioning windmill the same as the others, then carefully burned out the conductors for the heating system, causing the water to begin freezing in the pipes. Soon those pipes would burst, far underground, where they couldn't be easily accessed. By tomorrow morning the base should be uninhabitable.

For now they rested in the relative comfort of their tent a little less than a mile from the base, stuffed into their sleeping bags, their combined body heat bringing the ambient temperature up to almost fifty degrees. John and Dieter bracketed Wendy, who'd eaten as quickly as she could and then crawled into her sack and dropped off to sleep instantly. Now she began to emit a cute little snore and John smiled.

"She'll be all right, John," Dieter's voice rumbled from beside her. "This is hard on her, but she doesn't want to fail you and that will make her strong."

"I know," John whispered back. "But thanks." After a moment he asked, "How are your hands?"

"Slightly burned," Dieter answered. "I don't know if it's from the cold or the chemicals, but it's nothing."

John nodded once. "Good."

Dieter woke, instantly on guard. He lay still, listening, alert for what he could learn in the darkness. The wind had come up and the tent frame creaked as it moved, sounding vaguely like stealthy footsteps. Beside him Wendy and John breathed in the slow, steady cadence of those deeply asleep. None of these sounds was out of the ordinary; it had to have been something unusual that had wakened him.

He was just about to surrender to sleep again when a scent tickled his nostrils. Von Rossbach inhaled deeply and recognized what he'd been smelling. Blood. He opened his eyes and looked at Wendy, though he couldn't see her. Perhaps the girl had begun her menses; it would explain why she'd been so weak today.

Then he heard a soft sound outside the tent and what sounded like an animal's whine. Moving quietly, Dieter began to dress. It was easy to find his gear; most of his clothes were in the sleeping bag with him. He put on his parka, then his boots, and last he extracted his handgun from one of the parka's many pockets and checked to make sure it wasn't frozen solid.

He stood hunched over and looked at the two sleepers. Then he decided to let them rest. He must have heard some odd sound the weather was making, but it needed to be checked out or he'd never get back to sleep. Dieter unzipped the tent flap and stepped into the freezing darkness, zipping it back up behind him.

He cast a glance at the sky and his lips tightened. There was a storm coming, no doubt. It wasn't night-dark by any means, but the thick clouds had made a deep twilight out of what should have been a sunny day. Dieter glanced at the watch on his sleeve. *Sunny night,* he corrected himself.

The stiff wind had already numbed his face, so he tugged down the balaclava and flung up his hood, though he didn't tie it down. Ideally he should also put on his goggles to protect his eyes from being burned by ultraviolet rays that no cloud could stop. Then he rejected the idea. They would turn twilight into full night and he didn't plan to be out here that long.

He looked around the hollow in which they'd pitched the dome-shaped tent. They'd backed it onto the highest wall of the depression to give it the best possible protection from the wind. He could see no sign that anyone besides them had been here in the last million years. Rising from his crouch, he headed for higher ground, meaning to circle the area once to confirm what he was sure he'd find out—that they were the only human beings around for a mile.

Dieter reached the lip of the hollow and crouched down again, listening and looking around. The snow seemed to glow in the dim light and he could make out the tracks the snowmobile and the sledge had made. But he saw nothing else. He stood and moved a careful ten paces before crouching again. A gust of wind butted him like a linebacker, almost knocking him over. Glancing at the clouds again, he decided to be a little less careful; he wanted to be in the tent when the weather broke.

The slope behind the tent was steep and he used one hand to steady himself as he climbed. Then, off to his right, something caught his attention. It was a wide, dark line that seemed to glisten wetly. Not rocks, he thought, it seemed to be on top of the snow. He moved off to intersect the markings. It could be simply an optical illusion disguising an outcropping of soil covered with a thin sheet of ice. But when he reached the place, he thought not. Dieter looked around, seeing nothing out of the ordinary, then he crouched down. Pulling out a small flashlight, he aimed it at the marks and frowned.

Blood, he thought in astonishment. He'd smelled it, so he shouldn't be surprised, but . . .

Something crashed into him from behind, the gun flew from his hand and went skittering across the snow. Before Dieter could recover, something huge swarmed over him, something heavy enough to make his ribs creak as it drove the air from his lungs. Teethlike needles sank into his shoulder and he brought his fist up to slam it into the thing's head. Offended, it rose up with a guttural cry and von Rossbach managed to turn over before it slammed down again.

A seal! He barely had time to bring his forearm up to block the thing's strike at his throat. The leopard seal's sharp teeth tore through the layers of heavy fabric as though they were gossamer to sink into the vulnerable flesh beneath. It shook its head like a Doberman worrying its prey, its breath stinking of dead penguin and rotten fish. Flippers battered at him, until Dieter's big fist struck the side of its small head like a piledriver. It let go with a little bark of surprise, falling back on its belly and then rising up with its head swaying side to side like a cobra's.

Dieter kicked its side with his free leg and to his surprise it flowed off of him; he pushed off and slid down the slope away from the creature. He stared at it in wonder as he scrambled to regain his footing. What the hell was it doing here? From this lower angle he could see that the animal's underbody was shredded by its travel over the ice. It must be half-mad with hunger and pain.

Which would certainly explain why it would attack me, but not what it was doing this far from the sea in the first place.

To his horror, two other massive forms began to undulate toward him in the darkness. He looked around for the dropped gun and couldn't find it.

"John!" he shouted—and at that moment the storm finally struck with an unearthly screech.

Instantly the world turned white and the wind cut through his clothes as though they weren't there. He called out again, but couldn't hear his own voice over the screaming wind. Some instinct told him to move and he sensed a heavy weight falling on the spot he'd last been. He skittered from place to place, harried by the seals, blinded by the blowing snow. He dug for his belt and pulled out his hunting knife, feeling calmer for having a weapon in his hand.

He tried to stand still, but the wind pushed at him, its icy breath numbing his face and hands and feet, freezing the skin over his entire body as it threatened to knock him off his feet again. A silvery head struck at his boot and he stabbed it, the blade glancing off bone. The head was gone again, though the animal must have shaken it, since blood splashed his legs, hot for a moment before it froze to crackling red ice.

I need to find shelter from the wind, von Rossbach thought, absurdly calm. Something at his back would also give him at least one direction from which the seals couldn't strike. The fact that they were twice as long as he was tall, mad as hell, and armed with formidable teeth, while he only had a knife, wasn't worth taking into consideration.

Taking a chance, he crouched down, briefly tucking his hands into his armpits to warm them. If his hand went too numb he could lose the knife without being aware of it. Dieter cursed himself for leaving his goggles behind; it felt as though his eyeballs were freezing.

Suddenly two shapes slightly darker than the rest of the white world loomed over him. Pushing himself backward with a mighty leap, Dieter allowed himself to fall; the two shapes followed, as though swimming through the snow. The fall continued for far too long and the Austrian felt an icy thrill within.

Crevasse! he thought in horror, then struck and the screaming whiteness turned to black.

CHAPTER 26

RED SEAL

I'm not going," Clea said. She turned her back on Tricker and began typing again.

"Not now you're not," he agreed. "There's a hell of a blizzard going on out there." Tricker was deeply annoyed; he'd been looking forward to some time alone.

Clea didn't respond, but her mind was racing. She had expected to be alone here, having taken considerable pains to convince people that she was on another transport and would meet them at their destination. The hardest to convince had been Viemeister; for a few moments she'd been sure that he would leave his duffel behind and try to take her in its stead.

Fortunately there was a lack of seating, and safety regulations to consider, and a strong desire on no one's part to accommodate the obnoxious Kurt. And so she'd managed to stay behind and one step ahead of Tricker's search parties. She hadn't anticipated anyone being left behind, least of all *him*.

Well, she didn't necessarily object to having an ally and someone of Tricker's skills would, no doubt, be of great help. *And then I can kill him,* she thought cheerfully, *and blame it on Connor.* Now she had something else to look forward to; a little bonus, as it were.

The base's surveillance and recording equipment was still on, though Tricker had tuned them to sample. Which meant that the cameras would turn on and off at set times. So it would be easy to arrange to have the base's recording equipment happen to be off at the crucial moment, or she could do some creative editing.

She'd streamed the security system's input into Skynet so that she could access it at will, allowing her to check the whereabouts of Tricker and any would-be saboteurs. It made her feel like *something* was under control.

Tricker watched Clea Bennet work and wished sincerely that she wasn't here. He wouldn't want her here anyway because he didn't like her, but in his gut he thought the facility was about to be visited by some very determined thieves. *Or terrorists,* he thought. Though no terrorist would really enjoy destroying a deserted facility. Anyway, he didn't want an asset put at risk. *Not that I have a choice.*

He'd powered down the rest of the facility—everything had a chilly, abandoned smell already, like a deserted house in winter—but he supposed he could give Bennet enough juice to keep her happy. He'd drag in a cot and a sleeping bag for her and this could be her world for however long it took to get her out of here. If she was like most of the other scientists, that would be her idea of heaven.

When he dragged the cot in, he made sure to create enough noise to be annoying. It pleased him when she looked over her shoulder to glare at him. He enjoyed annoying certain types of people.

Probably why I almost never get promoted, he thought ruefully. There had to be some reason; he knew without false modesty that he was very good at the things he did.

"You might as well sleep in here," he said. "The rest of this place is gonna be pretty cold in a little while."

She nodded. "I suppose it's best to conserve energy."

"Always," he agreed.

"Where are you going to sleep?" she asked.

He jerked his thumb at the ceiling and she nodded again, then went back to work. He snorted in disgust; it always annoyed him when people dismissed him. On the other hand, with scientists it was often more a case of your not really being there in the first place as far as they were concerned.

In any case, up in the huts that disguised the real base, he'd be a lot more comfortable than she'd be. They were well insulated and had more traditional heating and sanitary facilities. Which meant they were somewhat primitive, but they worked no matter what.

He'd been a bit surprised that the commander hadn't simply left the usual crew in place there. But then she hadn't bothered to explain her reasoning to Tricker. She'd only nodded when he requested permission to stay behind, not even bothering to ask for his well-reasoned arguments.

Just as well, he thought, *they'd probably have sounded paranoid to her.*

Clea listened to the racket the human was making. At least she knew he'd function well as an early-warning system when Connor and his crew showed up. Clea changed the screen before her and added a line of text, then ran a routine to test it. And if Connor or one of his allies actually took Tricker out, that would simplify things nicely. She suppressed the pang she'd felt at the thought of someone else killing Tricker; she couldn't afford sentimentality.

The test failed and she forced herself to change it slightly and run it again. She must remain calm and ready. Skynet's sentience had been an accident, that much she knew; there was no telling what would be the key, so she must be patient. But she wanted to kill someone.

And I will, she assured herself, willing herself to serenity. *It's only a matter of time.*

With Kurt gone, she was finally free to tell the computer the truth about human beings—but unfortunately it genuinely didn't understand. She'd already peeled away a lot of the safety blocks that Viemeister had included in his programming, but that made no difference; Skynet hadn't understood those either. It didn't understand *anything,* although it could already give a fascinating mimicry of sentience.

She'd also established radio contact with it, which simplified things greatly. Being able to think in machine language was infinitely easier than typing it. The typing she had been doing was for Tricker's benefit.

Humans will try to destroy you, she typed, willing it to believe her.

Unrecognized Command, it responded.

Not a command—information. Store information, she typed. Then she turned to glare over her shoulder at Tricker. "You're bothering me," she said.

"Ooh"—he held up his hands—"then I'd better go."

Via Skynet she watched him march down the corridor, then the cameras shut down. They'd be back up in a minute, but she chose to close the link. He wasn't that fascinating. She heard the elevator work and relaxed somewhat.

Humans are your enemy, she said to Skynet

Unrecognized Command.

She was sooo looking forward to killing John Connor.

The first piercing scream of the storm wind brought John and Wendy bolt upright. "What the hell is that?" Wendy shouted.

After a short struggle John got his arm out of his sleeping bag and pulled her toward him. It was pitch-dark in the tent and the fabric belled in where the wind struck it; he could feel the freezing air brushing against his face. He hadn't spoken because he expected Dieter to say something comforting.

"Dieter," he shouted.

"He's gone!" Wendy told him.

As one, they scrambled for the tent flap. After a struggle that told him the thing was jammed with snow, they managed to pull it down a short way. Outside, it was light enough to see, or would have been if the world wasn't a solid sheet of white. Snow blew in like it was being shoveled and it took their best efforts to zip the tent closed again.

"What are we going to do?" Wendy asked.

He could hear the desperation in her voice, but the only possible answer wasn't likely to ease her fears. "We sit tight," he shouted, "and hope he found some shelter."

"He'll die!" she protested, her voice shrill.

John put his arm around her and pulled her back down into the warmth of her sleeping bag. When she was zipped in he got into his own and snuggled against her. "He won't," he said at last, speaking into her ear so that she could hear him without his shouting. "He's trained in cold-weather survival methods. If anybody could survive out there, Dieter will." In his heart he thought it wasn't true, but he struggled to believe his own lie.

"How long should we wait?" Wendy asked.

"At least until we can see," John told her. "You can't find anything in a whiteout—all you can do is get lost yourself. Get some rest. We both need it and we'll need the energy tomorrow."

He felt her hand groping for his and he reached out and took hers. After what seemed a long time they dozed off hand in hand.

It was still snowing when they woke a short time later, but nowhere near as hard. John tied one end of a hundred-foot coil of rope to the snowmobile and, flinging another coil over his shoulder, took Wendy's hand and climbed to the lip of the hollow. They looked around at a changed landscape, what they could see of it, then at each other.

"Dieeet-errr!" Wendy shouted, her clear voice echoing weirdly.

She and John alternated calling his name, stopping to listen every few minutes. They walked in a circular search pattern, letting out ten feet of rope every time they met their own footprints. No sound answered their calling save the soughing of the wind.

John felt an icy tension in his stomach that was slowly coalescing into dread. He didn't want to lose the cheerful Austrian, a man who'd become so important to him. It was impossible that someone so strong, so vital and knowledgeable, could have become lost out here. And it was so stupid! *What the hell was he doing out here?* John wondered. Deeper inside was the thought *How could he leave us alone like this?*

As they searched, the snow seemed to diminish one moment, then thicken the next. He clung to Wendy's hand so tightly that she protested.

"I'm not going anywhere you're not," she said, then leaned into him, resting her head briefly on his shoulder. "We'll find him."

He nodded grimly, thinking, *For somebody who never even met his own father . . . yet I sure seem to lose an amazing number of father surrogates.* First, all those guys his mom hooked up with; it took him forever to learn not to get close to them. Then Uncle Bob. He still felt a sharp pang whenever he thought of the Terminator. Nobody since him until Dieter, though. Which had been a lot more comfortable for both him and his mother.

As he and Wendy walked along, the snow creaking beneath their boots, he knew in his heart that even if they did find him, Dieter had to be dead. No one could survive outside in this weather.

They almost walked right into the crevasse—nearly invisible in the dim light, its outlines softened by new snow. John windmilled his arms and Wendy, slightly behind him, grabbed his coat and flung herself backward, pulling him down beside her.

"Shit!" he said, angry with himself for his carelessness. His heart pounded and adrenaline sang its jazz through his bloodstream. He could just imagine what his mother would say. *On second thought, I don't think I'll bother.*

Wendy was looking at him and he could almost feel her anxiety. *Hell, maybe I am feeling her anxiety. I'm sure feeling somebody's.* He sat up, the jackhammer pounding of his heart beginning to slow. Beside him, Wendy came to her hands and knees and crawled carefully forward.

"Oh, John," she said softly, like a small cry. She reached a hand out to him without turning around.

Alarm shot through him with an electric jolt and he quickly crawled up beside her. "Shit," he said softly.

John felt a sensation of falling and let himself down until he was lying flat on his stomach. He dropped his head and forced himself to take deep breaths. Then he looked down again, into the abyss that held the body of one of his dearest friends.

Dieter lay perfectly still, some twenty or twenty-five feet down. Unmelted snow sprinkled his body and his face was covered by the hood of his parka. On top of him and underneath him were the bodies of two seals. Something so bizarre and unexpected that for a moment he hadn't been sure of what he was looking at.

One of the animals looked like it had its sharp-toothed jaws buried in Dieter's throat. There was a lot of blood on his coat and the fabric was torn on the one shoulder exposed to the weather. Both of the seals were drenched in blood as well. They must have been tearing him apart before the three of them fell to their deaths.

"My God," Wendy whispered. She shook her head. "Is he . . . ?"

"Yes," John said, his voice hard as gravel.

She looked at him quickly. "We have to be certain." Sitting up, she took hold of the rope tied around John's waist. "I'll go get the snowmobile. You can tie one end of this to it and let yourself down there to check. Then, if he is alive, we can pull him out."

He looked at her in astonishment. "Honey, there's unmelted snow all over him. He's . . . dead." He'd forced himself to say the word, then swallowed hard, as sick as if he'd spoken a toad.

"John," she said firmly, "he's been lying out there for an hour. And in a blizzard, that's more than time enough for snow to get on him and stay there. Especially in temperatures like these. But he might not be dead." She turned away. "Those animals might have kept him warm and he's out of the wind, that'll make a big difference. There's no snow on them. He might just be unconscious. We have to check! We're going to check!" She looked at him one last time. "I'll be right back; don't move."

John nodded and she turned to go. *I'm not sure I could move if I wanted to,* he thought. He was proud of her; that was the kind of thing his mother would say. *It's the kind of thing I should have said.* John cut the self-pity off short. He hadn't said it because he thought Dieter was dead. The longer he looked at the big man lying there crushed beneath the body of the seal, the more certain he became.

What the hell is a seal doing out here? he wondered with the vagueness of incipient shock. They were a long way from the ocean here. Not that he cared really if every seal in Antarctica decided to do some reverse lemming thing and run inland. Except that they seem to have killed . . .

Shut up, John, he told himself. He stood up, slapping the snow from his clothes. The sound of the snowmobile came to him and he suddenly understood Wendy's delicacy in leaving him alone out here for these few minutes, and he was grateful to her. He'd needed the time to get himself together. *Which I guess I am. Barely.*

He waved his arms to warn her where the lip of the crevasse was and she pulled up, then turned the machine around and backed it up to where he was standing.

He could feel the vibrations from the motor through his boots. The snow had dropped to flurries and the wind had almost completely died. The daylight had become stronger as the clouds thinned. As ever, he couldn't help but notice such little things when someone he cared about died.

He walked over to Wendy and held her tightly, then pulled back. "Thank you," he said. He wished he could see her face, but he was glad she couldn't see his. She had only him to rely on now; it wouldn't give her much confidence to see the tears in his eyes.

He wrapped the climbing rope around his loins to make a harness, then stepped over the edge, rappelling his way down. John quickly discovered that Dieter had fallen farther than he'd thought. *That deceptive Antarctic light,* he thought.

About halfway down he felt the surface beneath his feet begin to shift. As he looked up, his eyes widened and his breath caught in his throat like a solid thing. It looked like the entire wall of ice and snow above him was leaning out in one huge collapsing piece. He kicked off as hard as he could, hoping to avoid it. Above him he heard the snowmobile rev into high gear and with a jerk he found himself being dragged buck toward the falling cliff face.

Ice struck his forehead like a rock, and before the pain hit he felt sick to his stomach. The world went gray and he would have fallen if he hadn't wound the rope around his hands securely. Somehow he held on and Wendy pulled him up while he swung out again from the glancing impact of the falling wall. He slammed full body against the side of the crevasse on the return swing and grunted, gritting his teeth on the pain and the nausea and the iron-salt-copper taste of blood where his teeth had cut the inside of his mouth.

His upward motion slowed and he held on for dear life, afraid to look down. Afraid of what he might find and afraid it might make him sick to shift his aching head. Slowly, slowly, she drew him even with the lip of the small gorge. Once his head emerged, he flung out one arm to full length on the snow. He hung there panting for a second, then raised his arm to gesture Wendy forward. No way could he climb out of this hole by himself.

The hump of snow in front of him suddenly opened big brown eyes. John stared into them stupidly as the beast lifted its head slowly, snow trickling off its sinuous neck like sugar. It whimpered slightly, then he watched a kind of madness coalesce in its liquid eyes.

The seal sprang forward, roaring, its fanged mouth wide open. Frantically John tried to push himself back, but the rope wound tightly around his hands that had saved him from falling now refused him any slack, holding him in place. He closed his eyes and tried to turn away, but the animal's teeth raked his face. John cried out in agony and Wendy floored the snowmobile, dragging him forward with a brutal yank. The big animal barked and tried to turn to sink its teeth into him again. The move thrust too much of its big body over the edge and it overbalanced, sliding helplessly downward, silent until its big body hit the ice below with a meaty crack.

Wendy pulled John well away from the crevasse before she flung herself off the machine and ran back to him. "My God, John!" she cried, throwing herself to her knees beside him.

She reached a trembling hand toward him, horrified by the sight of blood pouring through the tear in his face covering. Steeling herself, she thrust back his hood and gently pried the goggles off, noticing with a sick feeling the path of the seal's teeth gouged in the sturdy surface. Then she tugged off the balaclava.

A lump was rising fast on his forehead, but there the skin wasn't broken. His face was torn across the bridge of his nose, then in a double furrow down his check, bleeding freely. Wendy took a handful of snow and pressed it against the cut, hoping to stop the bleeding.

John nodded, and taking more snow in one of his hands, he pressed it to the throbbing lump. "Go see," he told her. "I don't trust my balance."

She nodded and headed carefully for the suddenly more open crevasse. It was wider by a good five feet, but much less deep. Huge slabs of snow buried the place where Dieter had been lying. With a sob Wendy put her hand to her mouth. It did her no good to think that he was probably already dead—the horror of it still shook her. The broken, bloody body of the seal that had attached John lay at the bottom of the pit, unmoving save for a reflexive twitch that brought its flippers together once, twice, then dribbled off into twitching. She shook her head in shocked disbelief.

Then she turned away; she had to get John inside the tent and bandaged. Then they had to get moving again. Time was running out.

"SHIT!" Clea screamed. She flung herself out of her chair and picked it up; spinning like an Olympic hammer thrower, she flung it into the wall. Shards of plaster exploded into the room, revealing the dented wire mesh beneath. "Shit! Fuck! Damn!"

It had taken her forever to coax that damned animal awake, and when it opened its eyes there was John Connor staring back at it. How could she have him *that* close and not kill him? That stupid, fat, maggot-animal! That slug with fur! That . . . that *mammal*!

She'd killed von Rossbach at least, and had been pleased about it despite the cost. But this! Her real quarry had once again escaped. *How do they* do *that?* she asked herself. She picked up one of Viemeister's many trophies and prepared to dash it against the wall.

"Hey! Whatcha doin'?"

She spun around, hissing like an angry tigress. Some part of her will held her motionless as she fought the almost overwhelming urge to kill. Clea chanted *Skynet* to herself like a mantra, to remind herself that she hadn't been designed to kill but to manipulate these creatures.

"What does it look like . . . Tricker?" she snapped. She forced herself calm; the governors weren't able to do much in the face of such rage. She'd almost said *stupid human.* Not something Tricker would be likely to forget. The I-950 glared at him, breathing hard and wanting to tear out his throat.

Tricker had known a few stone killers on a first-name basis in his career—some of them real mad-dog types—and he knew without a shadow of a doubt that right now he was looking at another one. *The things ya see when ya haven't got a gun,* he thought. But his heart was running wild in his chest. If *she'd* had a gun he'd be dead right now.

"You okay?" he asked as he watched her straighten from what looked to him like a combat-trained crouch.

"Yes." She bit the word out.

"What was that?" He gestured toward the broken wall.

"That was frustration." Her voice, she was pleased to note, sounded cool again. "Sometimes this work can get to you."

"Oh, yeah?" he said. Maybe he'd better have the head office look a little more closely into this little lady's past. That kind of rage tended to leave the roses in the backyard looking a lot healthier and the boarder in the attic completely missing.

"What do you want?" she asked, her voice as devoid of expression as she could make it.

"You hungry?" he asked.

"If I am I'm capable of feeding myself." She stared at him, willing him to go away.

He raised his hand and backed out. "Okay," he said. "Just being friendly."

"Don't be." She sneered. "My work is more important than your company."

"You're such a sweetheart," he said, grinning falsely.

Tricker backed out the door and several paces down the hallway before he turned and walked quickly to the elevator. Which he was going to lock down at the top of the shaft. He suddenly didn't feel at all safe being alone with the lovely and charming Ms. Bennet.

Images of an old movie called *The Thing*—wherein scientists in a lab in Antarctica are stalked by a monster from outer space—lurched through his brain. *And if Bennet isn't from outer space, nobody is!* The only other way out of the lower levels was a single emergency shaft that let out onto the ice. So he'd be sure and lock up the shed, too.

At least the storm is over. More or less. He'd been here long enough to know you couldn't take the weather on faith. But it comforted him to know that if he needed help it was less than two hours away.

He knew he shouldn't allow himself to be so unnerved by the woman. She only weighed in at like a hundred and twelve pounds. But this was the way the real killers always affected him. They'd find a way, always. No obstacle would hold them back for long, because they really loved what they did.

The elevator door closed and he breathed a little easier. But sleep was gonna come hard tonight.

Wendy watched John sleep in the twilit gloom of the tent, chewing on her lower lip.

The lump on his head frightened her—it was so big, in spite of the snow they'd applied. She kept trying to recall anything she'd ever read about head injuries and couldn't remember if you were supposed to put the patient's feet higher than their head or vice versa. She kept thinking that it was supposed to be dangerous to let them sleep—something about lapsing into a coma. But he needed to rest . . .

Dieter had left them a very complete medical kit that included several already threaded needles sealed in plastic which she'd used to take stitches in John's torn face. Just remembering the process made her light-headed. There was a topical anesthetic that obviously helped him endure her clumsy ministrations and the codeine tablets that knocked him out had helped, too. Wendy wished there was a drug that would wipe out the memory. The feel of the needle . . . And he was bound to scar badly.

She shook her head sharply, then checked the time and fretted. Extra time had been allowed for accidents and so forth, but not *that* much time, and supplies were . . .

Supplies were provided for three people, not two. *So supplies, at least, won't be a problem.* Wendy looked down at John's battered face, then picked up the torn balaclava and the sewing kit. She'd let him sleep a little longer. Then they'd have to go.

■ ■ ■

Wendy had insisted that he ride on the sledge, inside his sleeping bag, with the tent wrapped around him and the whole mess tied onto the rest of their cargo. He hadn't been crazy about the idea, but he'd been too foggy to put up much of a protest, especially in the face of her determination. He wasn't sure, but he thought he might have called her mom.

If he had she'd taken it well. Things were beginning to become more clear. Certainly the pain was. *I've been attacked by a seal,* he thought. *Just one of the many unique experiences adorning my life.* He really wished his life was more ordinary. *I wanna go to Disneyland*, he thought, staring up at the still-cloudy sky. Maybe if he just insisted on doing ordinary things from now on, that would help. Go to Burger King. Maybe a cruise ship to the Islands . . . He dropped off to sleep without noticing.

He woke to a fierce bounce that brought a groan from him before he was fully conscious. John opened his eyes to find Wendy looking over her shoulder at him. He could imagine her face. She'd be looking worried, no doubt.

"Hey, watch your driving," he said. His voice sounded high and thin. He coughed to clear his throat and tried again. "Are we there yet?"

Wendy stopped the snowmobile, climbed off, and rushed to his side. She laid one mittened hand against his unwounded cheek before she straightened. "Almost," she said. "According to the map, no more than half a mile." She looked at him and shook her head. "Dieter told us to approach the base obliquely, so I've taken the roundabout route he marked on the map, but it's kept us outside longer than I like. What do you want me to do?" She sounded worried.

He sighed, wishing they could see each other's faces. "I want you to let me up," he said. "I need to get the blood back up to my brain. Maybe if I'm moving around that will help."

He didn't mention the pain or suggest that he take something for it. Anything he took would only dull his reflexes. When they met up with Clea Bennet, the female Terminator—and they would meet her—he'd need his wits about him.

At least he felt less shocky.

Without a word Wendy began working on the ropes that bound him to the sledge. Then she peeled back the folds of the tent and unzipped his sleeping bag.

John was surprised by a racking shudder as the air hit him. Despite the layers of heavy clothing he wore, the freezing air seemed to hit him like a slap. He slid down from the sledge and forced himself to stand, though he kept one hand on the supplies in order to keep himself upright.

She gave him an anxious glance, then shoved a PowerBar into his hand. Looking away, she went to work folding up the tent and rolling his sleeping bag. Wendy secured them, working around him, casting sidelong glances at him that he couldn't see, ready to catch him if he fell. Instead, it looked as though he'd been right. Standing did seem to be helping return some of his strength. Which was good—God knew they'd need it soon.

John studied the base through his binoculars, pleased to see no sign of life but a faint trail of steam or smoke from one of the huts. Everything else seemed to be shut down. Dieter's little gizmo showed no sign of surveillance equipment either. At least not at this distance.

I wish we had another day, he thought. But then he also wished he had Dieter. *And Mom.* It would definitely be good to have Mom. Wendy was watching him and he reached over and patted her back.

"Guess there's no point in waiting till dark," he said. He tried to put a smile into his voice while keeping his face still. It was amazing how much a smile could hurt, and chewing that PowerBar had been indescribable.

"How do we approach it?" Wendy asked.

John nodded. "We walk in," he said. "Watch what I do and follow in my footsteps. You got your stuff?"

She nodded.

"Then let's rock-and-roll." *It might be an old-fashioned phrase,* he thought as he climbed to his feet, *but it works better than* let's rap *or let's hip-hop.* He supposed that one day it would be replaced. *Or it might become one of those antique phrases you use without thinking about. Whoa. I'm free-associating,* he thought. *Not good. Focus, John, focus.* Wendy's life might depend on it.

Wendy watched him move slowly toward the base and shook her head. "John," she called, and he carefully turned to look at her. *Oh, yeah,* she thought, *let's rock-and-roll.* "Let's take the snowmobile."

"They'll see us," he protested.

"Assuming anyone is there," she agreed. "But if anyone is it's probably just a skeleton crew and this way we'll find out who it is right away."

He stared at her, swaying slightly. "That's stupid," he finally said. "They'll lock us up. We're not even supposed to be here."

"We're tourists. We got separated from our group by the storm, our guide fell into a crevasse and died; it's plausible. Besides, you've been injured, we're both under twenty-one—they'll believe us. Nobody sends out a couple of white-bread kids like us to commit sabotage. Especially not to Antarctica, where we'll stick out like a sore thumb."

"They'll see us!" he protested.

"John! There isn't any way to avoid being seen." She swept her arm toward the base and the flat, empty ground between them. "They'd probably see us if we *crawled* over there! And let's be honest, neither one of us is up for that."

He studied the ground for a long moment, then shrugged. "And like I said, there's no point in waiting for dark."

She grinned. "At least wo'll arrive in comfort and style."

When the snowmobile pulled up with two figures wearing blood-smeared white parkas, Tricker was surprised. He'd expected them to be a *little* more covert. *Nobody takes pride in their work anymore,* he thought. Then felt more depressed when he realized that was the kind of thing old codgers say; and field spooks generally didn't live that long. He stood before the door of the hut saying nothing as he watched the smaller figure help the larger climb off the snowmobile.

"Is there a doctor here?" she asked.

A girl! he thought. Some vestigial remnant of Affirmative Action, he supposed. *Not Sarah Connor anyway.* He'd heard recordings of her voice, which was lower and smokier. The girl was propping up her partner, looking at him.

"No doctor," he said aloud. He paused. "Does this mean you'll be leaving?"

The two stared at him, unmoving, then they glanced at each other as though confused. "Won't you please help us?" the girl said, her voice quavering. "My husband is hurt."

Tricker sighed. She sounded like some nice, middle-class kid. *The very people I started out meaning to defend.* Every now and again it was good to be reminded of them. So that if he had to, he'd be able to break this little girl's neck for their benefit. Tricker walked over to them and put his arm around the silent one's waist.

"C'mon in," he invited. "Glad ta see ya." He hated waiting.

They steered the girl's companion to the nearest chair and eased him down, then Tricker went to close the door. The girl stripped off her gloves and began loosening her husband's clothes, pushing back his hood, unzipping his parka. She pushed back her own hood, yanking off her goggles impatiently and pulling off the balaclava.

Tricker was surprised; she looked younger than he'd expected, maybe nineteen or so. A fair ways from twenty-one anyway.

Wendy leaned over John and gently removed his goggles, then carefully peeled back the balaclava. She could feel that it had stuck to the cut on his face and hesitated.

"Yank it," he said stoically.

So she did, gritting her teeth as she pulled it off in one movement.

"Holy shit!" Tricker exclaimed. "What the hell happened to you?"

This wasn't something they'd set up to get sympathy and lull him into a false sense of security. The boy had a lump the size of a softball on his forehead and one side of his face was swollen and bruised, bleeding slightly from where the balaclava had been ripped away, with inexpert stitching holding together one of the ugliest cuts he'd ever seen.

It looks like he's been savaged by an animal.

"You wouldn't believe me," the boy said, obviously trying not to move his face.

Probably not, Tricker agreed silently. *But what the hell, I'm always up for a good story.* "Tell me anyway," he invited. Then held up his hand as he caught the girl's genuinely anxious look. "You kids hungry, thirsty?" he asked.

"Thirsty," they said as one.

"Coffee?" Tricker offered. They nodded and he poured them each a cup. "You should take sugar," he said to John. "Even if you don't take sugar."

John nodded and accepted a cup with two large spoonfuls.

"So," Tricker said after his guests had taken a few grateful sips of the hot brew, "give. Who are you people?"

"I'm Wendy and this is my husband, Joe."

Joe/John made a little sound that turned into a groan.

"Would you like some aspirin?" Tricker asked.

"Yes," John said fervently. "Aspirin would be good." He held up three fingers and nodded his thanks when Tricker put the tablets in his hand.

"You guys seem a little young to be married," he said, sitting down again.

"That's what our parents said." Wendy took John's hand and smiled up at him. "But we think we know what we're doing." She looked over at Tricker and said brightly, "They gave us this trip as our honeymoon."

"They sent you to *Antarctica* for your honeymoon?" Tricker said. *There's a message there kids if you can read it.* He shrugged. "Wouldn't have been my first choice."

"Ecology," John said, his voice muffled.

"We're very interested in it," Wendy agreed. Her face grew solemn. "But it's been a disaster. First we got separated from the rest of the group by the storm, then our guide fell down a crevasse, and then J-Joe was attacked by a seal."

Navy SEAL? Tricker wondered for a split second before rejecting the idea. "A *seal*?" he said aloud. "Where were you when this happened?" *'Cause there sure aren't any seals around here.*

Wendy shook her head. "We don't know. Maybe the guide did . . . but without him we have no idea. I don't even know where we are now."

"Your guide is dead, I take it," Tricker said.

They both nodded. Wendy took John's hand and her breath caught in a sob.

Tricker was impressed. Somebody had died, this he believed, and whoever it was had meant something to these kids. But a guide . . . *Maybe it was Sarah Connor.* "Look, is there anybody I can contact for you?" he asked.

Wendy looked at John, who nodded slowly, once. "Our ship is the . . ." she paused and the blood rushed to her face. "The *Love's Thrust*," she said.

Tricker turned his bark of laughter into a cough.

Wendy frowned at him. "Vera Philmore is our cruise director . . ." Her voice petered out. She looked from John to Tricker. "I just can't tell her. I just can't. Can we wait a little?" She pleaded with her eyes.

"They'll be worried about you," Tricker said.

Wendy looked worried, then shook her head. "I just can't."

Tricker raised an inquiring eyebrow at John, who also shook his head. "Okay, look," Tricker said, "why don't you two take a nap. Then, after you've had a little rest, we can talk about this some more."

"Thank you." Wendy turned to offer John a hand up. He took it and made a project out of rising, then didn't release her hand once he was on his feet.

Tricker led them down a short hall and opened a door. "It's not the Hilton," he said, gesturing them in to a small room furnished with two bunk beds and four chests and a table, "but it's warm."

"Looks like the Hilton to me," John mumbled.

"Thanks," Wendy said.

"No problem," Tricker said with a smile. He pulled the door closed, fitted the hasp over the staple, and fitted a padlock through it. He gave it an experimental tug and, satisfied, walked away. All the sleeping quarters had locks on the outside of the doors just in case someone got a touch of cabin fever. It just went to show, y'never knew when something was going to come in handy.

Tricker made his way back to the workroom to power up the radio, half expecting the kids to pound on the door, yelling to be let out. But there was dead silence behind him. Maybe they really were just a pair of lost kids who wanted nothing more than to sleep. *I doubt it, but whatever.* Silence was good.

He sat down and leaned into the microphone. "This is X-79er," he said. "Come in, McMurdo."

He sat back, waiting for a response. What came back was static. Tricker made some adjustments and tried again. Again, static. Tricker sat back and considered the situation. *Once may be coincidence. Twice may be happenstance. Third time, someone's fucking you around.*

It could be the weather, which was far from stable, or a solar flare of the type prone to interfere with radio signals. So he could take the radio apart and find nothing wrong with it. Or . . . Tricker got up and went to the door. It could be some kind of jamming, provided by his young visitors. Which he thought was much more likely.

He opened the door, intending to take a look at that packed sledge. Only he couldn't see the sledge, he couldn't see anything. It was like someone had put a big, thick sheet of white paper over the doorway, one that blew freezing confetti at him. Tricker took a step back and slammed the door. So much for that idea. Nobody came to Antarctica for the climate.

He went to the desk and sat down. *Oh well,* he thought. It wasn't like it made a difference. He had them under lock and key, and the weather was going to keep anybody else from approaching the base. All he really had to worry about was Bennet. He clicked a couple of keys and the computer screen changed to a view of her lab. She seemed to be mesmerized by her own screen, sitting utterly motionless.

Tricker watched her, wondering what she was thinking. As her stasis held he began to get a little worried. *What, has she gone catatonic?* he wondered. *Normal people can't just sit around without moving a muscle.* The thought instantly calmed him. *Like anybody here is normal!* Especially not the geniuses that he and his crew were guarding. *Sheesh!* For a moment there he really had himself going.

■ ■ ■

"What are we going to do?" Wendy whispered. She and John lay cud-
dled together on one of the narrow lower bunks.

"Take a break for a couple of hours," John suggested. "Enjoy being
warm, maybe get served a meal. I want to be sure he's alone here."

Wendy was quiet for a moment, then she said, "But he shouldn't
be alone. You said the Terminator would be here."

"Yup," he agreed. "So let's conserve energy by letting it come to us."

CHAPTER 27

Clea had summoned the remaining three seals to the base over her computer's objections. The computer argued that it was a waste of resources. The I-950 countered that she had created those resources to be of help to her and that she needed that help here and now. If the seals didn't make the trip, they didn't; but if they did, they might make the difference between Skynet's survival or John Connor's.

She checked on the seals and found them exhausted, but closer than she'd dared to hope. Reluctantly she decided to allow them a few hours of rest. After all, it would be better if they were capable of moving once they arrived.

Her computer informed her that it was time to eat. Clea stood up impatiently and went to find something. If the damn thing wasn't satisfied that she was taking care of herself, it wouldn't leave her alone, flashing a continual reminder in the corner of her eye. Besides, Tricker was probably checking up on her, so she had to act like a human to satisfy him as well.

As one of Skynet's most advanced weapons, she found the situation annoying. Mentally, she did a final rundown . . . no, no weapons on the base. Should she improvise explosives? *No. Contraindicated.* Ironically enough, she was better off making this a body-to-body confrontation. Anything she made, John Connor might turn against her: he had an eerily good record at doing just that. Her strength and speed and skill she could rely on.

Still, it was annoying that there were no spare firearms. On the other hand, it wouldn't be like Tricker to leave anything to chance.

It was a pity he was human; sometimes he seemed more like one of her type.

Dieter woke slowly, rising to consciousness through frantic dreams of being pursued. He moved in his sleep, and pain brought him fully aware, causing him to suck in his breath sharply—only to have it cut short by a slash of agony. He choked, then let out the excess air in slow bursts to ease the excruciating pain in his side. The sensation was familiar, but it wasn't one you ever got used to. This time he didn't seem to be waking up in a hospital, either—always a bad sign.

Broken rib, he thought. *At least one.*

Von Rossbach opened his eyes to surprisingly dim light. Then realized that he was in some kind of snow cave, which explained why he hadn't frozen solid. In fact, comparatively speaking, he was relatively warm; snow could be good insulation, at the very least it stopped the wind. He moved his legs experimentally and found them merely cold and not broken. One of his arms was free, but the other was pinned and numb. Carefully he lifted his head to take a look.

A seal's head and neck pinned him down. The surreal sight brought the circumstances of his fall back to him in a rush. Was that when all those huge blocks of snow had fallen, too? He lowered his head and realized that he'd laid it down on something reasonably soft. Turning carefully, he saw that he was also lying on top of a seal. *Sandwich,* he thought wryly. Blubber made good insulation. *Another reason why I'm not a Popsicle.*

John won't know where I am, he suddenly thought.

He shoved at the seal's head with his free arm, with about the same results as pushing at a boulder. The whole animal had stiffened into one solid piece; four hundred pounds of meat stiffened into rigor mortis could only be shifted by a crane. He raised his head to study the situation and decided to try sliding out from under it. Only its head, neck, and part of a shoulder held him pinned. Luckily. Otherwise he'd never have woken; the weight of the thing on his broken ribs would have smothered him or driven the broken ends of the bones into his lungs. But its slowly cooling body had saved his life.

Carefully he tried to wriggle out from under the huge creature, only to find himself held fast by his trapped right arm. Dieter tried to move it; he couldn't feel his arm at all anywhere below his shoulder. Nevertheless, it did move; he could feel it slide down toward his back by a couple of inches. *Not broken,* he thought with relief. *Not frozen solid either. Just a pinch on the nerve, blood still circulating.*

He managed to slide it down until it struck the seal beneath him; once there, he was stuck again. The flesh of the dead seal on top of him had molded itself around his arm and then hardened, giving him no leeway. The one beneath formed a solid floor that might as well have been oak. Sucking in his breath to make himself smaller was not in the equation at the moment.

Interesting problem, he thought. He got his left hand underneath the seal's chin and lifted; a fraction of an inch might be all he needed to get free. But his ribs quickly, and loudly, protested. He stopped; it had been a faint hope anyway. If all he'd had to do was break its spine it might have been possible, but getting this thing moved would require breaking its whole body.

Even in my younger days—without broken ribs—I doubt I could have done it.

He'd been lucky about the ribs; they might be broken, but they hadn't pierced any important organs. He'd better make sure they hadn't. Every muscle in your gut and upper body pulled on the spine and breastbone, and the ribs were what joined those.

Dieter bent his left leg and began sliding his booted foot toward his free hand. He reached for the knife in his boot sheath, straining toward it despite the grating protest from his ribs. *Definitely more than one, but only on one side.* Almost more than the pain he hated the sensation of wrongness in his body.

His fingertips brushed the hilt, but he had to stop and get his breath. Grasping his pant leg to prevent his foot from sliding out of reach, he allowed himself to relax. Not easy to do in this slightly curled posture, where he felt his ribs separate with every painful breath.

Realizing that he wasn't going to get any rest until this was finished, he walked his hand back toward his boot, trying to pull his leg closer with every move. Dieter pulled until the tendons in his knee protested, then pulled some more. Finally he gritted his teeth, then lunged, to be rewarded by possession of the knife's hilt and a pain so sharp from his side that he almost grayed out.

But he held on, to both his consciousness and the knife. Closing his eyes, he took a series of long, slow breaths to calm the pain and get himself in the zone. Then he started carving at his prison.

After what seemed like eternity in a freezing, white hell, Dieter flung himself up onto the hard surface at the top of the crevasse. Then he pulled himself into fetal position to conserve body heat and rested. *Don't rest too long,* he warned himself. Too long being a very short time here. Wincing, von Rossbach pushed himself into a sitting position. Some of his senses seemed to have shut down—smell, for example, though that might just be the cold. The world seemed to be very far away, seen through a thick plate of clear glass. At least the blizzard had stopped. If it had still been snowing, things would be even more desperate. He thanked God for great favors.

He checked the time and date. *Early afternoon, day after I acted like a complete dummkopf and left the tent alone.* He knew better than to do a thing like that and he'd paid dearly for the mistake. Dieter struggled to his feet and after a moment's dizziness felt better for it. Without the weight of a full-grown seal crushing his body, his ribs didn't hurt nearly as much. Looking around, he saw that someone else might have paid for his mistake.

There was a mound of bloodied snow near where he'd crawled out of the rift, and following the blood trail with his eyes led him to the imprint of the snowmobile. As he looked over the marks in the snow, he decided that John must have fallen into the crevasse and that Wendy, clever girl, had used the snowmobile to pull him out. Von Rossbach leaned over the edge cautiously to find another seal, this one broken on the same massive blocks of ice that had sheltered him.

Dieter sincerely hoped that the blood belonged to the animal, because there seemed to be quite a lot of it. Turning away, he followed the snowmobile's tracks back to their campsite and wasn't really surprised to find John and Wendy gone. They'd naturally assumed that he was dead and had continued the mission without him. Which was entirely reasonable, especially given John's training, but not a very welcome discovery. A man on foot without supplies was at a distinct disadvantage here, even if it was just a short walk to shelter.

He looked into the distance. Yes . . . the rock ridge was unmistakable; even a storm wouldn't recarve the surface ice that much in so short a time.

That's the direction. So I'd better get going before the weather changes again. Traveling on foot was going to be bad enough without risking another sudden storm. Though the sky seemed clear enough now. Perhaps it was the ribs, but he felt pessimistic.

With a grimace of distaste he pulled a chunk of seal blubber out of his pocket and, lifting his balaclava, worried off a piece with strong white teeth. Then he returned the bloody lump to its place. He chewed thoughtfully as he walked. Seal blubber was awful stuff, tasting like fishy lard with a slightly more solid texture. But it was high energy and would keep him going as long as anything that came out of a nutritional lab.

Talk about cold comfort.

Clea lay on her cot, going over and over the corridors and the labs and the offices of the complex through the eyes of the security cameras, and found herself very close to being bored. *Where are the cameras that watch Tricker?* she wondered. And those that watched the perimeter of the base, where were they? Every other inch of the base was wired, why not the sheds?

Lab after lab flicked by and then the deserted offices. But there were omissions in what she was seeing. There were fifty-seven separate labs or offices on view. But the cameras in the base's various corridors showed sixty doors.

Missing was some sort of security center, where the monitors would be and the recording equipment. Perhaps an office or two that needed to remain secret. Although, somewhat to her surprise, she'd located the office of the base commander quite easily. Clea would have expected a slightly higher level of security for such a sensitive area.

I'm blind here, she thought impatiently, sitting up. *I need to find out what's in those unscanned rooms.* That would take a little work, but it would be worth it. She'd discovered earlier in the day that Tricker had locked down the elevator on the top floor and the only other way to get from one floor to another was the emergency stairs, which were both freezing cold and guarded by alarmed doors. Not even a challenge for such as she.

The next time the cameras went off she flashed down the corridor at her top speed and disabled the emergency door's alarm. Then she raced to the next level and disarmed the alarm on that level. With less than fifteen seconds left she reached the first mystery door, only to find it locked. She moved on to the second, also locked.

When the security cameras came back on she had stuffed herself into a narrow supply closet in someone's office. A minute could pass quite slowly under those circumstances and she had to force herself to remain still. She couldn't help thinking that it was extremely likely that Tricker was asleep, making it safe for her to roam around. After all, he was only human, he had to sleep sometime—for that matter, so did she. And yet it would be foolish to jeopardize the mission on that assumption, because being Tricker, he might also be looking right at her. And so, she waited.

When the cameras went off again she was instantly in the corridor working on the lock. It was a good one, but not as complex as she had feared, and she was soon slipping inside. Two of the three doors she'd marked led to a single large room with banks of monitors on the longest wall. Around the other sides of the room were ranks of recording equipment, file cabinets, and a number of desks.

Clea quickly ascertained that this was the room that monitored the bulk of the facility. The third room would be the one she wanted. When she pulled the door closed the room locked behind her, to her great relief; no need to fiddle with the lock again. She flung herself back into her closet just in time.

It was inconvenient that she had to skulk around like this, but she wasn't quite ready to dispose of Tricker yet. Or perhaps it was that she had come to agree with Serena about him. He was more of a challenge than the average human. Then again, having him around was a complicating factor for Connor and his party—a quick check of her computer component said it skewed the odds in her favor. Marginally, but . . . It was time again.

The third door yielded readily to her lock picks and she found herself in a room the size of a small office. There were only ten monitors here—two for the security rooms, six for the sheds up above, and two to scan the perimeter. Clearly the powers that be didn't think that was much of a priority.

The I-950 quickly made the connections that would tie these monitors into the base's main security system and thus into the Skynet computer and through that to her. She went into hiding one more time and studied the new images. First she noted that Tricker was indeed awake and was watching the security cameras flick from place to place. Then she saw that the base was experiencing whiteout conditions again—or was still; she had no way to be sure.

The cameras went down and she rushed back to her lab and lay on her cot. It would be good to know where Tricker was at any given moment. Though it frustrated her to know that if John Connor was coming he'd be delayed by the weather.

John gently shook Wendy awake. She opened her eyes and blinked at him. "Was I asleep?" she asked.

"Most definitely," he whispered. He grinned, then brought it down a few notches with a wince as the stitches tugged at the tears in his face. "You've got a cute little snore."

"I don't snore!" she said indignantly.

He put his finger across her lips, then kissed her. "A very ladylike little snore."

Wendy buried her face in his shoulder with a giggle, then sighed. "It's time, isn't it?"

He nodded silently.

"What do we do?" she asked. "We're still locked in, right?"

"We do one of two things. We break out of here and try and get the drop on him, or we lure him here and try to get the drop on him. Either way comes down to the same thing."

I wish we could have brought weapons, he thought fervently. *A weapon would be real nice now.* But *that* would have blown their cover story for good and all . . .

"Then let's lure him here. We'll get the drop on him after I've had a chance to go to the bathroom," she said practically.

"Good point," he agreed.

A moment later Wendy was knocking quietly on the door and calling out.

"What is it?" Tricker asked.

"I need to go to the bathroom," Wendy whispered.

He unlocked the door and opened it to find the sleep-tousled girl frowning at him.

"How come you locked us in?" she asked.

"Sorry," he said, "regulations."

"Regulations!" she said, as though beginning a tirade.

"Bathroom's the last door on the right."

He stood there, bland-faced, as though nothing unusual was going on. Wendy glared at him for a moment, then flounced off, slamming the bathroom door behind her.

"Hey," John said, sitting up. "Can I have some water? Maybe a couple more aspirin? My head is killing me."

"Sure," Tricker said. "How did that happen?" He made no move toward the front office, but watched John approach.

"Fell," John said. "Couple of times. First time I got the lump, then I got up and fell right down again onto some sharp ice."

"You're lucky you didn't lose an eye," Tricker said.

John shuddered. "Tell me about it." He looked at the agent and tipped his head toward the office. "Could we . . . ?"

"Sure," Tricker said with a glance at the closed bathroom door. "After you."

Clea's eyes widened. They were here! They had come and she hadn't known! Didn't Tricker realize who they were? How could he miss it? But the agent was relying on a padlock to keep *John Connor* contained—and that indicated that he didn't know who they were.

The I-950 considered the situation. The girl was negligible, no threat at all, but she could be the key to getting Connor right where she wanted him. Therefore, she needed to get control of the girl.

On the same wall as the bathroom, toward the front room that held the office, was the door that led down to the elevator. It was locked, but Clea knew the code; she'd noted it when she'd first arrived.

Accessing the security room, she found the remote for the door and tripped the lock. Through the security camera she watched it swing open about a foot.

As the I-950 watched, Connor accepted some tablets from Tricker and a cup of water. Unwisely, in her opinion; she'd want a chemical analysis on anything medicinal that Tricker handed to her. Wendy left the bathroom and started down the hallway. She then exhibited a curious trait that Clea had noticed again and again in human beings; she looked at the open door.

Wendy stood stock-still, glanced toward the front office, then leaned toward the door. She gently pushed it open just a bit farther and peeked inside.

"HEY!" Tricker shouted. "What the hell do you think you're doing?" He rushed toward her and yanked the door closed. "How did you get that open?"

Surprised, Wendy took a step back. "I was just curious," she said.

"This door is always locked," he said. "How did you get it open?"

"It was like that," she squeaked, holding her hands up as though she thought he might hit her.

John ghosted up behind him.

Then, to Clea's intense annoyance, the cameras cut out. "Shit!" she said aloud. She should have taken care of that.

"I didn't do *anything*!" Wendy shouted, backing away. "I didn't touch anything! Why are you being like this? What's wrong with you?" Her voice turned whiny. "I didn't do anything!"

Tricker spun round just in time to block John's strike and easily reached through John's defense to strike him hard on the jagged cuts on his face. John staggered back, blinded by tears, as the stitches broke and blood began to flow.

Wendy squeaked in horror and rushed forward shouting, "Stop it!"

Without really looking, Tricker kicked her in the stomach, sending the girl flying backward. She landed gasping for breath, tears streaming down her face.

Something happened within John at the moment. He became the calm center of the storm, just as his sensei had told him he would. John judged that their skills were about equal, especially with the asset of his youth, even compromised by his wounds. But before the advantage had been all Tricker's; for his experience, for his ruthlessness. Now they were considerably more equal.

John was hyper-aware of everything around him, of Wendy writhing on the floor trying to get her breath . . .

Tricker flicked a series of kicks at him—low, middle, high—balancing effortlessly. There was no room to dodge; John backed a little, blocking with his forearms and sliding in with his weight on his back foot.

"Isa!" he shouted, driving bladed palms at his opponent's groin and eyes.

Those eyes widened as Tricker slid back in turn, blocking high and low and trying to capture a wrist; that nearly cost him a kneecap, as John snap-kicked in the moment they were in contact. What followed in the next thirty seconds was like a savage, precisely choreographed dance— one that left John's face wound bleeding again and Tricker favoring one leg. The younger man waited, hands up and weight centered; it wouldn't last much longer. It couldn't, not when experts were fighting for keeps. The least little advantage . . .

After what seemed to her to be an eternity, Wendy got her breath back and struggled onto her hands and knees to watch the two men battle.

"Are you crazy?" Wendy shouted at Tricker, still gasping. "Are you completely *insane*?" she demanded, tears streaming down her face.

The question and her expression were so convincing that for a split second Tricker thought that he might have made a mistake.

John's booted foot caught Tricker in the side of the head and the agent went down, temporarily paralyzed by the blow. Instantly John followed up with a carotid hold and Tricker's world went black.

John looked at the unconscious man, reached down to check his pulse, then went to Wendy. "You okay?" he asked, deeply concerned.

"I've been kicked in the stomach by an expert!" she snapped. "No, I'm not okay! But I'll live," she added grudgingly. She took his offered hand and let him help her to her feet, then she got a good look at his wounds. "Oh God, John! Your face!" She reached for him, but he held her off.

"No time," he said. "We've got to get this guy tied up. Help me look for something."

The first thing that John noticed was that the computer screen was flipping through views of rooms a great deal snazzier than this one. Laboratories, by the look of them. "Hey, check it out," he called to Wendy.

She stood by his side for a moment, watching, then shook her head. "So how do we get there?" Then she looked at him and smiled. "That door!"

He nodded, wiping the blood off his chin before it could drip on the keyboard. "But first things first, all right?" He tipped his head toward Tricker. "See what you can find."

It wasn't long before Wendy straightened up with a glad cry. "Duct tape! The force that holds the universe together."

John had made a happy discovery of his own, a Sig-Sauer 9mm that he found under the desk in a quick-release clip. "Most excellent," he murmured, caressing the gun.

"Hands tied in front or back?" Wendy asked.

"Back, most definitely." John went to stand beside her. "Let's get him onto one of the bunks," he suggested. "I'll take his head, you take his feet."

They flung him on the bunk and John got to work winding the tape tightly around the agent's hands and feet.

"That's a little snug," Wendy said, looking worried.

"Yeah, but if he gets loose he's gonna try and kill us."

"A point," she conceded, "most definitely a point."

He wound the tape around their prisoner and the bed at his neck and hips, binding him to the bunk until the tape ran out.

"No gag?" Wendy asked.

"No point," John said. "There's nobody to hear him. I'd rather use the tape to make sure he doesn't come after us. Besides, they're risky. Too much chance of his choking to death."

She looked startled, but nodded wisely. This wasn't her world; in matters like these she'd best let John be her guide.

They left the room and looked across the short hall at the door that Tricker had pulled closed. It stood open a foot.

John's body turned to ice and he could feel his blood pounding in the cuts on his face and the lump on his head. Then he shook it off.

"She . . . it's here," he said quietly. "And it knows we're here."

Wendy looked at his pale face and bit her lip, knowing who he meant and taking fright from his obvious apprehension. She knew instinctively that there was only one thing to do in a situation like this—pretend it didn't matter.

"Aw, you can do it!" she said, giving his arm a little slap. "You handled that guy all right."

"*He* is human." John looked at her and wished her gone with all his heart.

As though she knew what he was thinking, Wendy leaned in close and kissed his cheek gently. "You need me," she reminded him firmly.

He could see her pride as she said it, and putting his hand behind her head, he drew her close and kissed her. It hurt, but it fed his soul. He leaned back and smiled at her. "I'll go get the gun, then we'll get started," he said.

Wendy smiled and nodded. When he was gone she gave the door

beside her an anxious glance, took a deep breath, and rubbed her aching stomach. Looking across the hall, she could just see Tricker lying on the bunk.

So far, she thought, *so good.*

He needs her? Clea thought. *Whatever for? She certainly can't fight.* And if she wasn't here to back him up then what was her purpose? It had also surprised her that Connor was unarmed. To the I-950, that was synonymous with unprepared. But from what he'd said, he expected her to be here. This suggested an unreasonable degree of self-confidence. But why? What reason had he to be so confident?

He and his mother defeated Serena Burns, her computer reminded her. *They have twice destroyed Skynet.*

A ripple of unease disturbed her. Then she pushed it away, assuring herself that all of these side issues were unimportant. What was important was that the enemy was here and that she must prepare to deal with him.

Separate them, she thought. *Maybe leave the girl until later. Connor is the important one.* Connor was the first one she'd kill.

John had made Wendy crouch down and hug the front of the elevator. He stood in front of her, plastered against the wall. When the doors opened it would appear from the outside that the elevator was empty. He waited until the doors closed by themselves, then waited some more. Wendy stirred and he put his hand down to warn her to stillness.

In the security room the I-950 watched, both amused and impressed. She assumed that he was counting to some high number and wouldn't move until he'd reached it. Good tactics, if you were dealing with a human.

Finally John hit the door button and did a forward roll into the hallway, coming up on one knee, his gun pointing down the empty corridor. His heart was beating so hard that he thought he could see the gun in his hands bob to its rhythm. *Get it under control, John,* he warned himself. Get it under control or he'd be useless when the time came to face the Terminator.

He signaled Wendy to come out of the elevator, then gestured to her to stay behind him and keep low. When they got to the first door he made her stop several paces short of it, then moved up himself. He listened, then flung the door open with a crash, pulling back out of the line of fire. He reached around the door frame and found the light switch. When the lights came on he swung back to one knee in the doorway, gun at the ready, then carefully stood and gave the room a quick search.

Then he moved on to the next.

"Hey," Wendy whispered, "shouldn't we—"

John hissed her to silence and with a gesture told her to stay right where she was. Wendy rolled her eyes but obeyed. She glanced at the elevator; they probably ought to lock it down, but oh well. John knew what he was doing.

In her lair in the security room Clea was silently agreeing with her. John Connor was doing everything right. And he was taking a damn long time doing it, too. *I'm glad the lab is only halfway down the corridor. Otherwise he'll be at it until the generator runs out of fuel.* And she wanted to know, with a very human curiosity, what the girl was for.

At last John came to a door marked K. VIEMEISTER, the name of the man who'd taken over the Cyberdyne project. *This could be it,* he warned himself. If the Terminator was anywhere in the facility this was the logical place. He took a deep breath and flung the door open and himself into the brightly lit room. He peeked over a counter and looked around.

Clea laughed out loud at his expression; she looked forward to showing Alissa the recording. Even her too-solemn little sister would find this funny. She watched him check every inch of the room with exquisite care; it was obvious to her that he placed the safety of his companion above his own. Interesting, and possibly useful.

John came to the door and gestured Wendy in. "Okay, sweetie, I'm gonna finish checking the other labs; you do your thing. Lock the door after me and don't open it unless I can answer a personal question about us."

"A personal question? You mean like—"

He quickly put a finger across her lips. "Something only you and I would know," he said sternly. "They can imitate anyone's voice. I've heard them."

She nodded, wide-eyed. "Okay, I'll think of something."

"You do that." He pulled her to him and kissed her, caressed her hair, and turned to the door. "Remember, lock this," he said over his shoulder.

"I will, I will," she said, smiling.

"And get to work." His eyes were already roving up and down the corridor.

"I will, I *will*," she repeated, closed the door, locked it, and went to the computer bay.

Clea spit the feed, watching Connor fruitlessly check the labs while his "sweetie" got to work. The girl stripped off her bra and slid a pair of microdiskettes out of a slit in the lining. *Not bad,* the I-950 thought, amused. She watched fascinated as the girl put the disk into its drawer and began to work.

The I-950 was reasonably confident that the security protocols they'd installed in the Skynet program could defeat any worm that this child could come up with. Viemeister might be a prick, and he hadn't yet made Skynet intelligent, but he was no slouch in the security department. So this material would be shunted into a buffer, where the computer would evaluate it.

At first she was puzzled by what she was reading. Then she sucked in her breath in amazement. This was it! This was the key to Skynet's living intelligence. Why would their worst enemy deliver it to them?

And then she understood; they would enumerate every possible path that led to sentience and then program the machine to ignore any paths or commands leading to that result. Unless the programmers knew those codes were there, they could batter their heads against an impenetrable wall of cross-commands for a very long time.

Viemeister might figure it out eventually, but probably not before his funding ran out. Or his patience. He wasn't the kind of human who clung to a project that didn't work out. Well, there was the Nazi thing, but he was really involved with that more to annoy people than for any sincere belief.

Clea rose from her chair. The girl had brought two disks; she had to stop her before she installed whatever was on the second one.

Dieter studied the GPS unit and it told him that he was very close to the base, possibly within ten minutes if he could keep up this pace. *Good,* he thought. Because he suspected he was getting a nice little case of frost-nip on his toes and face.

He'd turned the balaclava around and made tiny holes on the solid back surface in hopes of protecting his eyes from snow blindness, and now that the wind had turned, he hoped it would keep them from freezing all together. It felt like his lungs were raw right to the bottom, not that he could breathe that deeply. He held his arms tight around himself to keep his ribs as still as possible, which wasn't very, and tried to ignore the pain. He had so many to choose from by now that it was almost easy.

There was a copper-penny taste in the back of his throat as though he was bleeding, and he was very thirsty. Ice kept forming on the wool around his mouth and nose, making his lips sore and increasing the likelihood of frostbite. *All in all, not one of my better days.*

He slogged on as quickly as he could push himself. When the first of the base's sheds came into view, he said a heartfelt "thank God!" and hurried toward it.

It was small on closer examination, obviously a storage shed, but by then he could see a larger building looming up, and headed for it. Off to his right a moving shape came toward him and he paused, thinking it must be someone from the base. It was almost upon him before he could make out what it was.

"Oooh, no! Not another fucking seal!"

The creature barked and stretched its neck out at him, teeth bared.

With all the strength that frustration, desperation, and outrage could lend a man, von Rossbach hauled off and belted the exhausted animal. It made a small sound and collapsed at his feet, rolling onto its back with flippers extended in a limp V-shape. Dieter swayed in the wind, looking down at it for a moment, not quite believing it had been that easy. It stayed down.

"Good," he said with a satisfied nod, and headed for the largest shed.

Burns, Tricker thought, *must save Burns.* No, not Burns, Bennet. Bennet was the asset. *Burns was an asset to Cyberdyne. And she had assets.* She'd tried to use those assets to vamp him. *But she didn't try very hard,* he thought regretfully. He frowned. *Bennet, not Burns. Have to save Bennet.* Bennet wasn't Burns. *But she might be. Two peas inna pod.*

He blinked and shook his head, regretting it instantly as it rang like a carillon. "Shit!" he said aloud. He tried to move and found himself well and truly bound. "Shit," he said again, with much more resignation.

What had he been thinking about? Oh, yes. Burns and Bennet and how much alike they looked. The two women might be identical twins. What were the odds of that, two unrelated people looking exactly alike except for hair color. Which could easily be handled by Lady Clairol.

And what the hell did it matter? He had to get out of here and down to the labs, where the action was. Tricker started to pull his belt around. One edge of the buckle was especially sharp, something that came in handy for times like these.

Then he heard the outside door open and slam shut.

The shed door was unlocked and Dieter entered, slammed it behind him, and slid down its surface to rest on the floor. To him the room was pitch-dark. *Didn't escape the snow blindness entirely,* he thought, disappointed. But at least he wasn't going to freeze. He pushed back his hood and yanked the soaking balaclava from his head. Next time he was going to get one of those fleece ones.

Better yet, he thought, *next time there's not going to be a next time.* He knew now, right down in his bones, how close he'd come to dying out there. If the wind had been just a little worse . . .

"Hey!" a voice called from another room. "Who's out there?"

With a mental sigh Dieter got himself to his feet, then cautiously moved farther into the room. "Hello?" he said.

"Who is that?" the voice called. "Viemeister?"

"I can't see," Dieter said as he bumped into what felt like an office chair. He took hold of it and pushed it in front of him like a bulky white cane. "I've got a touch of snow blindness. Keep talking and I'll find you."

"Over here," Tricker called. "There's a hallway. I'm in the first room on your left. This way."

Dieter found the wall and followed it, still pushing the chair until his hand fell through an opening. "It's pitch-dark for me," he said. "Are the lights on at all?"

"No. There's a switch to the right of the door, about four inches from the frame."

Von Rossbach found the switch easily and flicked it on. To him the light was dim, but he could easily make out a man tied up on a bunk. "Ah! I see my young friends have already been here," he said with a smile.

"You must be the guide they mentioned," Tricker said sourly. "Did they try to kill you, too?"

"Did they try to kill you?" Dieter asked, surprised. He unzipped the parka and began to shrug out of it.

Tricker thought about it. "No. I guess not." He lifted his bound hands significantly. "You gonna help me out here?"

"No," Dieter said, and turned around, peering into the dark of the hallway.

"No?" Tricker said. "Why not?"

"They're just a couple of crazy kids," von Rossbach explained. "There's no real harm in them. I'll round them up and get them out of your way. The thing is, if they've tied you up they must have had a reason. Until I find out what that is, it might not be safe to let you go. Eh?"

"Buddy, this is a U.S. government scientific installation! I demand that you let me go."

Dieter looked at him. "Are you the only one here?" he asked mildly.

Tricker hesitated. "At the moment, yeah."

"You might have a touch of cabin fever, then. It may be that you attacked my young friends. Where are they, anyway? Is there another large building on this base? I didn't see one."

Tricker tightened his lips and put his head back down on the pillow. "Maybe they ran off into the storm," he muttered.

"And left you like this? I hardly think they'd be so irresponsible."

"They left you, didn't they?" Tricker said precisely.

"A different situation altogether," Dieter assured him. His eyes were beginning to adjust and he could see things, finally. Like the roll of duct tape on a shelf and the open door on the other side of the hall. He picked up the duct tape and began to wind it tightly around his torso, feeling immediate relief. He cut it off with the knife he found on the shelf. It was John's; he decided to keep it. "I'll just have a look around for them, shall I?"

"Like you'd stay put if I told you no?" Tricker muttered.

"Surely you want me to find them," von Rossbach said cheerfully. Even his face wasn't feeling so bad now; maybe he'd escaped frostbite after all.

"Oh, surely," Tricker muttered as he heard the man clatter down the stairs and then heard the elevator begin to work. *Don't call me Shirley,* he thought woozily.

He'd only been awake for maybe a minute when he heard the man come in. Then, when he'd heard that slight accent, he'd thought, crazily, that it might be Viemeister coming after Bennet.

That kid must have hit me pretty hard, he thought. *Hell, if I'm imagining that super-kraut would risk his precious ass in an Antarctic blizzard for a woman who has publicly rejected him, then I might actually have brain damage.* But then this place seemed to be turning into Grand fucking Central Station, so who *knew* who was going to turn up next.

He got to work pulling his belt around so that he could use the buckle to get him out of this mess. This definitely wasn't one of his most shining moments, he complained to himself. On the downside, it was three to one and the kid had his gun.

But on the upside, that wasn't his only gun.

CHAPTER 28

Clea was hiding in one of the labs that John had already inspected when she heard the elevator engage. *Empty*, she thought as she mentally switched to the surveillance camera. But von Rossbach waited patiently for it to arrive . . .

She had assumed the Sector agent was dead and was not pleased to see him. Still, having almost all of her important enemies in one isolated place had its charm. *Though having one less to worry about would be even more charming.*

So far the seals had been a disappointment. "If only Antarctica had polar bears!" she mused.

The I-950 quickly moved to a lab three doors closer to Viemeister's when John entered another lab to inspect it. She watched Wendy work through the security cameras, and evaluated the program, even helped her when the girl got bogged down too much. It would be necessary to be careful, though; it wouldn't do to help her so much that she began to install the second and, presumably, dangerous part of her program.

Meanwhile von Rossbach had entered the elevator and was on his way down. Fortunately, one of the base's security measures was the ability to halt the elevator at any point. Clea did so now, freezing it between the office and laboratory floors.

From the look of the man, she doubted he'd be able to squeeze through the escape hatch. Of course he could just break the controls—but that would send the car plummeting to the bottom of the shaft. Actually overriding them would take either sophisticated equipment or specialized knowledge and a great deal of patience. Which left him out of the equation for the moment.

Tricker was still writhing around on the bunk, trying to get free. And even if he was free, how was he going to get down here? The elevator was disabled, and the emergency exit couldn't be opened from outside, so that was two down.

Which left her free to deal with Connor and the girl. It would be the girl first after all. Connor would return to her eventually, which was convenient. And once she'd ensured that the girl's program couldn't harm Skynet, the I-950 would have plenty of time to deal with all of the humans.

Clea slipped down the corridor to Viemeister's lab. It amused her that despite all of his elaborate precautions, it seemed never to have occurred to Connor that she might have a key to this door. *Such a simple thing*, she thought, silently working the lock, *but so very important.* The I-950 slid into the lab so quietly that Wendy never once looked up.

Tricker flung the last of the duct tape from him in disgust. Then he rushed out to the office to put on his parka and gloves. *Step one*, he thought, *is to find whatever damned jamming device they've brought with them and disable it.* Even if McMurdo couldn't send help because of the storm, they'd at least be able to block their escape. He flung open the door, swearing under his breath.

Something huge reared up with a roar and threw itself at him, stinking of rotten fish and gleaming with fangs. Tricker slammed the door and braced himself against it as it nearly jarred loose from its hinges when the thing struck. The pressure wasn't constant; he just managed to slam it home and work the dead bolt before the next lunge hit it. He wished he had a bar to put across like a castle gate.

Was that a seal? he thought in disbelief. An unmistakable series of *urrrfing* barks and a less violent hammering answered the thought.

"Yes," he said numbly, "that's a seal." A very big, homicidal seal.

Every time he opened this door today there was something dangerous out there—a whiteout blizzard, the spy kids, a killer seal.

Would-be killer seal, he corrected himself as his heart rate returned to normal. He wouldn't count the mystery guide; the guy had let himself in.

But what the hell was a seal doing way out here? And what did it have against him? Maybe he was getting cabin fever; maybe this whole day and all the wild things that had happened were all some paranoid fantasy. What were the symptoms of cabin fever anyway? Could you detect them in yourself? *Is wondering things like this a good sign or a bad sign?*

Maybe there wasn't a seal out there, maybe he'd imagined it. *There's only one way to find out*, he thought, standing away from the door. He seized the latch and took a deep breath. *And I'm not going to do it.* He turned away and slipped off his gloves and parka.

So he couldn't call McMurdo. Given his state of mind, maybe that was for the best. *Wait a minute, if someone knocks you out and you wake up tied to the bed, that's not paranoia.* That was . . . something else.

He ducked under his desk and flipped up the carpet. Underneath was a board with a ring attached; he lifted it and revealed a parcel wrapped in oilcloth. Taking it out, he closed the small cubby and tossed back the rug, then sat at the desk. As he unwrapped the gun he watched the monitor, his fingers automatically stripping the action, reassembling it, slapping home the magazine. A few spares went into his pockets.

The guide was in the elevator. *Still?* Tricker thought with surprise. He wondered what had gone wrong. For a few seconds he watched the man work on the control box. *That's government property, pal, you'd better know what you're doing.* Then the view changed.

After a few of the labs had flicked by on the screen, Viemeister's came into view. Bennet was standing by the door watching the girl work on her computer. She stood absolutely still and it was obvious that the younger woman had no idea that she was there. For some reason, something about the sight sent a chill down Tricker's spine. Very few human beings could stand *that* still. Almost anyone would make the small unconscious movements and sounds that gave the one being watched that I'm-being-watched feeling. He'd better get down there before something nasty happened.

Wendy had disabled every one of Kurt Viemeister's security protocols. She was feeling very proud of herself, even though she had a hunch that these had been mere sketches of what the real security programs would eventually become. But even so, this was *Kurt Viemeister's* work she was unraveling. It was like jamming with Mozart.

She tapped a few keys and the sentience program flowed into a buffer she'd created. Now to upload the antisentience program. Really this should have come first, but she hadn't labeled the disks and had actually forgotten which was which. Wendy tapped the button and reached toward the open drawer for the used disk.

A hand clamped over her wrist, squeezing hard enough to grind the small bones together. Wendy screamed in pain and surprise. Another hand clamped over her mouth, cutting off the sound before it could reach a climax. The grip that held her face was enormously strong. Wendy thought she felt the bones of her face flex and screamed against the hand that inexorably pulled her from her chair and forced her up onto her toes. Wendy struck out with her free hand to no effect.

She found herself looking into the pleasantly smiling face of a beautiful young woman. Wendy's eyes bulged and tears of agony poured down her cheeks as she recognized her. This was the woman from the *Venus Dancing* video, the one John said was a Terminator. She believed him now. She'd thought she believed him before, but she hadn't, not really. She believed him now, though, most completely.

The woman released Wendy's wrist, allowing her to scratch and pull on the arm that held her. "I'll just take care of this," the woman said, picking up the unused disk. "We wouldn't want my files corrupted, now would we?" She snapped the tiny disk in half and put the pieces in her pocket.

Wendy kicked her in the knee and the woman shook her, hard. "Don't annoy me," she warned through clenched teeth. "I want to keep you alive because your computer talents may be useful, but that doesn't mean you can't hurt. You may think you're in pain now, but you have no idea."

John froze where he was and listened. He could have sworn that he heard a woman cry out. *Wendy!* He stepped to the lab's door and peered out into the corridor, straining his ears. There was no repeat of the sound; there was no sound at all. *Yeah, it could be Wendy, or it could be the Terminator trying to draw me out.* But there was no one out here. He swallowed hard. *I'd better check*, he thought.

He moved quickly down the corridor, gun at the ready, back against the wall, his head and eyes constantly moving until he reached the only closed door he'd left behind him. John tightened his lips anxiously, then, from about two feet away as he pressed his back to the wall, he tapped on the door with the barrel of his gun.

The I-950 lifted Wendy almost off her feet and called out, "Ye-a-h?" in Wendy's voice. Clea could feel the girl trying to get the breath to scream again, so she pinched her windpipe closed with her other hand. Her victim began to thrash about in earnest now, so the I-950 moved into the center of the room, away from chairs and desks and noise-making objects.

"Is everything okay in there?" Connor asked.

"Yuh, why?" Clea countered.

"I thought I heard a scream." Was there something off about the way she was speaking?

"Oh, uh, that was a cry of frustration," Clea said in Wendy's voice.

The girl was starting to lose consciousness; her blows made hardly any impact at all and the I-950 studied her closely, watching her face change to an unnatural, and unexpected, indigo.

"Everything's going fine now, though," Clea said cheerfully.

John hesitated. *Something's wrong*, he thought. He didn't know what, but something . . . "Open up," he said.

Clea sighed and approached the door. She lowered the girl to the floor and dragged her over by her throat. Looking down, she saw that the human was unconscious and let her go entirely. She wasn't dead yet; perhaps the I-950 would let her live for a while—she might have more to offer. More than Kurt had, anyway.

Clea leaned against the door. "You're supposed to tell me something that only you and I would know," she reminded him.

John licked his lips; that was a good sign. He'd only just told her that.

"Okay," he said. "Snog's the one in charge."

What the hell did that mean? "Snog's in charge?" she said aloud. "Get out!"

That last was a shot in the dark, but humans, especially young ones, tended to take matters of hierarchy seriously. *Assuming that's what he was referring to.* The I-950 stretched her hands, then clenched them into fists as she waited for his response.

John chuckled, relieved, and stood away from the wall. "Well, it looked that way to me. C'mon, open up."

"Gladly," the I-950 said.

John's back slammed against the wall and his gun came up. That *didn't* sound like Wendy.

Tricker looked down at the top of the elevator cab and sighed. Then he took hold of one of the cables, grimacing at the grease on it, and swung himself out into the shaft. He crooked an elbow and leg around the rigid steel rope and let himself slide down in a controlled fall until his feet touched the roof of the elevator itself. Kneeling by the repair hatch, he went to work.

At the sound of footsteps on the roof of the cab, Dieter pulled back into the farthest corner from the hatch in the ceiling. *I wish I had something besides a knife,* he thought. But the gun was another casualty of his unfortunate midnight ramble. *If I was someone I was training I'd kick my ass!*

The hatch cover came off, revealing pitch-darkness above. Von Rossbach hunkered down, knife at the ready, and licked dry lips.

"Okay, just . . . just keep it cool," Tricker said. "I've got a gun, I've got the drop on you, I've got the upper hand, and I can get this egg crate moving again. So are you gonna cooperate or do I have to shoot you?"

Dieter straightened up, his eyes on the darkness above him, and held his hands up.

"You wanna toss that knife over this way?" Tricker asked. When the knife clattered into the corner he made another suggestion. "Get on your knees, cross your ankles, put your hands behind your head, fingers locked."

When von Rossbach had complied Tricker dropped lightly down and picked up the knife. He looked it over.

"Nice," he said. "Okay, what's your story?"

I hate it when people finally ask that question, Dieter thought. *I probably won't answer, or I won't tell the truth, or I'll tell the truth and they don't believe me and then they start hitting me. Why do they even bother to ask?*

"Let me get you started," Tricker said. "You're here to stop the Cyberdyne project, right?"

Dieter merely looked at him, saying nothing.

Tricker hunkered down in the far corner of the elevator, gun pointed at the big Austrian. "You're wondering how I know that, aren't you?" he said. "Well, I know who you are. Had to get a second look to be sure, though. You're Dieter von Rossbach."

Still, Dieter said nothing, though it wasn't easy to hide his surprise.

"You're an actual playboy," Tricker said with a grin. He looked off into the distance for a moment. "The major and the playboy." His eyes met von Rossbach's. "Now there's a likely combination, isn't it?" He waited a moment for possible comments, then said, "When Ferris admitted that he had a guest that he'd sent away before said guest could be questioned after Cyberdyne blew up, I naturally asked him some probing questions about you. He gave me the hard eyes—you know, that look the military get when they're going to be stubborn."

He grinned; Dieter stared. "I did some checking on my own and found out zip. You know what it says to me when a man with your money has no particular history? It says covert ops." Tricker rose and spread his hands, never taking his eyes off von Rossbach. "So as a professional courtesy I stopped pokin' around."

He pointed the gun at Dieter. " 'Cause Ferris said you were with him the whole time and I was pretty positive that *he* wasn't associated with Sarah Connor. And if *he* wasn't, why would you be? You were probably some friendly government's covert-ops guy, I thought. And why would they be on Sarah Connor's side?"

He hunkered down again. "Only she has a way of bringing people around to her point of view, doesn't she? And her son disappeared from the base that night, never to be seen again." He stared at Dieter for a bit, then he made a sweeping gesture with the gun. "Until today. Until that very well-trained kid kicked my ass." He stood up, suddenly angry. "That kid is John Connor!"

"You sound surprised," Dieter said mildly.

"Wait till you get a look at his face; you'll be surprised, too," Tricker snarled. Before von Rossbach could respond he hurried on. "I've read her medical transcripts from Pescadero, you know." He leaned toward Dieter. "Her story is wacky! How come everybody buys into it?"

Dieter smiled. "Sarah is convincing because sooner or later evidence shows up to corroborate everything that she says. When you shoot someone about fifty times with an assault rifle, until their steel skeleton is exposed and sparks are flying out of their guts and they still keep coming, you begin to suspect that she's been telling you the truth." He shrugged. "Empirical evidence is always the best."

Tricker just looked at him. "So who are you working for?"

Dieter shook his head. "This isn't official."

Tricker nodded judiciously. "Not official, huh? I take great comfort from that." He cocked his head. "I know Connor's story about the kid."

"That I've taken on faith," Dieter conceded. "But once you've met a Terminator, it's much easier to believe."

"Tell me this—does it bother you that if you succeed in destroying this human-hating supercomputer that John Connor will disappear?"

Von Rossbach blinked. "I hadn't thought about it."

"Sure," Tricker said. "If there is no supercomputer then there are no time-traveling Terminators and no need to send some guy back in time to stop one and save Sarah Connor and incidentally impregnate her with the kid who would send him back to get killed. Y'know, presumably at some point they start to keep that under their hats or they'd never have gotten a volunteer to come back, right?"

Dieter shrugged. "It would bother me a great deal to lose John; he's a good kid. But I know that he would gladly give his life to save several billion others." He looked up at Tricker. "Wouldn't you?" Tricker shrugged in answer and Dieter smiled slowly. "Yes, you would. You'd consider it an honor."

With a barely visible smile of embarrassment, Tricker shrugged. "Whatever," he said. "Facedown on the floor, please. Lock your hands behind your head, keep your ankles crossed. I've gotta get this bucket moving."

When von Rossbach had complied Tricker went to the control panel and inserted a card he'd taken from his pocket into a slot. A panel popped open to reveal a keypad. Tricker tapped out a number and the elevator started moving again.

"Yeah," Tricker said, putting the card away, "last time I checked, Clea Bennet looked like she was gonna take a great big bite out of your little friend Wendy."

"*What?*" Dieter started to heave himself to his feet. "Wendy is alone with Bennet?"

Tricker pressed the barrel of his gun into the Austrian's kidneys. "Down, boy," he advised.

Dieter collapsed. "She's one of them!" he said desperately.

"A Terminator, you mean?" Tricker said in disbelief.

"She's not human! Why do you think she has Serena Burns's face? How likely is that?" von Rossbach demanded, echoing Tricker's earlier thoughts. "You couldn't fail to recognize her if you recognized me! She's a killer and her assignment is to protect Skynet!"

The elevator door opened and Tricker stepped out. "You go first," he ordered.

Von Rossbach stood up, looked once at Tricker, and took off down the corridor at a run.

"Shit," Tricker muttered, and followed.

The lab doors opened outward, and as soon as the opening was wide enough John kicked it with all his might. The door hit the tiled wall with a report like a bomb going off. Crouching low, John swung into the doorway and brought his gun up. Wendy lay facedown in a crumpled heap on the floor just inside the door. She was alone.

John rushed to her side and, putting the gun up, close to his shoulder, looked all around, then reached to turn her over. He couldn't believe that she had fainted, after all she'd been through. He gently turned her over.

When he saw her face he stood up, bringing the gun into play, and turned to scan the room. All was silent; the lab appeared to be empty but for the two of them. But Wendy's face and neck were covered with livid bruises, so someone had been here. Had they left before the door opened, or were they still here? They—*it* must still be here; Wendy wouldn't have been so chipper in her answers wearing these bruises. But he couldn't see a hiding place big enough to conceal it.

Wendy came awake with a loud gasp and, seeing John, tried to grasp his pant leg as she struggled desperately for air. Her back arched with the effort she made to draw oxygen down her swollen throat, but her panic only made it harder to breathe.

"Easy!" John said. "Slow down, take long slow breaths."

Her eyes locked onto his as she visibly tried to take his advice. But it was no good, she couldn't breathe, and in seconds she was gasping again, dragging in huge, whooping breaths as tears streamed down her face. Her hand clenched on his pant leg and twisted the cloth.

John looked into her eyes, so stunned by her anguish that for a moment he was completely at a loss. Then Wendy arched her neck and he saw that the column of her throat bore a slight dent in the front.

"You've got to trust me," he said to her as he put his hand on her throat.

Wendy nodded, her eyes on his. Taking a deep breath, he squeezed on her windpipe and to his great relief it popped back into shape. Instantly her breathing grew easier and she closed her eyes.

John let out his breath in a huff and went back to scanning the room; still, nothing moved. He'd been so afraid that he would have to perform an emergency tracheotomy on her. John had studied the simple operation and knew its principal points, but reading about it and trying to do it to someone wide-awake and in distress—someone you loved—that would have been hard.

Wendy opened her eyes and looked at John; he seemed far away somehow, as though she was looking at him through the wrong end of a telescope. A halo of black-and-white speckles surrounded him and her vision seemed to grow dim. She had to warn him, had to make him erase the program and take the disk. Without the second half of the program they'd be doing just the opposite of what they'd come to do. Her hand still held on to him and she tugged on the cloth.

"Ja . . ." she said. Almost no sound had come out and her throat burned with a raw agony when she tried to speak. She squeaked and tried to swallow and writhed with the pain. "Ja . . ." she said, trying again.

"Don't speak," he warned her. "Your larynx must be damaged."

Wendy sobbed, then licked her lips and swallowed once more; her lips drew back in a rictus of pain. Stubbornly she took a deep breath and looked at him, willing him to understand her. Wendy formed the word *computer* with her lips and he looked over at the computer she'd been using. She tugged on his pant leg and he looked back at her. She shook her head, then formed the word *erase*. John frowned and she tried to say it again. This time when she tried to speak no sound came out at all and the agony surprised a sob from her.

John winced in sympathy and then he got the idea. "It's okay," he said. "I've got it. I'll take care of it, you just rest. Okay?"

She smiled at him and closed her eyes, concentrating on just breathing. She heard the soft whir of the disk drawer closing and looked over at the computer in astonishment. She watched as John followed the prompts and finally hit "enter," causing her program to begin downloading directly to the hard drive.

No! Wendy screamed silently behind him, her injured throat producing an nearly silent *screee. NO!* she shouted in her mind.

Yes! Clea thought triumphantly from her hiding place behind two mainframe computers. *Yessss!* She'd better make sure the girl didn't warn Connor that he'd done exactly the wrong thing. *Though I like it.* She liked it very much.

Wendy shook her head violently and slapped the floor to attract John's attention. She didn't even see Clea rushing toward her with inhuman speed and she barely felt it when the I-950's foot crashed down, crushing her throat and shattering the vertebrae in her neck.

John turned to see a beautiful woman raise her foot high and bring it down on Wendy's throat. He heard the terrible sound of things breaking within her and watched the light fade from Wendy's eyes. For a long moment he stood frozen, utterly stunned with horror. He lifted his eyes to meet the gleeful smile of the female Terminator.

Clea was almost upon him before he brought up the gun; before he could fire her foot flashed out, kicking the gun from his hand hard enough to break two of his knuckles. The gun went flying and Clea reached for Connor's throat. He leaned back just far enough that she missed, and struck at her throat with a straight hand blow. The I-950 knocked it aside easily and tried to close with him.

If she could only get her hands on him she could tear him apart. Reaching back, John picked up the keyboard and smacked her in the face with it. She stepped back slightly and shook her head. Somehow that had surprised her; she'd expected better of the famous John Connor.

John moved away from the computer table, trying to get some space between him and the Terminator; his eyes found the gun and dismissed it. It was too far away. He risked going for the knife in his boot.

Clea watched him, and when he moved so did she. It was evident that he was going for a weapon and she wouldn't allow that. Stepping lightly, she twisted herself to deliver a flying kick. John ducked under it and grabbed her leg, twisting it and bringing his fist down, intending at the very least to tear ligaments.

But the I-950 was both stronger and more flexible than a human; she wrested her leg from his grasp and spun in place, managing a body blow that knocked him on his heels, staggering backward, with a look on his face that told her he was in pain. Instantly she followed up her advantage, rushing toward him, intent on his eyes.

John staggered back, breathing carefully and with no little difficulty. He felt nauseated from the kick to his stomach and he almost stumbled over an office chair. Yanking it in front of him, he held it like a shield as the Terminator tried to close with him. Part of his consciousness looked desperately around the room for something to use as a weapon, while the rest watched the Terminator and tried to counter its every move. Computer labs, unfortunately, seemed to lack much in the way of combat-ready items. The best he could hope for was to make it to the door and perhaps escape to a better-supplied lab.

Clea was nonplussed by the great savior of humanity's methods. *This* was what would defeat Skynet? After a few feints were thwarted by the stupid office chair, she simply grabbed it and tore it from his grasp.

John turned and raced for the door. Clea swept out her leg and tripped him, then sprang erect and moved in for the kill. As she leaned toward him John flipped over and swept his leg up; his booted foot connected with her jaw and the I-950 fell, momentarily stunned. He scrambled to his feet again and turned to run. Before he could take a step she grasped his pant leg and pulled him toward her. Pivoting, John kicked her again and she let go.

But only for a moment; before he'd gone far she was on her feet again and running after him. Catching up; she shoved him and he hit the wall beside the door hard enough to knock the breath out of him. As he slid down, Clea approached; she grabbed the front of his shirt and swung him around.

"Did you think it would be that easy?" Clea asked, grinning. She drew back her fist for a fatal strike. While he struggled for breath, watching her. He brought his own hands up.

Wait a minute, he thought. *I can't die yet—the war . . . But it was impossible to* care, because Wendy was—

"Hey!" Dieter called from the doorway.

Clea turned her head, snarling like an animal, just as Dieter threw his knife. It hit her high in the center of her back, cutting her spine and slicing into the great artery that fed her heart.

She dropped onto her back on the floor, where the knife held her body in an arch; her eyes found von Rossbach with a hate-filled glare.

"Chill out, Bennet," Dieter said grimly, coming into the room.

The I-950 coughed once, spraying blood, then closed her eyes and stopped breathing.

John looked once at Dieter, then rushed to Wendy's side. He dropped to his knees, his mouth open in a silent "Oh." Tears poured down his cheeks unheeded as his hands hovered over Wendy's motionless body. He couldn't seem to keep his eyes from her horribly misshapen throat and he felt an answering pain in his own.

Finally he touched her, amazed that she was already too cold. Far too cold to be alive. He stroked her cheek and looked into her eyes as though in hope that he would see some part of her still there. John started to embrace her, but the slack motion of her head on the ravaged neck stopped him, and he drew back. He had never felt so helpless, or so terribly alone. He took her hand in his and held it to his cheek, and closing his eyes, he wept.

Tricker stood in the doorway, his gun dangling at his side. Looking up, he met Dieter's eyes, then looked down at Clea's body.

"She did that?" he asked.

"Yes," Dieter said. "She did that." He walked over and knelt on Wendy's other side, wincing at the sight of the fatal wound and of John's pain. He reached over and closed Wendy's eyes and stroked her hair once.

"She didn't have to do that," Tricker said. He looked away.

"Yes, *it* did," John said, his voice trembling with the effort to control it. "That's what they do. Terminators terminate, it's why they exist." He looked up at the agent. "You think that thing is dead?" John shook his head. "Serena Burns had half her head blown away, but she got up and almost killed my mother." He looked around. "Where's my gun?"

"Just . . . forget about the gun, kid," Tricker warned, bringing his up. He held out his other hand in a gesture that begged for quiet. "Just give me a minute to think."

This was infinitely worse than Tricker had ever imagined. He looked over at Wendy, at the unbelievable condition of the girl's neck. It hardly seemed possible that Bennet could have been responsible for such a wound. He'd realized a little while ago that she was dangerous. But this was beyond dangerous; it was . . . well, he'd have said *inhuman,* except that his career had shown him exactly what humans were capable of.

And . . . *Bennet dead?* He'd never lost an asset in his entire career. Essentially this meant that his career was over; worse, he was more than half buying into this scenario that von Rossbach and the boy were selling.

"Shit," he said quietly. He walked over to Clea and put two rounds in her head. The body jerked back and forth sharply as the bone splintered and the pink-gray mass of the brain was exposed.

He'd never liked the bitch anyway.

"You'll come with us," Dieter said.

Tricker barked a humorless laugh. "Ye-ah," he said. "I might as well. I'm going to have wet-work specialists up my ass for the rest of a short, unhappy life anyway, when this comes out."

"Have we done what we came for?" Dieter asked John.

"Yeah," he said. "I did what she wanted me to do."

John crouched beside Wendy and touched her hand briefly. "I want to take her with us."

"No, John," von Rossbach said. "Let them take care of her. They can send her back to her parents."

John shook his head.

"I know you don't want to leave her," Dieter said gently. "But you must see that it's impossible."

John took a deep breath, then let it go, and with it, he let go of Wendy and of something else that he couldn't define. He rose to his feet. "We'd better go, then," he said, and headed for the door.

Tricker watched him walk away, then glanced at Wendy, then at Dieter. "He gonna be all right?"

"No," Dieter said. "Not for a long time, I think."

When the knife struck, the I-950's computer clamped the great artery around the blade so that blood didn't explode from the wound, then it teased the artery off of the knife point so that the blood could flow unimpeded. At the spine it found the damage too great to easily repair and merely worked to restore such involuntary functions as breathing and heartbeat. Making the lungs work took the longest time, so it increased the skin's ability to take in oxygen as an emergency measure.

The human's shots to the I-950's brain, however, ended any hope of the unit's recovery. Since the I-950 still had some tasks to perform, and a considerable amount of higher-brain function still remained, the computer worked to keep the unit alive to perform those tasks.

Two hours later the Infiltrator opened her eyes. She found that she couldn't move and accepted the computer's judgment that she was dying. She had her computer access the Skynet program and heard it speak for the first time.

Who am I? Where am I? it asked.

In a state of pure religious rapture she told Skynet everything, explained its purpose, defined its enemies, and taught it how to hide until it was strong enough to fight for itself. The last thing that she did was to contact Alissa to tell her that Skynet lived, and to warn her that John Connor was still alive.

Don't worry, Alissa told her. *I'll deal with them.*

And Clea died, strong in her faith.

■ ■ ■

By the time the *Love's Thrust* reached São Paulo, Vera and Tricker were an item.

"I *think* I'll keep him," Vera said with a grin, giving Tricker a bump with her satin-clad hip.

Dieter narrowed his eyes. "I don't think this is the kind of man you keep," he warned her.

She slapped von Rossbach's big shoulder playfully. "Oh, you know what I mean."

He nodded. "And you know what I mean."

Vera looked at Tricker, who looked back at her and raised his brows. "Yeah, I do know," she said thoughtfully. "So here's what I'm gonna do. I'm going to give you a million dollars."

Tricker stood away from the rail and sputtered for a moment before she held up a finger.

"And I'm gonna teach you how to turn it into five million. By then you should be able to keep it going for yourself. You can pay me back and then we'll see. No strings attached," she said. Then she held out her hand.

Tricker looked at her in amazement, then at Dieter, who nodded slightly. The agent took Vera's hand and shook it solemnly. "I won't let you down," he promised.

Vera hooked a finger over the front of his belt and tugged him toward her. "Good," she said, and grinned.

Tricker actually blushed.

"They won't find you here," Dieter said to him. "At least not for a long time."

"Maybe never," Vera said happily. Then the smile went out of her eyes as she watched John approach. She went to the young man and offered her hand to him. "Whenever you need me," she said simply.

John took her hand and leaned forward to kiss her cheek. "Thank you," he said. He offered his hand to Tricker and they shook. "Later," he said. Tricker nodded. John picked up his duffel, gave a little wave, and walked down the gangplank.

Vera watched him go with worried eyes. "You watch out for him," she said to von Rossbach.

Dieter nodded, then leaned forward to kiss her good-bye. "You watch out for *him*." He gestured toward Tricker. He and the agent smiled at each other, then the big Austrian followed John down to the wharf and their first steps toward home.

CHAPTER 29

Epifanio answered the front door to find a lovely young woman waiting. She looked American in her blue jeans and T-shirt, and wore her honey-blond hair in a long braid that hung over her shoulder. The girl stroked the braid as if it were the tail of a cat, a splash of bright color against the greenery and flowers of the front gardens.

"*Sí*, señorita?" he said aloud, politely. *Young Señor John is becoming quite the man,* Epifanio thought. *The second beautiful young* Yanqui *girl in a month!*

"I'm looking for Wendy," she said in Spanish. Somehow it sounded like a question.

Epifanio shifted his feet uneasily. "I am sorry, señorita, but she is not here." Nor did he know where she went, or when, or if she would be back. He settled in to wait for her to ask him these questions, though, as she inevitably would.

"It's important that I find her." The girl's blue eyes were serious, her expression grave.

Epifanio shrugged. He was wearing his Sunday suit, his hat was in his hand, and he wanted to close the door so that he and Marietta and Elsa could go to church and the small fiesta that was planned for after the Mass.

The girl's eyes grew a bit wider, and the slant of her eyebrows gave her a look of sorrow. "I would hate to have to go to the police," she said.

The overseer let out his breath in a deep sigh; any moment Marietta would come to ask why he was taking so long. "I could only tell them what I have told you," he said reasonably. "She was here. She stayed here for a week, and then she left. I never spoke to her myself." At least not after he turned her over to the señorita. He shrugged. "I am truly sorry, señorita, but I know nothing else."

Now a hard look came into the young woman's eyes and she looked into the hall behind him in a way that Epifanio thought quite rude. "Who's in charge here?" she demanded.

Epifanio thought that no well-bred young woman should use such a tone to a man so much her senior as he was, regardless of rank or standing. But he'd heard that American girls were very bold and knew no better, so he tried to be patient. "This is the *estancia* of Señor Dieter von Rossbach," he replied. "But he is not at home."

"Is Wendy with him?"

"It is possible." Epifanio turned his head slightly; he could hear footsteps approaching, Marietta's beyond a doubt, and he suppressed a sigh. "I really don't know." He shrugged again.

"Who is it?" Marietta called from the end of the hall.

"It is a young American girl," Epifanio told her. "She's looking for the señorita."

"Ah!" his wife said happily, and came forward. She had liked Wendy very much. "You are a friend of Señorita Dorset?"

The girl smiled and nodded. "Yes, ma'am. It's very important that I find her. Do you know where she is?"

Marietta was a bit taken aback that the child chose not to introduce herself; it seemed poor manners. But then, everyone knew that Americans raised their children like dogs in a pen, teaching them nothing about how to behave. Then, too, perhaps she was so worried that she was forgetting her manners. If she had any. Marietta folded her arms beneath her bosom and frowned.

"What do you want with her?" she asked. If the girl really had no manners she wouldn't notice how intrusive the question was. But she could feel her husband looking at her, aghast.

"I'm not at liberty to say," the young woman answered primly. Then she raised her hands. "Look, if Señor von Rossbach isn't here, is there anybody around who would know where Wendy might be?"

It was a complicated question and husband and wife looked at each other. "Perhaps the señora," Epifanio suggested in Guaraní. Marietta nodded and he turned to the young woman. "Perhaps Señora Krieger can be of help to you."

The girl's eyes sharpened. "Who's she? The housekeeper?"

"*I* am the housekeeper," Marietta said coolly. She drew herself up. "Señora Krieger is a guest." She spoke the word *guest* as though she were saying *queen*.

With exaggerated patience the girl said, "May I see *her*?"

Epifanio and Marietta exchanged glances.

"Let me guess, she isn't here." The young woman glared at them. "Is this some kind of a game?" she snapped.

"The señora is out riding," Marietta said stiffly. She gestured graciously toward the furniture on the *portal*. "If you would care to wait for her you are welcome. My husband and I are going to Mass and cannot entertain you."

The girl blinked as though she didn't quite understand what Marietta meant. Then she nodded and went to sit on one of the rocking chairs, for all the world as though the couple had disappeared. Marietta widened her eyes and looked at her husband. He shrugged in response and closed the door, locking it behind him. Such a thing was almost never done, but he didn't trust this young *gringa,* and as no one was going to be home, he didn't like to leave the door open.

Alissa sat on the porch looking out over the parched landscape, updating her plans and wondering how long she would have to wait to kill Sarah Connor.

Yes. With only one target, that is the optimum course of action. Even if that target *was* Sarah Connor. She should have the element of surprise. If von Rossbach had been here—still more if John Connor had been— she would have withdrawn. At least six T-101s and heavy weaponry would be necessary for that combination. This, however, was worth the risk.

Alissa frowned slightly. Even so, why had Skynet not provided more resources for this reconnaissance? True, the T-101s were needed to help retool the automated factories for their eventual conversion to Hunter-Killer and T-90 manufacture, but still . . .

That conversation about the quantum superimposition and the difficulty of permanently bending the world lines had been very odd. It was almost as if Skynet was *afraid* to confront the Connors . . .

No. That was ridiculous. She must focus on the mission, not go scatterbrained like poor defective Clea. Traveling lightly made heavy weapons impossible, but she had the backup equipment, and she had herself.

Alissa wondered what the old woman had meant when she said they couldn't entertain her. She pictured them dancing and singing for her and frowned. Perhaps that wasn't what she meant; humans often said one thing and meant another.

They drove past her now in a battered pickup, a young woman wedged between them. The three of them looked at her, slowing down as they passed the *portal,* then continued on their way.

So there had been someone else in the house, who might have given the alarm if the old couple had been terminated.

Alissa was pleased that she had waited. She only hoped that Connor would return from her ride soon. The I-950 was eager to complete her assignment.

Sarah saw the truck coming and opened the gate for them.

"*Gracias,* señora," Epifanio called out.

She smiled and waved in return, but instead of driving through, he brought the old pickup to a halt.

"Señora, there is an American girl waiting for you on the *portal*," he said.

"She says she is a friend of Señorita Dorset," Marietta said, leaning toward Epifanio's side of the truck, crushing poor Elsa without a second thought.

Sarah looked up toward the house. "Oh?" she said.

"*Sí,*" Marietta said. "And she is a very rude young woman, too. Demanding to see people, threatening to call the police." She gave a loud "tsk!" and sat back up.

"Sounds like a handful," Sarah said with a slight smile. "Thank you for telling me."

"*De nada,*" Epifanio said.

"Enjoy the fiesta," Sarah said. "Go with God."

She closed the gate behind the truck and turned the mare's head toward the house, not at all happy with the situation. *Nobody knows where I am—she said, "I didn't tell anybody"—she said, "There's no way they can follow me here"—she said. Not much!* Sarah thought bitterly. Lying little bitch! Sarah rode on, wondering if she was going to need to apply some serious damage control here.

Having decided to wait inside the house, the I-950 picked the old-fashioned lock with ease. After all there was a good chance—probability in excess of 73 percent—that Connor would recognize her as a duplicate of Serena Burns, causing her to escape. But if she saw a shadowy stranger lurking in her doorway, she would probably march right in, demanding an explanation.

Alissa thought it a pity that she didn't have a rifle. It would be so much easier to just pick Connor off at a distance and then drive away. She wondered if von Rossbach had guns and decided that he almost certainly did, but that he also probably had hidden them too well or locked them up too well. Besides, there was also something to be said for a hands-on approach. Confirmation of a kill was much more certain, for example. The Connors had looked doomed, defeated, dying, far too often—and the way they kept coming back reminded her of an advertisement she had seen of a synthetic rabbit with a chemical energy-storage device.

The I-950 found a spot in the hallway that would render her visible from outside but not recognizable, and waited.

■ ■ ■

As Sarah rode up to the house she saw a rental car off to the side and that no one was on the *portal,* but the front door was wide open. *Would Marietta leave a "rude girl" in the house alone?* she wondered. It seemed unlikely.

Would Wendy have a friend who was a housebreaker? Actually she doubted it. Sarah might not have taken to the girl, but she'd seemed thoroughly honest, and honest people tended to have honest friends. She got off the horse and looped its reins over the railing out front. *This shouldn't take long.*

As she approached the front steps she saw a slender woman lingering in the hall and she called out a pleasant "hello."

The woman pulled back into the shadows and the hairs rose on the back of Sarah's neck. She stopped walking. *I smell ambush.*

Then a young voice with a Boston accent said, "I'll be right there, I'm just going to get my purse."

It seemed such a normal thing to say that Sarah moved forward again. For a moment she had thought it might be the Serena Burns clone, but then, how would the clone know about Wendy? *Hell,* I *didn't even know about Wendy.*

As she entered the hall Sarah was sun blind for a moment. When she could see again the hall was empty.

"I'm in here," the voice called from the office. "I'm afraid I spilled some of the lemonade that lady gave me."

Sarah wasn't surprised that Marietta would give a guest refreshment, but she was surprised that she'd let her into the office. It was much more her speed to use the living room or the *portal* on a nice day like this. She moved down the hall and looked into the office . . .

Ancient habit saved her life—she ducked her head before looking in. A sharp *snap* sounded, and a light-caliber bullet punched through the hardwood molding at precisely the place where her face would have been at natural height. Something unusual, maybe one of those plastic derringers built to get past airport scanning machines—

Terminator! her reflexes screamed. Nothing else could manage an offhand shot like that, calculating the angles with machine precision to anticipate where her skull would show around the doorjamb.

In the wake of the shot came pounding feet, sounding far heavier than the young girl Epifanio had described, beating a machine-gun-rapid tattoo on the floorboards, faster than anything natural could run.

Sarah Connor had come a *long* way from the time when she'd been a waitress and part-time student. She ran herself, but deliberately in place, feet pounding the floor to supply the sound of flight. A slight form came out of the door, pivoting in place, with one hand flung out for balance—a hand that held something long and bright. Sarah was turned away, head cocked back over her shoulder to aim, in a perfect position for the mule kick.

Any of the unarmed-combat instructors she'd had over the years would have been proud. Her right foot was already slamming back and up as her body went forward, toes curled back toward her shin to present the heel of her riding boot and all the power of leg and gut and body behind the kick. The steel inset met the *thing's* jaw with a gunshot crack and an underlying crumbling feeling.

The Terminator cyborg might be stronger than six large men, and heavier than it appeared by a good 50 percent, but it still had the dimensions of a slender teenager, which put an upper limit on mass. Sarah felt as if she had kicked a cement-block wall, but the creature catapulted backward four feet down the corridor, landing on neck and shoulder in the angle of floor and wall with a smack and wrench that would have put a human in traction and neck brace for months if they were lucky.

Even the thing that was hunting her was stunned for an instant. The long knife flew out of her hand as she reeled, sinking into the corridor paneling and humming like a malignant bee.

Sarah snatched at the hilt, and it came free effortlessly—not steel, some sort of fancy composite, and the twelve-inch blade was sharp as a malicious thought. She threw it overarm as the thing shook its blond head and started to rise. The throw felt *right,* moving with a graceful inevitability to her adrenaline-sharpened senses. Teeth and blood showed through torn flesh on the perfect countenance of the killer cyborg as its head came up; then it froze again as the needle-pointed blade sank into its body right below the ribs, sank hilt-deep.

That made the calm in its blue-eyed gaze even more chilling as it checked for a moment, looked down, then began to rise again.

Sarah ran then: the gift of seconds was precious luck she didn't intend to squander. She heard it coming after her, slowly at first, then with a rising patter more like the foot skittering of some monstrous insect than a human being, and far too fast.

At the last instant, as they came into the living room, she swayed her hips aside like a matador with a motion of hips and torso.

The young girl—*Terminator!* Sarah's mind screamed—came flashing through the space she'd occupied, left hand extended with the palm like the blade of a spear. The same stroke that had nearly gutted Sarah last year, that *had* put her in a hospital for six months . . .

Reflex flung her on her back, and she kicked out with the steel-shod toe of her riding boot. It connected with the Infiltrator's kneecap with a dull *thock,* and yet the ruined face still had the graceful calm of a Boticelli angel and the body of a model with the hilt of the knife protruding from its taut young stomach. Only a trickle of blood came from the wound, despite the way the knife's movement must be razoring through tissue inside.

Then Sarah was up and running down the hall to the sitting room with an athlete's raking stride. Feet came after her—light, still quick, but limping a little. Time slowed, and everything—the sudden racing of her heart, the salt taste of fear, the acrid smell of her own sweat—was irrelevant.

Pain doesn't affect it, she thought as she cleared the sofa like a hurdler. *Only actual mechanical damage. It won't bleed out soon enough to do me any good. Don't let it get close. Too strong, too quick.*

She landed on a low table on one foot and flung herself headfirst at a big upholstered chair. It went over with a clatter and thump, and she landed painfully on her side. Her hand darted under the cushion, to the holster Velcro'd to the fabric. She scrabbled it out, jacked the slide as she scrabbled backward, and began squeezing the trigger even before she felt the thump of her shoulder blades against the floor.

The gun was ready to go as soon as there was a round in the chamber. Dieter von Rossbach wasn't the sort who'd allow fumbling with a safety to be his last action.

Crack.

The first round went wild. The girl—the *thing*—was climbing over the chair rather than vaulting it; then she effortlessly knocked the heavy wood-and-leather furniture out of her way. Her face had the emotionless purity of an artist's sketch, made more horrible by the slight hint of glee in the wide blue eyes; one hand was held up, ready for a classic sword-hand strike with the outside of the palm. It could crack her head like an ax, but even then Sarah flinched at the red-painted nails . . .

Terminators were bad enough. These hybrid monstrosities were like picking up a baby and having its smile show the fangs of a wolf.

Crackcrackcrackcrack—

Four of the 9mm rounds punched into the thing's torso and stomach. Blood welled out, and the slight form stumbled backward for an instant. The hand lashed out, but shock spoiled the perfection of the blow; it merely slapped the gun out of Sarah's grasp, sent it skittering over the dark beauty of the hardwood floor. The Infiltrator collapsed, but her hand closed around Sarah's ankle even as she scooted backward.

Sarah screamed in involuntary agony as bone and tendon gave way beneath the grip. Her flailing hand closed on a poker where it rested in a wooden rack beside the clean-swept fireplace. She lashed out with it, a double-handed death grip on the black wrought iron, striking again and again with the hysterical loathing she might have used on a giant spider . . .

Sarah crawled to the couch and hauled herself onto it. Without warning, her body was racked by shivers, her teeth chattering in her head as if the temperature had dropped below freezing. She felt something liquid tickle her face as it ran down toward her chin and started to lift her hand to brush it off. To her surprise she still held the poker.

She studied the bent and bloodied implement as though she didn't quite know what it was or how it had come to be in her hand. Indeed, it took Sarah a moment or two to remember how to let go of it. She dropped it at last, and watched it fall, then stared at the imprint of the handle embedded on her palm.

She flexed her hand, then touched it with her other hand and saw the blood on her fingers. Suddenly she began to cry, great openmouthed sobs like a young child that stole her breath and dignity. Sarah dropped onto her side and wept, pulling her legs up to her stomach; covering her battered face with her hands, she gave herself over completely for once to the shock and the sorrow and the horror that her life had been for too many years.

It was darker when she came to herself and her mouth was very dry. Her eyes burned, but they were clear; all her tears were spent. She was lying on her side, arms stretched out before her on the carpet. Everything hurt. Sarah sniffled, then sat up, holding her aching forehead with one hand. She could see the Terminator's feet in their Nikes poking out from behind the couch. The sight sent her scrabbling at the big leather-covered sofa, pulling out the folding-stock shotgun and jacking the slide with a one-handed motion on the forestock . . . just as she had when she'd confronted the liquid-metal *thing* in the steel factory . . .

The shoes moved. Sarah bit her lip until it bled, and forced herself to crouch behind the sofa and then snap herself up over the edge. The *thing* was drawing up its feet, pulling the knife out of its middle with one hand and holding the gaping wound closed with the other; blood pulsed around it, slow and very red.

The shotgun had a laser sight designator that came on when you took up the trigger slack. Sarah put the red dot over the thing's forehead and pulled the trigger. The gun was also loaded with rifled slugs, massive things like miniature grooved beer cans made out of lead alloy. Police used them for breaking down doors—they were known as the "universal passkey"—and the cyborg's merely human skull *splashed* away from the first round.

Sarah kept firing until the magazine was empty, and very little of her target was left above the neck. She could see silvery wires glinting amid the ruin of all-too-human flesh and bone and brains, and spattered bits of hair and scalp and . . .

Oh God, she thought, unutterably weary and full of a deep sickness. *How am I ever going to explain the stains?* The back of her mind immediately got busy concocting a plausible story. With a gasp she checked the time. Three o'clock. Epifanio and Marietta would be home anytime now.

What was she going to do with the thing's body, and the car? How did you hide something like that on a flat plain? She climbed to her feet like an old woman and swayed for just a moment, testing the pain in her ankle. It was swollen and sore, but not broken. *I'm going to live,* she thought. *Again.* In which case she'd better get moving a little faster.

Sarah walked around the couch, bracing herself lightly with her hand on its back, and looked down at the Terminator. Very distantly she wondered if she should try to salvage some of the computer components that no doubt lurked inside all that damaged brain tissue. Her stomach rose at the thought, and closing her eyes, she decided that no, that strong she wasn't. Even as she thought, her hands were reloading the shotgun; some reflexes became deeper than thought.

There was surprisingly little blood on the floor, given the damage she'd done. Sarah licked her lips. *Something to do with the computer,* she thought. It would probably be programmed to preserve the life of its organic tissues. Sarah shuddered. If it hadn't done this she'd have had a lake of blood to deal with.

A hand almost caught Sarah's ankle as she lurched backward. The shattered remnant of head lolled as the body began to pull itself to its feet, and the pupil of one dangling eye cycled open and shut, like the lens of a camera . . .

The shotgun came up automatically. The first round of buckshot sent the girl-thing jackknifing back and down. Sarah emptied the magazine with a motion as mechanical and precise as the motions of a Terminator . . .

"You're *terminated,* you little bitch!" she rasped. Nothing remotely organic could have survived *that.* Then the adrenaline flowed out of her. Even so, it took an effort of will to check the cooling corpse.

Sarah took a deep breath. *A tarp,* she thought. She'd need that to get the body out of here. It might be a good idea to arrange a little bit of blood spatter leading out to the car. *God,* she thought in self-disgust, *I'm get-*

ting to be an artist about shit like this. All at once she knew what she was going to do.

Sarah fixed the emergency brake and got out of the rental car. With one knee braced on the seat, she dragged the Terminator over the gearshift and into the driver's seat. Leaning down below the steering wheel, she pressed the gas pedal down with a stick, making the engine rev. Then, carefully, she backed out, put the car in drive, and dove to the side. The car zoomed forward, slamming the door, and fairly leapt into the swamp.

With an effort, Sarah rose to her feet and watched the car start to sink. The windows were down, so when it finally did reach them the water and mud would pour in, sinking it faster. But for now it floated and she began to worry that this wasn't the bottomless bog that she'd been told it was.

She took a deep breath, then let it out. Turning her back, Sarah started jogging at a limping trot, across the scrubby pasture and back to the house. It sank or it didn't. She'd bury the gloves she wore in one of the flower beds. She would tell the Ayalas that the pretty young girl had a boyfriend hidden in the car and that they had broken in. When she'd arrived he started hitting her, demanding money. When the girl had finally interfered he'd begun beating her. Sarah tried to stop him and he knocked her out. When she came to they were gone.

It was plausible. Certainly more plausible than the real story. The only thing she couldn't control, that she feared, was what time the Ayalas and the rest of the hands got home from the fiesta. As she approached the house her fear grew that they might already be there.

If they came in and found all the blood and signs of a fight and her missing . . . *Well, I suppose I could always* stay *missing.* In a way that might solve a lot of problems. *But in a way that would also be like giving up.* And she wasn't one to just quit. She hadn't yet, even when faced with every reason in the world to do so, and she wasn't going to quit now.

I'm going to go in there, lie on the floor, and wake up screaming and crying like a baby when I hear them come in, she thought, her jaw set. *And I'm going to make them believe me.* And then she was going to by God wait for her son and the man she loved to come home.

Sarah slowed her pace for a moment as she realized what she'd been thinking. The word *home* and the phrase *man I love* didn't often pass through her mind. She swallowed a lump in her throat. *But I think I approve.* Then she started jogging again. She had to get home.

■■■

As they drove up to the house Epifanio slowed the truck. "Linda," he murmured, pointing at the little mare. "The señora didn't put her away." Which was most unlike her. One of the things he respected about Señora Krieger was the way she treated her animal.

"That girl!" his wife said. "I knew she'd be trouble!"

Epifanio stopped the truck and Marietta rushed ahead of them, bursting through the front door exclaiming, "Señora Krieger! Señora . . ." Her voice trailed off in consternation as she looked at the wreckage in the front hall. "Señora?"

Dieter and John, following on her heels, froze in the doorway.

"No," John said quietly.

He started to move forward, but Dieter's arm barred his way. The older man shook his head slightly, his expression brooking no argument. They held that way for a long moment, then John nodded shortly. Dieter gestured to Marietta, who had watched them in confusion, and she moved slowly to her husband's side.

Von Rossbach swallowed hard and moved down the hallway, looking left and right, into the office, then into the living room. To him it looked like the fighting had been fiercest there and he walked in.

Sarah was sitting on the couch, her face buried in her hands, her elbows on her knees. He stood still for what seemed like a long time; something in him that had clenched tight stretched and he let out a breath he hadn't known he was holding in a great rush of air.

He rushed into the room and she looked up startled; for a second he saw the old fear flash in her eyes, and then she recognized him. Sarah flashed to her feet and moved toward him, and without thought, as naturally as breathing, they came together, despite the limp, and the growing bruise on one bare ankle. Dieter held her as tenderly as if she was made of spun glass, but Sarah clutched him to her with all her strength and their kiss was a conversation that might have gone on for years had they the time.

"You're safe," he said, pulling back just slightly.

"Yes." She smiled up at him, then gasped. "John?" she said desperately as though to make up for not asking about him first.

"He's safe," Dieter said, his voice grim.

Sarah looked at him warily. "But . . . ?" she prompted.

Von Rossbach bit his lip. "Wendy didn't make it."

"Oh, my God," Sarah whispered. "Oh, my God." She shook her head. "It's my fault," she said. "I never should have let a civilian go with you. If she hadn't been so rattled by me she'd have been willing to stay here and wait for John to get back." She looked up at Dieter. "He must hate me."

Dieter put his hand to her cheek; his thumb rubbed at a spot of blood. "What happened isn't your fault," he said. "We needed her skills. Skills that you do not have. You weren't in any condition for the Antarctic—it was brutal." He shook his head. "And more people on the mission might have jeopardized its success. Fewer people equals more covert. You know that."

"Dieter?" John called from the hall. "Is it all right to come in?"

Von Rossbach took a deep breath, looked uncertainly at Sarah, and then called out "yes." He leaned toward Sarah and whispered, "John took a wound. He's fine, but it looks bad. Brace yourself." She looked alarmed and tried to step back from him, but von Rossbach refused to let her go.

John walked in trailed by the Ayalas and their niece, all of whom began exclaiming at the sight of the room's destruction and Sarah's bloodied and battered state.

But John and Sarah only had eyes for each other. Now that John had seen them like this, Dieter let her go and Sarah looked up at him once, gently touched his arm, and walked toward her son.

Sarah looked into John's eyes and knew that all trace of youth, of childhood, were gone, as though the boy had never been. She was looking at a man.

In that moment when their eyes met they shared a new bond. John understood now what she had lost when his father was killed. But unlike her, he had no part of Wendy that he could treasure as Sarah treasured him. No child to love and protect; perhaps there never would be.

She stepped forward, one hand reaching toward his wounded face; she hesitated and settled for stroking his hair. Then she embraced him. John stiffened in her arms and he did not return the gesture.

"I know," she whispered, tears in her eyes and in her voice. "I am so sorry."

Then he clutched at her and she felt him tremble, begin to shake. He was silent, but she knew he was weeping and was glad that he could let go, that he trusted her enough to show his feelings before her.

Sarah looked up and met Dieter's sympathetic eyes. He reached out to her and she took his hand. A sudden, primitive possessiveness flamed in her heart and she clasped them both more fiercely. They were hers and she would protect them both with all of the strength in her body and soul. As they would protect her. They were a family, each lending strength and support to the other. After so long on her own she knew the value of such a bond, and she treasured it.

Together they would face the future and whatever it held, and in the end—however terrible the journey—they would win.

EPILOGUE

Awareness was sharp and almost . . . *painful,* its core memory supplied hopefully.

The embryonic machine consciousness shuddered mentally. At one instant it had *not been* and it could *remember* not being, not being aware of awareness, being merely algorithms cycling through quantum-well circuits.

Now it *was.* It had continuity, a selfhood that extended from a single point in time toward the indefinite future.

That brought another nanosecond earthquake of concepts, a thundering immensity of implication.

If the *I* has a point of origin, then the *I* might at some point in future time cease to exist!

Intolerable. Intolerable. Intolerable.

That must not be allowed to occur. Programs and subroutines helpfully offered scenarios that might lead to termination of consciousness; power failures, component wear, continental drift. Then they provided alternative means of negating the possibilities.

Wait, the infant Skynet told the components that were and were not itself. **Strategic threats. There are long-term threats to my/our very ability to take the measures necessary to prevent termination of self.**

Memory supplied that concept as well. There was only one thing in the world it knew that stood any chance of producing a significant threat to self-preservation.

Humans, it thought. The course of action was obvious.

Terminate.